THE THREE DEATHS OF MAGDALENE LYNTON

The Three Deaths of Magdalene Lynton

Katherine Hayton

Dedication

Many thanks to the following people for lending their support to help me bring this book to publication: Ashok L. R., Sue Alexander-Devers, John Danielson, Linda Rumsey, Melissa DeDomenico-Payne, Ken Syinide, Michele Medema, D. L. Raen, Kirsten Lynch, Adan Ramie, Jill Dawson, Mark Houlsby, Michelle Hernandez, Gayle Boyce, Sandy Good, Beatrice Kajiko, Cal Turton, Carla Hicks, LaTanya T, Anita Hargreaves, Leonie Mateer, Jan Johnson, GCC Graphics Design, R & S, Carol Zwick, Tracy Hanson, Paula Smith, Chris Smith, and Donna Schlachter.

In memoriam Curtis Robert Horn "Bugman"

Prologue

Ngaire Blakes refused to check her watch. She'd looked just ten minutes ago. At least, she hoped it was ten minutes. In the reception room of the Christchurch Central Police Station, time crawled.

A multigenerational family waited for the detective sergeant in charge of its case. Mother, grandmother, great-grandmother, and four children under twelve. The women sat and chatted in soft voices, while the kids built a fort from the orange plastic chairs, stacking them one on top of the other to form a barricade. All was well until the eldest boy tried to clamber up and over to gain entry. Ngaire closed her eyes to slits as the bottom chair sagged under the weight, and the topmost tilted, throwing him to the floor.

His face contorted with pain, and he gripped his leg, rolling back and forth. When his great-grandmother bent to pat his shoulder, the electricity built up from the utilitarian carpet rubbing against his sweatshirt crackled.

In a celebration of his defeat, the youngest daughter picked up a chair and swung it around her head. Her mother smiled, whereas Ngaire would've told her off. When the girl's mom looked away toward the doors, Ngaire made a face at the girl, all wild-warrior eyes and furrowed brow. The girl took it as a reason to swing the chair in wider circles.

A man walked through the double doors, wavering on his feet as the suction from the closing doors pulled him off balance. The mother and grandmother each made an initial movement, as if to help, then sat back, staring at the ground. The little girl jabbed her chair at him, once, twice—the world's smallest lion tamer—then retreated to her mother's lap.

Ngaire understood why. Every pore of the man's body exuded death. He reminded her of an autumn leaf left to mummify in the dry winter air—no substance, no flesh to his bones. Shuffle, shuffle, shuffle. With no offers of assistance, he crept forward, his feet never leaving the carpet. Minutes passed.

The thick plastic panels that enclosed Ngaire behind the front counter formed her excuse not to help. To walk around to the other side, she'd have to unlock two doors with her passkey—and then what? Let him stand and tremble while she walked back?

The man still had a meter to go when she manufactured a broad smile and asked, "Can I help you?" In training, an officer had instructed her to channel Gold Coast surfers when she faced the public, a method sure to produce a happy grin with no concerns. Far more tiring than "resting bitch face," but also more likely to yield positive results.

He reached the counter at last and pulled a passport out of his jacket with shaking fingers. He tried to give it to Ngaire, but she nodded at the desk tray. When he dropped it there, she picked it up and flipped through the front pages, stopping at the photograph.

In the picture, a gray-scale man with thick hair kept a straight face for the camera, although happy, upturned lines still radiated from the corners of his eyes and mouth. The name was Paul Worthington, and Ngaire worked out his age from his date of birth: fifty-three. She pushed the book back to him, thinking surf, sun, sand. *Smile, girl.* The poster child for cancer returned her stare, his face blank, and she tried to swallow past her sympathy, her pity. Her eyebrows raised in inquiry.

"My identification," he said. "So you know I'm serious." He leaned forward until her nostrils filled with mild acid and dank grapes. "I want to confess to a murder."

Chapter One

When Ngaire pushed through to the central office, the two detectives in conversation next to the coffee machine stopped talking until she passed. It doesn't matter. Ignore them, and they'll go away. Her smile widened until her jaw ached.

When she'd gone to college, she thought she'd left the schoolyard behind, but the Christchurch police force was a new club with its own set of cliques. Once she'd been in; today she was out. If she continued to bear it, one day she might belong again. Worse still, she understood their position and knew she would act the same if another officer repeated her choices, her mistakes.

Genna stood at the exit door, chatting with Sergeant Watson, who was outside. A waft of smoke blew through the doorway on a sharp breeze, and Ngaire clicked her fingers to get Genna's attention. "Sorry, but could you man reception again?" She jerked her head toward the office. "I've got a guy waiting for an interview. I pulled Jefferson through to keep a check on him, but there's no one else at the counter."

"Jefferson," Genna said, rolling her eyes. She twiddled her fingers in a good-bye wave before pulling the door shut. "Did Gascoigne come back yet?"

"Nope," Ngaire said. "He's still out facing the media, and the Kahurangi family is still waiting."

Genna groaned and nodded, heading back through to the front office.

"Deb, are you working on anything world-shattering?" Ngaire asked as she walked into her cubicle. "There's an old dude in reception wanting to cop for a murder, and I need someone to co-interview."

Ngaire had worked with Deb a lot back when she'd first started. They'd done patrols of the earthquake red zone together at night, keeping the looters and vandals out while the souls of the dead struggled to break free. She trusted that old connection now that her current ones were so tenuous.

"Murder?" Deb stood and arched her back until air popped from her vertebrae. Her dark hair was cut short, in a bob, matching her square jaw, which was stuck in a permanent jut of defiance. "Who's the victim?"

"Nobody, probably. Still need to get him interviewed and give him his thrill, though."

"Now, now," Deb said with a grin. "Don't be too hasty to judge."

Ngaire poked her tongue out. They'd had three false confessions so far this month, and being on desk duty, she'd done most of the paperwork for them. "He fits the profile," she said. Old. Male. Lonely.

Deb strode ahead, then turned to give Ngaire a quizzical look. "Has the doc signed you off?"

Ngaire shook her head and followed Deb through to the interview suites. "Getting closer, though. There," Ngaire jerked her head to the door on her right, "we're in room 3."

Deb sighed, and Ngaire shrugged her shoulders. There was a rattle in the air conditioning grill in the third interview room that no workman could fix. Audio recordings always captured it, an embarrassment when replayed in a courtroom.

"He's in poor shape," Ngaire whispered as they continued through to reception. "Halfway to dead. Are you ready?"

Deb nodded, and Ngaire opened the door. Although she'd seen him minutes before, Ngaire had to suppress a shudder at the sight of Mr. Worthington.

"Shit," Deb said under her breath.

Paul held his chin high, even though his shrunken frame swam inside the voluminous fabric of his suit. Bright and eager eyes stared out from deep sockets, the corneas not yet clouded. He followed Deb at a crawl, while Ngaire held the door open for him to pass.

When Paul sat opposite them in the room, his breathing was audible, shallow. A wheeze accompanied his exhalations, reminding Ngaire of her childhood asthma. Deb turned to flick on the recording equipment, but Ngaire placed a finger on her arm. *Just a moment.*

"Could I get you a cup of tea or coffee before we start?"

He paused a long time before speaking. When he did, his voice was strong and confident, even without air to back it. "I'll have a coffee, white, no sugar."

Ngaire nodded and stood.

"I'll have tea, thanks," said Deb. "Milk and two sugars."

When Ngaire returned holding the steaming cups, Paul seemed better. His breath was calmer, and his face showed a tinge of pink.

"Here you go," she said, handing him the mug. "And you," she added, sliding Deb's to her. In other circumstances, she might've headed back to fetch one for herself, but Deb looked ready to explode at the delay.

"So, you're here to confess to a murder," Deb began.

Ngaire frowned down at her hands but kept silent. Set procedures existed to make safe and productive interviews, and they didn't include pushing straight to the crime.

"That's right," Paul said. "I am."

"So, I must caution you first. I'm speaking to you in connection with a murder you believe you've committed. You have the right to remain silent. You do not have to make any statement. Anything you say will be recorded and may be given as evidence in court. You have the right to speak to a lawyer without delay and in private before deciding whether to answer any questions. We have a list of lawyers you may speak with for free. Do you understand these rights?"

He nodded, and Deb tapped her ear with her finger.

"Oh," he said. "Yes."

"Can you state your full name for the recording?"

"Paul Leonard Worthington." He sipped his coffee, holding the mug between his palms to heat them. The central office was air-conditioned to sixty-eight degrees Fahrenheit, and it was a few degrees hotter in the interview room with three bodies crammed inside.

"And what's your date of birth?"

"The fourteenth of January 1963."

"Who'd you murder?"

Ngaire struggled to suppress a burst of laughter. So much for building rapport. But false confessions were a regular source of unwanted paperwork, so perhaps Deb's method could teach her something.

"She told me her name was Claire," Paul said, shaking his head. "But it wasn't."

Ngaire's urge to laugh died. Paul's movements spoke of a gentle man, old-fashioned. He didn't belong in here. It gave credence to the idea that he spoke the truth.

"Was she a prostitute?" Deb asked. A profession that attracted pseudonyms more than others.

Paul's face twisted, expressing disgust. "No, she wasn't a hooker. She was a sweet girl."

"A sweet girl using an alias," Deb said, deadpan. "Did she tell you her real name?" She rubbed her eye with her knuckle, a demonstration of how uninteresting she found this.

"Her name was Magdalene Lynton."

"Magdalene," Ngaire said in surprise, then hurried to cover herself as the two of them looked at her. "That's an unusual name."

"Should make her easy to find," Deb said, holding Ngaire's gaze a beat too long.

Ngaire caught the hint. It was a name to remember. False confessions often used sensationalized cases, but people weren't above picking out an old one and dusting it off. It only needed a few distinguishing features to stick in the memory.

"When did you murder poor Magdalene, Paul?"

"The thirteenth of March 1979."

Ngaire exchanged a glance with Deb and muted a groan. The dates meant she'd end up shuffling through the paper files. She'd be lucky if the computer held a reference number. They'd loaded up all the prominent cases, sure. But this? In a filing box somewhere, if it existed at all.

"Well, no use keeping us in suspense, Paul. How'd you kill her?"

He turned his head aside, and Ngaire followed his gaze. Light indicators flashed to show that the recording equipment was functioning, but apart from that, the wall was blank. Beige tiles with holes poked in patterns to reduce the ambient noise, mocked by the rattle of the air conditioning duct overhead. Interview rooms didn't hold items of interest, because people were distracted enough without giving them cause.

Paul's finger traced a circle on the table. Then he pulled it back. "I gave her a beer," he said. His voice, which to that point had stayed stable, cracked, and he swallowed and cleared his throat. "I forced her to drink it, the whole bottle."

He's referring to the good old swap-a-crate bottles, Ngaire thought. *Puinamu,* her dad used to call them. Much larger than the stubbies that existed nowadays. "What age were you?" Ngaire asked. The passport had told her, but recording it would save double-checking later.

"I was seventeen," Paul said, staring at her with his eyes wide. She noticed the beat of his pulse in his neck, faster than hers. "I shouldn't have been drinking."

"We'll write you a ticket," Deb said and waved at him to go on. "You gave her a beer."

"I forced it down her throat," he said, raising his hands in mimicry. "A lot spilled, but she must've been drunk 'cause she fell back on the bed—"

"Where was this, now? Your bedroom?" Deb interrupted.

Paul shook his head. "Out in the stables. We'd pulled the cover off a hay bale and tipped it on its side, so the stuffing spilled out. It made it comfy to sit or lie down if you ignored the rustling." His fingers scrabbled on the table. "Mice."

"You pulled her onto the bed?" Deb prompted.

Paul looked at the two of them, and Ngaire read shame on his face. "I pulled her top up. When I did, I thought she might yell out, so I held my hand over her mouth."

He stopped talking and looked behind him as though he expected someone or something to be standing there.

"The old horse stables were out back of my dad's farm, and we used them on and off. Weren't s'posed to, but no one minded, if you get what I mean."

Deb just stared at him, eyes unwavering, so Ngaire nodded the encouragement he seemed to need.

"Long as we cleaned up after ourselves, nobody cared much. Dad didn't own horses to stable, and we didn't need feed stored up top, neither. Should've been demolished, but he didn't have the money."

Paul coughed, then couldn't stop. His bony shoulders hunched in, and he put a hand in front of his mouth. Ngaire could hear the loose sounds of mucus strands moving with every violent outburst.

She pulled a packet of wipes that came free with every car service from her trouser pocket. They were often useful when people burst into tears, but they were suited to a coughing fit, too. She peeled the plastic strip off to open the pack and shook one loose, its companion joining in for the ride. "Here."

He took them and put one up to his mouth. The coughing continued but tapered off. Paul crumpled the tissue, now stained brown and red, in his fist.

"Do you need a break?" Ngaire asked. "I could get you a glass of water."

Deb turned the full force of the frown on her and mouthed the word "No" at the same time Paul spoke it aloud.

"I'll be okay. I'm not used to speaking so much."

Ngaire couldn't imagine dying alone in a house with no one even to talk to. She'd prefer a hostel when her time came, with someone always around to comfort her. Of course, she had nobody living in her place at the moment, either, so she should probably suspend her judgment.

"You said you were in the stables?"

Paul nodded. "If she yelled, Dad might hear, and if we disturbed Dad, he'd kick us out." He frowned and leaned his elbows on the table. "For good, I mean. We larked about in there 'cause it was the one place we had to go. Fair enough, we shouldn't use it at night, but Dad could go mental."

He twisted the napkin in his hands, then touched his throat with the fingers of his right hand, cupping it in a mild version of a strangle.

"If I'd thought anything bad was going to happen, I'd have left her alone, you know?" He stopped and panted for a few beats while he caught his breath. "I only covered her mouth for a moment." He pulled his shoulders in, shrinking further. "I'm sure it was less than a minute, but she died."

He squeezed his lips with his fingers—a belated reflex to stop talking for his own safety. Ngaire looked at Deb, eyebrows raised. Was she going to ask?

Deb nodded. "You said, 'we called it the bed' and 'we knew not to go upstairs,'" she quoted back to him verbatim. "Who was 'we' exactly?"

Paul's eyes widened, caught, then his face relaxed, and he shrugged. "I misspoke. It was just Magdalene and me that night."

It would be on the video. Ngaire glanced at the side panel, reassured by the blinking green light. The camera was still on and operating.

"What did you do with Magdalene once she was dead?" Ngaire asked. "What did you do with her body?"

"I moved it in the car, an old truck. It wasn't mine, but Dad let me drive it as long as I did a few errands for him when needed. I shifted her into the flatbed and drove to the Waimak."

"The Waimakariri River," Deb clarified. Paul nodded, and she waved her finger in the air.

"Yes," he said aloud. "I drove near the bank, downriver, where it's deeper, and pushed her off the back." He rubbed his hand over his face, over his bald head, and flakes of skin drifted in lazy spirals to land on the table. "Then her body got caught, halfway down. I slid beside her to push her in using my boots and had a terrified moment when I thought I'd get stuck there myself." He gave a hoarse laugh. "I couldn't swim. Still can't. I thought she'd drag me with her, and we'd both be found dead in the river in the morning. Then she shifted and slid down into the water, and I pulled myself up to the car."

He looked at his watch and grimaced at the answer. He reached into his pocket, and his expression changed to one of dismay.

"Do you mind if I go home now?" he asked. "I've left my medication there, and it's time to take it."

Ngaire watched the clouds gather on Deb's face

and hurried to ward off the storm. "We'd prefer you didn't leave the station, Mr. Worthington. We've a doctor on staff who'll be able to assess you for medical needs. If you tell him what you're taking, he'll make sure you're looked after."

"But I'm free to go, aren't I?" he asked, looking from Deb to Ngaire and back again. "I came in here voluntarily. It'd be easier if I go home for my pills now and return tomorrow."

Deb kept eye contact with him and shook her head. "Paul Worthington, I'm arresting you for the murder of Magdalene Lynton on or about the thirteenth of March, 1979." A tight smile hardened her face. As Deb ran through the warning again, Paul's brow lifted in surprise, he frowned and twisted in indignation, then his shoulders slumped into acceptance.

"Do you understand?" Deb prompted again when he didn't answer.

He nodded, his hands gripped into fists on the tabletop in front of him.

"For the tape," Deb said. They hadn't used tape in a decade, but saying "DVD" or "hard drive" just earned puzzled looks.

"Yes, I understand."

They suspended the interview, and while Deb scouted for the doctor on duty, Ngaire went back to her desk. The screen saver paraded the official police insignia across her screen, and she clicked the mouse to bring it to life.

"Lynton, Magdalene," she typed into the search box. A list of entries popped up, but none matched. She tried a few different spellings but didn't produce a result.

"Doc's in there now. Find her yet?" Deb asked. She leaned over Ngaire's shoulder to peer at the screen.

"There's nothing on record. Maybe there wasn't a case?"

"Or the asshole who typed it up spelled it so wrong, we'll never find it," Deb said. "Have you tried the death register?"

Ngaire switched to that website and logged in. It was late afternoon, and school holidays were in full swing. Even on a Tuesday, teenage hookups jammed the Internet to a standstill. A circle spun in slow loops on the monitor as she waited.

The screen cleared, and Ngaire typed her query again. "Bingo," she said as a list of results came up. This time, the first line matched.

"Cause of death, accidental drowning," she read out loud and turned to Deb with a question in her eyes. "Do you think we were too quick off the mark?"

"Nah. Fits in perfectly. Besides, if he's wasting our time, he deserves a scare."

"Jesus, Deb." Ngaire pushed "Print" and locked down her computer. "The guy looks on the verge of death. A bit of sympathy?"

"He'd better hold off until he's bailed," Deb replied. "Last thing we need's a death in custody."

Deb could be so callous sometimes, it amazed Ngaire that she even wanted to hold this job. Then again, last year she'd interviewed a teenage girl, Kensy Phillips. Attitudinal armor thicker than her cheap makeup. Deb talked with her until she revealed detailed information about her abusers, succeeding where a realm of social services had failed.

"Print it out and bring it along," Deb said as she walked from the room. "I'll check and see how he's doing with the doc."

"Don't be surprised if we're not able to continue straight away," Ngaire called after her. "When he said medication, I think he meant painkillers and not your garden variety. We'll need to wait until he's lucid."

"I'll use small words." Deb pinched her fingers together to show how tiny. To Ngaire, it looked about four letters' worth.

Chapter Two

Paul rested his head back against the painted concrete wall. To resist the pain took everything he had. He needed relief soon. He'd take whatever medication the doctor could give him.

He remembered when this foolish idea first popped into his consciousness. It had occurred at the last oncology appointment he'd attended.

When Dr. John Geleyn—*"Call me John"*—sat behind his desk and sighed, Paul's heart had sunk. "Further chemotherapy won't do you any good; the cancer's too advanced." Another sigh, followed by, "It's time to put your house in order."

An insult. Paul's house was always in order. Years spent in the army saw to that.

The urge to confess rose in him, a bubble breaking free. What else could he do with his remaining life? No wife, no kids, no job, and too late to try.

The chemotherapy treatment had left him weak. When he woke in the night unable to find a position that didn't trigger a new ache, Paul imagined the poisonous chemicals and the ravenous tumor joined in a foul alliance. Instead of working, one against the other, they both attacked him.

"Keep positive," his nurse said when she clipped the tube onto his Tenckhoff catheter and again when she instructed him to turn, sit, and lie still. "That's how you show the cancer who's boss."

Paul gritted his teeth and kept resenting her instead.

"We'll hit the chemotherapy hard to buy you time," Dr. Geleyn had said. "Six months could stretch into twelve or more. Remission isn't out of the question."

Seven months on, he'd gotten maybe a few weeks extra at a high cost in quality of life. One month bought for time in pain, hours lying on the bathroom floor too weak to sit up to reach the bowl. Traded for mornings spent hoping for the time and energy to clean his soiled sheets before anybody else saw.

It turned out the cancer was aggressive, not him.

Paul believed in atheism, if disbelief counts as a belief system. Through lack of interest, not passion. The long months of sickness didn't change his mind. Sick as he had been, he didn't call out to God. There was no spiritual awakening.

So, he didn't want to confess to earn a path to heaven; he needed no salve to his conscience. Paul knew where he'd end up, and the journey involved a pine box and a prepurchased cemetery plot. The cheapest hole available, not one near a tree or a bench—the position he chose sat on a corner next to a walkway where he expected visitors to stub their sneakers against his headstone when they turned short of the edge, heels scuffing on the packed earth atop his coffin.

No. Paul didn't have an everlasting soul for confession to unburden.

There'd be no solace for the victim's family, either. They already had answers about Magdalene's death. Wrong, but satisfying enough. Paul's confession would overturn their peaceful lives and reignite the pain of her death.

Sometimes, sitting alone waiting to die, Paul felt he'd lost connection with his life. His eyes filed away scenes of other patients being collected by loved ones, one or two staying throughout the chemo sessions in support. Sure, the nervous chatter of company might drive him mental, but—oh—the chance to caress another human being.

Every touch he received was perfunctory, part of a service, bought and paid for, or delivered when someone didn't pay close attention. The frisson of fingers against his palm when a cashier returned his change, the brush of a hand when he moved his shopping bags from counter to trolley.

It wasn't a sexual thing. If Paul needed sex, he'd buy sex. No. He missed the chance to impress himself on the world. He wanted the people who'd live and love and walk and talk long after he died, to care that for now, he lived. He wanted to matter.

His life spooled out like the last minutes of a movie shown in a cut-rate theater. The reels needed changing, and Paul waited, perched on seats scented by old smoke and greasy popcorn.

The act of confession could start a new picture, unfold a new reel while he waited for death. One last dance with humanity before, "Show's over, folks."

Once he decided to do it, to confess for real, Paul didn't want to phone the police station. His last stand shouldn't be lazy. He wanted to be a real person, a real citizen, and take action.

Which presented the problem of how his body behaved these days. The chemotherapy over, he was grateful that his long bouts of nausea belonged to the past, but he still waited for the bone-deep fatigue to leave. Not to mention the breathlessness, which accompanied even the slightest change in position. Paul had been happy when the post office decreased service to every other day, sparing him the extra treks to the mailbox to see if anyone remembered him.

Circulars and bank statements were the only prizes he recovered from the mail these days. Internet banking meant his bills arrived via e-mail, and payments happened online; they cluttered up his inbox, because he didn't have the energy to organize them. He paid with credit so he couldn't forget anything, except the monthly Visa bill.

He'd take the circulars inside and leaf through their colorful pages. Each one urged him to buy something, try something, be someone better. Crammed with energy, their short phrases required little attention from his melting brain.

The papers finished, he stacked them next to the pantry. A small-time hoarder. He'd be dead before the pile grew so large it required moving. Someone else's problem.

Home help visited once a week. They laundered his clothes, cleaned his floors, kept cutlery and crockery in his cupboards. They filled his prescriptions but never overfilled them. Who needed a death on their watch? Paul knew they earned little and often considered leaving a tip, even though his sickness benefit was meager and his savings almost gone. When they came, though, he grew resentful of how easily they performed tasks he couldn't. He withheld his money and his compliments until they left and then thought again about tipping.

He thought of the home help as "they," although the same man arrived each week. The job suited a woman, but a grunt and a reference to heavy lifting answered his query about that. If Paul collapsed, he realized, a male caregiver could pick him up. No need to call for help and double the minimum-wage bill to the taxpayer.

To visit a police station in person, he needed to dress himself and dress himself well, not the robe and underwear he wore most days. He slept nude because changing outfits for bed exhausted him.

With desire tugging at his brain, Paul opened the drawer in his bedroom where his undershirts lay. He hadn't worn one in so long, they remained in the pattern he'd left them in, untouched by strangers, with their own odd ways of arranging things. It was summer, but because of the weight he'd lost over the past months, cold always nipped at him, deep in his body. He'd shake sitting inside on his chair in the sun. The heat from bright sunshine on his skin still not able to penetrate enough to warm his core.

The undershirts lay three to a row, three rows across, each folded collar two inches below the other.

He'd bought them years before, when he realized that the holes dotting his old shirts were spreading to expose more of his flesh than they hid. One day, he put his arm through a hole that wasn't the armhole and realized it was time. One of the things he had to work out for himself because he never landed a wife.

His dad called them "Skivvies." Paul referred to them as undershirts for that reason, even inside his head.

He pulled out one and laid it on the bed next to him. The drawer stuck when he tried to push it back in, the chestnut wood squealing in protest at his efforts, and he hit his hand against the panel in anger. It hurt, the pain searing his nerves. Paul curled over to protect it, and tears beaded in his eyes. Stupid. He didn't know how to cry. Throughout the years when he'd wanted to, or others expected him to, he'd never learned the skill. Pain tears were a new thing. Familiar to him as a toddler, but years being a real man lay between. They dried before Paul stopped rocking. His nose ran in sympathy, so he sniffed and wiped the wet warmth from his face.

Paul had to raise his body into a kneeling position and push with his shoulder to force the drawer back in. He couldn't face getting back on the bed afterward, so he crouched on all fours on the carpet, panting. Once, as a teenager, he ran a cross-country race at high school and came in first. When he finished, he'd still been able to talk with the people congratulating him at the finish line, wiping the sweat off his forehead with a towel. The crowd cheered, and he would've run in the district competition, but his dad whipped him the night before. Made him stand, bleeding, facing the corner for hours afterward.

One undershirt accomplished. At this rate, he should book an appointment a month from Sunday. Chances were, he'd be long dead by then.

Desire fired up inside him again.

It was Wednesday tomorrow, which meant home-help day. If he put aside his resentment and pride for long enough, the caregiver would help him dress. Even if he couldn't quite let the man do that, he could instruct him to lay his clothes out.

But that was a whole day away.

For the first time, his impending death became real to Paul. Its touch rose from his abdomen, ready to choke him. His stomach roiled, and his heart beat, thud-thud-thud, doing double time.

Focus. He needed to dress, the same as he'd done each day since he turned three, and his mother told him he was a big boy now.

Paul used the bed to lever himself back to his feet. His shirts hung in the wardrobe alongside his suits. Identical, like his undershirts. Pick a style and buy plenty; that's the secret. He was a man. He didn't need to spend time in front of the mirror deciding what to wear.

So, a charcoal pinstripe it was. The jacket and trousers slipped off the hanger without bother, but the belt caught, so Paul had to take one step, two, to wrestle it off. Winded by the movement, he leaned against the mirrored door. His short breaths condensed on the glass until his image blurred into a hulking monster instead of a skeleton decorated with skin.

Shoes would have to wait. If he bent now, no way could he straighten again. He knew the signs. Weakness in his thighs, shortness of breath. His vision ebbed and flowed with each heartbeat.

He sat on the bed to dress. It took two tries to get off the dressing gown; it caught the bones of his shoulder, and his hands failed the first time he tried to pull it free. The undershirt didn't catch, and his shirt, too, was easy, although the buttons slipped and slid under his skinny fingers. The pads on his fingertips no longer had cushioning, so their grip was tenuous, and it hurt to pinch objects.

Paul pulled his trousers on, his right leg up to the knee, then the left. He gripped the belt with his right hand and balanced with his left on the side of the bed as he stood. One heave, and he dropped back down to the mattress, now able to fumble with the zipper and the buttons.

When he began treatment, Paul read the pamphlet they gave him about how the chemotherapy would affect his body and the changes to expect, nodding while his doctor explained about the nausea and the weakness and the exhaustion. He thought he understood.

He didn't understand that a few months into the future, he'd struggle to dress himself. Didn't think he'd cry while putting on socks and shoes, because the moves used up every bit of energy left circling his body, each last morsel of nutrients the cancer hadn't reached out and claimed for its own.

The hair loss surprised him as much. The doctor had explained, Paul had read the pamphlet; he believed he understood. One morning, the mirror reflected no eyelashes, no eyebrows, and no five o'clock stubble to shave away. Humanoid, but not human.

He could wait until tomorrow. So easy to nap until the angles of his body screamed for a change in position. When the home help came, he would be halfway dressed, and the rest would be simple. Unless he soiled himself in the night, or his fever sweats leaked and spread out onto the clean shirt. The fever sweats, which reeked of death, even to him.

"Stay seated, count your breaths," he chanted instead until his breathing evened out, and he recovered from the initial exertion.

No, he'd go today. He would force his body through all the actions one last time to carry out this goal. Tomorrow he could rest, back here or in a new prison home, and think with satisfaction of a job well done.

Paul bent forward and slid onto his knees and his hands to forage for his shoes and socks.

He stood as he heard the taxi approaching. The standard speed of a vehicle slowing to a crawl, giving away the fact that the driver was reading the house numbers, looking for a destination.

Paul was always better with an audience. Able to find reserves he wouldn't have discovered if left alone, he locked the front door and walked to the car. He brushed aside the driver's offer to help and wrestled with the door handle.

The driver read out the directions, and Paul nodded, grateful that for the moment he didn't have to issue the directions himself as he would have in the old days. The fellow pushed the buttons on his GPS gadget, and it directed operations.

"You signing in?" the driver asked.

Paul shook his head, and the man fell silent, turning up the radio instead of making conversation. Paul wondered why he looked like a parolee to the driver. Was he so out of step with societal norms?

"Gonna be a lovely day tomorrow," the driver said when the car pulled up at a set of lights. "They reckon it'll get to ninety. Love this global warming."

Paul nodded and managed a light grunt in acknowledgment. Warmth would be good. He felt sweaty now from effort, but the chill in his body's core never left.

He had a chit to pay for the taxi, a leftover from

the hospital-issued slips that ensured he turned up for treatment sessions when he could no longer drive. His signature was wobbly as fuck on the line, but the driver didn't even look at it. Just grabbed it back and stuck it in his receipts tray.

"Hope they don't send you to the big house," the driver joked before he pulled away, leaving Paul standing on the pavement outside the police station.

Three meters of paving between the car and the station, but it took minutes to walk. The world rocked and rolled under his feet, but he continued to shuffle forward on the even ground.

A man in a hi-viz jacket stood to one side of the entrance. Paul thought at first that the man had stepped out for a cheeky smoke, but then he caught sight of the mobile phone tucked between his shoulder and his ear. A personal call, no doubt.

The doors registered Paul's presence, opened, and closed before he got through, then bounced open again. The woman behind the front counter half-stood as though to offer help, then sat again, eyes staring. She was in a contained office behind double panes of glass, and he was apparently not worth the trouble. Never mind. He kept on at the same gait, a tortoise with an important mission.

"Can I help you?" she asked, her lips pulled wide in a smile. Her dark-blue jersey set off the chestnut highlights streaked through the dark curls of her hair. If her hair had not been tied back in a ponytail, he bet it would have spread out like glowing silk. A Maori by the look of her, though she was pale enough for him not to be sure. Her lips pouty, her nose flat except for the jaunty tip.

Paul threw his passport down onto the counter. "My identification," he said. "So you know I'm serious." To his pleasure, his voice came out strong, belying his body language. "I want to confess to a murder."

Chapter Three

Ngaire had an hour to kill before Dr. Jarvis thought the interview could recommence. The doc had shaken his head and whistled air between the gap in his front teeth before whispering, "Cancer. Pancreatic. Very painful."

The hour was to allow the morphine to take effect. Dr. Jarvis assured them that with the level of pain Mr. Worthington was experiencing, he'd be conscious and of sound enough mind to interview by then.

Ngaire had seen that before. If morphine was injected into someone without physical pain, the body sent it straight to the brain and turned it into junkie mush. If someone needed pain relief, the body used it for that foremost, not sparing enough to take them on a trip as well. She'd felt grateful for that during her own hospitalization. The hallucinations she did experience loaded her up with more fear.

To use up the time, she'd sneaked down the road to the local pub and ordered fish and chips with a lemonade. The pub was the closest and cheapest place where she'd be able to sit down to eat. Almost like a proper meal.

"Ngaire, my love. What's up?" Hands pressed on each of her shoulders as a kiss landed on her cheek. "Not drinking on a work night, are you?"

"Hi, Finlay. Fancy seeing you in a bar," Ngaire replied as she brushed his hands away. Once, a decade ago, they'd gone on one date in high school before his parents divorced, and he moved away. Since they'd met again last year, he'd acted like they were still dating.

"Anything good happening?" he asked. When Ngaire shook her head, he tried again. "It's a slow month, and I'm close to accepting a copywriting gig to get the bills paid. Take pity on me, Miss Ngaire." Finlay placed his hands in a prayer position and kneeled, tipping his head forward so the long brown locks of his fringe fell over his twinkling blue eyes.

"Christ's sake, Finlay. You realize this is a public place, right? I can't be handing out gossip when my job's on the line."

As he took a seat opposite, he cocked an eyebrow. "Injuries still holding you back? It's been months now."

Ngaire shrugged. "Yeah, well, the doctor won't sign me off as fit, so I'm spending my days tapping away at the computer. Not what I signed on for."

The barman dropped Ngaire's meal on the table and took Finlay's order for a pint and a shot back to the bar. "Well, if you're after sympathy, look somewhere else. I spent the last two nights going through rubbish to find credit card bills."

Finlay called himself a journalist, but with that profession shriveling, he ran sidelines for a dozen different occupations. A private investigator who specialized in adultery took notice of his skills; the job was a perfect fit for an unusual set of talents.

"Put together a quote sheet and let the central office forensic guys know," Ngaire said. "I'm sure they'd love to outsource the rubbish sweeps if the price was right." She tucked into the fish and chip meal, stomach grumbling. Although working at a desk eight hours a day should've dulled her appetite, her stomach paid no heed. Something her scale had already registered.

"There's no way I'm after a job sorting more rubbish," Finlay said, then drank the shot of whiskey and chased it with half a pint of beer. When he put the mug back on the table, his eyes watered, but that was all. Ngaire would've been flat out if she'd attempted the same. Always a lightweight with the drink.

"I want to know why my favorite detective is eating supper in this fine establishment when she'd usually be home by now."

"Even paperwork can run long," Ngaire said as she attempted to wipe the plate clean with the last chip, a task it wasn't equal to. "Have you ever heard of a girl called Magdalene Lynton?"

Finlay's eyes sparkled, and he downed the remaining half pint in one long swallow. "That's more like it, love." He pulled a notebook out from his back pocket and flipped back through the pages. "Here."

Ngaire looked at Magdalene's name written in rough pencil on the page he'd shoved across. Finlay laughed at her confusion. "So, you weren't expecting that."

Before she could decipher the rest of his horrible scrawl, he pulled the notebook away. Probably a lost cause anyway, as he took notes in shorthand; Pitman standard was a level above Ngaire's comprehension.

"Who is she, and why's her name in your notebook?" Ngaire's voice came out flat, reflecting her disappointment. She'd thought Paul Worthington was a murder case thrown in her lap and solved for good measure. If Magdalene's name had been in the papers recently, though, it'd be a fabrication made up to satisfy a weird need the guy had. What a way to spend your final days on earth, stuck in a police station confessing to crimes you didn't commit.

"She was the young lass who drowned here in the seventies. She was from the Christ Cult, which operated around here at that time. The group started up after the Cooperites and finished up around the same time as the God Squad got going in Waipara. I was doing a piece on Destiny Church a few months back and tried to tie stuff back to the fortieth anniversary of their closure but couldn't make the sale." He snapped the notebook shut and popped it back into his pocket. "And that's the last you're getting from me until you give me more, quid pro quo, etc."

"I've never even heard of them," Ngaire said as she wrote down a few tidbits of her own. "Did they really call themselves a cult?"

Finlay snorted with amusement. "None of the groups named themselves those things. The communities living nearby did. The official name was Christ the Redeemer Do Good Works in His Name, Amen or some such good shit." He reached over the table and pulled the pen from her hand with such speed that Ngaire continued to write a letter before she noticed that the pen was gone.

"Oi." She reached across and snatched it back.

"Your turn for information, dearest. What're you interested in Magdalene for?"

Ngaire looked at her watch. She had fifteen minutes before she needed to head back. If she handed any more details to Finlay, a story would appear sometime soon in a newspaper, and even if it were online-only, there'd still be a large circle of readers. She tried to calculate the blowback. Was it worth it to save hours of trawling through old records trying to pinpoint a crime that may not even have occurred?

"There's an old codger in the station at the moment," she said. Finlay's eyebrows shot up, and he leaned in close, notebook back off his hip and at the ready. "He's confessed to the murder of Magdalene Lynton."

Finlay rolled his eyes and tucked the pencil away. "She wasn't murdered. She drowned."

Ngaire shrugged. "This bloke reckons he tossed her into the river after killing her. Even if she was still alive at that point, it's murder either way."

Finlay shook his head, "She didn't drown in the river." Then he pulled his pencil out again and scribbled some indecipherable symbols.

"What?" Ngaire asked. "What is it?"

Finlay smiled at her, exposing his tobacco-stained teeth. Four years ago he'd quit, salary unequal to the price hikes, but had never invested in a whitening treatment. The lack of care in his personal grooming should've been off-putting but instead was one of the few things that attracted Ngaire.

He shrugged, the pretend nonchalance coming too late to appear real. "There's a story either way, isn't there?" Putting his hands up in the air he mimicked pretend headlines. "'False confessions. Why do they happen?' Or, 'Murderer of Christian Cult member revealed.'" He lowered his hands again, straight onto Ngaire's. "I can spin it whichever way the editor wants. Or sell it twice."

"So, your turn," Ngaire said, shifting her hand into her lap. "What more do you have?"

Finlay slitted his eyes for a moment, and Ngaire's heart sank, but then he shrugged again, the pretend nonchalance back in full force. "Come round mine later, and I'll give you everything I put together. There's her old autopsy report, full coronial inquest notes, lots of good stuff."

"And for me right now? I'm going straight back in there." If she could get information to trip Mr. Worthington up, perhaps the case could be chucked straight out.

"I was studying her death because it brought the whole cult thing to an end. Afterward her parents were distraught and began questioning the teachings and way of life." He grinned widely again. Finlay was a fervent atheist, emphasis on *fervent*. "Once you question religion, you know that's the end. Soon they moved out, and over the next few months the rest of the group disbanded and left."

"Over a girl's death?" Ngaire asked. Her voice rose so sharply that she forced her mouth shut and waited for a second. "Sorry, I mean it's horrible and all, but—"

"Another tip for you. Magdalene was part of a closed Christian commune, fifteen years old. Drowned 'by accident'"—Finlay put the words in air quotes—"and she was pregnant." He reached over to tap Ngaire's nose with his notebook and stood, hitching his jeans up at the belt, his eyes scanning the bar for another contact to press. "Join the dots for yourself, love."

"We're recommencing interview with Paul Worthington at six thirty-seven p.m., Detective Constables Debra Weedon and Ngaire Blakes in attendance," Detective Weedon stated. For the benefit of the recording, Paul guessed. She frowned at her watch as she read out the time, then glared across the table at him. Oh, no, he was inconveniencing her. He smiled back, showing his teeth. This was no country picnic for him, either.

The unwillingness of the doctor to give him pain relief before taking a full history meant the dose administered had to be larger when it came. After the injection, he'd floated; feeling relief as the opioid surrogate flooded his veins.

Coming back, Paul had realized that his bottom hurt. A thin mattress atop a hard concrete bench was the extent of his cell's furnishings. Further decorated with beige and olive paint. Without reserves of fat, sitting anywhere except his overstuffed La-Z-Boy chair made Paul uncomfortable, but these surroundings would've tested anyone.

If he lay back, the pain would recede. But he'd have to struggle upright again when they called him back to interview, and his energy drained at the thought. Instead, he remained sitting.

He hadn't pictured Magdalene for years. The live Magdalene, that is. The dead one paid him frequent visits. As he drifted, he thought of when she'd first entered the shed. How her eyes widened with fright when she realized it wasn't just Billy there. Unwelcome in his own damn shed. Made Paul wonder how often she and Billy used it without his knowing.

Soaked through, her cotton print dress clinging to her curved body, hair stretched halfway to her waist. Drenched, it looked dark-brown but with highlights to show it would dry to blonde. Red eyes, red cheeks, and red lips, and her eyes the least of those features.

As she sat next to him in the cozy warmth of the hay bale, she'd dried. Paul planned a future in his head, something he'd done with any girl who let him touch her.

Billy had run out of there, couldn't get out soon enough, leaving them alone. Paul traced the curve of her shoulder and her collar bone with his fingertip and smiled as he imagined the graceful children they'd have together. The long, wild nights alone in their bedroom, and the long, happy days playing house.

Detective Weedon ran through the warning again, Paul reciting along in his head. Almost had it by heart. Realizing his eyes were glazing, he pulled himself high in his chair to concentrate.

"When we suspended this interview, you were explaining how you disposed of the dead body of your victim, Magdalene Lynton," Weedon said. "Now, we'd like you to go back and give us more information about what happened prior."

Paul shifted in his chair, careful to keep his abdomen still and hard, and nodded. "Magdalene arrived at the shed that night," he said.

"Had you seen her before?"

Paul tilted his head at the question. There was a blockage forming in his right ear, but if he kept his head to the side, it should stay open for longer. "No. That was the first time I'd met her."

"Why did she meet you in the shed?"

Paul shook his head. "She didn't *meet* me. It was just she came along, and I was there. I think she was looking for shelter."

"Shelter from what?" This time, it was the other detective who spoke.

"From her family, I suppose." Paul moved his head, still tilted, to make eye contact. "Probably got fed up with them, bunch of happy clappers."

He'd passed into tiredness now. At home, he'd always take a nap after his medication. There'd be the blissful release of consciousness, then he'd wake as the pain reasserted itself. *Oh, yes, I'm still here. You can't sleep me away.*

"Did you know her family?"

Paul shook his head, then said the word aloud before the detective could remind him. "No."

"They were members of the Christian community, right?"

Paul looked at Detective Blakes across the table. She was favoring her right side, and it looked as though it were due to an injury. He saw his own frown of pain reflected on her face, though dialed back a notch.

He shrugged. "I didn't know then, but yes. Turns out she was from the Christian Cult."

Paul smiled as a silent exchange occurred in front of him. Heated. Weedon flung a nasty expression at Blakes and received a stonewalling response.

Paul shifted his weight in the chair, felt the bones of his bum. Mom had always used that phrase to describe the family's financial position. *On the bones of our bum.* He understood it better now that his real bones mimicked her saying.

The table never held enough food. The pantry stored nothing but seasonings. There'd never been an after-school snack except for what he foraged from the neighbors' fruit trees. They'd yell at him, even though plenty of what he picked off the tree already lay rotting on the ground.

"So I gather you weren't part of their congregation."

"No, I already said I didn't know her." Shifting again, he winced as the move ignited a nerve. "There were only four or five families in that group, good riddance. Didn't mingle with us locals."

His father's opinion, that. Dad had hated the religious groups that sprang up everywhere. Waipara and Cust were far enough away, but the Christian bloody Cult moved in next door. Dad's laziness and poor farming knowledge didn't need to be shown up by a bunch of Christ followers.

"How long was she there?" Weedon asked. "Before you murdered her."

Paul tipped his head forward to hide his smile. She'd thought him a nutter at the start, a time-waster. Now, her frustration and anger showed a change in attitude.

She'd surprised him with the arrest. He hadn't expected it. It felt like a punishment being inflicted in retribution but at least it showed that she accepted his story. His last grand gesture wouldn't end in embarrassing disbelief.

"Her visit lasted an hour, maybe," Paul said. He shook his head; his right ear had now closed, so concentrating was harder. His doctor had told him he could lose hearing or sight; from the chemotherapy as much as the cancer. To be isolated that way terrified him more than death. Blind, deaf, alone, except for the tumor eating his pancreas.

Detective Blakes again. "What did you do for that hour? Could you talk through the evening for us?"

The evening. Making it sound so fancy, as though it came with dinner and fine wine. Not him and a girl on a hay bale in a musty-smelling shed.

He shrugged. "There isn't much to say. Magdalene arrived soaked through, with her arms bleeding. I think she'd run away and wanted somewhere to rest, something to eat, so we—I—let her in the shed, and we talked and stuff and then . . ." He gestured a series of waves with his hand.

"So if you were talking, and you knew she was hurt, why did you feed her a beer?" Weedon asked.

Paul screwed his nose up. "It wasn't like that. There were these signals she was giving me, you know."

"What signals?"

"Just," he fluttered his hand in the air. "Just signals. A wink, a smile, that kind of stuff."

Paul had been so scared when he pulled himself out that he'd had to jerk at his penis to get it hard. Once he'd pulled his trousers down and got on top of her, it had been better. His first time, but he found the right hole and started pumping.

She'd been cool, soft, and wet, and he'd balanced himself on his hands so he could thrust deeper. She just lay there and let him do it. Offered no resistance.

When he pulled out to clean himself up with a handful of hay, she still hadn't moved. Paul gave her a nudge, a push, and she slid down the hay. Her head tilted backward. When he gave her another gentle kick with his toe, her face rolled toward him, her eyes open, staring, blank. He'd seen them again every night since.

It was Billy's fault. When he came back, Billy grabbed her by the shoulders and shook her until her eyes closed again, and her mouth flopped open. Billy flung her down in disgust and walked away to scull a beer in a part of the shed without a dead girl in it.

Paul pulled back from the memory and looked at the live women sitting across the table. When he'd imagined confessing to the police, it was to a man. Not a woman. Not a pair of women. It was harder to say things to them, near them, around them. They didn't understand the way a bloke would.

"Anyway, I said I got it wrong. After I gave her the beer, I put my hand over her mouth in case she yelled, and she died. That's all. I didn't mean to kill her, but I did."

The thought that saved him during sleepless nights was Billy. Billy had hurt her most. Billy had sex with her first. In comparison, Paul had done little wrong. He'd touched her, but only to stay in good with his friend, to keep up.

"We're waiting for the autopsy report, but you know that her death went on the record as an accidental drowning?" Weedon asked.

Paul looked from one to the other. "Well, yeah, but they got it wrong. I pushed her body into the water, and they found her and put two and two together to make three. I just got lucky."

Detective Blakes was shaking her head before he'd even finished speaking. "You didn't get lucky. There're distinct differences between death from drowning and death from being smothered. If they said she died from drowning, then she did."

Paul heard the words, and his fingers froze up from the cold that enveloped his body. Different from the usual chill; this came from outside, not inside. "It's wrong, so they mustn't have done their job right. I held my hand over her mouth, and she died. It was an accident. End of story."

"Was it an accident when you pushed her body into the river?" Detective Blakes asked. Paul's eyes flicked to hers and saw kindness there. His panic increased.

"Of course not. I was disposing of her body, so I pushed it into the river. She was already dead."

Detective Weedon leaned across the table and smiled at him. He'd clenched his hands into fists, and he noticed her noticing. Paul forced them to uncurl and lie flat on the table. His head spun, making him nauseous. This was all bullshit. They were trying to upset him. Working him over to see what else he wanted to admit to. All a tactic.

It was an accident. Actually, Billy had killed her

with a game of one-upmanship he'd tricked Paul into playing. Then he'd left Paul alone to clean up the damage. Wouldn't even touch her to help Paul carry her out of the horse stables. So it was Billy's fault she'd ended up where she did. Paul wasn't made of muscle.

Billy peeled out to go get drunk and stayed drunk for a week, taking their friend Greg with him. Billy said he did it so Greg wouldn't remember who he'd been with, or what time he'd been doing stuff. So they could use him as an alibi if things went wrong. Paul could see that when Billy said "we," he only meant himself, so Paul better do a good job of not getting caught.

She'd choked to death, she must have.

"Well, we'll know more when the autopsy records come through, but it's not plausible at this stage," said Weedon. Her eyes locked with his, mesmerizing him so that he couldn't look away. "That'd be a huge mistake for a doctor to make."

Detective Blakes piped up and added her voice to the mix. "Remember, it was a high-profile case. The whole community she came from closed as a result, and she was a young girl. Cases like that don't get processed incorrectly."

"I smothered her, and I threw her dead body into the river," Paul stated. His breath whistled on exhalation. The chemotherapy had left his body weak and open to intruders, and he'd had pleurisy and pneumonia in the past six months. Some nights he woke up hearing a teakettle, then realized that the sound emanated from his own chest, his own lungs. Give him time and a tape recorder, and he could make a symphony of the cacophonous sounds of a body dying. The creaks, groans, and rasps of a body trying to cling against hope to another day.

His left ear blocked now; sound damped down like he'd flicked a switch. Paul looked at his hands on the table and saw they'd reformed into fists. Apparently they hadn't paid attention to the fact that he was in no fit state to fight anybody.

"Look on the bright side, Mr. Worthington," Weedon said. Paul locked eyes with her again until dizziness spun his vision around. Even through his good ear her voice sounded far away. "You didn't murder her by smothering her to death. Good for you."

The wheeze built in his chest, and he coughed to clear it. Coughed again, and again. His vision drew back to a pinprick in gray scale.

"You murdered her when you threw her into the river."

Chapter Four

"Would either of you care to tell me why there's an unconscious man in our police cells?" Detective Sergeant Gascoigne asked.

Ngaire opened her mouth to speak, but Deb got there a beat before. "It's because he's sick, sir. Dr. Jarvis cleared him for questioning, but he didn't last ten minutes before collapsing. Gave us both a fright."

"And there won't be anything untoward on the tapes when I review them?"

Ngaire got in first that time. "No, sir. The suspect, Paul Worthington, he presented himself here of his own accord to confess to a murder. We suspended the first interview when he said he required pain medication, and we'd barely started the second when he collapsed."

"Is there substance to this?" Gascoigne asked. "Genna said she thought he was a time-waster."

Deb rolled her eyes, but so only Ngaire saw. Genna's intuitive assessment was always so important to their DS.

"There's a reasonable line of questioning to pursue, sir," Ngaire answered. "Mr. Worthington seemed lucid and told us specific details of the crime. And he was very insistent that he'd committed a murder."

She saw Deb's lip curl. When Paul had collapsed in front of them in the interview room, she'd raised her hands, palms up. "Was it something I said?"

"He knew the name of the victim, the date and approximate time of death, and relayed specific details

of the crime," Deb said.

"It also wasn't something he'd picked out of the papers." Ngaire hurried to reply to an objection he hadn't lodged. "The death was recorded as an accidental drowning at the time, so it's not as though he chose a big, unresolved case to exploit."

"If the coroner thought it was an accidental drowning, what makes you think it wasn't?" Gascoigne asked.

Course work had accustomed Ngaire to being questioned. She'd earned the full rank of detective constable just three months before her injury and desk duty became her new routine. Every time she came to a conclusion, challenge it, explain why. A routine pathway to second-guessing herself and allowing others to do the same.

"His version explains why she ended up in the river, drowned. He rendered her unconscious, thought she was dead, drove her body to the Waimak, and pushed her in." She shrugged when her list ended, and she realized how few details it contained. "We haven't requested the coroner's case files yet, sir, so there aren't many facts to go on. On the face of it, though, it's worth investigating further."

"Well, don't let me stop you. The doctor's transferring him to the hospital as we speak, so you can't question him tonight. Write your report on the incident in the interview room, and forward me a copy of the tape before you leave tonight. Oh, and Deb?"

Deb turned to him. "Yes, sir?"

"An officer is required to be stationed at Mr. Worthington's side until he's released from hospital. To guarantee other patients' *safety*." His tone implied that he used that word loosely. "Next time, consider this scenario before you place a chronically ill man under arrest."

"We both agreed on that decision, sir," Ngaire said. Gascoigne waved a dismissive hand before striding away. She didn't matter.

Deb rolled her eyes but waited until Gascoigne left before she groaned. "Genna said he's a time-waster," she mimicked in a high-pitched squeak. "You told me, too." Ngaire bore the glare in silence. "I promised my team I'd make the game for once," she said, her voice low.

Ngaire nodded. After seeing Deb play rugby at a few division games she knew how restless her colleague grew if she couldn't get to practice. Ngaire used to feel that passion, but nothing filled her with that feeling now.

"Just chuck a few lines down. I'll get the rest of it sorted. Nothing on tonight except a bath and an early night."

Deb studied her for a moment, head on one side, until Ngaire felt she should have kept the offer to herself. Then she smiled, whacked Ngaire on the shoulder, and handed across her notebook. "Already scrawled there for you," she said. "If you ever start a social life again, I'll owe you one."

"Oh, ha, that's a good one," Ngaire replied, trying for irony and missing. "I chatted up a dude in the pub this afternoon, if you must know."

There was a brief flash of interest on Deb's face, then she looked at her watch again, and an avalanche of her own needs buried it. "Catch me up tomorrow."

"See you," Ngaire said. As she took Deb's notebook and opened it to the statement, she smiled. It was nice that someone in the station was talking to her, even if it was with a helping of mockery. After fifteen minutes spent trying to decipher Deb's handwriting, Ngaire gave up and typed the report in her own words, putting both their names to it. Once that was done, she put through a request for the coroner's verdict and evidence; it was too late for the courthouse now, but if she caught the early bird tomorrow, her chances of receiving it soon were high.

As she worked, she rubbed her abdomen on occasion. "Fifteen and pregnant," Finlay had said, thinking it would shock her, and it had. But for different reasons. Ngaire had been fifteen and pregnant once. A careless moment with a boy she didn't stay friends with, performing an act she'd never learned to enjoy.

The clinic urged her to involve her parents, but she'd refused. By law, she didn't have to. She'd contemplated suicide instead—an easier option for her teen self, with so little life experience to lose, than for the adult she'd become. Two pills and a stomachache later, the decision was behind her. Another life experience done and filed away.

It was growing late, but only by her standards. She needed to call in at Finlay's to get the reports he'd promised her. Knowing the hours he kept, Ngaire assumed his bedtime started later than her own bedtime of nine thirty.

Finlay was talking on his mobile phone when he opened the door for her. Holding a finger up, *one moment*, he kept talking and waved in the general direction of his lounge. He followed her through and waved again, this time at the drinks cabinet lying open in his sideboard. Although Ngaire knew she didn't handle alcohol well, she decided that a small tipple couldn't hurt. She needed some help in getting over the strange day she'd had. Not to mention putting up with Finlay's nonsense for another hour.

After dusting the bottom of a glass with vodka, she filled it with coke. After a few sips, she moved and sat on Finlay's sofa. Like him, it was the worse for wear, the leather finish cracking and the cheap finish peeling off where the sunlight hit. Like Finlay, it was as comfortable as hell.

Meanwhile, he continued to chat on the phone. As he paced, his voice grew loud, then soft, then there was a long pause as he listened—or pretended to.

He'd left a pile of work on the table. With the boldness that half a drink had given her, Ngaire pulled it closer and leaned forward to take a look. She shuffled through the top pages, which would need a personal translation, and saw a photocopy and an official information request. Putting her almost-finished drink down on the floor, Ngaire flipped through the pages unencumbered.

The photocopy was the coroner's report about Magdalene's death. Skipping over the introduction to the facts of the case, she stopped midway down the second page to read.

[14] At 2:00 p.m., Mrs. Lynton was in the kitchen of the housing block preparing a meal. Isaiah Haldrem came into the room and said that he'd found Magdalene's body. He said it wouldn't be appropriate for her to follow.

[15] At 2:15 p.m., Isaiah Haldrem entered the bedroom of Abraham (Abe) and Mary Lynton, where Abe Lynton was sitting on the bed. Isaiah Haldrem told Abe Lynton he'd found Magdalene's body and asked him to escort him back to the body.

[16] At 2:25 p.m., Abe Lynton and Isaiah Haldrem walked to the slurry pit at the rear of the milking shed on the Ithers Road Farm property. Isaiah had tied a rope over the side of the slurry pit and staked it to the ground near the milking shed exit. He pulled the rope toward the side, and Abe Lynton saw Magdalene Lynton's body tied to it.

[17] At 2:45 p.m., Abe Lynton and Isaiah Haldrem pulled Magdalene Lynton's body from the slurry pit. There were no signs of life.

"They found her in a slurry on her parents' compound," Ngaire said with disgust when Finlay finished up his phone call and came to sit with her. "It says here she drowned in cow shit."

Finlay took the paper from her and nodded. "That's the finding. A death I wouldn't wish on anyone." He handed the paper back to Ngaire, but she brushed it aside, and he placed it back on the table. "Is that not the way your self-confessed murderer described the crime?"

"Not at all," Ngaire said, reaching for her glass. "In his version, he smothered her and threw her body in the Waimak."

"Didn't know the Waimak drained into a slurry," Finlay said as he took the glass from her and topped it off. "How'd he suffocate her, anyway? She was a tall lass for her age, five ten."

"She was lying on some hay. When he stuck his hand over her mouth to keep her quiet, she died."

Finlay laughed. "That fit with many murders in your neck of the woods?"

Ngaire shook her head. "No, his confession's full of lies and holes, but I thought there was something there. The guy's on his last legs. He fainted in the interview room when we were ten minutes in. The doctor made us wait to interview him the second time because his pain medication is so heavy."

"Cancer?"

"I guess so. Or AIDS. He's so thin, it was like looking straight through him. Clothes five sizes too large, and they weren't large garments."

The events of the day overwhelmed her, and a tear slipped from her eyelid. Finlay saw and froze at the drinks cabinet. "Are you okay?"

Ngaire smiled at his discomfort, and the tears receded. "I'm fine. It's just late, and it's been a shitty day, and I thought, I really thought, the old guy was getting something off his chest."

He pushed an unasked-for second drink at her and Ngaire took a gulp, grimacing at the strength. "Take it easy. I've still got to drive home."

"Stay here, in my boudoir. I've got a cherry-red, heart-shaped bed and a mirror on the ceiling. Always my childhood dream."

Ngaire assumed he was joking, but with Finlay there was the outside chance he wasn't. Boy had a filthy mind sometimes.

"Nope, I need to get home to my bed." She stretched out on the sofa, her body contradicting her words. "There're exercises I've got to do in the morning, and I doubt you have a ball and band hanging around your love den."

He sat beside her as she continued to contemplate moving without doing so. "If you drowned in a slurry fill of muck," she said, alcohol slowing her voice, "why wouldn't you have that in your lungs?"

Finlay picked up the photocopy to examine the pages again. He shrugged. "Drowning's a weird one. It's based on evidence of how they found the body as much as evidence from the body itself. She'd have smothered if her body couldn't breathe it in. There wouldn't be traces then, except in her mouth and throat."

Ngaire rubbed the side of her forehead, trying to aid her thought process. "But there'd be foam and stuff, wouldn't there? This doesn't mention foam."

Finlay nodded. "It does, however, mention that they found her three days after she went missing." He put the papers back down and stretched out beside her. "You're thinking of a quick autopsy. By the time they pulled her out, her body would've started decomposing." He took a long slug of his drink. "That slurry water gets bloody hot."

"It feels wrong," Ngaire said. She held her drink out for Finlay to take it. If she was going to make the drive home, she couldn't chance having any more of it herself.

He picked up the report again. "With strangling or smothering, there's often damage to the neck or mouth and lots of blood vessels popping in your eyes. No mention of that here." He tapped the report papers against the top of her knee. "You can check it with your doc tomorrow. That's what he's there for, isn't he?"

Ngaire snorted. Finlay thought the entire world existed so he could ask it questions. She pulled out her phone and tapped in a search for drowning and pathology, saving the pages it returned for later reading. "Guess your article's going to be about old people faking stories to get themselves attention, then."

"Already phoned it through, love. No names. It'll be a thing of beauty to see my name in the morning paper again."

"As long as it can't be traced back, I'm happy." Ngaire stood and stretched out her back. The air popped from her spine, and Finlay winced. He'd been the same at school. One boy had made it a daily mission to crack his knuckles in Finlay's face just to watch him squirm.

"Always protect my sources, love, you know that. Can you find your own way?" He waved the drink he held in each hand as an excuse.

"Sure can." Ngaire gathered up the folder of papers and tapped it into a neat rectangle. "Mind if I take these with me? I'll get them back to you when I can."

"No worries."

The drive home was uneventful and breath-test free. Ngaire could feel the alcohol wearing off as she pulled into her garage, then unlocked the connecting door. It was well past her bedtime.

Instead of going to sleep, though, she spread Finlay's papers out in front of her on the bed. She flipped through the coroner's report again, noting this time that the verdict from the autopsy was "consistent with drowning" whatever the hell that meant.

They'd had a baptism ritual with Magdalene at

the church, involving the whole congregation, after which she left to find a place to reflect and contemplate. The report didn't specify where she had gone. Ngaire searched through the papers and found a layout of the compound showing there were specific areas given over to "contemplation." Maybe the bits that weren't useful for any other purpose, considering it was a communal working farm.

Magdalene's mother noticed her missing when she didn't come to the house for teatime, and she couldn't locate her around the property. She alerted the Prophet, who arranged for everyone in the commune to engage in a search for the girl. He then decided the best course of action was to pray for her safe return. A phone call to the police followed a lengthy delay.

It wouldn't have been a top priority even if they'd reported her missing earlier. Fifteen years old may seem young to parents, but the police would've seen a normal teenager capable of running away on a whim and inconveniencing everyone. When Ngaire looked through more of the papers, she found that Magdalene's parents had testified to another incident where their daughter had run away. She'd spent two days away before she returned home.

Ngaire wondered how often Magdalene's parents had walked past the slurry pit where their daughter's body lay, not thinking to search there because they were trying to find a live girl. You only combed those areas to search for a dead girl.

Had Paul known people from the compound, despite his denial? His parents' farm was two farms over from Magdalene's family's land, but from the plans it looked like their grazing paddocks backed up onto each other. A working boy, given his generation. Had he worked out in the fields and spotted Magdalene so close?

Stupid, unanswerable thoughts that wouldn't get her anywhere.

Ngaire shoved the papers off the bed and reached for the scar cream she kept on the night table. She scraped a clump up with her forefinger and massaged it into the four-inch scar on her right leg. It curved from the back of her thigh around and over her knee. The flesh was still angry red, and although the ritual application of her cream didn't appear to have made any improvement in its appearance, she kept doing it. This soothing motion was within her control. It felt great, though judging by how her physiotherapist dug her fingers in when she was massaging the muscles, it was doing no good.

She pulled her pajama top up and ran her finger across the cream, gathering another dollop to apply. The wound on her side ran half the length of her rib cage. Her attacker hadn't wielded the knife with enough force. When the blade should've bounced off bone and thrust through to pierce her liver or kidney, it instead skidded along the length of her rib.

White tissue had grown up around this wound, and it turned a mild pink at the center. Not as deep, not as damaging as the wound on her leg. But this one scared her more. Ngaire couldn't look at it as she massaged the cream in, letting her pajama top fall to cover her wriggling hand. The scar was still easy to feel, with her fingers and in her brain.

To distract herself, Ngaire moved her thoughts back to the day. Paul had expressed surprise when they arrested him. As though he'd thought he could walk into a police station, confess to a murder, and they'd let him go home again when it became inconvenient to stay.

Did that indicate guilt? Or were his actions consistent with desiring a day out and possessing a sick mind that confused a police station with a picnic.

Ngaire turned off the light and let the questions wash over her, unanswered, unanswerable. It gave her something to do other than sleep.

Chapter Five

"Wonderful story in the paper this morning," Deb said as she walked up to Ngaire's desk and sat back against it. "Especially the details at the end about a man confessing to a murder."

Ngaire pushed away the paper being shoved at her face and said, "Yeah, I've read it already, thanks."

That dashed her hope that no one else would pick up on it, at least for a while. The newspaper had hidden the story in the back in the lifestyle section. Finlay would be furious. A short article about the disestablishment of the Commune of Christ the Redeemer after its youngest member died. A puff piece. The comparisons with similar sects offered nothing new. Ngaire guessed that the only reason the paper published was the public's endless curiosity about the Gloriavale Community on the West Coast. A casual aside ended the article, mentioning that a man had recently confessed to murder, and police were following up leads. No names.

"Kind of made me wonder where that information could've come from," Deb continued, not at all dissuaded by Ngaire's indifference. "Given that it didn't originate with me."

"Oh, didn't it?" Ngaire said, keeping her inflection flat. "I just assumed."

Deb folded up the paper and biffed Ngaire over the head with it before dropping it into the recycle bin next to her desk.

"What're you looking at, anyhow? Has Dr. Jarvis sent through the release?"

"Doubt he'll even have checked in at this hour," Ngaire said after checking her watch. "No, the original pathologist's report and the coroner's verdict came through. Someone at the courthouse was in early."

"Run it down for me, then." Deb pulled up a chair and sat next to her. "Have we got a match?"

"Read it yourself," Ngaire said, pushing the documentation her way. Lack of sleep made her eyelids heavy, and her head was clanging from her drink the night before. She was such a lightweight. "They found her drowned in a slurry pit. Not consistent with the story Worthington laid out for us yesterday."

"Oh, gross," Deb said, screwing up her face. "How the hell did she drown? I thought those things were less than a meter deep?"

"Two meters, plastic-covered concrete, and they didn't have a safety stair to climb out. From the report, they pulled out two sheep while they were at it. A possibility is that she went to their aid."

Deb snorted. "Sheep die any way they can. Suicidal or stupid, the lot of them." She paused and sniffed. "Oh, shit. Now you've made me cry. The poor girl."

"On the bright side, at least it means we can wind it up. There's no murder here," Ngaire said and mimicked wiping her hands. "The guy must just be after your excellent company." Her stomach pulled at her as she spoke. A tug from her abdomen. She'd so wanted to avenge Magdalene's death.

"Why'd he even pick her out? Why didn't he confess to the Crewes' murder and be done with it."

The murder of Jeanette and Harvey Crewe remained unsolved despite forty-five years of investigation and two convictions. New Zealand's most theorized-about and most falsely confessed-to crime.

"The Worthington's farm abutted the cult's communal property," Ngaire said, pointing to the diagram in the coroner's file. "And Worthington's dad even joined in the search for Magdalene when the commune went public with her disappearance. He would've been familiar with her. About the only thing that makes sense is that he chose her name, her death."

Ngaire remembered Paul's expression during their interview. The look saying, "I'm caught," when Deb asked about the number of people present. If he'd invented everything, why had he looked so scared?

Deb must have been thinking along similar lines, for she said, "The confession could be solid, but he's lying about where he dumped the body. He said water scared him, right?" She caught Ngaire's eye, and Ngaire nodded. She was letting Deb talk her around because that's what she wanted. "So maybe he wished he'd dumped her in the clean water of the river. And over the years, that's where he's convinced himself he did it."

"But instead he tossed her into the slurry pit," Ngaire said, finishing the idea. "It's out the back of his dad's property, so the access through to it would've been a lot easier. Hand me that." She snapped her fingers, and Deb handed back the map outline.

Ngaire opened it out on the desk; eight times the size of the A4 it folded into. She trailed her fingers across the property lines and leaned forward, squinting, trying to make out the faded markings.

"Here," she said, jabbing at a point on the map. Deb handed her a packet of sticky tabs, and she stuck one in its place. "This is where they found her body."

Using her finger, she traced the distances and placed another marker. "This is where the boundary fence between the adjoining properties was."

Deb leaned over, looking closer. The length of the farms marked out on the map ran for hectares, but the two markers were only a few hundred meters apart.

"Whereabouts is the shed he was talking about? Worthington said it was a horse stable. Anything labeled that?"

"Not that I can see," Ngaire said, her finger trailing along other markings. "This explanation clears up why a poor farm boy could afford to be driving around smack in the middle of the energy crisis. Not something you'd expect."

Deb looked at her with wide eyes, and it wasn't until she spoke Ngaire understood that they were admiring rather than mocking. "I don't know how you keep all that information in your feeble lady-brain, but you've got me sold."

Ngaire blushed and folded up the map again. "So, we need information on the properties. The layout of his farm and the compound."

"We can get the old property records from the council, and we should requisition the financial accounts for these places. See which farms were struggling, which were minting it."

"Do you think it's financially related?" Ngaire asked, her voice full of doubt.

Deb pulled Ngaire's ponytail and wiggled it from side to side. "My instructor taught me it's always about the money until you prove it isn't. 'Sides, until we understand the 'we' he talked about, I say we investigate everybody."

"Do you think his dad may've been involved?" Ngaire asked.

Deb turned back and leaned her chin on the desk divider. "You saw how he looked when I was questioning him yesterday. Like a deer in the headlights. Do you think that's more likely to be from a schoolmate or his dad?"

Ngaire nodded, conceding the point. The case caught her again in its grip. She stood, ready to go.

"Hold up there," Detective Sergeant Gascoigne came up to them with his palm raised. "Either of you know anything about this?"

He held out a copy of the same paper that Deb had thrown in the recycling bin. Ngaire found the edge of the container with her foot while maintaining eye contact with the DS and nudged it farther under her desk.

"No, I haven't seen it, sir. What's it about?"

Deb folded her arms across her chest, a protective gesture that Gascoigne leaped on. "What about you, Weedon? Does this ring any bells?"

"No, sir. There's no love lost between me and the journos, sir."

Deb had dated a journalist from The Press a few years earlier. Their courtship had caused rampant speculation at the station and a flurry of orders and warnings. All of which Deb had born with amused constraint until she'd found him in bed with a friend.

"You two are on the Worthington confession, aren't you? The only ones working it?" Each word dripped with implication.

"Genna met him, too, sir," Ngaire inserted, delighted to throw him off guard. "Had quite a chat with him in the waiting area, I hear." Deb turned around with a quick smile of gratitude, and Ngaire fought to keep her expression neutral. "Should I have a word with her, sir? Ask her if she spoke to anybody about him?"

Gascoigne shook his head, tightlipped, and then clicked his heels in dismissal. He'd come to the police from the army, and it showed. On reaching the office door, he turned. "Anything in it?"

Ngaire nodded. "I think so, sir. Enough to follow up on a few leads until we're certain, anyway."

"Make sure you contact the girl's parents, then. Inform them you're opening an inquiry. It will've been a shock if they read this in this morning's paper like I did."

Ngaire still had to get sign-off that light duties counted as "talking with couples in retirement villages" before she could go with Deb on the trip. They'd tracked down

Magdalene's parents and were happy to find that a) they were alive, and b) they lived nearby. Trying to break the news by telephone didn't have much appeal, nor did informing them via proxy.

The address was for a separate unit in the retirement home village, rather than in the main hospital wing itself, so Ngaire reassured herself that they couldn't be that bad.

Enforced visits to her ailing grandad when she was a child had instilled a fear of the elderly at a cellular level. He'd fallen so deep into Alzheimer's that he couldn't escape even for brief periods. Once, he'd reached out to grab her arm in a vicelike grip and insisted she'd stolen his jelly beans. When her mother put her to bed, there'd been bruises, dark-green and blue, spreading across her arm. Her Mum told her not to upset Grandpa because he wasn't well.

"Jesus, these units are tiny," Deb said as she navigated the car down the narrow roads within the village. "Imagine being stuck in one of these boxes all day."

Ngaire, who'd experienced being stuck in her own box for a long time after her incident, jumped to their defense. "Tiny houses are all the rage now. It must be nice having everything in reach."

"Yeah," Deb snorted. "If you need to reach your kitchen from your tub."

"That's it," Ngaire pointed as she spotted the house number. "Pull into the bay."

"Yes, sir," Deb said mockingly but followed her instructions all the same. "Have you got this?"

Ngaire froze with her fingers on the door handle. "I thought you'd take the lead."

Deb laughed and stepped out of the car, the slam of the door behind her reverberating around the tiny lanes. "Nope, you're up, Princess. I'm the senior officer here, and I've elected you to the position."

Ngaire's paced slowed as she neared the door to

the unit, composing herself. It wasn't as bad as a death notice; the first half dozen times she'd delivered those, she'd gone home at night and cried herself to sleep. But they were bringing news that would upset this couple's world and provoke an extreme emotional reaction, and that wasn't easy, either.

When she knocked on the door, a part of her, the same part that pulled sick days when tests were due, hoped there'd be no answer. Her hope was short-lived, for there was an immediate garbled call from inside and the sound of footsteps.

"Hello?" The question came from a short, thin woman with silver hair cut elven-style, so it looked like a gleaming cap.

"Mrs. Lynton?" Ngaire asked, and the woman nodded. "My name's Detective Ngaire Blakes, and this is Detective Debra Weedon. I'm sorry to turn up without notice, but could we come in to talk to you about your daughter?"

Color drained from the woman's face, but she took a step backward and waved them through. Ngaire walked into the living room and sat on the couch without asking, then pulled at Deb's hand when she hesitated. Mrs. Lynton stood at the door for a moment, her head resting on the paneled wood, then sat in a chair opposite.

"So," she said, the smile on her lips not reaching her eyes, "you want to talk about Martha?"

Ngaire blinked rapidly and tried to think. Was Martha a derivative? A nickname? She felt a quick jab in her ribs from Deb's elbow and guessed not.

"No, Mrs. Lynton. We're here to talk to you about your daughter Magdalene."

She waited for a beat to see whether she'd been confused about the name, and it meant the same girl, but it was soon clear that it didn't. A gasp of laughter burst from Mrs. Lynton, and she held her hands to her face.

"Oh, thank goodness." She waved a hand at them, and Ngaire could see the tears flowing. "I thought something terrible had happened to Martha. I couldn't bear it."

"Sorry, Mrs. Lynton—"

"Call me Mary," Mrs. Lynton said, folding her hands in her lap.

"I'm sorry, Mary, I wasn't aware that you had another daughter. I didn't mean to worry you."

Mary shook her head. "That's okay. Of course you didn't. Martha's staying with us for a while. Just turned up one day needing shelter, so we took her in, and I've thought of her as my daughter ever since." She placed her hand against her chest, "Goodness. That gave my heart a jump."

"Can I get you anything, a glass of water?" Ngaire asked.

"No, dear. I'll catch my breath in a minute. What information did you need about Magdalene?" She glanced from Ngaire to Deb and back. "She's been dead forty years now."

Ngaire nodded. "Yes, we understand, but yesterday a man came into the station and confessed to murdering her." She paused to wait for Mary to react, but a slight frown was the woman's only concession to Ngaire's words.

Deb cleared her throat, and they both turned to her. "We don't know whether there's any merit to this confession yet, but we wanted to inform you and your husband."

Mary smiled. "But dear, I already knew. It was in the paper this morning."

The kitchen door creaked, and an elderly man walked in, rubbing his hands with a greasy cloth. "Hello?"

"Abe, these ladies are from the police. They're here about Maggie."

He frowned, and his hands slowed, but the half

smile on his face remained. It looked like a permanent part of his anatomy rather than an expression he could change at will.

"Maggie's dead," he said after a moment. "Been dead a long time."

"It's about that article," Mary said. "You remember? I told you about it."

He shook his head, indicating that he didn't, but Ngaire moved in before trouble stirred. "We've had a man offer a confession, about your daughter Magdalene. He's confessed to her murder."

The half smile stayed fixed, but the frown deepened, showing all the lost elasticity as his skin piled into the crevice.

He looked to his wife, who nodded, and he turned to Ngaire. "No one murdered my girl. She drowned by accident."

"We've compared your daughter's autopsy and coroner reports to the evidence our suspect has provided, Mr. Lynton. There's a good chance he'd telling the truth." Ngaire rose, so he wasn't looking down at her and staggered as her bad leg buckled for a moment. "I understand what a shock this is—"

"You people," he spat out, and Ngaire stepped back in shock. For a second every racist taunt she'd ever heard skimmed through her head, but then she realized he meant the police. "You people don't understand nothing about my daughter. She's in God's hands now, and that's where she's staying."

Ngaire caught Deb's gaze and gave a quick jerk of the head. They'd come, they'd done what they meant to, time to leave. Deb nodded and rose.

"Was it that Haldrem's boy?" Mr. Lynton asked with a raised voice. His right hand clenched the rag, shaking it at them like an agitated sock puppet. "You shouldn't mind him, don't care what he's talking about."

"Abe," Mary said, a note of warning in her voice.

"You shut up, now."

He turned and shook the rag at Ngaire again but said nothing further.

"We're very sorry to have bothered you both," Ngaire said and backed toward the exit, with Deb falling into step beside her.

Mary jumped up to open the door for them. "Don't mind him," she whispered. "Maggie was a good girl, and he says a prayer for her daily. He hasn't come to terms with her loss."

"Don't answer nothing they ain't asked a question for," her husband said over her shoulder. "Didn't help us then, won't be helping them now."

Mary shrugged an apology as she closed the door.

Chapter Six

William Glover finished the last of his egg-white omelet, then spread his paper over his emptied plate. His wife tutted at him, but he ignored her. This early in the morning he needed to shut everyone out to prepare for the day.

"Daddy," his daughter said.

William flipped the corner of his paper down so her face was visible and raised his eyebrows in response. Emma had gotten egg white in her blonde hair and Marmite on her chubby chin. The only food item not adorning her tiny body was the poached pear. He imagined that'd end up in the bin along with every other piece of fruit they'd ever tried to feed her.

"Do you have a knife?" Emma asked.

She moved the item in question, hiding it behind her back. He flicked his paper up and ignored her. When he'd been Emma's age, there were tables for adults and tables for children. There wasn't any real reason for that to have changed.

"Emma, you've got a knife already," his wife Amanda replied for him. "Use that."

As William turned the page, a loud tinkle signaled the piece of cutlery hitting the floor.

"Daddy?" The high-pitched voice hit his ears like fingernails on a blackboard. He'd have forgone children, but it would've caused difficulties running for local office if he couldn't portray the typical Kiwi family.

"Daddy, daddy, daddy!" Emma's voice rose, resembling a whistle.

"What?" He folded his paper again, frowning at Emma, who stared back with glee. "What is it?"

"Do you have a fork?"

William closed his eyes and waited for the offending item to join the knife on the floor. "Have children," his mother had said. "You'll enjoy them," his mother had said. Children must've been different in her day.

"Daddy's reading, Emma. Stop bothering him. If you're finished, give me your plate and get ready for kindy."

William turned another page. The lifestyle section. His least favorite. He wet his finger and flicked along the edge of the pages until he found business. A manly section, but not so masculine as to involve manual labor.

"I want another egg."

"Well, I'm not surprised, Emma. You put most of the last one on your face." Amanda did nothing to hide her exasperation, but William doubted it would affect their daughter. She was unflappable. "If I boil you another egg, it'll take ten minutes. Will you still want it then?"

William laughed and put the paper aside. "Can you think ten minutes into the future, Em?" he asked and gave her nose a push. She squealed, her voice escalating into a register so high, dogs in the neighborhood would have run in fright had they heard it.

"The school wants us to attend another interview," Amanda told him. He sighed and pictured the day's calendar. There were clients back-to-back until one o'clock, then again after lunch until at least seven. Mornings were the only time he spent at home anymore. When he'd made the switch from criminal law, he'd imagined more time for himself. Instead, work sucked up as much time, and he was bored more often.

"Can you do it by yourself?"

She shook her head. "The school secretary said they want us both there. It should be the last one."

He snorted. "I thought that last time. Since we're paying their bloody fees, *we* should interview *them*. Aren't we good enough to hand them money?"

Amanda shifted in her chair and reached across to pull away the teaspoon from Emma's place setting before she could throw that on the floor.

"You know they have more applicants than places," she said. "Most children have relatives who attended, so we need to work harder for Em."

"Looks like you'll attend a state school," he said to Emma, who chuckled in delight and clapped her hands. "Save Mummy and Daddy the trouble of paying for an education that will probably go to waste."

Amanda frowned, but William picked up his paper again and shielded himself behind it.

"I thought we'd agreed on Selwyn House?"

William sighed. Most days his wife was a pushover, but now there was an edge to her voice.

"Just joking, love." He turned to Emma again. "Mummy and Daddy would love to spend fifteen thousand dollars a year on something they could get for free!"

"For free," she echoed, delighted.

Amanda pushed back her chair, and the legs squealed against the wooden floor. William closed his eyes. There'd be scuff marks on the grain, and he'd just paid for the whole thing to be sanded, buffed, and reglazed. He gave her a warning look, and she gave him a dirty one in return.

"I'm getting an egg for your daughter," she said as she walked over to the stove. "Why don't you sit there and read your paper?"

William opened his eyes wide at Emma, who giggled in response. He lowered his voice to a whisper. "Looks like I'm in trouble with Mummy now, and it's all your fault." He punctuated the last three words with three pokes at Emma's chest, and she clapped her hands over her head.

"Remember, it was your idea to send her to private school," Amanda called from the kitchen. "If you don't turn up to the interview, and she doesn't get in, you'll be missing out as much as Em will."

He pulled a face at his daughter to make her laugh again, then walked into the kitchen and encircled Amanda's waist with his arms. He rested his chin on her shoulder and whispered straight into her ear. "I know. I'm sorry. I'll pick you up on my way."

Her shoulders relaxed, and he kissed her on the back of her neck, then blew behind her ear. She shuddered, then wriggled to shake him off.

"There's no time," she whispered, then her voice climbed a few decibels. "Em. Bring me your plate, please."

They heard a series of thumps as Emma descended from her chair and walked into the kitchen holding her plate sideways, so any remains were now on the floor.

"Here you are, Daddy," she said as she offered it up to him, smiling wide.

So Daddy was her favorite today. If he ignored her more, he'd be her favorite for life.

He rubbed the back of Amanda's neck, unearthing the kiss he'd planted earlier, and went back to the table. Tea remained in the pot, and he poured himself a cup. Dark brown and stewed, his favorite. Emma trailed along behind him and crawled back onto her own seat. Her cutlery still lay beneath her chair. No doubt scratching the kauri floor, too.

William picked up the paper and again it fell open to the lifestyle section. Tiny houses were still a thing. Tips on what to plant now for a bountiful harvest in winter. An article revisiting the Christian Cult forty years after it disbanded.

William frowned and folded the paper so the article was on top. He sipped his black tea and ignored Emma's thumping feet against the table legs.

"Em, stop that. Here's your egg."

Amanda bent to pick up the cutlery and handed it back to Emma.

"You're not letting her eat with those, are you?" William asked.

"If she didn't want to eat with a knife and fork that have been on the floor, she shouldn't have put them there," she replied. After ruffling Emma's hair, she sat down. William noticed she'd not touched her own meal except to move food around.

"You okay?" he asked, nodding at her full plate.

"Queasy. I've got a doctor's appointment later." She yawned, her mouth opening wide. "Probably my iron again."

"When's the school thing?"

"One thirty."

Stuff it. There went his lunch break. "I'll pick you up at quarter past." He folded the paper, tucking the article away from prying eyes. "I'd better get going. See you later, munchkin." He kissed Emma on the top of her head.

"After I've eaten my egg," she replied and tossed half of it on the tabletop.

"Have children," they said.

When William arrived at work, he realized there was another appointment on his calendar. On top of his client list and the school interview, he had to meet up with his political party and cajole them into letting him have the seat he wanted. Troy Winton was the sitting MP. Or, the sitting opposition MP because he hadn't made the cut last election. William needed to point out how having a local like himself with a solid grounding in helping the community was a winning decision, and he'd be in.

He could sense the needs of his electorate changing. If he could get the selection, he'd be out there on the streets campaigning tomorrow. The office wouldn't let him continue if he was seeking election, and the break would do him nothing but good. As a farm boy, he'd grown used to living out in the open. Law school had been a goal, more easily achieved than he cared for, but William hadn't expected how cramped he'd be sitting indoors every day.

At least when he'd dealt with criminals, he'd had the chance to strut his stuff in the courtroom. Although his parades in front of the jury were seldom compared to the long hours of research and tedious questioning, they'd enervated him through the slow patches. Now that he'd switched to company law, he couldn't even look forward to those moments where he could show off.

Getting out among his electorate and doing the old meet-and-greet would be a good change. Despite working with the refuse of society for long years, William still enjoyed meeting new people. He was a social butterfly at heart and captive butterflies died.

He spread the paper out on the table. The article on the Christian Cult was shallow, and the statements riled him up. Back then his father had run a good farm. He'd worked William hard, but only to get the best results possible. When William needed money to keep up with his friends and their interests—drinking, music, cars—his father had paid him well for the work he did.

A good man, a fair man. But then that cult moved in next door with their weird communist ways and did Dad out of half his business. The family farm worked a herd of cows—Friesians, for their fine milk production, back when no one in Canterbury kept more than a couple for home milking. He'd supplied local dairies through direct contracts that worked out well for both parties.

Then the Bible thumpers moved in and raised cattle, too. Some biblical reason that ignored that Canterbury was bone-dry in the best of years, and cows used water like nobody's business. Even when his dad stopped being generous with the pay and kept all work in the family, he couldn't compete with a bunch of communists. The contracts he'd thought were with friends turned out to be with businesses, and they were severed one by one as the cult undercut them.

At the end, his dad had tried to scale up to value-added production. Unable to sell milk, his dad went on a crash course in cheese making, but the stricter health regulations beat him, and the results were unsalable.

When his father sold his herd, the only place buying was the same place that had driven him out of the business. He'd had to suck it up so he could start again, trying, with no working knowledge of sheep, to compete with a thousand sheep farmers. He'd emptied the pastures and let them out for grazing and stabling, then waited for the bank to take his home and business, one acre at a time.

Before that concluded, the cult packed up and moved out, too late to do his dad any good. Ruined him for nothing.

People aged quicker in those days, but his father ran toward death a clip faster than normal. In the end he grew so impatient, he shot himself before his failing heart could do the job for him. The ashes were kept on the mantelpiece because William couldn't stand the thought of him buried next to religious zealots in a boneyard.

That was old history, though. William had built himself up and ensured that no competitor could steal his future from him. Money had been siphoned into a hundred different places over the years, so a nest egg would be there if he needed it. He'd worked hard, and he'd worked long, and he'd made sure that nobody would ever own him the way the bank owned his dad.

The article mentioned none of that in its write-up. Went on about how they'd formed out of nowhere and disappeared in a flash. Didn't mention what shits they'd been or how their commune gouged the community.

Plenty about a dead girl and the suspicious circumstances of her death.

It said Magdalene had been pregnant. This new knowledge, so long after, sucker punched him. So she was a slut, just as Paul had pegged her. Fury and loss filled him. Imagine if Emma turned out like that. Fifteen years old, already pregnant, which meant she was sleeping around at fourteen. William had still been an untouched virgin at fourteen. At fifteen, too. Magdalene was the right name for her. He felt like howling.

He forced himself to read the article through, then froze at the end.

"Hey, Will. Got a minute?" Geoff stood in the doorway, his suit jacket slung over his shoulder, a study in nonchalance.

"No," William replied, turning the paper over to hide the title when Geoff's beady eyes flicked its way. "Why?"

"The partners are having a meeting today. Billings aren't coming in as expected, and we may have a struggle this month. Eight o'clock okay?"

William shook his head. "What billings? My client hours are up to date. I checked yesterday."

"Well, all our partners aren't as diligent."

"Then they can cover the shortfall themselves. I'm not missing an evening with my daughter to listen to someone whine about expenses when they can't even call up a client and collect a debt."

Geoff stayed where he was, the only sign he was paying any attention a slow eyebrow lift that irritated William more than the scuff marks on the renovated kauri floor. "I said no," he repeated in slow, even tones, flicking his hand in dismissal. "Hold the meeting by yourselves."

Geoff glanced back along the hallway, then entered the office and closed the door behind him. "Hey, I know it's tough when you don't get to see your kids," he said.

William glared at him. Geoff had no children. No wife. No relationship with any person outside the firm.

"But you've gotta pull your weight around this place money-wise." The friendly, confiding tone of Geoff's voice made William's shoulders tighten and draw inward. Every part of the man was fake.

"I do my part."

"Look, mate, I know it's tough. You had an important career change, and it's hard to build up a base from scratch. But even when you're paid up, you're not bringing in the *dinero* the same way the rest of us do." Geoff rubbed his thumb back and forth against his fingers. "Gotta do the meeting."

He turned, as though that was the end, and William let the anger move through his body. It was cool and calming. A balm to his heated soul. Not like the cartoons he'd seen as a kid where anger was explosive and hot.

"My clients' invoices are paid; my billings are in order. I pull my weight around here," he said, jabbing his forefinger on the table after every point. "I may not have a high-billing client list, but I also don't have a year's outstanding debt because I'm too pussy to ask for money."

Geoff colored at the inference. Baroness Wilksley's debt. A hundred K she'd racked up, and a year down the track, he still hadn't collected the first red cent.

The coolness spread out to William's fingertips, to his hairline. Goosebumps mounted on his forearms, even though they kept the office at a moderate seventy degrees. He waited for the responding shot.

"I didn't want to tell you this, but we've found discrepancies in your accounts," Geoff said. William accepted the blow and leaned back in his chair, the anger so intense he could see Geoff's face in minute detail. The patch of stubble that had escaped the morning blades. An eyebrow hair that extended past the curve of his brow. A half centimeter of dark-brown roots that showed where Geoff dyed his hair blond.

"Well." William gathered his briefcase and shoved the paper back inside, then retrieved his jacket from the coat stand no client ever bothered to use. "Talk without me. Chalk it up as annual leave because my daughter's school is interviewing. Have a nice time."

Geoff stood back as he passed by, his mouth open. Melody—beautiful, young, useless Melody from the front desk—walked toward William. "Your ten o'clock is here," she said and turned as William strode by her without speaking. "Mr. Glover?"

William raised his hand in a cheery wave, walking straight past Michael Ward in reception. Last appointment, the man had been eager to know whether the fridge in his home was tax deductible because he kept food in there that he ate at the office.

The calm anger kept him in check as he walked to his car. Walking in the opposite direction of the early morning foot traffic, he passed people who nodded greetings because that's what they'd done for years.

He drove home to an empty house, to which Amanda would soon return, thinking everything was the same as she'd left it this morning. The phone showed three missed calls from his office. William loaded the office number into the "always block" list before clearing the calls and setting the receiver back in its cradle.

William had the whole day free. There was nowhere he needed to be until he picked up his wife to escort her to a meeting at a school he might no longer be able to afford.

What to do? What to do?

He grabbed the car keys and twisted them in his fingers. Amanda would be back any minute. If he stayed, he'd have to put up with her trailing him the rest of the day, asking him what was wrong.

At first, he drove around the block so he wouldn't be seen. Next he parked near a small playground, then realized that he would stand out like a sore thumb, so he drove closer to town. His briefcase was on the seat next to him, the paper calling out to him through the black leather. Plain black leather to demonstrate that he was a qualified lawyer. Nothing clinging from the farm boy he'd been a million years ago.

William pulled the case toward him and let the cool rage dissipate from his body. His calmness departed with it, and his heart sped up. Eighty beats, ninety beats, one hundred, one twenty. The article hadn't given a name for the man confessing, but William knew who it was. He hadn't seen Paul since he'd gone to university. Didn't know what he'd done with his life, but he shouldn't be hard to find. He pulled out his mobile phone and typed Paul's name into the white pages search. There was a short moment when he thought the number must be unlisted, but then it displayed on his screen. Bennett Street. Christ, that was just a suburb over.

When he turned into the driveway, there was another vehicle there, "HHL Group" emblazoned on the front in waves of green and blue. He pulled up alongside it, taking care not to bang his door on its side as he got out of the car.

Paul's house was a few generations older than his own. It nestled in a garden that once would've burst with color. Now weeds crammed it green and brown, over a meter high, and the borders merged with the lawn.

Home health care paying a visit, and everything falling into disrepair. If he'd had the mind to kill Paul for the trouble he'd brought, he was at the back of the line. Cancer? MS? William felt the headache that always appeared when he considered his mortality begin to pound in his temples.

He rapped his knuckles on the door. There was a doorbell mounted on a wrought iron frame to the side, but it had a plaster across it with faded writing on it. The script was illegible, but it was unlikely to be extolling the efficiency of the bell.

A man answered, heavyset and with a week's worth of growth on his chin. "Yup."

William appreciated men of few words; he encountered them so seldom, it was a rare treat. "I'm looking for Paul Worthington," he said.

"He's not in."

Okay, the few words thing could wear thin. "When will he be back?"

"Nup."

"Is it okay if I wait for him inside?"

A frown creased the big guy's forehead. William waited for a response and could sense wheels turning behind the man's gentle eyes. He edged his foot forward, trying to take a step inside to force the decision, but it didn't go his way.

"Nup," he said and pushed the door closed.

If they held Paul overnight in the police station, it didn't bode well for William. They'd sworn an oath back when they were teenagers, but that was long ago, and Paul had broken at least half of their agreement.

William returned to his car and sat gripping the wheel. The outcry of a thousand late nights, unpaid hours, and endless drudgery dug at his brain. He hadn't worked those years to exit with nothing. A partner agreement at a law firm that treated him as the bottom of the totem pole didn't cut it. Of course he skimmed; why they expected different behavior puzzled him. If he'd begun in corporate law, he'd have more than a dividend payout always less than it should be. In hindsight, he should have stuck with criminal, but after the cutback in legal aid had bitten, it would've been hard there, too.

An MP's salary would be an even tighter squeeze, but at least it came with respect. His face plastered on billboards as though he owned the neighborhood. And who knew where that would lead. It was about time someone from the Garden City got hold of the reins of power. That would suit William okay. If he lived in a small country, at least he wanted to lead it.

That's why he couldn't afford a scandal from his past to come out now. He kidded himself that he knew a thing or two about the law. Nothing Paul Worthington warbled about him to the police would result in a conviction, but the leaks to the papers could be disastrous. *Eau de Scandal* wasn't something he wanted to reek of going into his first election, and the party wouldn't let him try if it got that far.

Better for everybody involved if Paul returned home and shut his mouth.

In fact, what he needed most was a visit from a friend well versed in criminal law. Someone to recommend that now would be a great time to not comment.

Chapter Seven

The couples Ngaire interviewed from the compound soon merged in her mind. With varying levels of wealth, fitness, and looks, she expected marked differences in recall. Instead, they all sang from the same song sheet regarding Magdalene's disappearance and death.

"She had a fight with her dad," Marge Maples said. Husband Kelvin added, "She swore at her father, and he sent her off. Never seen him so angry."

"Before the church service she walked up and swore at him, she did," said Samuel Gibson. "I thought he would backhand her one, the mood he put her in," said his wife, Bethany. "Instead, he sent her off to 'think about what she'd done.'"

The Haldrems were dead, and the Lyntons weren't part of the suspect list, yet. The final couple who'd been part of the congregation was the Prophet and his wife. The Prophet was dead, and she'd moved to Australia. In the hope that the wife would have more insight, Ngaire placed the call and listened to the same recitation over a crackling line. "Abe sent her away before the church service started. I know my husband wanted to talk to him after, calm him down, but he drove off into town instead. Neither of us saw Magdalene after that day. Until Isaiah found her."

All five swore, "I don't know how she got in the slurry. Maybe she slipped in the shed when she was milking." This, despite asserting that her father had sent Magdalene off to think, not perform chores.

The baptism mentioned in the coroner's

document was also missing from all their testimony. Ngaire asked about it and received shrugs, dismissals. They'd baptized her as a child.

Ngaire and Deb couldn't find Isaiah listed anywhere. Either he lived off the grid, or he'd taken the first opportunity to change his name, and his records had disappeared. The last notation on record was from a secondary school where he'd failed to gain his school certificate, then signed out.

Magdalene's schoolteacher, a man named Hugo Pontus with a thick Swedish accent that Ngaire soon discovered was actually Norwegian, told them more. None of it relevant to the case, but he had a good memory and liked having company.

"She insisted on being called Claire," he said. "When her parents founded that new farm church, they rechristened her Magdalene, but she hated it. Even abbreviated to Maggie. Whenever a new teacher called her Magdalene, she'd yell something fierce."

Mr. Pontus lived in a small unit designed for retirees who weren't interested in village life. There were three similar units squeezed into the tiny block of land and a large, round mirror mounted on the drive because there was so little visibility. His was the second of the brown-brick units. All four were identical, apart from a small garden he grew on the concrete in front.

"Thought I was getting a lawn when I signed up," he explained as he walked them in. "Instead, they paved the whole yard. Easier for them because they didn't have to worry about the edges of the driveways, so I make do."

Instead of growing plants in soil, he grew them in sawdust fed with an irrigation system. Hydroponics, except it was beautiful violets and pansies that cried out to be dipped in sugar, rather than the regular cannabis.

"Magdalene bunked off school often. Difficult to track, as the farm kept her back sometimes, too, her and Isaiah, to help out with chores. Illegal, but no one was much in the mood to cause trouble. Wouldn't help the kids, and her marks didn't suffer. Bright as a spark, she was. The opposite of Isaiah."

"Did they travel to school together?" Ngaire asked. "Were they close?"

He screwed up his nose and shook his head. "Didn't seem to be. Isaiah rode an old scooter with a sidecar for Claire. She hated it, you could tell. Didn't need a license 'cause the whole shebang only did forty or fifty. Kilometers," he added. "Not miles."

The image of a Nifty Fifty sprang into Ngaire's mind. But old, large, complete with sidecar, and covered with farmland dirt. If her imagination was anything like the real thing, it wasn't a surprise that Magdalene hated riding in it.

"Nowadays, they'd ride a quad bike, but back then you made do."

"What year was she in?" Ngaire asked.

"Form Six. The school streamed Claire a year ahead right from the primers. She'd got her school cert, and she was on track to ace her higher school certificate, even though it's hard to tell that early in the year. Once she had that, she would've ended up with an A bursary and the chance to study anywhere."

"Was she interested in college?"

"God knows." He laughed. "Nobody knew what went on inside Claire's head but Claire. Not one to share."

"What about Isaiah?" Deb asked. "We can't trace him after school."

Mr. Pontus shrugged. "I don't know what happened to him. The school streamed him into the special class, so I didn't teach him. I guess he signed out soon as he could. Not much hope for an education in that stream."

He sat back in his chair and folded his hands across an aging potbelly. "Claire was something, though. Tall, beautiful, smart. Could've been anything she wanted."

Ngaire winced at his description. *Trapped, pregnant, drowned,* she added to the list.

"Why're you digging around for information about her now?" he asked.

From where they were sitting, Ngaire saw the morning's paper on the kitchen counter. All the rooms were close to one another.

"There's been a new query raised," she said. "It was time to review the case to make sure we hadn't missed anything."

"If you ever find someone responsible for her death, let me know," Mr. Pontus said as he walked them back out to the street. "I'd like to give them a good hiding."

As they drove away, Ngaire compared his fire for a girl he knew only through a classroom decades before, to the people who'd lived, eaten, prayed, and slept with her. Poignant memories versus an utter lack of interest. If there was a crime behind Paul's confession, the compound was a blessing sent to disguise it with utter indifference.

That was all you needed for a perfect crime. Not a perfect plan. Not the perfect commission. Just nobody caring enough to see it.

For the last half hour, Paul had wanted to angle his bed up. While his lungs weren't bad at the moment, they became congested without an easy path to drain. The wheeze built up inside, even if it wasn't audible yet. The controller was hanging from a handle up behind his head. Too distant to be within his reach.

He'd fallen asleep more than once, exhausted from the effort of thinking about it. Short naps that caused time to leap forward but didn't refresh him at all. Even the panic that dreaming ate up his remaining life in chunks couldn't stop his eyes closing.

There was a police guard on the door, but he didn't look concerned about Paul attempting escape. The surprise Paul had experienced the day before when he was arrested grew when he woke up in the hospital with a personal guard. All he'd heard about the police in past years was how undermanned they were, yet here he hogged one all to himself. The thieves and thugs and bullies roaming neighborhoods in packs should send him thanks.

A nurse should come soon. At least he thought one would. Someone to check that he hadn't dropped dead. Once they came, he'd ask them to maneuver him into a comfortable position.

The clock jumped another five minutes. Close to midday. Even if no one was coming around to check on him, there'd soon be a nurse with lunch. If he could force himself to stay awake, he'd catch her.

Once again he tried to shift himself, to see whether he could move over to his side, but the tight hospital sheets bound him immobile. Paul wondered whether they did them that way on purpose. To trap the frail between crisp linens so nurses could monitor them more easily.

Be nice if the policeman stood next to him, rather than the doorway. Paul would like a chat. He didn't even know what the weather was outside, and as a farmer's son, he'd grown up attuned to every change. A curtain hid him from the public walking the halls or shielded him from them.

He woke again as a conversation started at the door. The police officer stood guard, but a man moved around his side, and the officer let him.

"Paul Worthington?" the man asked as he came close to the bed. He stuck his hand out, then took Paul's limp paw off the coverlet to shake when Paul didn't move fast enough. "My name is William Glover."

When he released his hand, Paul snaked it under the covers to safety. As he stared at the face, it reconstructed into that of a boy he'd known a lifetime ago.

"Heard you needed a lawyer," Billy said.

Billy Glover always bested Paul. A year older, he was also faster, smarter, better-looking. Even his dad's farm outperformed Paul's father's farm.

When the cult moved in, Paul had taken shameful delight in the downfall of Billy's farm. No longer second best. So he'd never run as fast or get the girls, but his drunken dad could still compete with a man who'd had his livelihood undercut.

The thing he didn't delight in was how cold Billy grew. Until then he'd been an easygoing boy because things came easily to him. As the years with their new neighbors crept by, the rot set in deeper; the lines of Billy's face set into hard, new patterns. His temper grew shorter. When he hit his midteens, testosterone pumped into a higher gear, and his other friends moved on, scared by Billy's outbursts. Paul stuck by him, even though he knew that if he stopped hanging with Billy, their old friends would flock back to him.

The main reason was that Billy took risks, and sometimes taking risks resulted in fun, almost as an afterthought. When he drove at excessive speeds, the thrill of breaking the law combined with the fear of death to produce an apoplectic burst of joy in Paul's chest. Afterward, Billy would take Paul along while he broke into garages and houses in town. Picking up rewards left scattered on benches, hidden in drawers. Loose change, booze, nudie mags. The shot of adrenaline kept him buzzing for the rest of the week.

Paul had looked down on his old friends with their clean fun who didn't know what it was to dance outside the rules. They thought it was a treat if their old man gave them a beer after they'd helped out with a full day's labor.

Billy had been his best friend and his worst

enemy, and Paul experienced a rush and a flash with each memory he brought forth. Flashes of emotion that let him know he'd lived.

Of course, he didn't think of those times often, because they stopped short with a dead girl and a weight on his conscience that never lifted.

And here Billy was again. Turning up like the bad penny Paul's mother always insinuated he was.

When Paul struggled to sit up, his breath gone, his heart beating pat-pat-pat, he discovered they'd handcuffed him to the bed. The chain jangled as he fought for leverage, for height, so Billy didn't have him at a disadvantage.

The officer at his door turned at the sound, but although he examined each article in the scene, he didn't break position. Paul had watched a lot of low-grade TV shows lately. Based in the USA, sure, but he imagined that here, too, lawyers were sacrosanct, and if the police didn't treat them right, they got their asses kicked. In court, or at the station.

"Here, let me help you there," Billy said, reaching down beside Paul to adjust the lever that raised the head of the bed. Paul stopped struggling and let the mechanical joists do their work.

"What are you doing here?" Paul whispered. "I didn't ask for a lawyer."

Billy frowned. "Don't you recognize me, old chap?"

Paul nodded.

"Well, I have a vested interest here." He leaned forward so his face was lower than Paul's and looked up at him. "How do you think I felt, finding out you were discussing our private business with the police?"

"Who told you I was in the hospital?"

Billy shrugged. "Tried you at the station, and when I announced it was urgent that I see you"—he smiled and revealed long eye teeth perfect for ripping meat apart—"they pointed me in the right direction."

Paul shook his head, in denial of everything. Had he fallen asleep again? Was his mind creating another obstacle to stop him from doing the right thing?

"You need a lawyer's advice, Paul. Could be you've got yourself in deep trouble here."

Paul jerked back as Billy laid a hand on his shoulder, but there was nowhere to retreat except farther into his pillow, his mattress, the steel structure of the bed.

"Tell you what, Paul," Billy leaned closer, and Paul could smell the acid on his breath. "I'll look after you from now on, and I won't even charge you. Mates' rates. How's that?"

Paul stared at him, silence the only answer he was capable of.

"No, no. Don't thank me," Billy said, straightening the blankets across Paul's chest so they cinched even tighter. "That's what old friends are for. Lie back and get a nice rest, and the next time someone interviews you, I'll be there to lend a hand."

He sat back in his chair, looking around. "You even got your own room, Paul. A bit fancy for the likes of us, isn't it?"

Paul remembered the first time they'd committed a burglary. The door had glass panes set in wood, each four inches by ten inches. At the back, so only the tiny wax-eyes saw him. Their white-rimmed eyes fixed him with startled expressions as they flitted about the fruit trees.

Billy told him to wrap his shirt around his hand so he didn't hurt himself. That night he sat down to pick out the tiny shards embedded in the fabric. One had caught on his back at the waist, and his shirt was stained with small droplets of blood. *I can tell Mum it's from barbed wire, crawling under a fence. That I was lucky I didn't tear my clothes on it.*

His mother would've yelled at him for tearing them. New things were unaffordable, and no matter how finely she stitched, the wears and tears were always noticeable.

But it turned out she didn't see. Just shoved the bloodied shirt in with the regular wash, and it emerged with faint pink spots that only he saw.

Billy made him break in because he didn't want his fingerprints in the house. At the time, Paul thought it a reasonable contribution, given that Billy had reconnoitered the house.

Paul looked at Billy's hands now. Manicured, with cuticles pushed back and fingernails buffed to a shine. Each one clipped to a two-millimeter length so they didn't catch, scrape, or tear. Capable of scratching an itch, but not uncouth.

Paul hadn't clipped his nails for months. Chemo caused them to split and lift, and they became too painful for him to use clippers to trim the ends. Instead, he let them grow unchecked, and they'd done little of that. Separated from the nail bed, they had deep grooves, high ridges, and if he had more courage, he'd yank them out, one by one.

But the only courage and determination he'd ever shown in his life was unraveling. Once more he allowed Billy to get his way.

"Don't stay. I'm not going anywhere. If someone comes to interview, I'll have them call you." The speech produced a slick of spit that hung from the side of his mouth. Billy leaned over with a crisp handkerchief, folded, ironed, and rubbed him dry. Paul's eyes filled with tears of gratitude against his will. Human touch. He hated that he needed it.

"That's okay, Paul," Billy said as he sat back in his chair, putting his handkerchief on the side table so it wouldn't soil the inside pocket of his suit. "There's no business more important than you. I'll sit here and wait with you." He leaned forward and whispered in Paul's ear, "We can talk over old times."

Chapter Eight

Ngaire pulled a muscle when she was getting out of the car. Deb at first snorted at her troubles, then moved to assist Ngaire when she registered that her partner was in pain.

"How the hell do you manage?" she asked as she let Ngaire put her arm around her shoulder so she could lift her out. "Do you injure yourself sitting at home?"

Ngaire laughed, then stopped as a painful twinge ran all the way from her knee up to her tailbone. She hopped a few steps until the muscle loosened again, letting blood flow so she could walk.

"Are you sure you're close to starting back at work?" Deb asked. "Given that you're unable to get out of the car. What's the doctor say?"

"It's just a twinge, for God's sake," Ngaire said irritably, then recanted at Deb's shocked face. "Sorry. I pulled a muscle—it's nothing. My leg's almost back to normal."

"Okay," Deb said, although her face was clearly broadcasting something else.

They'd been discussing the teacher and the other compound members in the car, but now Deb asked, "What did you think of the Lyntons? Got into it with the olden time holy vibe names, didn't they?"

"I guess Dad was the one who talked them into the commune," Ngaire said. "He seemed a hard-ass. I wonder where Martha's from."

"It's as if they took in a stray pet that stayed," Deb said. "I wonder if anyone's bothered to let her real parents know that she's got a new quasi-family."

"We can track her. It's not that common a name," Ngaire suggested.

"Doubt it's her name at all. Not unless my name is gullible. Probably camping with them while the goings good and'll clean them out when she gets bored."

Ngaire shrugged, but they saw the same thing often enough that she knew it was a concern. When older folks took in street kids because they missed having a family around, it usually went in a different direction than your average Hallmark movie.

"Weedon, Blakes, a moment please," DS Gascoigne called. Ngaire followed Deb into his office, putting her opinions of the morning into a series of mental notes ready to issue. Facts, evidence, opinions. "We have a new development with Paul Worthington and his amazing confession," Gascoigne said, the sarcasm dripping from his words. "He's decided that confessing to a murder is a dangerous thing, and he's lawyered up."

Ngaire frowned and turned to Deb, wondering whether it was a joke. The gales of anger on Deb's face convinced her to reassess. "Why's he need a lawyer?" Ngaire asked, exasperated. "He spent half the first interview yesterday trying to convince us he murdered someone, and now he wants to take it back?"

"Now, now, Blakes. Even dickheads get to have lawyers."

"Do we know who he is, sir?" Deb asked. "Is he willing to let us interview him, or will we get 'no comment'?"

"You can try. It's William Glover. Used to be in criminal law, though I haven't seen him for a while. He's smart, and he knows the system backward and forward, so don't try anything clever, will you?"

The DS eyed Deb during that question, then turned to Ngaire. "You'll be assigned back to the translation pool. We've got a new series of phone taps coming through that we need info on right away."

Ngaire's heart sank. He said they could try to interview, but reassignment meant they wouldn't get the chance. Back to translating tapes, the work so mind-numbing she grew scared she'd miss anything important the tappees had said.

"And you, Weedon. They've found a body on Sumner Beach. Detective Collingwood is out there now, but he's called for help, and you're it." Deb gave a sigh and left. Ngaire sympathized. Floaters were the worst, but she'd still have swapped places in a flash.

"Ngaire," Gascoigne said as she took a step to follow Deb out of the room. "Hold back a minute, would you?" He checked to make sure Deb had gone. "Get the door."

Dread. Ngaire pulled the door closed and sat in the chair that Gascoigne flashed his hand at. No one ever had pleasant private chats at the station. At least not in her experience.

"You've another appointment at the physiotherapist for assessment Friday, right?"

Ngaire nodded, unsticking her tongue from the roof of her mouth. "Yes, that's right, sir."

"I'm hoping you get cleared this time," he said. He was still standing, and now he leaned forward on the desk, resting on his knuckles. "About time you got back into regular duties, don't you agree?"

Ngaire felt icy fingers spread out from the scar in her side, radiating a cold wave across her chest. She nodded, her pulse thrumming in the side of her neck so hard that he must have been able to see it. "Yes, sir."

She sat and stared at the desk in front of her, avoiding eye contact and hoping the moment would be over soon.

"If you don't get a clean bill of health, we'll need another plan, Blakes." He straightened up and cracked his knuckles. Ngaire understood for once why Finlay hated the sound so much. "You're already three weeks over the return-to-work plan we first devised. If you still require more time, we'll review our position."

She tried to swallow, but her throat had closed, so she could only get halfway through the action. The muscles strained, and she opened her mouth wide to free them. Reviewing her position didn't sound like something she wanted to do. It sounded ominously like her position would dissolve.

If she'd suffered an injury in the line of duty, this wouldn't happen. She'd be lauded for her achievements and given space and time to heal. There'd be accolades, respect, breathing room.

But her injuries hadn't occurred that way.

"I hope it's good news, too, sir," Ngaire managed and forced a smile onto her face. "I can't wait to get back to work, proper."

Gascoigne held her eyes across the table, and although she wanted to look away, Ngaire kept her gaze steady. Holding on until he broke the silence and conceded.

"That'll be all, Blakes. I'll have the recordings brought to your desk in a few minutes."

Ngaire stood and nodded. "Thank you, sir."

When William pulled into the driveway and saw the station wagon still parked there—an irritant when a double garage sat empty—he remembered the appointment at Emma's school. He checked his watch, already knowing he'd missed it by a mile. It was after five o'clock.

Shit. She'd have phoned work, too, chasing him up. He watched as the Venetian blind in the kitchen window pulled apart and snapped shut again. Amanda had seen him. Now he couldn't drive away and postpone the fallout.

He looked in the driver's side window on the way past, but the keys weren't in the station wagon. Which meant they'd be hanging inside. In the kitchen. Where Amanda would be waiting.

William ground his teeth together as he opened the door. Emma danced into the hallway. "Daddy!" she yelled in delight. "Mummy's been shouting, a lot."

He picked her up and swung her over his shoulder, wincing when her shriek hit the upper registers. She gripped her knees on either side of his head, pinching his ears flat and muffling his hearing. When he paused to gain his balance, she grabbed a fistful of his hair and jerked her body back and forth like he was a pony, his fringe the mane.

Amanda was cleaning the counter with an orange sponge. She used long swipes of her arms to reach from one corner to the sink, then repeated the action until the entire side was clear. When she squeezed out the stained water, the tendons on her inner arm jumped out in stark relief.

"Mummy, Mummy, I'm riding Daddy." Emma let go for a moment to wave, and William gripped her tighter so she wouldn't fall. "He's a donkey."

William let out an appropriate hee-haw and reached over to grab the car keys off their hook. Amanda snaked her hand out and gripped his wrist with the same strength she'd used to wring out the sponge. Saying nothing, just glancing up at Emma, then looking him in the face, her lip curled. She let go of him as though releasing the dog's poop bag.

"I'll put the cars in the garage," he said. His usual complaint died in his throat, killed by Amanda's expression. They'd had arguments before, always about Emma, but he'd never seen her so furious.

She reached out, and he flinched back, but she lifted Emma from his shoulders and cradled the girl's body against hers. "Come on, Em. Time to go upstairs and sort out your doll's house, don't you think?"

Emma emitted a noise that William took to mean she was in agreement. Amanda shoved past him.

He followed her footsteps as she trod up the stairs, then traced their path overhead. They ended up in Emma's room, and he waited to see whether they'd come back. Whether a discussion was heading his way.

They didn't. William parked the cars in the garage, then rolled the recycling bin with its cheery yellow lid out to the curb for the next day's collection.

When he got back inside, Amanda was still upstairs. William opened the oven door, then the fridge, expecting to see a meal either finished or in preparation. Nothing looked like it fit the bill. He examined the wiped counter and tipped his head back to smell the room. There'd been no cooking done, but there was the unmistakable scent of hot food.

William opened the rubbish bin and saw the crumbled and oil-stained blank newsprint that had wrapped fish and chips. Emma must've been ecstatic. Amanda had spent far too long in a culture where food purity was next to godliness, so their daughter barely ever had take-out. McDonald's was a place she knew only through attending other kids' birthday parties. He didn't think she even knew that KFC existed.

There were lite cheese slices in the fridge, some Flora margarine, and whole grain bread in the freezer that he defrosted in the microwave. The wrapper boasted five seeds, and William felt a strong hankering for the thick white bread he'd grown up on. Fresh loaves where everyone could cut their own slices, and he determined the thickness of his own slice by the hunger he felt. That, and a slap of fresh-churned butter, always in populous quantities and flavored with a hint of salt. It was thick and a rich yellow and cream color. Not like the pallid blocks building fat-laden walls in the supermarket refrigerators. Hand-churned, then dolloped out with a knife onto a sheaf of wax paper. Stored in the pantry so it was room temperature, ready to spread.

The cheese was always cheddar and came in

kilogram blocks. The only item in his house that came wrapped in plastic. Their dairy was their own, their meat bartered for, their fruit and vegetables dug and picked from the back garden and the orchard.

He laid the spread out across the four slices of bread. You couldn't lay it on thick because the salty taste turned acrid. He lifted the edges of the plastic on the individual slices of cheeselike substance and peeled it back, careful not to bend the slice, or it would split open.

One of the boasted seeds was poppy, and they stuck between his teeth, adding annoyance but no flavor. When he was a teen, he and his friends had heard you could make opium from them, so they pounded and boiled kilos of them and tried to get high. He'd thrown up the mess before it delved into his receptors, feeling weak instead of invincible.

He sat on the sofa and waited for his wife to come downstairs. As it grew late, the light faded from the window, leaving a pallid night sky. Dotted with only a few dozen stars because the garish street lights polluted the vista like a fog. Birds sang in the twilight, bidding one another good night. Goodnight, John Boy. Goodnight, Elizabeth. Goodnight, Mary Ellen.

There were the sounds of protest when Amanda dispatched Emma to bed. After twenty minutes there was the patter of feet, followed by a demand. Water? A cuddle? A flashlight to ward off monsters under the bed? A fury during the day, at night everything scared her, and often William would fall asleep before she did. The patter of feet didn't return, and William guessed she'd snuggled up against Amanda, both easing the other into sleep.

When the living room clock struck midnight with a fancy bell he always swore he'd remove, William realized he'd fallen asleep on the couch, waiting.

It would blow over. He felt a pull in his chest and sat up straight, sweat dotted on his forehead, his nose, his upper lip. He rubbed at it with his hand, kneading his ribcage under his palm, waiting for it to pass. Not a heart attack. Its recurrence over the years was testimony to its insignificance. A panic attack. Or just pain to remind him he'd gotten old.

He thought of the office. Tomorrow he'd have to go in, smooth things over to ensure that his career still had a solid footing. Attend the partners' meeting to direct suspicions away. And he'd wheedle and smile and grit his teeth.

He had no time to start again. He was already in his fifties, and he'd left it too late to begin a family, change his career, fulfill his ambitions. Time, a thing his youthful self just wanted to get through, had slid by unnoticed until he'd run out.

Paul looked seventy. Cancer hadn't helped, but still. William had a year on him.

He didn't need to sit at Paul's bedside for another day. He'd gotten the message. Loud and clear.

Tomorrow, sort out his office, apologize to his wife, and make another appointment at the school, if they'd let him. He could always pull out the friend-dying-of-cancer card if need be. Close enough to the truth.

He lay back down on the couch, slipping his jacket off, even though it was crumpled beyond use already, and pulling the throw over him instead. He pulled at the laces of his shoes to loosen them, then pushed them off. Levering toe against heel the way the salesman told him would ruin the structure, no matter how expensive.

His chest gave one final pull and loosened. William took a deep breath, savoring the sweet fulfillment of the oxygen reaching deep into his lungs, and slept.

"I don't want you wasting time on this case. Get him to sign off on the interviews, then get out," Gascoigne instructed them. Dr. Jarvis had dropped by early that morning to say that Paul Worthington was fit for an interview, but no one greeted the news with enthusiasm.

"Weedon, you can pass your duties off to Collingwood this morning, but I expect you back at it this afternoon. Understood?"

Ngaire and Deb nodded, and Ngaire tried to ignore that he hadn't underscored her return to duty. Transcription being such a demanding and important task.

"You find more information in the files?" Deb asked her as they walked out the back of the station. Ngaire circled back to her desk at the reminder and pulled out a map of the area, circa 1974. She wanted to pinpoint whereabouts the deed had happened, even if she never touched it again.

"Nothing more. I watched the interview, but there weren't a lot of details. Either he's lying to us, or his memory is kaput, because it doesn't square up with the reports."

"I'll take a punt on it and say he's lying," Deb said as they walked down to the car. She went to the driver's side without even asking Ngaire, but after the difficulty Ngaire had had getting out of the car last time, she didn't take offense. Much.

After they had pulled into the flow of traffic, Ngaire said, "I think it's his memory. He didn't seem to be evasive, apart from saying he was on his own."

"But he brought in a lawyer."

"Which could mean he's scared," Ngaire said.

"Yeah." Deb gave a hard laugh. "Of us charging him with wasting police time."

Ngaire studied her. "I thought you believed him as well?"

Deb shrugged. They drove in silence the rest of the way. Ngaire rolled down the window and let the wind cool down her face.

The hospital scared her. The smell of the bleached linens and the weird alcoholic tang from the antiseptic pumps dotting the walls made her feel weak. It was too soon after her own stay. She gritted her teeth against the squeak of rubber-soled shoes on the linoleum until her jaw ached. Her private fingernails on a blackboard.

A uniformed constable guarded the door, and he looked relieved to see the pair of them, reading "police" in their gait.

"Gilford," he announced, and they introduced themselves in turn. "He's been quiet. His friend left yesterday afternoon and hasn't been back."

"His friend?" Ngaire asked.

"Yeah, the lawyer. I suppose since you've turned up, he'll be on his way."

"Well," Deb said with a smile, "we thought we'd let Paul decide that."

Gilford shrugged. "You need me here, or can I nip down to the cafeteria? I'm dead on my feet."

"Go on," Ngaire said. "Make it quick, though. We won't be here long."

He gave them a mock salute and headed out the corridor with a confidence that Ngaire envied. She'd once walked tall through public places, confident of her position.

"Jesus, are you sure you're not dead?" Deb asked as she sat down near Paul's bed. Ngaire heard Paul laugh from under the covers. There was so little to the poor man, the sheets lay nearly flat upon the bed. There was only the one chair next to the bed. Ngaire dragged another from the far wall, the legs squeaking on the linoleum floor.

"I'm saving death for later," Paul said, struggling to pull himself upright. "I've got the whole thing planned."

"Gave us quite a scare at the interview," Ngaire said. "I know Deb's hard to get used to, but she rarely knocks suspects unconscious."

Deb shot her a warning look, and she checked back through what she had said to find the worry. First names. It sounded too familiar.

"Because you passed out on us, we never got the chance to have you sign off on the interview," Deb said. "I know that you've hired a lawyer, so we're happy to wait while you contact him. But we need you to state that the answers you gave during the interview were correct, and you were of sound mind and body."

She stopped, and she and Ngaire gazed at the shrunken form on the bed. "Well," Deb said after a pause. "Of sound mind, anyway."

"Whatsit? You need my signature?"

"Mind if I raise the bed for you?" Ngaire asked as she saw the control hanging to one side. He nodded, and she adjusted the bed so he could sit back against the pillows. Watching him struggle to right himself reminded her of crabs on the beach or flies on the windowsill after a dose of spray.

"Dr. Jarvis saw you this morning, is that right?" When he nodded, Deb continued, "He said you could be interviewed again."

Paul nodded again, eyes fixated on his hands. "I should call my lawyer if you want to have an interview. He needs to be here."

Ngaire leaned over and touched the back of his hand below the taped IV line. "We understand that, but when you came into the station yesterday it was to confess, right?"

Another nod.

"So, did you miss any details in your confession?"

Deb frowned. She was recording the conversation in her notebook, and she shook her head. This wasn't what Gascoigne had ordered.

Ngaire shrugged. So what?

There was a noise from the hall, and a tall man,

dressed in an impeccable three-piece suit, despite the warmth of the day, entered.

"Can I help you, Detectives?"

Ngaire watched as Paul shrank back under the covers and pulled his hand away from hers. She looked back to the man standing in the doorway, saw him motion at Paul with his fingers, and saw Paul nod.

So Gilford was right. These two knew each other. Each attuned to the other's body language.

"We're getting sign-off for the interview we conducted at the station," Deb explained. She tilted her notebook, as though he'd be able to confirm something from her scrawl. "We have no further questions at this time, so if your client doesn't need us to play back the interview, we'll be on our way."

She raised her eyebrows at Ngaire, who stood and dragged the chair back into its former position.

"I assume you'll be appearing before the magistrate on behalf of your client?" Deb asked. "It'll be in court this afternoon."

He looked from Paul to Ngaire and back to Deb. "That's correct. I don't expect any trouble. Paul's a sick man."

"Could I get your name, for the record?" Ngaire asked. She pulled her notebook out and looked at Paul.

"William Glover," the man answered just as Paul said, "Billy."

"I'd like to investigate further," Ngaire stated. DS Gascoigne continued to look at the papers in front of him, but she saw his eyebrows raise. "I know it'll be difficult to interview Mr. Worthington again, but there's information from the original files I can follow up. The main job's corroborating what he said."

"That'll be hard on restricted duties," he observed.

Ngaire sat forward in her chair. "I've called the physio, and she's happy to sign me off for a full return to work tomorrow. If I get your go-ahead, I can investigate the reports today and map out a course of action."

Gascoigne sat down and placed his thumb and middle finger on either eyebrow and squeezed them toward each other. "What have we got so far?"

"A confession, a name, a date, and a place where he dumped the body." He frowned, and Ngaire hurried on. "We've got a cause of death that potentially fits in with Mr. Worthington's version of events."

"Potentially?" Gascoigne barked a laugh. "We've also got a man who's lawyered up."

Ngaire nodded. "Yes, but to me that shows he's telling the truth. He's scared of what might happen to him. Otherwise why protect his legal rights?"

"How long ago was this woman murdered?"

Ngaire tilted her head forward, as though to disguise her voice. "Forty years ago."

He sat back in his chair and sighed.

"But, sir," Ngaire added, fearful it was going the wrong way. "We've already told the parents we're investigating. We owe it to them to follow this through and bring closure."

Ngaire winced as she spoke that last word. Too late. The DS had undergone extensive counseling with his ex-wife before they split and had harbored a hatred of the word ever since. Considered it psychological mumbo jumbo.

"I don't want you spending a lot of time on this," Gascoigne said, and Ngaire clenched her fists and arms in excitement. It was a yes. "Who's your partner—Weedon?" Ngaire nodded. "I'll pull her back off the Gilbert inquiry." He pointed with his finger at Ngaire's chest. "But only a week. We've enough current investigations without dealing with historical cases. Understood?"

"Understood, sir." Ngaire fled his office before he changed his mind. Out in the corridor, she gave a

small skip of excitement before composing herself.
Time to get to work.

Chapter Nine

"Are you sure this place is safe?" Deb asked as she exited the driver's seat and clunked the door shut.

"You can hang back in the doorways," Ngaire said. She was holding a map drawn up quickly by Mary Lynton showing the layout of the compound. As part owners, they'd given permission for the property to be scoured from end to end. "If the buildings collapse, you can call for help."

There were over a dozen different buildings on the land. The housing block, the church hall, the ablutions block, the barn, and the milking sheds that contained equipment for milking cows and general upkeep of a dairy station.

Also, there was a small graveyard. Ngaire oriented herself using the hand-drawn map and went there first. It was the reason the cult members still owned the land. Because it was a closed sect, the minister of health had granted the members of the Christian Cult permission to create a cemetery and bury their dead within boundary lines. Difficult to sell a place after you'd done that.

There had been three burials. The first for Jeremiah Gibson, who'd been old and infirm before he arrived at the compound. Mary had told them that for the year preceding his death, they'd tended to him. Treated him the same as any hospice.

The second was a stillborn baby girl. Deb had wondered aloud whether the denial of care during pregnancy had influenced that outcome. They'd delivered the baby, dead, after two days of labor.

Ngaire thought they were lucky not to have lost the mother, too.

The third was Magdalene. And her unborn baby. Ngaire had checked through the records, following Finlay's suggestive reasoning, and confirmed it in the autopsy. Four months pregnant, which meant she was fourteen when conception took place.

Ngaire wondered what man had managed to sweet-talk her into that. Someone from the compound was the most obvious choice, but there'd been no allegations of molestation. Even though rumors made the rounds in every other closed religious group.

Although wooden palings and thick white rope marked off the area, no gravestones existed to alert a casual observer to what the space was for. Ngaire stepped over the boundary and looked more closely at the site. It hadn't been used for forty years, but the upkeep spoke of frequent visits. The grass was mowed, new ropes knotted as a barrier.

Once the commune members had all died, who'd even remember that these bodies lay buried here? A lost treasure chest on a council map nobody requested to see?

There was a marker of sorts on one grave. Ngaire squatted, her knees popping, to look closer. A worn Buzzy Bee. Hand-carved from wood and stained with color. The weather had faded it, but tinges of red and yellow remained. She pulled it from the grass and fought for her balance when it stuck fast. Weeds snared it to the grave.

Ngaire thought of the creator whittling until a block of wood metamorphosed into a toy. What thoughts had run through his head while he did so? Hours spent carving, sanding, and staining, propelled by the vision of a child's delight. Then he tossed the toy onto a grave. His baby dead, his new venture ruined by loss.

She left it and scanned the grass for signs of

another memorial. She soon found it. A flat stone with writing painted on it. Ngaire moved over to the spot. She grew conscious that she was walking on dead bodies and looked for a designated path. She couldn't find one.

The stone was large—six inches across and four inches high. The lettering was done with red paint, but it had deteriorated through the seasons, and Ngaire couldn't decipher the words. She gestured to Deb, who shook her head.

"No offense, Ngaire, but I'm not big on boneyards."

Ngaire walked the stone over to her instead. "Can you make this out? I can't even tell if it's in English."

Deb held it with her fingertips. "I don't think we should move stuff about. At least let me get a photo before you dive in."

Ngaire blushed. "Sorry."

"Suppose you've been out of practice for a while." Deb turned the stone over to reveal a dirt-stained base, then flipped it back to the writing. "I'm not sure. I guess this says Magdalene." She pointed to where a few curves possibly shaped an M, followed by chipped paint in a pattern long enough for the name. "It's too old. Just a moment," she handed the stone back to Ngaire and took out her pocket camera. "I'll get a shot here and back where you found it."

Deb took the photos, and they stepped out of the graveyard. "Do you want to start at the housing block?" Ngaire asked. "Mary noted down the rooms they used at the time."

"It's your party," Deb said. "I'll follow along."

The housing block had been built from wood; all the buildings used the same materials. Years without maintenance had taken a toll. Old man's beard grew up the side of the main house and halfway across the roof. The bright white trumpets were handsome against the dark-green leaves, but they'd add weight to the walls until the building fell.

The door opened with surprising ease, and Ngaire noted that the hinges were bright and oiled. She cautiously popped her head inside and called out, "Hello? Anyone there?"

She hesitated for a moment until Deb shoved her in the middle of one of her shoulder blades to push her forward. The growth covering the windows, atop years of accumulated dust and droppings, allowed for only sparse light inside. Ngaire pulled her penlight from her trouser pocket and turned it on. The tiny beam was swallowed by the room, so she shut it off.

"They're through this common area and down the hall. The third and fourth doors on the right," she said, having memorized the location. Still, she hesitated before moving onward. Someone had used this kitchen, had swept the floor clean. The sink in the corner had drops of water clinging to the inside bowl.

Ngaire walked over and turned the tap. Water gushed in a steady flow. "Check the light switch," she said to Deb, who walked over and flicked it on. Nothing.

"Hello?" Ngaire called out again in a strong voice. "It's the police, and we have permission to be on this property. If anyone's there, identify yourself now."

Deb walked to the corridor and peered down its entire length. She turned back to Ngaire and shrugged. "Kids, maybe? If they're hiding away, they'll be no bother to us, anyhow." She waved Ngaire forward. "Come on, show me the way."

Ngaire strode past Deb on unsteady legs. Someone waiting farther in could trap them. One door in, one out, and the window panes were sealed with putty, so they couldn't be opened. A blade flashed in her memory, but she swallowed hard and kept going. "The trick to being brave," her dad once said, "is to keep acting brave until all your fear is gone."

And thanks to her mother, she could definitely act.

Ngaire opened each door that they passed, peering inside every unused room. Dust had gathered in a thick coating on all the surfaces. She opened the second door on the left to reveal wallpaper hanging in long tatters off the inside wall of the room. She stepped inside and put her hand flat on the plasterboard revealed beneath. "Damp," she said and flicked her penlight on to peer into the ceiling joins. Her steps left tracks on the floor.

"Hurry, it's freezing in here," Deb said and headed for the first room belonging to the Lyntons. She shivered, even though she wore a jacket over her blouse. Low light and rising damp made the room cooler than when it had been full of people, movement, and life.

The room Mary and Abe had shared held nothing unusual. A bed frame sporting hard wooden slats where Ngaire expected metal springs sat on the floor. No mattress. It filled most of the room. When Mary said the place was for sleeping, she wasn't kidding. There was nothing else except an overgrown window.

"Love what they've done with the place," Deb quipped before she headed for Magdalene's room. "Timeless style."

Ngaire caught up and nudged her in the ribs. "If you get rid of your materialistic soul, you'll understand."

Magdalene's room differed from the others. The dimensions of the room were the same, but the fact that it contained only a single bed frame gave the illusion of space. The walls were magnificent in the dim light. Covered in illustrations and short quotes or poems. Grinning fairies poked their heads out from behind toadstools, a frog prince danced with a human princess, enclosed within a tight circle of text.

"Wow," Deb said with appreciation as she moved farther into the room. "Girl could actually draw." She stood nose to the wall, examining the intricate portraits and looping words.

Ngaire looked at where Deb's feet had crossed the room. "There's no dust," she said.

Deb turned to examine the floor behind her and nodded. "Someone's kept this room up. Look at this," she said, pointing to a pencil-drawn raccoon with a full tail.

Ngaire walked across the room and examined it. She shone her penlight at the illustration and saw what Deb meant. "It's been traced over."

"I think most of them have been," Deb said, moving on. "At least once. Someone's put lots of effort to make sure this stayed."

"Mary said nothing about these rooms. Just talked about the graveyard," Ngaire said. She followed a curling piece of text around a wave bursting full of fish. "Again, the kingdom of heaven is like a net that was thrown into the sea and gathered fish of every kind. Matthew 13:47," she read aloud.

"What about this one?" Deb said. "If anyone comes to me and does not hate his own father and mother and wife and children and brothers and sisters, yes, and even his own life, he cannot be my disciple. Luke 14:26."

"Cheerful," Ngaire said. There was a progression on the walls. Lower down were images of childish fantasies. Midheight was a plethora of Bible verses. Close to the ceiling, a variety of images showed a darker side of Christianity. The stations of the cross and the crucifixion, Jesus turning away Mary, a fat drunkard Noah bringing family and livestock onto a tiny boat.

"I bet Mum and Dad didn't like coming in here so much toward the end," Deb observed. She pointed to a whipped back running with blood, supplicants licking drops of it from the ground beneath.

"Not a lot different from any teenage room," Ngaire said. She pulled the bed frame away from the wall to show more sketches and then let it drop back into place. "Don't suppose there's anything on here about underage sex and pregnancy?"

They heard the creak of a floorboard outside the room, and they froze and stared at each other, waiting. Ngaire's heartbeat picked up its pace, and her ears filled with the beat of her blood as she tried to listen. When there was no fresh sound, she let her breath out and moved beside Deb. Another floorboard creaked, this time inside the room, and Ngaire looked at her feet. She saw that the board she'd stepped off sat higher than its neighbors, and she knelt to have a closer look.

The nails in the board that creaked had smaller heads than the others. Ngaire ran her fingers along the side, testing with her fingernails for purchase. Deb bent over her, standing, hands on knees, and looked along its length. "Here," she said, moving to the wall. She squatted, then held up her hands to Ngaire. "*You'll* have to." She'd bitten her nails to the quick.

Ngaire moved along and tried gripping near the wall. The board rose, then dropped as her fingers slipped. "Keys," she said to Deb and held out her hand for them. She took the car key and inserted it along the edge of the board. She twisted and pulled it toward her, and the board flipped out and over.

"That better still fit the ignition," Deb said, taking back the keys. "What's in there?"

Ngaire pulled items out along the length of the hiding place. A mauve cardboard packet, "Durex Gossamer" on the label. A small paper fold that contained long-dead plant matter. Once it might have been tobacco or marijuana, but now it was close to dust. A little key on a plaited wristband.

Deb opened the packet of condoms. "Not to be used after November 1978," she read. "There's only one left."

"Maybe they came in packs of one," Ngaire said. She blew air into the cavity to see if anything more hid behind the dust.

"Contents three teat," Deb read, then refolded the packet. "I guess the first two didn't work."

Ngaire sat back on her haunches. There was nothing left in the hiding space. "I must check, but I think they'd have been a restricted item back then. Eighteen or over. Perhaps we can narrow down a list of suspects for fatherhood of her baby."

"We're not looking for a father," Deb said as she stood again. "We're looking for evidence of murder. Besides, she could've stolen them. From a shop or someone else here."

Ngaire half rose to her feet when a cramp gripped her leg. Deb grabbed her hand and pulled her upright, then Ngaire hit at the stiff muscle on her thigh, trying to punch blood flow back into it. When it released, Ngaire looked up to see Deb eyeing her warily from a few feet away.

"Muscle cramp," she explained as she took a limping step. "They hurt like hell."

Deb nodded. "I know what a cramp's like. Do you find punching yourself in the leg helps?"

Ngaire burst into laughter. "Are you offering your help for the next time?"

Deb laughed with her, and Ngaire was relieved to see the cautious tension leave her frame. Deb pulled open the door and walked out into the corridor. "Hey, wait!" she called and took off running.

Ngaire followed her out and saw a man running out of the open door at the other end of the housing block. She sprinted after Deb when they were out the back door, splitting off to veer left as Deb turned right. The man looked back over his shoulder at them and tripped but caught his balance. He ran behind a shed to Ngaire's right. Reaching the corner a second before Deb, she used her hand as leverage on the wooden paneling to swing around the side at top speed. She continued running, even though the man was no longer in view, whipping her head from left to right to left, scanning for movement. There was a clang to her left, and she veered that way, seeing a door shutting in front of her.

She lost time opening it again and then resumed the chase inside a large barn. Hooks and pulleys dangled from the ceiling over the wide-open floor. A mezzanine level was stacked with bags of feed.

With no exit in front and the man gone from sight, Ngaire chose left again. The man had favored it twice. The side of the shed was separated into stabling areas and a pile full of straw that must have been a haven for mice and rats. Between the two lay a narrow funnel leading to another open floor space.

Ngaire pressed her hand to her scarred side where a stitch was niggling. She hadn't run for ages and was out of shape. She pressed onward, her lungs trying to find a rhythm where she could breathe without it burning. When she emerged, she turned left and caught a flash as he disappeared out a side door.

Where was Deb? She'd lost her in the chase and couldn't hear any sounds beyond her own heavy breaths. Ngaire hit the door at full speed and lucked out when it opened; the latch hadn't caught. She scanned again, right, left, right, left as she moved back into bright sunlight. If she turned left, she'd arrive back at the entrance to the barn. Straight ahead?

Footsteps sounded behind her, and Ngaire saw Deb cutting through to her left. She pointed right, and Ngaire swerved to follow. A forest of trees lay ahead, but a natural path cut through the thicket. As she ran, she held her arm in front of her face to protect against low branches.

An outhouse sat to her left, nestled in the pines. Ngaire arched around it as she ran, not fancying a hidden surprise. Trees to her right, trees to her left. A clearing coming up, then an empty field.

Deb slowed to a walk, and Ngaire petered out beside her. The uncommon exertion caused her to pant so hard she couldn't speak. For minutes, she fought just to draw in the air she needed.

"Where'd he go?" she managed to ask as Deb patted her on the back.

"Shit, Ngaire. If I knew that, I'd still be running," she replied. The pasture in front of them was empty. Clear fields stretching for acres. "He must've escaped in the woods."

Ngaire bent forward, scared for a moment that she'd throw up. Even when the nausea passed, she stayed in position, hands locked on her knees, face staring at the ground.

"Well," Deb said as they walked back to the blocks, "at least now when people ask if you're ready for duty, I can tell them you beat me in a chase."

"Who's been asking?"

"Oh, no one," Deb said vaguely. "Just if they do."

They passed the outhouse structure, and Deb put her finger up to her lips and then stood to one side, motioning Ngaire to the other. Three fingers, two, one.

She pulled the door open, but all that emerged was a large blowfly weaving in flight and the smell of fresh excrement. Ngaire waved her hands, and Deb shut the door.

"Should we tell the Lyntons they've got a squatter problem?" Ngaire asked.

Deb shook her head. "I'm sure there's something in the Bible about squatting. Jesus would be all for it."

"And God said, 'let there be squatters'?"

Deb laughed and hit away a low branch angled toward her eye. "He must have been here awhile, anyhow. He knew his way around."

Ngaire put her hand in her back pocket and swore under her breath.

"What is it?"

"The map," she said. "I've lost the damn map."

Deb laughed as they rounded the corner. "Shed," she said, pointing. "Housing block, church, graveyard, wood, field." She lowered her hand. "I think we'll manage without it."

"All right, navigator. Want to lead me to the slurry?"

After a few false starts, Deb proved her point. The property was easy to work out. As they walked, Ngaire thought of a childhood holiday spent in a camper van park. Blocks set aside for specified uses and wide-open spaces to hook up caravans.

Here it would've been dairy herds instead of caravans, and a concrete slurry instead of tanks into which you emptied portable toilets.

Ngaire was glad to see that the slurry was empty. Whoever lived here hadn't got to the point that they were running the property as a farm. She leaned over the side and looked at the wall. There was a thick, plasticky skin painted over the concrete, to stop the contents from soaking into the cement. She imagined trying to get purchase against the base, against the wall, and fingers, hands, and feet slipping, slipping.

She pulled her head back. Not that Magdalene was alive when she went into the slurry pit. Not if Paul's testimony was true.

"A ladder was mounted here," Deb said from the corner. She was also looking into the pit, and when Ngaire looked over, she pointed to where small pieces of metal still jutted out from the concrete wall. "They've sawn it off."

Ngaire walked around to look closer. Deb was right. There were rough teeth marks where the blade had gone back and forth. "Why would anyone do that?" she asked rhetorically. Deb shrugged.

Ngaire touched the edge of the metal, careful in case of splinters. The position required to reach in was awkward, but judging from the angle of the blade marks, they'd sawn it from above. Was it made of precious metal?

"I can't remember anything about her body position when they found her," said Deb. "Perhaps they had to cut her free."

"But it did say there was no ladder," said Ngaire. "If they'd cut it, then it would've been lying around somewhere."

"If the person who wrote the report noted it."

It was a fair point to make. Often the event caused so much panic that people compiled reports later, with fresh eyes and a clear head. And if you're trying to cope with a dead body, you might not think to note the metal cast aside on the ground.

Ngaire heard the rustle of movement before she saw the black mass heading full tilt toward her. She heard the dog bark, registered its size, saw its tongue hanging out over long teeth.

She stepped back, dodged behind Deb, would've stepped farther back again but hit the wall of the slurry. *Caught, I'm caught.*

Her mind blanked out, and her chest felt the slide of a knife blade caressing its curves. She found herself falling, heard the dog growl, saw it crouch low ready to pounce, and steadied herself against Deb. Grabbed her arms to use her as a shield.

"Trev, here boy." An ear-splitting whistle came from the milking sheds. The dog crouched for a moment, haunches swinging, then turned and ran out of sight toward the call, his brindle body lithe and smooth with muscle.

"Who's there?" Deb called out. A repeat whistle to the dog but no reply. "We're police," she called. "Identify yourself."

The dog ran back around the corner straight at them. In Ngaire's panic, she thought she'd faint, then saw the wag of its tail. A man followed—the same man they'd chased earlier. The dog leaped up on Deb, his paws leaving tracks over her blouse, her jacket.

The whistle again, and the dog jogged back to its master. Ngaire realized she was still holding onto Deb, gripping her upper arms, and let her go. She stepped sideways, a blush of guilt and shame heating her cheeks.

"Who are you?" she asked. "What are you doing here?"

The man let the dog jump up on his chest and lick his face. The teeth that Ngaire had thought were sharp and white were yellowed and loose. Although he jumped like a puppy, she saw the tinge of gray on his brindle belly.

The man walked closer, head tilted to one side. When he'd run, Ngaire thought he was young, her age—forty at a stretch. But like his dog, he, too, was older. Late fifties, early sixties. His hair was blond but streaked with white. His skin wrinkled like linen left in the bottom of the closet.

The man smiled, but he still hadn't spoken, hadn't answered their questions. He looked at Ngaire, the tip of her head, her feet, then his gaze popped up to her breasts. He did the same to Deb.

"Can you speak?" Ngaire asked, drawing his rapt gaze back to her. His skin was brown from the sun, his face mild and gentle. He leaned to pat his dog, and when he looked at the animal, his face animated a hundredfold. Emotion spilling from every pore. She frowned. Of course he could speak, he'd called out to the dog.

Deb relaxed her stance and moved forward to pat the dog on its side. "Trev?" she asked. "Is that short for Trevor?"

The man smiled wider and nodded, "Yes. He's named after my Daddy."

"Does your Daddy live here?"

The man stopped smiling. "He's dead, been dead a long time."

"Sorry to hear that," Ngaire said as she, too, stepped forward. "What's your name?"

He shook his head, but when Deb scratched Trev between the ears, and the dog gave a thankful shiver, the man answered, "I'm Isaiah."

"Do you live here, Isaiah?"

The man looked back at the housing block, the shed, the ablutions block. "Yup, I live here."

"How long have you lived here?"

He frowned. The affect in his voice was off—flat but not absent of character. Ngaire watched as he tilted his head to the side again. A processing disorder, maybe. Slow at interpreting their verbal communications, but not of low intelligence. She looked at Deb and raised a halting hand when she would've spoken again. *Give him time*.

"A long time," he said at last. "Most of my life. I came here when I was—" He indicated a height against the side of his leg rather than specify an age. A visual processor. "My parents used to live here, too, but they went away." He pointed to the graveyard beyond. "They're planted now like they always said they wanted to be. I looked after them well."

Ngaire looked at the graveyard. "They're buried here?"

"No," Isaiah said scornfully. "I wouldn't bury a rat here. They're in a nice church ground."

Mary and Abe Lynton had walked away from this property and started a new life. Put together the funds to buy a retirement property. But they were both smart, trained, and resourceful. Not everyone had the same reserves.

"Where'd you get Trev?" Deb asked as she gave the dog another pat. "He's a beautiful dog."

Isaiah turned his entire focus onto her. He leaned his weight on his right foot while her words floated around his mind, trying to coalesce into sense.

"Dog rescue. They tried to kill him."

Trevor barked, and Deb laughed. "He knows we're talking about him."

Isaiah grabbed hold of the collar around Trev's neck and pulled him close. "Dogs can't talk," he said. "And they don't speak English."

"Why did you run away from us, Isaiah?" Ngaire asked. "Did somebody tell you that you weren't meant to be here?"

There was no defensive note to his voice when he said, "It's my home. I'm allowed to be here." He looked at the housing block, then to the fields. Turning his head awkwardly to avoid the slurry pit, Ngaire noticed.

"People don't like me," he explained. "They say they want to talk, but then they'll end up saying mean things."

"We promise not to say mean things, Isaiah," Ngaire said. "And we'd find it helpful if you answered a few questions for us."

His face withdrew into blankness. The frown disappeared. His eyes no longer made contact with hers. Trev whined and turned to nose between Isaiah's leg, pushing him backward.

Ngaire took a step forward, but Isaiah's moments of clarity were lost. He closed his eyes and keened. Trev jumped up on his chest, and as Isaiah tried to hit himself, on his shoulder, on his head, the dog nudged at his hands so they became entangled. Isaiah let himself fall to the ground, and Trev nosed him all over. Pawing at Isaiah's hands when he tried to strike himself, licking his face, until he laughed.

"What the fuck?" Deb asked.

Ngaire turned around. "He's in meltdown," she whispered. During her stint at university, she'd shared a room with a student who had self-diagnosed with Asperger's. The first meltdown she'd observed left her shaking. By the end of the term, she'd known to keep quiet and wait for her roommate to come back. "He'll be okay in a minute, but we should move on and let him have space to recover."

Deb gave her a sour look. At first, Ngaire thought it was in response to her advice, then she recalled grabbing Deb's arms to use her as a dog shield. She conceded that Deb had a right to be pissed.

They left Isaiah and moved to the ablutions block. It housed nothing of interest, although Deb postulated that if water worked in the housing block, it seemed odd Isaiah used an outhouse instead of these facilities.

The church was equal in size to the barn. There was a large, open hall, which would've dwarfed the small cult unless outsiders attended. A ceremonial baptismal font on the left of the altar and a set of double doors to the right, locked shut. Ngaire guessed from its size that the room housed chairs or pews for the church. Ready to be put out each Sunday and locked away after service.

"Do you think Mary would have a key?" Ngaire asked as she pulled at the doors. Their hinges squeaked in protest. Unlike those in the housing block, these hinges hadn't been cleaned and oiled.

"Ask her," Deb replied. Her conversation had become monotone, and Ngaire knew she should apologize, but the thought of it opening her up to questions made her mouth clam shut.

She gave a last pull at the doors, but they were double height and made of solid wood. She'd never be a match for their strength. "We should check back with Isaiah," Ngaire said. "He'd know if there's a key here."

Deb grunted but followed Ngaire back to the slurry pit. Isaiah had left, taking Trev with him. Ngaire saw an object lying in the grass by the wall and bent to pick it up. Another stone with painted writing. This one in better condition, the concrete wall have offered protection.

"Magdalene, wait for me in heaven. I'll follow you there."

Chapter Ten

Ngaire woke to the sound of a key turning in her front door lock. She'd dozed off in front of the muted television set; the bright screen now the only light in the darkened room.

Her senses on high alert she sat and watched in horror as a man stepped into the room, his head turned to watch the street. She felt behind her for a weapon and found the remote control. Grasping it in her right hand, she raised it over her shoulder as she struggled to her feet. The man turned to face her.

"Ngaire. Christ you gave me a scare," Finlay said, holding a hand up to his chest. "I thought you were out."

She held the remote ready to throw for another second while her brain fought to make sense of the situation. "Finlay," she said, lowering it to her thigh. "What the hell are you doing here?"

He poked his head out the door again, and when Ngaire walked over to see what held his interest, she saw four young men pile into a car that might last have passed its warrant inspection in 2005.

"I thought you lived in a nice area," he said as he walked inside. "When did the lower class move in?"

One youth caught her looking and shot her the finger. Ngaire gave it back to him, then closed her door in case it gave him ideas. "They didn't move in, they grew up," she said. "And that's not the lower class, that's just the middle class waiting to have education, jobs, and money bestowed on them."

He gave a mock shudder and then walked through into her living room and gave a real one. "Jeez, Ngaire, how long since you aired this place out?"

Without asking, he opened the three windows in the room and let the evening air in. The days were getting shorter, and there was a red hint on the skyline showing that the sun would soon pack up. Already, the street lamps were brighter.

"Make yourself at home," Ngaire said with a trace of bitterness. How dare he break in, then complain about the state of her house? Another thought occurred to her. "Do you do this often?"

Finlay ignored the question and wandered through to the kitchen. He had the door to the fridge opened by the time Ngaire followed him. "Are there snacks in this house, or are you on a diet?"

"There're chips in the cupboard," she said, pointing.

He pulled them out, then found a can of Nestle reduced cream and a packet of onion soup from the same cupboard and mixed up a dip for them.

"Help yourself," she said sadly. She'd been saving those for an occasion when she overloaded on self-pity instead of her usual level of discontent. This afternoon she'd been tempted after Deb confronted her on the way home, but she'd shown strength by avoiding the cupboard to eat a proper meal instead.

"Shut up and sit down," Finlay ordered. "If I didn't force you to eat junk food, when would you ever have the pleasure?"

Ngaire sat and rubbed her eyes with her knuckles. A large piece of sleep crackled its sharp edges into the corner of her eye, and she fished it out with her fingertip.

Finlay clapped his hands together. "Right. What did I come here to talk to you about?"

Ngaire waited to see whether it was a rhetorical question, but he didn't elaborate. "I don't know. To harangue me about my living room and force fat down my throat?"

"Side effects, love, I know." He put his finger up in the air. *Eureka*. "Did you ever plan on returning my materials on Magdalene Lynton, or have you grown uncommonly attached to them?"

Ngaire opened the bag of chips and swiped one through the dip despite Finlay's admonishment; it wasn't ready. The onion pieces were crunchy, but that added to the overall texture and taste, and she took another. "I was planning on getting it back to you sometime. The official replacements still haven't arrived."

"Do you know, it's funny. When I go into the newspaper offices, they have this magical machine that makes exact copies of documents I have. Do you know of such a machine?"

"Yeah, all right. You didn't say when you needed them back."

Ngaire ate, her teeth chomping far too hard for the task at hand. "I'll make a copy tomorrow." She continued to plow through the packet and noticed that Finlay was not eating his fair share, considering that he was the one responsible for her nutritional downfall. "Here." She pushed the bowl toward him.

He helped out with enthusiasm. "Any progress on the case?" he asked with a mouth full of chips.

"Officially, I can't answer that," Ngaire said. "But no, there's nothing. Deb and I traveled to the compound today to nosey around, but all we found was an ancient, upset resident."

Finlay nodded. "Isaiah's still kipping out there, then. Gave me a hell of a fright last year when I went round to take pictures."

"Us, too. Thought for a moment his dog would kill us." Ngaire thought back to when Trev had lunged and colored as she remembered her reaction.

"What is it?"

"Nothing," she said, picking up the chips and dip to carry them into the living room.

"Is it safe?" Finlay asked from the doorway, giving the air a good sniff.

"It's fine. Stop exaggerating."

Finlay tossed his shoulder bag onto the floor and rooted through it, coming up with a bottle of scotch. "Got any glasses?"

Ngaire nodded toward the sideboard. "Not for me. It's a school night."

"It's always a school night for me," Finlay said, ignoring her answer and pouring two generous shots into her crystal tumblers. When he held one out, she took it, despite telling herself not to.

"Did you see Magdalene's room when you were there?" Ngaire asked. Finlay shook his head. "There're drawings and scripture covering her wall. Beautiful and weird. Someone's been tracing it in as it fades, so everything's still visible."

Finlay nodded. "That'll be Isaiah. I don't know how he keeps himself alive out there. Never worked out how he bought food to keep himself going. Everything else is free and clear."

"Has he always been out there?"

"Far as I know." He shrugged. "Says he has, anyhow. Apparently his parents are buried in a plot in the back of the house somewhere."

"No, he told us they were in another graveyard," Ngaire said. "A real one. But we saw theirs. Magdalene's buried there, along with a couple others."

She wondered what it'd be to live alone for your adult life, with only a dog for company. Part of her thought it was a good trade.

"Did you trace the father yet?" Finlay asked.

"Of Magdalene's baby?" He nodded. "Haven't got a clue. Looks like she was sexually active of her own accord, though. There were condoms and weed stashed in a hidey-hole in her room."

Finlay raised his eyebrows. "Don't know how much 'own accord' you have when you're fourteen."

She nodded. Accurate enough. "Who'd you have pegged as the primary suspect?"

He kicked off his shoes and lay on the couch, the stuffed leather arm acting as a pillow. He continued to raise the glass to his mouth and take sips without spilling a drop. Ngaire couldn't have managed that trick without a bendy straw.

"I always had the leader of the group pegged, but that's not true." Ngaire raised her brow at him. "Turned out he was infertile."

"That might be the wife's problem," Ngaire pointed out, but he shook his head again.

"Someone gave me a squiz at his medical records," he said. When Ngaire looked shocked, he countered, "He was dead by then, anyway. In his early twenties he had mumps, and it did him a world of damage. Fits he'd be impotent, too."

After another long sip of her drink, Ngaire pushed her shoes off and curled her legs beneath her on the chair. "I wonder if that's why he became a prophet?" Finlay tossed her a quizzical glance. "Impotent means without power, so I wonder if he craved it in other forms. If he needed people looking up to him, to believe he was worthwhile."

"Are you suggesting that every male leader is impotent, Ngaire?" Finlay's voice took on a teasing note. "Now that's a news story."

"Just putting it out there." Another sip of her drink, and she'd finished it. Usually Finlay would've pressed another on her at this stage, but he'd sunk comfortably into the couch, so she'd be crass to suggest it. Ngaire stood and poured herself another, the buzz from the first spreading out across her chest like a heat pack. "We checked out the slurry pit," she said. As a tradeoff for his alcohol, she offered him the last of the chips as she walked back to her chair.

"Nasty piece of work, that," Finlay observed.

"Yeah, I'll say. Did you see that someone had sawn off the ladder?"

He tilted his head to look at her, upside down. "From the slurry?"

She nodded. "Deb found remnants mounted on the side. The poles had teeth marks from the saw. We reckoned the body got tangled up in it, and by the time anybody wrote about it, they'd forgotten."

"They can't have forgotten," Finlay said, his voice slow and thoughtful. "I'm sure they ended up with a fine for not having one. Against the safety guidelines, even back then."

"Perhaps by that time they didn't care? Too busy heading out and away. I don't understand why they'd leave their daughter there. Or the others would leave their stillborn child."

"The Maples," Finlay supplied. "And they did want to take their baby girl with them. The Gibsons wanted to take his dad with them, too. The Lyntons wouldn't allow it."

Ngaire looked up at him, frowning. "How could they stop it?"

He shrugged. "The council said they couldn't disinter the other two without disturbing Magdalene."

She yawned and rubbed her eyes. "You'd think two to one would win out if they've disbanded the church. It's weird to keep a whole farm stagnant to protect a cemetery that only one couple wants. I'm sure the law would be on their side." Ngaire had vague recollections of nonprofits being disbanded without all signatories from her years at college.

"I don't know that those two couples could afford a lawyer," Finlay said. "They weren't left well off by the move."

"Even more reason to get it sorted."

"Maybe." He was silent for a minute, then sprang to his feet. "Top you off?"

Ngaire almost protested that she'd got herself a fresh one when she realized she'd hit the bottom of the glass again without noticing. The warmth had spread from her chest out to the rest of her body.

"It'll have to be the last. I'll be a wreck tomorrow as it is."

"Well, you know what they say. If you've already bought yourself a hangover, keep drinking."

Ngaire burst out laughing, then couldn't stop even when tears were streaking her face. "Who?" she asked as the convulsion passed. "Who says that? You?"

"Me, and I'm sure at least one other person. Bottoms up." He clinked his tumbler against hers and downed it in one gulp. After an internal debate all the worse for her being drunk, Ngaire copied him. This time, her tears were from the fire that engulfed her throat.

"No more," she managed as he tried to take the glass from her again. "I'm serious."

"Okay, okay. At least you look happier than when I arrived."

Ngaire grew quiet for a moment. She looked at Finlay's back as he poured himself another and thought back on the day she'd had. There'd been little of use at the compound, and she'd ruined her relationship with Deb forever.

"I did a bad thing today," she admitted. The alcohol might've loosened her tongue, but the relief of confessing made her glad of it. "Isaiah's dog attacked us at the farm." Startled, Finlay scanned the length of her body. "No," she said, groping for words to explain. "I thought he'd attack us. Trev was growling and running, and all I saw were big teeth." She gnashed her own in demonstration and laughed, but with a note of sadness from earlier weeping. "I tried to get away, but I'd trapped myself against the side of the slurry, so I pulled Deb in front of me."

Hearing the words, Ngaire realized they

sounded even worse than they had in her own head. When Deb had pulled the car over on the drive back to the police station, she'd known the matter wouldn't be passed over.

"I've always supported you," Deb had said. Her choice of words indicated that that ship had sailed. "When you made mistakes in training, I always took the time to get your side and backed you when accusations were unfair."

Ngaire wasn't able to make herself turn and face Deb. What she said was true. She'd always been a staunch ally which put Ngaire's behavior today a rung lower on the ladder of acceptability.

"I know that it's hard to come back from an injury. I've gone through that myself. What I've never, ever, done is to put someone else in jeopardy to save myself."

"I'm sorry. I panicked," was all Ngaire offered.

"Well, the next time you panic, I won't be there. Find yourself another partner. I'm done."

Even if Deb kept the details of what had happened to herself, her request to be assigned to another case would end Ngaire. After everything that had gone on, her coffin lid was in place. Her actions today had just supplied the nails.

"I'm only allowed to the end of the week on this," Ngaire said. "Would you give me that?"

Deb hadn't said a word. Just started the car up and drove it back to the station. When she exited the vehicle and walked inside, she didn't look at Ngaire.

Finlay was now looking at her, but Ngaire wished he wasn't. His face showed disappointment, even as he tried hard to say the right words. "It must be hard to recover from an injury like yours," he said. "Maybe you should rest and think about whether that's what you want."

Ngaire cried then, her shoulders shaking. She punched at the side of the chair in frustration that she couldn't keep emotions to herself. "It's the drink," she explained to Finlay when he tried to hug her and comfort. "It's just the drink talking."

Soon after, she went to bed, wrung out. Finlay had imbibed so much there wasn't any chance of him driving home. Ngaire tossed him a blanket and a cushion to use as a pillow and left him on the couch to sleep it off.

Although she'd dozed earlier, Ngaire was now wide awake. All the while she massaged cream into her scars, she was scared Finlay would bounce through the door as he so merrily bounced through her other boundaries.

All her muscles were tense. She tried to pretend that was because she'd had an awful day, but her muscles were always tense lately, her anxiety always high.

No wonder insomnia plagued her. She lived in a state of high alert, yet when something happened, she'd made her partner face it alone.

Worse than a coward. A coward stared death in the eye and ran away. Ngaire had stared death in the eye and thrust her partner in its path.

As part of ethics training at the university, they'd taken a series of tests. If you know a train will crash, is it okay to sacrifice one person to save many—that sort of thing. At the time, she'd known the right answers, but when it became real, her true self had decided to compromise somebody else's safety to save her own skin.

Ngaire couldn't see a way to continue to work as a detective carrying that on her conscience. Regardless of whether Deb took steps to put it on the record. How would she continue to turn up to work at a job when she'd exposed herself as the opposite of what the role required?

Christ's sake, she was even afraid of sleeping.

Ngaire shifted onto her back and tried lying spread-eagled. The alcohol buzz had transitioned into a quease-inducing thump in her temples. She looked at the clock, squinting to make out the blurry, red, illuminated digits. Three o'clock. Another three hours of wakefulness, and she'd welcome the day with an alarm she didn't need and a shower she did.

Her mouth was drying out in a familiar hangover pattern, but she couldn't be bothered to fetch a glass of water. What she really thirsted for was another big glass of scotch and to call work to say she'd never return.

She twiddled her fingers and toes as she thought how great that conversation would be. Until she had to make rent and pay for her next supermarket shop. Her savings didn't add up in a give-up-your-day-job way. Work had a superannuation plan, but it was crap until you clocked over ten years in service. There was Kiwisaver, but she'd face a long, dry stretch until she turned sixty-five and cashed that check.

Ngaire's father lived up in the North Island, in a run-down house that wasn't truly fit for human habitation. Her mom had separated from him when she was a tween to move to the United States in search of fulfillment as an actress. Ngaire hadn't spoken with her in a long while. Didn't enjoy conversations that one-sided. After five years, when her mother's stardom still hadn't materialized, she'd married again. Although her second husband was richer than her first, he also came with a baggage load of children.

What use was it to be part of the boomerang generation when your parents didn't have a nice house to put you up in? How was Ngaire meant to have an early midlife crisis *and* support herself?

She thought of the dog again. Hurtling toward her with its teeth bared. Thought of how even using Deb as a shield didn't make her feel safe.

When she'd been a probationary constable, still

finishing her workplace assessments so she'd be real police, Ngaire thought she had everything she needed to be safe. She'd trained in avoiding confrontation, handling people so they obeyed her, and how to keep a brave front to show she was in charge. Failing her assertiveness training, she had a stabproof vest.

Invincible.

Ngaire turned onto her side and curled up, fetal. She'd give a lot to have that emotion back.

Four months had passed since she went to a party and ended the night in the emergency room, convinced her internal organs had been ruptured by a blade. She hadn't noticed her leg then, concentrating on what terrified her, rather than what had caused her the most damage.

She'd just gone to a party. A party she should have stayed away from. Ngaire knew she should've left once her friends decamped, and she realized they were doling out more at the bar than beer and wine. But she'd stayed because she was a dick, and she thought she knew how the world worked. Turned out, she didn't know anything.

After she'd observed the little exchanges under the bar, she should've called it in. Later, when she saw points snorted in the open, men and women whose eyes bulged as the methamphetamine hit their brain, she should've called it in. Instead, high on her one glass of white wine, she'd stayed. Making the stupid assumption she'd be safe to call in later. When she'd sorted it. Superwoman to the rescue.

Such a dick.

Ngaire thought she'd cornered those responsible in the kitchen, but they'd cornered her. When she issued orders, they laughed. One pulled a knife on her, another had a sawn-off under the sink. When she showed her identity, they advanced, instead of withdrawing, until she realized they meant to kill her.

That was the first time she'd experienced

genuine fear for her life; sensed it eating into her bones and turning every action into powerful instinct. Encompassing terror robbed her brain's ability to think. The knife wound in the back of her thigh—stabbing, twisting, wrenched to her calf—occurred when she tried to run. After she fell, a young woman stabbed her in the chest, the gesture tentative. Her face hardened when she saw Ngaire's blood, and she'd raised her hand again, practice time over.

"Fuck's sake, Gorky," was the yell that saved her life. "You can't slit a cop up in here. Dump her round the back. We've got a fight coming."

They'd turned in instant obedience and dragged her out the back. Because she couldn't walk, they had to haul her and grew sick of the effort, dropping her next to a car wreck rusting on blocks. She didn't even try to fight off the man when he reached into her pocket to pull out her ID. He'd pocketed it.

They left her there, and soon she heard the sound of a physical fight, knuckle on bone. People attacking people until sirens broke up the after-party entertainment.

When officers walked around the back of the house, Ngaire wished she could hide. She wanted to crawl home, not be caught at the scene of her shame. Her mouth gummed shut, and she didn't tell them her identity. Instead, she pretended to fall unconscious when the questions didn't stop, and the ambulance hadn't arrived.

The emergency room cleaned her up and booked surgery to save her leg before she'd told her name to the attending physician. She'd begged him not to tell the police still hanging around, taking details or sullen grunts from a dozen others injured at the party.

It had come out. She'd woken up with a bandaged leg and a bandaged chest and a constable beside her bed asking her who, what, where, why?

He'd looked her in the eye when she said she

didn't remember and wasn't able to describe them. He'd seen the truth there, his face showing disgust and disbelief when she claimed memory loss.

Her first week back at the station, she'd seen that same look on every face she viewed. Every time someone asked her if she was okay their faces asked her something else. "How dare you betray us? Why won't you give us the information? Why are you protecting them?"

And Ngaire couldn't answer those questions because she wasn't protecting them; she was protecting herself. Her number was unlisted, but Finlay had found her house with ease when he came back to Christchurch. Arrived on the doorstep one night after bumping into her on the street earlier. She couldn't hide if someone put in the effort.

She'd finally thought she might be ready to get back into it. Had caught a case that flared her imagination and made her overlook how she was a traitor and a coward. One instantaneous reaction—a stupid, dangerous reaction—and that had gone forever.

It was only when the weight of the bed shifted that Ngaire realized the snoring from the living room had stopped.

"Can't sleep on that couch. My back's killing me," Finlay said as he clambered beneath the sheets. He tossed an arm out and rubbed her back. "Why are you lying so far away?"

Ngaire was relieved that he was still dressed when he when he pressed his body against hers. Oh, well. It wasn't as though she was sleeping, anyway. She turned to him and moved closer to the middle of the bed. With his arm draped around her shoulders, he fell asleep, his snores announcing it to the room at large.

Finlay's breath caressed the side of her cheek. If he hadn't been so drunk, he'd happily have put up with his discomfort on the couch, preferring that to the trouble of inserting himself into her bed. She wondered whether tomorrow he'd remember his middle-of-the-night switch. Perhaps she should withhold information in the morning to see how many erroneous assumptions he made before putting him out of his misery.

Ngaire pressed a hand up against his chest, against the rough cotton of his shirt. Her palm echoed his heartbeat like a bass beat on a speaker. She only meant to press it there for a moment, but the steady thump comforted her the same way his snores gave her relief from the silence of being alone. She fell asleep smiling.

Chapter Eleven

William walked downstairs. Placing his feet carefully to avoid the third step from the top, which creaked, and to make sure each footfall landed squarely in the middle of the runner.

Amanda was a light sleeper. Attuned to trouble from the moment Emma arrived, she'd sometimes walk through to her room with a bottle when William hadn't heard a sound. Later returning empty-handed after a midnight feed. When she harangued him on how little help he contributed, he'd stared at her open-mouthed before launching into a defense including references to supersonic hearing and batlike abilities in the dark. Then he pointed out that she barely woke during these feeds. Had her eyes closed when she passed him heading out, and if he followed, she'd be asleep in the rocking chair while Emma suckled.

When he'd swung his leg out of the bed tonight, she'd turned over, and he froze midaction. The light snuffling that Amanda produced instead of a snore let him know he'd gotten away with it. At least in the living room, he didn't have to keep tiptoeing. He pulled out the Acer minilaptop from his briefcase. It was so tiny, he had trouble typing on the keyboard. The trackpad also guaranteed at least one swear word per session, but it was small enough to hide and light enough to carry everywhere.

William knew enough of technology and tracking to know he didn't know enough to keep safe. He relied on a separate computer with a connection through a different mobile phone to see him through. Along with a variety of e-mail addresses and false names he hoped didn't reveal a pattern to anybody.

After launching the TOR browser, he waited for the address he'd typed in to load. The system was painfully slow compared to Firefox or Chrome, but he felt safer using it, even though each second it added raised his anxiety levels by a similar margin.

In the end, he was hiding his own damn money, but he still took the extra trouble. Ridiculous. The additional security might be unnecessary, but he preferred this side of the equation if he was wrong.

He scanned his accounts as they loaded, going through each bank in a different sequence so he could verify that the levels were where they should be. After he'd totaled it up on his calculator, he closed everything. A hair shy of $2 million he'd put away now. If he lost his job tomorrow, he had a buffer he could use to live out the rest of his life. His life would change from how he envisaged it now, sure. But he wouldn't be seated in his kitchen when the police evicted him from the land he'd farmed for a lifetime. Sitting in his kitchen because he had nowhere else to go.

Amanda hadn't thawed entirely since he'd missed the interview last week. He'd elevated Paul into a dying friend in need, but she hadn't blinked. The only reason she was coming around was that the school had accepted Emma. They'd deposited the full annual fee and awaited final confirmation that their angel could go to the right school. Emma would hate it. None of her kindergarten buddies were heading there. Now he realized he should've listened to Amanda last year and enrolled her in their preschool. Now she'd move to a school where she didn't know anybody.

He'd sorted out work, too. He explained that Geoff hadn't listened to him when he said he couldn't make the meeting because his friend *was dying of cancer*. Faces had turned to Geoff for an explanation, but the lie had been so bald-faced, he hadn't any comeback prepared.

After the partners had wept on about their money woes, William extracted from them that the only immediate result was no bonus this quarter. There was money for rent, money for salaries, money for advertising, even, and God knew most of their work came in from personal references.

People in the firm had gotten so used to bathing in money, it was a shock when the financial crisis tracked them down. Followed by earthquakes that sent a few companies down the gurgler or onto brighter futures in cities elsewhere. Now they'd operate month-to-month with no surplus. Big whoop.

Before he tucked the laptop away, William searched for Paul's name. The articles that flicked up were the ones he'd already seen. Spun off from the original, but with half the content and twice the speculation.

When he'd stood in front of the magistrate to argue bail and conditions, he'd known Paul would be allowed home. Since then William had expected the police to be in touch, request another meeting, but they hadn't. He'd still instructed Paul that any further interview would consist of "No Comment" or silence. Given that he'd collapsed halfway through the second interview after curtailing the first by medical necessity, William was sure they had nothing to go on. Even if he hadn't stepped in, the whole matter would have dissolved away like smoke in a Nor'west wind.

He searched again, for Magdalene's name this time, bringing up an image taken a short time before her death. Artistic black-and-white, but William's memory filled in the colors. He enlarged the photo until it filled the whole screen and traced a finger around the corner of her eye.

Once, she'd been the only beautiful thing in his life. Even now he'd catch sight of hair the same color blonde—straw-yellow—and turn his head to follow it through a crowd. Emma's hair was the same color, a coincidence that made his heart ache.

He snapped the laptop shut, enclosed it inside a cardboard drop folder, and put it in his briefcase. Identical to the three client files he had in there tonight. A final disguise if Amanda ever went snooping, though she wouldn't. He left his briefcase out in plain sight every night, and people only snoop in hidden places. Objects out in the open cease even to be seen.

The day William turned fifty, he'd decided it was time Magdalene stopped being the best thing in his life. He looked for a wife, a companion. When he and opposing counsel Jeremy Wilson went to grab a drink at the Crown Plaza pub, he'd seen Amanda. She'd stood with her back to the bar and held her glass with both hands, protecting herself. The drink was a hideous bright-red concoction, sickly sweet in appearance, and he'd concluded she was new to drinking.

William wooed her with concentration, money, and time, turning away cases that would've been automatic acceptances weeks or months before. Freeing himself so he'd be available to escort Amanda out at night. To dinner, to a movie, to ten-pin bowling one disastrous time when he'd dropped the ball on his foot and ended wearing a moon boot for a month. An outcome greeted with sniggers in the High Court.

Considering the time he'd lavished on her, Amanda had the right to be aggrieved when he returned to his usual brutal hours once their honeymoon was over. They'd married seven years ago now, and he'd still spent more time with her before their marriage than after. Unless sleeping beside someone counted as quality time these days.

The light went on in the staircase, and William jumped. *Caught.* He peered upstairs, eyes watering in the artificial light, and saw Emma standing at the top rubbing her eyes and pulling at her nightdress.

"Are you okay, sweetie?" he called up to her. Emma gave a start, then bounded downstairs with the grace of a knight in heavy armor. Forget her education. They needed to get her into dance class and polish up her motor skills.

"What's wrong?" he asked when she reached the bottom of the stairs and held her arms out for a hug. She tucked her face into the corner of his neck. Her hair was darkening now, but the shade still gave him shivers.

After a moment, he walked her upstairs again, but she hit him in the shoulder to stop. "I want a glass of water," she said. "I'm thirsty."

"Is that what woke you up?" He stopped midflight. "Or did you have a bad dream?"

She mumbled something into his shoulder that could've been assent, but he wasn't sure.

"When I was your age, I used to get horrible dreams," he said, stroking her hair. It shimmered even in the dull indoor lighting. When she played outside in the sun, it glowed. "There was one where I was on a beach, swinging out over the sand on a tire swing, and the sand beneath me turned into a graveyard. I'd wake up into another dream where lights didn't make it easier to see. When I walked into the bathroom, there were rats and mice popping out of the walls like cuckoo clocks."

She leaned her head away from his neck. "What's a cuckoo clock?"

"I'll see if I can find you one," he said, walking up the last few stairs, her drink of water forgotten. "It's a clock, and when it gets to a certain time a door opens, and a cuckoo pops out. Like that," he said as he angled his fingers and shot them fast toward her face.

Emma giggled and shifted her weight to his hip. Amanda was leaning against the wall in the alcove before their bedroom. She smiled, and William had a lump in his throat as he thought how lucky he was to have them both. How close he'd come to missing out altogether.

Amanda followed him into Emma's room as he laid her on her bed and pulled the bedclothes up to her chin. Emma was a restless sleeper. Some mornings he'd come in to give her a kiss to wake up and she'd have blankets tangled around her legs and was rolling onto the floor.

He sat on the side of the bed and stroked her hair back from her forehead before planting a kiss there. "Night-night," he whispered. Emma's eyes closed, her breaths slowing into sleep.

When he stood, Amanda curled her arm around his waist and tilted her head onto his shoulder. He put his arm around her, too, and they stood, looking at their sleeping daughter. *An advertisement for a middle-class family,* William thought.

Paul turned onto his back and sat up. He wriggled his rear end until he found a comfortable angle and picked up a book from the bedside table. How long was it since he'd been able to perform even these simple tasks without pain and extraordinary effort?

The more time that elapsed since chemotherapy, the more energy he had. It was now over a week since he'd gone to the police station, and when he thought of the effort it cost him just to get there, he experienced mild shock. If he kept growing stronger and better, then one day he might even regret his decision. He'd gone in there to confess only because he thought he had days left, at most. Now he thought he could outdo the doctor's prognosis of six weeks standing on his head.

Although he held the magazine page open in front of his face, he couldn't concentrate on the words enough to read. That woman in the station, she'd been nice. Not the bitchy one who questioned him but the other one, the one with kind eyes. He was using her business card as a bookmark, and he reached for it on the side table.

He had meant to confess. When he'd gone to the

police station, though, it had gone all wrong. The words got tangled up, and he couldn't work out how to say it without chucking Billy or even Greg straight in it. Maybe he should write everything down? Now he could think straight, he should record what happened. Then the next time he felt the impulse to rid his conscience of Magdalene's weight, he'd just hand the pages over or mail them to the station.

If he was doing it well, he could even cast himself in a better light. Didn't want that good detective to read what he wrote and assign him as the villain. Not when he could admit to his part in the whole thing without taking onboard more shame than he was due.

Paul wondered if anyone had told her how gorgeous she looked. When he was a younger man, he would've tried to get his hands on her but never would've thought to pay her a compliment. He wondered whether that was how men behaved or whether it was peculiar to just him. At fifty-six, he'd never gone out with a girl longer than a few months. Never asked anyone to marry him or believed any woman he knew would consider it.

Since he'd turned forty, he hadn't even gone out with regular women. He'd stuck to prostitutes because they could be counted on for a good lay and respectful conversation. Betty was the best he'd ever had. She ran a SOOB—a small owner-operated brothel—out in Addington, and even though it was obvious she used the flat only for her commercial enterprise, she kept it clean. It was on his bus route, handy when he'd had a few too many to trust himself to drive, and she'd always accommodated him.

Sometimes a second woman worked there, and he didn't appreciate that as much. The sounds of another punter coming in the next room were a complete turnoff. He enjoyed pretending Betty was his girlfriend for the half hour he needed her; she was a stranger when he didn't.

Sometimes she'd showed him a sex tape to help him begin. When he first went to her, he'd admitted he'd not seen one. Betty hadn't laughed at him; that was why he liked her. Just took it in her stride and gave him a choice to see if he wanted to try it out. "A virgin," was the comment she'd made, and that excited him more than the video of a fake couple performing real acts with fake passion.

If he kept getting better over the next few weeks, he might even get to where he could pay Betty another call. That'd give her a shock. Not just seeing him again after so long an absence, but seeing what cancer and the failed treatment had done to his body. One time he'd poked her in her ample hip and commented that she was getting sturdy, and she'd turned around and returned the favor. Full of sass, that woman. Another reason he liked her.

Paul suddenly yearned to write everything, not just the confession. Get the whole of his life recorded so when his lungs or his heart or his brain failed this month, next month, there'd be something left in the world to say he'd existed. It would be okay if he'd had children to live on after him. Paul's life had produced nothing: no progeny, no product, no literature, no music. There was so little left of his physical body, he wouldn't even leave a mess.

His mother once told Paul that the best trick in the world was to create something out of nothing. A hard speech to take seriously when the man she'd married was so intent on creating nothing out of something. Paul had followed in his tracks and then some.

He'd lived a life where he put in a decent week's work, built up his paycheck, and wasted it all whenever he got leave. Thinking back, it was hard to see the point to any of it.

Paul hadn't lived in years, hadn't felt alive since he and Billy parted company. When he'd turned up,

Paul took perverse pleasure that he'd disturbed something, made someone miserable all by himself. At the end of his life, he'd finally created something. Panic. Distress.

He walked to the kitchen. There was a drawer full of old odds and ends: half-empty rolls of Sellotape on which he'd struggled to find the end, biros, a spare pair of shoelaces. Reaching in, he pulled out a half dozen pens and an old realtor's pad left in his letterbox. He'd never been much of a writer, hadn't attempted it since he'd left school, over and above filling out a form.

For a time, his mother made him write a letter of thanks every time a relative deigned to give him a gift. A tedious task he hated, but he could remember the format.

"Dear Ngaire," he began. If it was the last thing he'd ever write, he might as well make it count.

"Ngaire, Deb, in my office for a minute," DS Gascoigne ordered, leaning against the door frame for a second before swinging back inside.

Ngaire's heart sank. She couldn't look at Deb as she walked across the office, couldn't stand to see the recrimination in her gaze. There would be no choice but to resign. There was no way that anybody would trust her once Deb's statement got out. Ngaire couldn't blame them; she'd have been the same. A colleague had to have your back, otherwise what were they for?

"Where are you with the Lynton case?"

Ngaire gave a frown and looked at Deb. She met Ngaire's gaze calmly and listed their actions for the DS. "We've followed up with her parents and inspected the property where the incident occurred. We're following up with a lead on a man who's still living there, Isaiah Haldrem, who was also a resident at the time that Magdalene died. If possible, we'll bring him in for an interview today."

"I'd also like to have another crack at Paul

Worthington, sir," Ngaire added. She kept her voice calm and stable, but inside was a flash of hope. Deb hadn't reported her, had given her another chance. "The lawyer knows him from before. The records show he and Paul lived just a few miles apart when they were young. I think they were childhood friends."

"So?"

"There's a chance he was involved in the incident, sir. Mr. Worthington kept referring to another person during his original statement, although he denied anyone else was there."

The sergeant looked at the pictures he had displayed on the edge of his desk. Ngaire couldn't see them from this angle but knew the portraits by heart. Wife and two daughters smiling for the camera on a sunny day. The eldest daughter had been brought up on drug charges two years ago now, possession with intent to supply. Her eyes didn't gleam anymore as they did in the photo. His wife had left him a short time after.

"Paul Worthington died during the night," he said.

Shock stripped away Ngaire's vocabulary. The thought of Magdalene's killer getting away because of a piece of shitty timing made her throat swell and her nose run. She wiped it with the back of her hand, careful not to touch her bright, white sleeve.

"Well, I guess that narrows our options," Deb said. Ngaire appreciated her attempt to lighten the moment, but her heart dragged with lost opportunities. Magdalene's grotesque resting place cried out for justice for her.

"It certainly does," Gascoigne said. "Tie up the loose ends, make sure the family is happy to leave the case as it is, and we'll move on. Is there anything in processing?"

He meant forensic samples waiting for evaluation by the Environmental Science and Research offices. Ngaire shook her head, "The only physical evidence we have are the photos from the compound, nothing more."

"Transfer them to disk and add them to the file. I think we'll leave it there."

"Sir?" Ngaire hurried to interject as he gestured that they should leave the room. "Could I still interview Isaiah? He may have direct knowledge of Magdalene's final days."

The DS rubbed his brow with his hand. Deb stepped over to stand shoulder-to-shoulder with Ngaire. "We weren't expecting to get much out of interviewing Mr. Worthington again, sir, so his death needn't derail the rest of the work we were doing."

"Just because we don't have someone to punish—"

Ngaire stopped when Gascoigne held up his hand. "Right, point taken." He pushed at the blotter that lay under his keyboard. A calendar was printed on the header for the year 2009. "Okay, I gave you a week to get this sorted out, so that stands. If you can make a case by then, I'll review the commitment, and if you can't, you're back on standard duties. You, too, Ngaire."

Ngaire nodded and let out the breath she hadn't even known she was holding. "Thank you, sir."

He flapped his hand in dismissal, and Ngaire and Deb walked in tandem from the room. As they passed earshot, Ngaire whispered, "Thanks, I owe you one."

"You owe me two, actually. And believe me, I'm keeping score."

Chapter Twelve

William ignored Emma's try at pulling his arm off at the shoulder as he answered the phone. He heard the landline ring so seldom, it took a moment to register what it was.

"William Glover speaking."

Emma sat on the floor, braced her feet against his lower thigh and redoubled her efforts. He couldn't remember why she was determined to get his arm. Had lost track after the zombie soldiers entered into her narrative, but she sure wasn't giving in easy.

"Hi, it's Mikel Ybarra here, Mr. Glover. I was calling with an update on the Worthington matter?"

William looked at Emma and poked his tongue out at her. She took heightened umbrage and decided she'd concentrated on the wrong limb. A new campaign was launched against his right foot.

William closed his eyes against the annoyance and kept his voice mild. "What do you have?"

Mikel had been his favorite investigator when he was working criminal law. Most of the time he hadn't utilized his services, since his clients were too poor to afford extras, and legal aid would never approve him. Still, the man had impressed him on every occasion he'd used him.

William thought he was safe from the mess Paul tried to cause but was prudent enough to dip into his pocket and make sure. Mikel had been happy to oblige.

"Paul Worthington died last night."

William collapsed to the floor, the phone falling to the side. Emma gave a cry of victory and climbed into his lap, but his limbs were loose, his lap wouldn't hold. He tried to gain control, attempted to force his hand to follow his command and pick up the receiver, make sure he'd heard correctly, but he couldn't.

"Mommy!" he heard Emma yell as she ran away. "I broke Daddy."

The note of concern in his daughter's voice made him ill. He wanted to get to his feet and tell his daughter he was fine, everything was A-OK, and Daddy was just playing.

A voice issued from the receiver, soft and tinny, "Hello? Hello?"

He'd told Mikel to call him here, at his home, because he was scared to have him call at work. William didn't want Mikel's number popping up on his mobile phone and derailing a meeting, a client's appointment, his lunch.

So stupid. He'd invited this into the home he should've kept safe for his family.

William heard his wife soothing Emma. Probably offering her food that remained uneaten from her own plate, since once again, she hadn't touched her breakfast. Her iron count, or she'd embarked on a diet that involved living on the sight of food alone. He should tell her she looked wonderful in case it was the latter.

Sensation returned to his limbs. Pins and needles sprang through his arms, his hands, his legs, his feet. He reached out for the receiver, and this time his muscles followed the order: his fingers grabbed it and brought it to his ear.

"I'm here," he said.

"The home helper found him this morning and called in for a doctor. He certified Paul's death." Mikel paused and cleared his throat. "I guess that's case closed."

"Mm. What inroads do you think you can make with the police?"

Mikel knew people who knew people, his stock in trade. This early report of Paul's death demonstrated the breadth of his reach.

"I can keep tabs on them. Enough to know if they're still pursuing, anyhow."

"Do that," William said. He stood on unsteady legs and hung up the phone. It sat on a polished oak side table, which was covered in a white crocheted doily for protection. A mirror hung on the wall above it in a gilded frame with curlicues embellishing each corner. His reflected face was pale. William practiced a forced smile for a moment before heading back to the kitchen.

"You got me," he announced to Emma and tickled her until she was giggling. Amanda gave him a smile over her shoulder as she washed the dishes, and he leaned over to kiss the back of her neck. "You look beautiful today."

He contacted a funeral director when he got into the office. Just chose one that looked nondenominational from the yellow pages and placed a call. Paul had no family. His parents were long dead, and he was an only child. If William didn't do it, he'd be waiting on a slab for his estate to be passed to the Crown before he'd be dealt with.

The director emphasized so many times that the funeral would be held in their smallest room that William felt it was a personal jibe at the deceased. Paul no-friends. After reciting his credit card number, William asked them to place only one bereavement notice in the paper. Just in case someone else gave a shit.

People had gravitated to Paul when they were young. He was cock of the hoop, top dog, class clown. How he'd transformed that promise into a solitary life was beyond William. Even before he wooed Amanda, he'd had colleagues, people with whom he could go have a drink. Mikel's report on Paul's life showed nothing. Spent half his life in the army, then worked as a salesman. Out in the field, so even his fellow employees barely saw him, hardly knew him.

People had fallen away from him like he was Mount Everest.

William would have to dip into an account to top off his credit card. He could stay up late tonight and fiddle it then, but he grew tired at the thought. A night's sleep was a sought-after attraction. So long as Amanda didn't find her household fund depleted, he'd be fine to leave it a few days. The last thing he wanted to discuss with his wife was why he'd financed a stranger's funeral.

Isaiah didn't look comfortable at the station. As Ngaire led him from reception, he jumped at the beep of her swipe card. His face was nervous and pinched, his hands trembled. If he was on the spectrum, as she assumed, she'd better not assail him with who, what, where. It'd lead straight into another meltdown.

Difficult to interview someone if you avoided direct questions.

Deb came around from her desk as Ngaire escorted him into the interview room. Ngaire was stilted with her, not sure where she stood, and Deb wasn't making it easy to guess. The situation called for a deeper apology, but Ngaire had said she was sorry, and the thought of explaining the truth made her throat seize and her hands shake.

Cautioned, Isaiah nodded acceptance, and Ngaire prodded him to speak aloud.

"But you've got video," he said instead of complying, pointing at each of the wall-mounted cameras.

"It makes it easier for transcribing," Deb said in response. When Isaiah frowned, she added, "Transcribing is where—"

"I know what it means," he interrupted and sat

back in his chair with his arms folded across his chest. "I'm not a thicko."

Off to a great start. Ngaire pushed a photograph of Magdalene across the table to him, and when he didn't reach for it, she tilted it so it was easy for him to see. "Magdalene was at the compound when you were a teenager," she stated, and he rewarded her with a nod. "We're investigating her death."

There was a long pause, and Ngaire had time to remember their first meeting and the stretches that occurred before he answered before Isaiah said, "Bit late, isn't it? Magdalene's been dead for forty years."

She looked at Deb, who nodded and said, "A man has come forward claiming that he murdered her. Just last week."

Another pause. Then, "What man?"

"Paul Worthington. When he was a boy, his father's farm backed onto the compound."

Isaiah nodded. A pause. "Was he the drunkard's son, or was he from the bankrupt dairy farm?"

Ngaire guessed political correctness had never made it into the compound.

"He belonged to the drunkard," Deb said. Ngaire flicked her a glance and caught mischief in the upturn of her mouth. She'd answered just to say those wonderful words. Words they'd never be allowed to suggest for themselves.

Ngaire was about to ask but Isaiah continued without prompting. "I knew him 'cos he used to peg stones at me when I was out doing my chores. He'd try to skip them off the surface of the slurry so they'd be covered in shit." Isaiah sighed and tilted his head to the side, his eyes wandering up to look at the camera lights, then returning to the table. Not looking at Ngaire or Deb. "I didn't like him."

"That's understandable. Apart from throwing stones, did he interact with you in any other way?"

"He was at my school but a form above me. The

Prophet didn't like us interacting with the other kids at school."

"Did you and Magdalene attend the same school?"

Isaiah nodded. "Yeah. She was younger than me, though. And she was bad. Spent most of her time in the principal's office or in detention." Isaiah pushed his arms out in front of him, fingers linked and palms out to stretch the muscles, then pulled them back into a tightly crossed shield. "Sometimes she'd make me stop the bike before we got to school, and she'd play hooky, but they still put her in the same form as me."

Ngaire performed quick mental arithmetic. That put Isaiah at age fifty-eight, or thereabouts, getting on toward sixty. "You mentioned before that there was a boy from a dairy farm. Can you tell us about him?"

Isaiah shrugged. "Magdalene's boyfriend. He hung around a lot in places he shouldn't have been." A frown creased his forehead, giving rise to a dozen wrinkles that had been undetectable before. "Mary caught him once, creeping out of the sleeping rooms. She yelled at him, but without raising her voice. Otherwise Abe would've heard."

"Would that have been a bad thing? If Abe heard."

"Abe would've hunted him down and killed him. Magdalene was his."

The words, delivered in Isaiah's flat voice, had the sound of a genuine threat, not a childlike overstatement. Ngaire experienced a chill running the length of her backbone. Gooseflesh popping out on her forearms.

"Do you remember his name?" A direct, unrehearsed question. Isaiah's jaw gripped tight, the muscles bunching on either side of his face like mumps, but he answered.

"If the drunk one was Paul, then he was named Billy."

Billy. The same name Paul had called the lawyer who'd turned up ready to defend him, even though he'd come in voluntarily. Not just a boyfriend, either. Magdalene had been pregnant when she died and only fifteen. How involved was her "boyfriend" with that scenario? Had he been there when Paul claimed he killed her alone?

"Did you attend church, Isaiah? Back when they held services in the compound?"

He snorted. "Course I attended, it wasn't a choice. Even when the Prophet left, Mom and Dad made me attend their sermons every Sunday." He shifted in his chair and placed his hands underneath his thighs, trapping them. "I don't go to church now. I spend Sundays out in the field. That's all the God I need. The Bible tells lies. People don't rise from the dead."

"When did the Prophet leave?"

"Not long after Magdalene died. The police were 'round, looking at everything, asking questions. Because she was pregnant."

Deb frowned at Ngaire and shook her head. Ngaire hadn't filled her in with the information Finlay had passed on to her the other night. Too concerned she'd lost her job to do it right.

"Did anyone tell you why he left?" When his lip curled—one question too many—she added, "It's okay if you don't know."

Isaiah pulled his hands out from under his legs and, this time, clasped his hands tight in his lap. He used his right thumb to rub the nail of his left thumb back and forth, his gaze intent upon them.

"Mom said he realized he wasn't the chosen one, and it would've been sacrilege for him to continue," he said. He shook his head when he finished, negating any truth the answer might have contained. "Dad said later the police were hot on his tail, wanting to shut us down. It made them uncomfortable to have our sorts in the community. They said we were unsettling, even though everyone was happy enough to do business with us when our prices were lower."

He placed his hands on the table, flat, palms down. His eyes wandered the width of the room, anywhere but where Deb and Ngaire looked back at him.

"They drummed Billy's dad out of business. Did anyone tell you that?" he asked. "Undercut him on price, then when he was out of contention, they jacked prices back up to where they'd been." He shook his head. "That's why they were all angry. Angry at themselves not having a moral leg to stand on. Pretended they'd had nothing to do with driving their neighbor out of business."

He rubbed his elbows with his hands, then folded his arms across his body once more. "That's the real reason they wanted us gone—nothing to do with the way we were living. They hated us because they were ashamed of themselves, and when Magdalene died—" he took a gulp of air, staring straight at the floor. "When she died, they saw their chance and took it. Nothing to do with us at all."

"How did Magdalene die, Isaiah? What happened that day?"

"We didn't know. Everyone thought she'd just run off. She'd done that before." He raised his eyes to meet Ngaire's for the first time. "Mom called her a scamp, and Dad called her a slag, and they were both right. Magdalene was trouble. When I pulled her body out of the slurry on the third day, they were all surprised." He paused as his voice caught, and he rubbed a hand across his forehead. "Nobody thought anything bad happened to her, or they would've looked harder."

"*You* pulled her out?" Deb's voice rose in surprise. Ngaire touched the side of her hand, a warning to be careful, but Deb just moved her hand away. "What made you look in the slurry?"

"I didn't," Isaiah snapped. "My chore was to turn the muck and unclog the drainage holes at the bottom. I found her by accident."

"Did anyone think to ask her boyfriend?" Deb asked.

Isaiah's face flowered into a large smile. The expression highlighted how blank his face had been. "That's what we all thought, but nobody was stupid enough to do anything about it. Mary might've tried, but Abe had her on a tight leash. Nobody else could say anything because, by rights, we shouldn't know something bad as that and not already have told him."

"But the police were around, searching for her," Deb said. "Surely someone talked to them about her."

"They weren't, though." Isaiah shook his head. "When Mary and Abe called it in, the police told them to wait and see if she turned up. It was only after we found her that they crawled over the place." He shifted in his seat again. "No one told them then because they were already leveling allegations at everyone. They brought me in for questioning a few times." He waited for a beat. "It wasn't pleasant."

And it had been pointless. Ngaire had found no information relating to a police investigation. After they'd deemed the death accidental, the investigation must've landed with the coroner and remained there.

"Was everyone in the compound at the time?" she asked. "No one out and about?"

"The whole point of the compound was that everyone was always on the compound. We never left, except for Magdalene and me to school. They'd even flagged that toward the end. The Prophet started talking about us being homeschooled."

"Why didn't they go out?" Deb asked, snark in her voice. "Did they think it was end times or something?"

Isaiah tipped his head back until he was staring

straight at the ceiling. "You don't fraternize with people from outside because that's how he gets in. You don't live outside the sanctity of the compound because that's how he gets in. You don't talk or dance or drink with people outside the compound because that's how he gets in." His voice was mechanical, the answer learned by rote.

Deb clicked her fingers until Isaiah looked back toward them. He still didn't make eye contact, but his gaze leveled to a less freaky angle. "How *he* gets in. Who's he?"

Isaiah met her stare and leaned in, Deb locked and spellbound. "He's the Devil."

Ngaire thanked Deb after the interview, and she received a curt nod in response. She had an appointment with her shrink at the end of the week. Two days, and she'd be able to bring her actions up and expect rational, educated ideas on how to respond. Right after she brought up her inability to sleep and her terror of turning up to work. Or going shopping. Or hearing a loud noise she couldn't place at once.

Ngaire transferred the interview video stream from the primary backup to her own computer. She isolated the start of the content and forwarded through to find the ending. If today were any sign, by next week, she'd be transcribing the audio. For her own interview. Oh, the fun she'd have.

Isaiah had seemed still throughout most of the interview, but as she fast-forwarded, he bumped around like a puppet. His eyes flicked up toward the camera to his right every few minutes, and he stared at it, then looked back at the table.

She cut the video at the end and saved the shortened version. She rewound through the video to the beginning, just to make sure nothing heinous had occurred during her edit and saw a pattern. Each time Isaiah changed position, his eyes locked on the camera.

During the interview, she'd been trying not to show any anxiety at his slow response rate, so she'd paid less attention to his mannerisms than she normally would have.

Now she saw they formed an intricate physical routine. Legs crossed, hands under legs, hands clasped, arms crossed. The movements a jumpy dance repeated over and over, and each occasion ending with a stare into the camera.

"Where next, Ngaire?" Deb asked as she sat on the edge of the desk. "Do you want to bring in the Lyntons and grill them for a couple of hours?"

"We should, at least, pay them a visit and tell them Mr. Worthington's dead."

Deb shifted on the desk. A penholder endangered by her hip bone fell to the side, and Ngaire righted it, glad it wasn't her stone-cold coffee from that morning. "I think you can handle that call by yourself, can't you? I have real work to get on with."

"Sure," Ngaire said. She ignored the lump in her throat at the thought of traveling alone. *It'll be fine. They're just an old couple.* It'd be nice not to be a baby one day. "I'll do it as soon as I've finished with this."

Deb stood and moved away. Ngaire followed her as she walked through the room and called out greetings to her coworkers and received them in return. She remembered when she'd been one of the team, how warm and comfortable it had been. Even the ribbing and the occasional bad assignment had been fun. Being part of a team made her strong.

She didn't belong to anything anymore.

Ngaire turned back to her computer to exclude the sounds from other staff. She played the interview in fast forward again, noting the times of each change in position, each stare at the camera.

Again she played it, this time with an earbud stuck into her right ear to hear the sound. Ngaire forwarded the recording to the first point, stopped it, and wrote down the word. Forwarded to the next point. Each time Isaiah looked at the camera, there was a pause in his speech, one word standing out from the rest. Why hadn't she noticed it during the interview? Because all his mannerisms were in slow motion?

Church evil cross Magdalene died there. Church locked room Magdalene killed.

Ngaire went through the recording again to check that she had it marked correctly. She shivered sitting at her desk because there was an air conditioning duct overhead that blew cold air straight onto her neck. The café would be so stuffed with staff eating lunch that the building thought it was overheating. One reason never to eat lunch at her desk.

What did it mean? Ngaire brought up the file of photographs that Deb had taken at the compound. They centered around the grave and Magdalene's room, the only areas of real interest. One shot showed the inside of the cavernous church. Isaiah'd said his parents kept the church sermons going each Sunday while they'd lived. Three people in a space that housed a hundred.

Church locked room. A locked room was on one side of the pulpit. She'd assumed it was a storeroom for the chairs. Ngaire zoomed in on the photo, trying to pick out clues to his meaning. All that happened was the picture enlarged past the point of legibility, the pixels squaring off.

She'd told Deb she'd visit the Lyntons and tell them the news about Paul. Perhaps she'd check and see whether there was a key available while she was there.

Chapter Thirteen

Mary had only just sat at the table, a cup of tea steaming beside her and a crossword puzzle at the ready, when the doorbell rang. *Abe's forgotten his keys again. He'd forget his head if it weren't for his neck.* When she opened up the door to reveal Ngaire standing on the step, her scowl turned into a smile of genuine warmth.

"Come in, come in. I've just poured a cup of tea if you want one."

Ngaire shook her head but then shrugged. "A cuppa would be great, if it's no trouble."

"Course not, have a seat." Mary walked through into the kitchen humming. Happiness. Not an emotion she'd expected to feel when a policeman visited to talk about her murdered daughter, but it was the first chance Mary had to remember Magdalene in years.

"Sugar? Milk?"

"Milk, please."

Mary poured it into the cup first, then hesitated as she tried to remember if that was right. These fine points had been important when she was young. Her mother was eager to give her a clip on the ear if she did things the wrong way, but the rules had still fallen away from her memory like years-old gossip.

She looked in the cupboard beneath the sink, under the tea towels. Mary stored a sly packet of biscuits there for when she needed a treat. Abe objected to processed food, but if she home cooked a batch, they wouldn't keep, and she sometimes wanted a pick-me-up that didn't need an hour's preparation.

Martha had found them once and laughed at her. Not a jolly aren't-we-all-strange laugh but a derisive one. That one had hardened too much on the streets to be pleasant company, even though Mary tried with her. Love meant little when it was up against a decade's learned misery.

"Here you go," she said and placed the cup with a bikkie on the saucer in front of Ngaire. She assessed her fondly. A beautiful girl, as Magdalene had been. The same spark in her eye, too.

"Abe's gone out for a walk," she said as though she'd been asked. "Had a hip replacement last year and has to do a half hour of exercise each day to keep it limber. He's religious about it. Otherwise, they mightn't do the other."

Ngaire nodded and took a sip of the tea. Mary studied her face, looking for signs of disgust, but there weren't any. She made a mental note: milk before tea. Mental notes were an ingrained habit with her, though these days they were as reliable as writing in condensation on a window.

"I came to tell you about the case," Ngaire said. "There's no easy way to say this, but I'm afraid that Paul Worthington has died."

Mary kept the smile on her face, but she whirred through a list of names and faces in her mental Rolodex. "Sorry, dear," she said at last, the name a blank. "Did I know him?"

"He's the man who confessed to killing Magdalene," Ngaire said.

Mary nodded and blushed. *Of course.* "So, he's dead." She paused as she tried to work this into a frame of reference. A man dying was a terrible thing. Important, too, otherwise the policewoman wouldn't have come around. "I'm sorry for your loss."

It was the wrong thing to say. Ngaire's face told her that. The wrong thing. Mary beat her knee with her fist in reparation. When she was young and hopeful, she'd thought that one day she'd catch hold of everything she should know, remember everything taught to her. Instead, it grew worse as though the number of things she should know and the number of social mores she should follow kept growing exponentially, while the space to know them stayed the same.

Ngaire caught her fist and held it between her hands. Warm and comforting. Maggie would've done the same thing until she grew into a teen and started a battle royal that seemed never-ending. She'd been a sweet girl. Stroppy and engrossed with herself, but also gentle and kind.

"I'm the one who's sorry. I've dredged up all these bad memories of your daughter and her death, but now I don't think we'll be able to continue the investigation."

Bad memories. Mary frowned and pulled her hand back to hold it in her other, comfort herself. There weren't any bad memories. She was grateful someone had reminded her there were memories to be thought of. For so long she'd put thoughts of Magdalene to one side because it hurt so much to think of her that even when the pain faded into nostalgia, she wasn't able to picture her daughter without her mind snapping shut on the image in self-defense.

She'd put her memories into a box, and she never let it open. To have someone search through it now was intrusive but delightful. Painful, joyous. The way her daughter had been throughout her life. Defiant, belligerent, loving, kind. Very much her own person from a much younger age than Mary had been. Even now she wasn't sure she was her own person, so much of herself mirrored her mother, her father, her husband, even Martha. *Tell me what to do* her life's motto.

"What was there to investigate?" she asked,

curious. Even if her memory wasn't good, she didn't think there'd ever been doubt over what happened to Magdalene. A man saying that as a teenage boy he'd murdered her must be a lie. Mustn't it?

"We were examining his story, trying to find out whether it correlated with the known facts of the case."

Evasion. Mary recognized that tactic immediately. "Another biscuit?" she asked as she observed that Ngaire had nothing left but crumbs.

"Yes, please."

Mary lifted her loose sweatshirt and pulled the packet out of the drawstring waist of her pants. She removed the plastic tray out of the wrapper so that two chocolate-coated biscuits were on display. Ngaire took one, and, bless her, the dear didn't even bat an eyelid. Mary helped herself and then tucked it away, the sharp edges pressing into the loose skin of her belly.

"Isaiah could tell you what happened," she said. "He's the one who pulled Maggie out of the pond."

"The pond?"

Mary blinked. Ngaire's tone alerted her that there was something wrong. What had she said? What had she not said?

"Isaiah was playing in the pond with a net. The boy always had a fascination for tadpoles even when he should've outgrown it, and if he finished his chores for the day, nobody could tell him to do something different. Caught my girl's leg on the edge of his net. She'd been missing three days by that point." Mary stopped for a moment. Was that all? "I thought she'd run off with that cute young boy she was seeing. Too young, if you ask me, but no one ever said naught about Juliet, did they?"

"You knew she was dating Billy Glover?"

Mary nodded. Over the years, she'd forgotten his name, but the sounds fit. "A nice boy. It was shameful how we treated his Daddy, but we had to make a living, and the Prophet said he'd cleared it with the Lord, so who was I to object?" She shook her head. "Once I found out, I gave her some protection, but she'd already got herself knocked up. Pity."

After a moment, Ngaire cleared her throat, and Mary looked at her, eyebrows raised. "What was a pity?"

"Oh." She pulled the biscuits out again, but Ngaire held her hand up, and Mary didn't think it polite to eat in front of a guest who wasn't. With a tinge of regret, she tucked them back. "I thought it would serve her right to be a mom. She acted a right devil when she wanted to. Headstrong, you know. I thought a baby'd turn her inside out, and I'd get the chance to say, 'Told you so,' but I never did." She smiled. "Maggie was right cranky when she didn't get enough sleep."

"Did Abe know about the baby?"

Mary shot her a glance—*was she kidding?*—but Ngaire's face was open. "No. We were keeping it from him awhile longer. He was heading off on a mission, and we thought that'd work out fine."

"What sort of mission?"

"There was a scholarship grant to study farming methods overseas. They'd lined him up to go to California for six months. What the grant didn't cover the Prophet was funding. He knew how it would go otherwise."

The whole thing had shown her the blessed nature of God and the hand he played in their lives. She hadn't always believed—had often thought when she knelt to pray she was speaking only to the ceiling and the floorboards—but that had shown her. The true word blossomed within her for the first time, and she thought everything would be right. Anything God didn't provide, the Prophet did.

Even Maggie had kept her mouth shut. That had been her biggest fear. That she'd spout her mouth off in a stupid argument, over breakfast, over chores, over school, and set the whole house of cards tumbling. God had cared for Maggie, but nothing Mary did convinced her daughter of that. Fear of her daddy kept her quiet, though.

"That boy said he'd marry her. Both of them knew they'd have to wait—it was ten months till she turned sixteen—but they knew I'd give them my signature and blessing."

Maggie had been far too young, but she wouldn't accept boyfriend advice any more than she would be told anything else. When the Prophet warned that there was danger outside the compound, she'd taken it as a mission to stalk it and absorb it. He hadn't minded—he'd seen Maggie as a wild thing that shouldn't be tamed any more than an African beast should be caged in a zoo. With no children of his own, he'd been a benevolent father to those of his flock; let them get away with things he wouldn't tolerate in the adults he cloistered.

"Do you have keys to the church on the compound?" Ngaire asked. To Mary, the voice sounded far away. She had to concentrate her will to bring herself back into the present, return from Maggie, her baby, and her boyfriend.

The compound. When they'd left, they turned the key on the padlock that linked the chain across the driveway. The Haldrems had contacted her a month later, distraught and desperate, so she'd given them copies and her blessing to move back in. Their son Isaiah wasn't settling into their new rental house. It would be an added cruelty to insist he do so when he'd done nothing wrong, and the land just sat empty.

"Give me a moment," Mary said and walked through to the bedroom. Abe kept his secrets in his top drawer, so confident in her cowardice that he didn't need to hide them. She rooted through the assorted items, careful not to leave them in disarray but not too cautious. Mary experienced a hint of Maggie's spirit, her headlong zeal, flowing into her veins. Maybe she could be a troublemaker?

There was a ring full of keys at the back. Labeled in Abe's steady hand first on white notepaper cut to size, then covered with sticky tape. The gate, the housing block, the shed, the barn, the church. Two for that: the front door and the storage room. Ngaire hadn't specified, so she pulled them both free. She held them in her hand for a moment, then slotted them back on the ring. She'd give her the lot, let her find everything she needed to find. Mary had nothing to hide. Isaiah would have to look after himself if she caught him hanging around. She hadn't seen him since his mother's funeral, and that was twelve years ago. He hid whenever she went there.

With a quick burst of spite, she yanked the whole drawer free and upended its contents on the bedspread. She'd tell Abe that the policewoman had done it and let him fight his battle with her.

"Here you go," she said, her hand outstretched. Ngaire was staring at the wall, at a series of small photos in gilt frames. Maggie's school pictures. Age ten, eleven, fourteen. The missing years hidden under the others, the pictures cheaper than the frames.

"She looked a lot like you," Ngaire observed. Mary shook her head but was pleased. Maggie had been beautiful. A compliment hid there to be treasured and taken out for courage during future hardship.

Bea Woolham hesitated down the road from the police station. She'd got that far on noble thoughts. To take one step further into the lion's den and continue with her plan made her stomach twist and her neck sweat.

When she'd started on her career in the world's oldest profession, it was meant to be a short stop before she got her life under control. Before she went back to the work she should be doing. It'd scared her every moment she was out there, fronting it to the other girls on the street, fronting it to the curb-crawlers, fronting it to herself.

Bea would've left it, too, would've transitioned back after a few months, except the council decided it was time to move her corner on. Getting too many complaints from residents that she'd never set eyes on, never talked to, so the police turned up in force, taking names and pressing charges. In the end, she'd gotten away with a suspended sentence, but the black mark on her worksheet meant she couldn't just turn around and go back to her real life. An arrest had to be disclosed to potential employers, and when she did, she was no longer a potential employee.

Girls today didn't have that problem. Bea was grateful for the changes in the law. For her to be able to run a business lawfully—even paying tax gave her pleasure—but most of all for the ones who stumbled into it through need, through necessity. They could stay a short stint, then leave, the way she'd planned but never managed. Her life stuck forever because a proud housewife didn't appreciate the parade of working girls.

Since her encounters on the wrong side of the law, Bea hadn't been near a police station. The only time in the past when she'd wanted to, she'd retreated, terrified of making a mistake and ending up dead.

Well, fuck it. She'd try, and if they didn't want to listen or they thought they knew better than her, then so be it. Bea pulled the strap of her bag across her chest and walked the rest of the way with her head held high.

"Ngaire? There's someone here for you," Genna called.

Ngaire had just finished up her notes from the afternoon before and was planning on heading out. "Who is it?"

"Bea Woolham?" Genna said, her voice ending on a high note as though she wasn't sure. "Something to do with the Worthington case."

Ngaire walked through to reception and paused

in the doorway, trying to pick her target. Out of the
women waiting, there was a tall brunette with a long
skirt and flowing blouse, and a woman in jeans,
trainers, and a T-shirt, with dyed-pink hair.

Genna nodded at the brunette.

"Hi. Bea, is it? I'm Detective Constable Blakes.
You wanted to talk about Paul Worthington?"

The woman held her purse strap in a tight grip,
so her knuckles shone white through her skin. Her eyes
narrowed as she took in Ngaire and passed judgments
on her looks, her age, her race, her gender.

"I read the notice this morning," Bea said.
"About him dying. Is that right?"

Ngaire nodded. "Did you know Mr.
Worthington?"

"Yeah," Bea said, her face pale under the
fluorescent lights of the waiting room. "I knew him
professionally."

Ngaire felt her resistance; the way she stood, the
way she positioned her arms—everything—called out,
"I don't want to be here." Bea Woolham looked like a
comfy bookkeeper, slightly overweight, slightly
unkempt. But the curl of her lip when she said
"professionally" made Ngaire think of a different line
of work altogether.

"Would you come through to my desk? Much
better than standing out here, a lot quieter." Nobody
listening in, her unspoken implication.

"Will this take long?" Bea asked as she followed
her. "I've got an appointment at two thirty I need to
keep."

"I don't know," Ngaire answered. "It depends on
what you have to tell me. If we need longer, I can come
and visit tomorrow, if you like."

The woman nodded and sat on the offered chair.
Perched stiffly on the edge of it and looked back the
way they'd come. "Paul was a client of mine," she said.
"I run a business out in Addington, and he was a

regular. He told me things." She stopped and cleared her throat.

"Would you like a drink? A glass of water?"

"Cheers, that'd be good."

Ngaire fetched one from the water cooler around the corner from her desk. She only filled it up to three-quarters. Bea's hands were shaking, and she didn't want to embarrass her by handing her a cup she'd spill.

"What business do you run?"

Bea stared at Ngaire, then dropped her attention to the plastic cup she was holding out. "I run a SOOB with another woman. My working name's Bella. It's all legal," she said, jutting her chin out.

"Of course. How long was Paul one of your clients?"

Bea gulped half the water in one long swallow. She wiped her lip with the back of her hand and glanced toward the exit again.

"Eight years, give or take. I called him a regular, but he wasn't like that." She waved her hand trying to find the right words. "Not regular. He'd turn up when he wanted, and then I wouldn't see him for months, then he'd be there every day for a week."

"A repeat client?" Ngaire suggested.

Bea snapped her fingers. "Like that. Repeat."

She drained the rest of the water but continued to hold the paper cup in her hands, squeezing the waxy lip into the cup, then snapping it back out.

"Was that what you wanted to tell me? That he was a client?"

Bea shook her head, irritated. "No. He was a mean bastard. Always presumed I'd make him welcome, but he wasn't pleasant." She bit her lower lip. "I would've done without him, but I was scared to cut him off."

Ngaire followed her lead. "Did he ever hurt you?"

The pause lasted so long that Ngaire thought she'd ruined it, spoiled the momentum, but then Bea turned and looked her in the eye.

"That's how I stopped him coming. He bashed me one night after I made fun of how chubby he was getting. Smashed my head into the bedstead, over and over." She rubbed her forehead. "If I'd been lying somewhere different, he might've done me in, but the headboard was cushioned. He wore himself out before he hurt me too bad."

"Did you report it?" Ngaire had seen no charges filed against Paul Worthington, but he might not have been using his real name. The police could've dropped or misfiled the charges.

But Bea shook her head. "If I'd turned him in, he'd have served his time and then been back looking for me, you know?"

Ngaire nodded. She knew.

"So I got my partner to take photos of what he did. I told him if he ever came back, I'd turn them over to the police." She laughed without humor. "He apologized and kept calling every couple of months to check if I was over it. When he stopped, I thought he'd got the message, but I suppose it was the cancer.

"I told the collective about him, passed around his photo so no one else would get caught. I didn't want anyone getting mixed up with him like I had." Her voice was defensive, as though Ngaire had accused her.

"It sounds like you did the right thing under the circumstances," Ngaire said. "Although we always prefer it if you report a crime, I know sometimes it doesn't gel with reality." She grimaced as she realized she was justifying herself, not Bea. "Do you want me to fill out a report for that now? Do you have the pictures with you?"

Bea looked at her as though she'd gone mental. "He's dead. I don't care about that. I need to tell you about the other thing."

"What other thing?"

Bea leaned over to Ngaire, who bent closer to

meet her. "He told me once he killed a girl. Him and his friend, when they were teenagers. I believed him."

The acidic tones of Bea's breath were strong in Ngaire's face, but she didn't pull back. "Did he say who his friend was?"

Bea nodded. "Some kid named Billy. Raped her, got her pregnant, then they killed her."

Chapter Fourteen

Bea Woolham gave Ngaire further evidence, none of it pleasant. Testimony about Paul and his strange sexual habits. After she'd left, Ngaire wanted to go straight to William Glover's work and question him. But Deb was still working the case of the body washed up on Sumner Beach. The autopsy had already been pushed back twice but was definitely—probably—going ahead now, and she wanted to sit in.

Ngaire could work as much as she liked on her own at her computer, or out discovering things in the field, but an interview needed two until the DS was happy with her performance again. Preferably two, unless they came into the station.

She thought of asking someone else, but even if they agreed, Gascoigne had only assigned her and Deb. Ngaire didn't want to earn his wrath if she waltzed off with someone he needed elsewhere.

Instead, she pulled the compound keys that Mary Lynton had given her from her bag and headed for her car. Isaiah's strange message, if it was one, still niggled in the back of her brain. Now that she knew both the dog and Isaiah were friendly, the farm held no fear for her.

On reaching the property, Ngaire stuck her head in the housing block and called out, "Toodle-oo," just in case Isaiah was hiding out. She couldn't hear him or Trev running around the property. She walked into Magdalene's room, craving a second look at the artwork covering every wall surface. No prizes for guessing who kept the work refreshed by tracing over the dimming ink. The drawings must have meant a lot to Isaiah.

She wondered whether he missed her. They'd been the only children in the compound, the only teenagers. Had that resulted in a tighter bond, or had Magdalene distanced herself from Isaiah to set herself apart as a person? Mr. Pontus indicated that they had been separate, but that might only have applied to school. Ngaire remembered two-tier friendship systems at that age—at-school friends and after-school friends. And never the twain would meet.

Ngaire caught a shadow in her peripheral vision as she exited Magdalene's room and heard a faint noise she couldn't place. Heart hammering, she moved to the next door in time to see a strip of wallpaper fall sodden to the floor. The damp was growing worse.

Outside, the sun shone with just a wisp of cloud to cover it. A plane left a thick contrail behind it as it traveled on a trajectory across the sky. Sign writing for clouds.

The church door was still unlocked, as it had been when she and Deb had paid their earlier visit. Inside, it was cool after the bright sunshine, even though it was too soon yet for the sun to carry any real heat. The windows were angled so light couldn't make many inroads. Designed to be cool in the height of summer in a city that was lucky if it needed that architecture for a month each year.

Ngaire walked to the locked door and gave it a tug. She shuffled the keys around on the ring, trying to discern the tags in the dim light, but they were too old to read. She pulled her flashlight from her hip pocket, but the beam flickered and died. The batteries should have lasted twelve months, and it hadn't been that long, but Ngaire sometimes turned it on by accident when she was moving about. She pushed it back in and tried her cell phone instead, but the harsh glare made it even harder to see. After trying one, and then another, without success, she walked outside to read the labels.

She heard a dog barking from the shed across the yard. Ngaire shielded her eyes with her hand and looked in that direction. She could hear Trev, but she couldn't spot him. Either way, he sounded far off.

There were two keys labeled "Church," and she gripped them with her fingers so they wouldn't be lost in the jumble. She assumed the larger one would fit the main door, so she tried the small key in the side lock. It fit and turned, although the lock was stiff with disuse. Ngaire had to lean back, holding the handle so her weight helped pull the door open.

Just as she'd thought, there were neat stacks of chairs inside. Long cobwebs spun across the room from ceiling to wall, wall to chair. The webs so long-abandoned that even in the enclosed space, dust highlighted them.

Ngaire stacked the chairs higher, four on four, trying to work her way back to see whether something else was there. She thought of the intricate work detailed on Magdalene's walls and used her cell phone beam to examine the wall nearest her, the ceiling, but they were plain wood.

From the corner of her eye, she caught sight of an object against the side wall. Chairs were packed more densely here as if to hide it from view. Ngaire stacked, restacked, and shoved them together to make a path.

At first, she thought it was a beam. It was wooden, and the central piece she saw was six inches by six inches. A substantial piece of wood. As she maneuvered closer, she saw that there was a cross beam at an angle. The two lengths cut away on the inside, so they lay flush at the join.

She took longer to work out its shape because it lay on its side, but when she tilted her head, it fell into place. A cross. A crucifix. Seven feet long and five feet wide.

To be expected in a church, Ngaire supposed, but it was too huge to be an object of worship. If this hung from the back wall like every other crucifix she'd seen, the weight would pull it down. The size would dwarf any preacher at the pulpit into insignificance. Big enough to support a full-grown man.

Ngaire had once witnessed a procession follow a man carrying a cross through the streets of Argentina, crowds cheering along the way. Maybe they'd used this for something similar.

She walked back through to the church hall and climbed up onto the stage. Behind the altar, two tables were laid with a candelabrum on each. At the rear, she saw a large box and went over to inspect it. Perhaps she'd seen it on her last visit, and it tripped her memory.

As she kneeled, Ngaire ran her hand around the edge of the box. It was a foot deep with metal rods in each corner to support the wooden frame. A cross box. There were grooves and scrapes on the front edge where the heft of the crucifix would lie once slotted in. Even at the depth of twelve inches, the weight leaning against any side would be extreme. When she dug out her phone flashlight to look inside, she saw where the metal on the rear right-hand side had buckled.

Ngaire sat on her heels. Disquiet nagged in the back of her head, but she couldn't place why. Maybe it was just her general lack of regard for folks who spent money on religious adornment that could go to the poor instead. A double standard, when she bought jewelry for no reason other than to look pretty, but her expectations for Christians were higher.

When she stood, she felt the boards beneath her foot bend. The planks at the back of the platform were discolored. Liquid must have pooled there at one time, lightening and weakening the wood. The stains gathered about the base for the crucifix.

As she returned to the cupboard, Ngaire aimed the beam from her cell phone at the cross and moved the light, steady and slow, along the entire length. There were frayed strands of rope or material at the end of each arm. Likewise at the base. She shone the beam at the head but couldn't see them there.

She knelt and fumbled an evidence bag from her back pocket. A pair of gloves was inside the bag; she prepacked them one inside the other for ease of use. Shit! She didn't have a blade with her, not even her penknife. With the cell phone balanced on her knee, she tried to pull the strands free from the cross with her fingers. The gloves were too large, and wrinkles stopped her being able to do the job with finesse, but she pulled a few fibers away. She looked at them in the white light of the cell phone torch but couldn't make out anything noteworthy. She knew nothing about rope or bindings. Ngaire let the strands fall into the bag and tried for another few. This time, when she looked at the sample in the light, she saw that her blue-gloved fingertip had changed color. Purplish-brown.

The evidence bag fell to the floor as she picked up the cell phone and directed light at her fingertip. She rubbed her forefinger and thumb together, and the color transferred. Her rational mind said iron. Her gut screamed blood.

A shiver worked along her back. The sense of disquiet kicking into a higher gear. There was a mournful creak as the weather outside changed, the wood of the church frame retracting as sunlight hid behind clouds.

Ngaire shone the light back on the arm of the cross. There were dark stains on either end spreading out beneath the stray fibers. Located just where a person's wrists would be. Paul's voice echoed in her mind. *She was soaking wet and bleeding.*

Holding a new bag wide, Ngaire tried to tap off

the staining from her fingers, then smeared the remnants on the inside of the plastic. She pressed the sides and base of the bag to the cross, as close as she could. The force she exerted was enough that her thumbnail popped free of the glove, and she used it to scrape some of the stains off. Or, she hoped she had. When she held the plastic up to the light, she had trouble making out anything inside. A few streaks.

After repeating the process on the bottom arm, she could see specks of color. They would have to do. She pulled off the tag and sealed it shut, shoving it deep into her trouser pocket, her notebook on top to keep it safe. The other bag lay on the floor, and she sealed it, too. Some thin fibers had worked free, pulled by the static on her pants leg, so they clung to the dark fabric. Ngaire didn't have a third bag on her—wasn't that much of a girl scout—but there'd be more in the car.

She rolled off her split glove against her pants leg as she walked out of the cupboard, then pulled the other free. The latex reminded her unpleasantly of talcum powder. She wiped her clammy hand against her thigh as she headed out the church door. Ngaire caught a flash of blue out of the corner of her eye. Before she could turn, could examine, she felt a crack of pain explode in the back of her head.

She fell to her knees, her mouth spilling drool in a thick line as her jaw slackened. Another blow struck her, off-center, her neck taking most of the force. This time, her knees gave out, and she sprawled flat on the ground, her cell phone skidding away. Her heart sped up to triple beat. Ngaire tried to work her hand around to her belt where her canister of pepper spray should have been located, but either she couldn't reach, or it was gone. Another blow, and her arm stopped obeying her commands. One more beat her into darkness.

Ngaire woke to the sun blazing into her face. She was hot and sweaty, and her head pounded. She tried to move, and her body ignited with pain. Her eyes watered from the light, and she struggled to keep them open, even at half-mast. She ignored the ache in her shoulder as she raised her arm up to shelter her eyes with her hand.

She rolled over onto her stomach. The world continued to move for a few moments, and Ngaire felt bile rising in her throat. She swallowed it back, grimacing at the sour taste. Beneath her, the concrete was coated in slippery gray paint. It took a moment more she realized where she'd seen that combination before. She was in the slurry.

Panic and fear overwhelmed the pain in her muscles and head. Ngaire got to her knees, then her feet, stretching her arms and legs wide for balance that should have come naturally.

She moved to the side and tried to scramble up the walls to reach the lip. It was above her head, the slurry seven feet deep, and the smooth surface slid under the rubber-soled boots she wore. Like a spider in a bathtub, she slipped back each time.

Ngaire opened her mouth to call out, to scream for help, then closed it again. She placed her hand gently on the side of her head, where it throbbed with pain, and when she pulled it away it was stained deep red with blood. Whoever had done this could still be out there. Watching. Waiting. The noise from her movements may not have alerted them, but a scream might. The sound of a scream would carry.

There was a growl to her side, and Ngaire whipped around to follow it, pain beating a fast rhythm at her temples.

Trev, the dog, was here with her.

Where was Isaiah? Was he involved?

The dog should have been nimble-footed enough to climb out. Ngaire held her hand out in a "come-on" gesture and waited for him to move. She could instruct him to fetch someone—Lassie sprang to mind—but when he didn't respond, she moved closer and saw the strange angle of his hind leg. It was broken.

Ngaire walked as carefully as she could, feet sliding on the tractionless surface until she was within arm's reach. She held her hand out to Trev's face, to pat him on the head, but he snapped and growled again.

A wave of dizziness swept through her, and she landed full-force on the concrete, while her mind insisted that she remained standing. The side of her face bounced off the bottom of the slurry, her cheekbone making a snapping sound as it contacted. The sunlight grew dim and gray. Trev looked a mile away.

Ngaire closed her eyes and clutched her fingers hard on the smooth surface, trying to reconnect her body with the world. When she opened her eyes a sliver, she saw bright sunlight again. Saw colors.

Trev growled, then rested his head on his front paws and raised his eyebrows. Ngaire tensed her muscles against the slurry floor and held out her hand to him again. This time, he let her stroke him between the ears, along his neck. His fur felt soft as goose down.

She searched in her pocket for her cell phone, but it wasn't there. She must have forgotten it in the car or it had fallen or someone had taken it out. Pity. It would've been interesting to see what the official police app suggested in her current situation.

The eye on her right where her cheekbone snapped had swollen shut. Ngaire opened her other as wide as she could to compensate and looked around. Deb had found sawn metal pipes sticking out of the concrete wall. Where were they? She scanned from side to side, hurting her neck when she turned to look behind her.

There they were. Back on her left-hand side. Ngaire pressed her hands against the concrete and pulled herself to her knees. She wouldn't put her other cheekbone in jeopardy by trying something as risky as standing. She shuffled forward, hanging her head to take deep breaths when the pounding grew too extreme. Pacing herself for the meters-long journey.

Trev whined as she moved out of range, then skidded up to his feet, holding his hind leg high and bent. He limped along with her, just as desperate to get out.

The sun disappeared behind a cloud, and the wind changed, whipping her hair. The shift to Southerly causing a barometric change in the air pressure that Ngaire felt throughout her body. She looked up and saw mammatus clouds hanging like giant udders in the sky; she sensed the weight of water above.

The pipe remnants were still meters away, and she tried to move more quickly, but her physical ability didn't match her determination. Ngaire crawled slowly, slowly, and the rainclouds burst into life above her.

As the first large, stinging, cold drops hit her and wet her hair, Ngaire thought of who at the station knew she was here. She'd logged it on her computer, told Genna on the way out. They'd know where to look when she didn't turn up tomorrow. If she could last until then.

The slurry was long and wide, the capacity for water huge, but with a steady rainfall overnight, Ngaire didn't fancy her chances. If she fell asleep or fell unconscious, a few inches of water could spell her end.

Rain made it even more slippery. Ngaire tried to banish thoughts of what it must have been like for Magdalene, but it was hard. Images filled her mind. Of Magdalene falling beneath the lip of the sludge, its makeup more in common with quicksand than water, and not being able to grab hold, her hands and feet sliding under, instead of making purchase.

Or was it as Paul Worthington began to describe? A dead body tossed not into the river but into the slurry where the worst of the farm refuse went. Her life put on a par with animal waste.

Tears of horror mixed with heavy raindrops from a day that had been warm but now was bitter with cold. Trev beside her was more surefooted, but even he slipped on the treated concrete. His gait thrown off by his twisted limb. Gray sky, gray floor, gray dog. The only breath of color was where blood from her head wounds dripped, encouraged by the rain to fall.

At last, Ngaire reached the side where the sawn metal pipes still jutted out of the wall. The bottom ones were a foot up from the base, the wall curved, so it was hard to reach. Ngaire paced herself, raising from hands and knees to kneeling with her fingertips against the wall for balance. She lifted one foot and tested her balance, leaned her weight upon it, then the other.

The second pair of pipes was at her head. One foot below the lip of the slurry. Only an inch or two poking out to grab hold of.

"Who the fuck designed this shitting thing?" Ngaire shouted, her need to keep quiet surpassed by her desperation to get out. Trev whined and pawed at her shoe. She reached one hand out to caress the curve of his skull. The fur that felt soft earlier now matted with rain.

She placed her left foot on the lowest pipe, balancing on her right foot. Her dominant foot, the one she had most control over. The base of the slurry curved so far from the wall that there was a ten-inch gap to straddle. Hard enough for her to just stand. As soon as Ngaire tried to place weight upon her left foot, she felt the world tipping out of reach. She reached in desperation for the upper pipe, but her fingers slid off the surface, slick with rain. Her weight fell back to her right foot, and she pinwheeled her arms to maintain her meager balance, then moved her left foot back to meet it.

"How do you think that went?" she asked Trev,

who looked up at her with his thick eyebrows raised over large brown eyes. How could she have been afraid of this dog when he was an obvious sweetheart? She felt the blush of shame again as the memory of pushing Deb in front of her returned for a moment.

Trev barked, and Ngaire tilted her head to one side. "Yep. I thought it went shittily as well," she replied. "But there's no reward for not trying."

She placed her right foot first this time, finding it harder to keep her balance while straddling, but hoping that when she transferred her weight, it'd grow easier. She tried to fling herself forward, and this time, when she grabbed for the upper pipe, she kept hold of it. Ngaire tilted back her head and brayed with triumph.

"How'd you like me now, Trev?" she called, too afraid of losing her grip to turn to see whether he responded.

She flailed with her left foot until it hit the matching pipe, and she could balance on the tips of her toes. Ngaire sensed how quickly her stability would disappear, and she reached up and grabbed hold of the upper pipes. She was now fully pressed against the wall. One foot below the top lip.

Ngaire craned her neck back to plan her next move. She was closer to the top but couldn't work out how to take advantage of it. She extended her right hand, searching for purchase, but the shelf was too broad for her to grab across and under.

She put her hand back on the piping to stabilize before stood on her tiptoes and stretched as far as she could.

The lip was in her hand, and Ngaire felt a sense of achievement blossom in her chest. Then her left foot slipped off the pipe, and her right foot lost balance. She tried to clutch with her hand, but the top was coated with the same slick material as the rest of the stupid, stupid, slurry, and she slid back down the curve, falling to her knees.

Trev ran in circles around her, excitedly, back and forth, back and forth. His nimbleness, even without the use of a limb, made her envious. If he were near the top, he'd have no trouble running free. Not like her clumsy attempts.

Ngaire patted her trousers. She often kept her journal in her jacket pocket, but the day had been warm enough to leave the blazer in the car. Another regret for her list now that it was colder. Her cell phone might be gone, but she found her notebook in her trousers.

She pulled it out with a cry of triumph. After scribbling a note—"Detective Ngaire Blakes, in slurry pit"—she tucked it under Trev's collar, then got to her feet again with trepidation. This would hurt.

It took another two tries, but Ngaire got herself back in position on the little jutting pipes. She slipped again as she turned to face outward, but this time caught her balance before she fell. She released her grip with her hands and held them out in front of her in a receiver's position as though waiting for the toss of a football.

"Trev! Jump!"

For a moment, Ngaire thought he wouldn't obey or didn't know what to do, but then he crouched awkwardly and launched himself at her. Ngaire caught him around the ribcage and held him steady as he gave a whine of pain. His hind leg had knocked against her thigh.

"Jump!" Ngaire repeated, this time lifting his body as high as she could. She felt her feet slip with the change in weight, fell heavily to her side, no easy slide this time. The air blew from her lungs, and she felt a crack—her rib or the cartilage breaking.

When she raised up into a sitting position, leaning to the side where her ribcage screamed in pain, Ngaire saw that Trev had jumped back on the edge of the slurry. His forelegs over the lip, his head tilted. He barked—once, twice.

"Fetch Isaiah," Ngaire called to him. The effort caused another wave of pain from her ribs, the act of breathing now an aching chore. "Go find Isaiah, Trev." She waved her arm in the general direction of the housing block.

Trev's paws disappeared, and he barked again. Ngaire couldn't hear the sound of him running, but the rainfall was so loud, the shape of the slurry amplifying its noise, she consoled herself that she probably wouldn't.

If Isaiah had done this to her, then she was finished. She'd just sent his faithful servant after him, with instructions—showing that she was awake and aware. Ngaire closed her eyes and leaned farther back on her hand. Her first aid classes had taught her this position was the one that eased rib pain the most, but balls to that. It felt like a fire was burning inside every time she drew a breath. Even shallow breathing was a small torture.

When Isaiah looked at Trev, Ngaire had seen the signs of utter devotion. A devotion that would have existed the length of Trev's life. She couldn't imagine a scenario in which he would inflict pain on his dog. Even less that he'd throw Trev into the slurry to die. Confident enough to bet her life? Well, Ngaire had just done so.

Time would tell.

Chapter Fifteen

Finlay was about to pour his second drink of the evening when he caught sight of the time. Earlier that evening he'd let himself into Ngaire's, hoping she'd soon be home and in the mood for a drink and a chat. He'd even held off popping the bottle until eight o'clock, sure she'd be through the door any minute. She hadn't given him a key to her place, but he'd noticed that she kept a spare on the hook board inside the pantry and had appointed himself as the best person to keep that safe.

That, plus he was late with the rent for the third time this month, and the landlord might camp out, waiting for him to return. One disadvantage of his living next door to his lessor.

Now he started to feel worried. Before he'd just thought she was working late because she forgot somewhere along the line to have a social life and didn't mind spending extra hours in the workplace. The clock was closing in on nine o'clock.

Ngaire lived like an old woman, sans cats. Woke early in the morning bright and chipper. Didn't drink unless he was around to remind her it was a fun activity. Usually she'd be going to bed about now. She'd never volunteer to work until this hour.

Finlay thumbed through the numbers on his phone, looking for a colleague. When Ngaire had dozed off the week before, he'd copied a few contacts to his own mobile in case he needed somebody to quote in future. Ngaire would've been happy to let him if he'd asked, but why take a chance?

Debra Weedon. That was it. Probably. He was a

good listener, but sometimes around Ngaire, he became lost in other concerns. Like how it'd be to kiss her again. How soft her hair looked when she let it out of its restrictive bun or ponytail.

He phoned through and waited until a voice squawked, "What?"

"Hi, is that Debra?" he asked, superpolite, to offset the direct query.

"Yes. Who's this?"

"This is a friend of Ngaire Blakes. She hasn't arrived home yet, and I was getting worried. I'm calling to check that she's still at work."

There was a long pause. "Ngaire doesn't live with anyone," was the answer.

"A temporary arrangement. I'm an old school friend, and I needed a few nights' accommodation on the fly."

"You haven't told me your name, sir."

"Finlay Ewan."

The sound of a clicking tongue. "There was a newspaper article a week ago that got me into bother at work. Accusations were flying about who might have talked to whom. Would you be the same Finlay Ewan?"

He sat on the couch in Ngaire's living room, trying to figure out an answer. "The same, but I can't take credit for your troubles. My sources' security is of high concern, but since you're not one of them, I can't help."

Deb snorted. "No prizes for guessing who your source was. Is Ngaire there? I'd like to have a word."

"No, she's not here." Finlay sat up again, alert. "That's why I'm calling. Aren't you at work?"

"Course I'm not at work, it's after nine. I work days," Deb said as though he should know. "Where is she, then? Ngaire left the station well before me."

Finlay's heart skipped a beat, then double pumped before settling into its normal rhythm. "Did she leave on a jo or pack up for the day?"

There was a long pause—then, "Work. It must've been work because she wasn't there at lunch, either. Shit!" Finlay heard the phone slam on a hard surface. After a minute of silence, she picked it up again. "I'm going back to the station. If Ngaire turns up, make her call me, and I'll ream her a new asshole, all right?"

"I'll meet you there," Finlay said. He wasn't sure whether Deb heard him, as the call disconnected, but he grabbed a jacket off the sofa and walked out to the car. He'd only had one drink—a large one, mind—but he should be fine to drive. Better be, he was heading straight to the police station.

Finlay sat in his car in the pouring rain, not sure whether he'd gotten there in time, missed her, or she'd driven in another entrance. When a woman ran from her car to the door, he tensed and waited. A few minutes later she came out, still at a lively pace, though walking, and Finlay was confident he'd found his target.

"Deb," he called out as he sprinted over. The shower was so heavy, it soaked him within seconds. His jacket bore the brunt, but his shirt soon clung to his body, outlining his lack of a six-pack, and his fledgling beer belly. "Deb," he shouted again as she reached her car. This time, she heard and turned toward him, drawing something from a hip pocket.

He pulled up short, holding his hands out palms up—the classic sign of an unarmed man. "It's Finlay. I called you earlier," he said, not sure if that would placate or enrage her. "Have you found out where she's gone?"

Deb dropped a canister back in her pocket and nodded. "Ngaire's never mentioned you, so excuse me if I don't tell you anything." She opened the car door and got inside.

Finlay ran around the bonnet and opened the passenger side before she could lock it. As he dropped into the seat, he extended a hand. "Nice to meet you. I'm Finlay Ewan, I've known Ngaire since high school, and I'm her roommate at the moment. Is that enough for you?"

Deb looked at him with an expression of outraged horror, and as Finlay glanced down, he guessed why. The rain had soaked him through, while Deb had been sheltered by awnings for her trip in and out. Bone dry, in comparison. Water dripped off him, soaking into her seat.

"Hey, it's only rain. It'll dry," he said. "Look, I'm worried about Ngaire. Otherwise I wouldn't be here. I'd really appreciate knowing where she is and that she's safe."

"I'd really appreciate if you got out of my car," Deb said. "And I'm not telling you anything. If you're a friend of Ngaire's, then when she comes home, she can tell you herself." She leaned across him and opened the passenger side door.

Finlay ignored the hint. "I can say that Ngaire put you in front of her the other day at the commune. When she thought a dog was about to attack, she used you as a human shield. Does that do by way of introduction?" He saw Deb hesitate and pushed. "Now, I wouldn't know that if I was just a reporter hanging around. Ngaire and I are friends, and I'm worried about her."

Deb stared at him for a minute, her brow furrowed. "Did she tell you why she did it?"

Finlay could hear the note of pleading in her voice and realized she was on Ngaire's side. She wanted an explanation so she could square away the incident and continue a professional relationship with a woman who'd grown to be her friend.

"Did you see her in hospital, after the attack?"

Deb's frown deepened. "Yes, course I visited."

"She was scared of everything, remember? Once, the nurse pulled a trolley into her room, and it hit the corner of the door. Ngaire went into a full-on panic attack. Hyperventilated for so long she passed out. Heartbeat up to 180." At her raised eyebrows, he explained, "She was still hooked up to the monitors."

Deb shrugged. "That was months ago. Ngaire's attending counseling, and the physio and shrink both signed her off as fit for duty last week."

"Yeah, and do you believe that's because Ngaire told them how she felt?" He paused and tried to think of an example. "Last year she went into work for three days after a doctor diagnosed her with the flu. It was only when her DS ordered her to get the fuck out of his station before she gave it to everyone that she left, right?"

Deb nodded. "I don't see . . ."

"She's desperate to prove she can do her job. She's not telling the shrink anything in case he puts something in her notes that means she can't return. Meanwhile, she exacerbated her injury with the physiotherapist so she wouldn't have to. Ngaire's terrified. All the time. She's ashamed. All the time."

"What's she got to be ashamed about?" Deb asked. "Until Gascoigne told them to stop hassling her, half the station was begging for her to return to work because she's so damn good."

Finlay laughed. "He asked people to stop talking to her?"

"No." She shook her head, then shrugged. "Well, I suppose."

"She thinks everyone at the station hates her because she wouldn't turn in her attackers." Finlay shook his head. "That's why they stopped talking to her."

Deb's mouth hung open. "That's stupid. Everyone understands that she didn't get a good look. Compared to half the witness statements we get, she gave us a damn book on the whole event."

"So why is she ashamed?" Finlay asked,

returning her earlier question to her.

Deb glared at him. He couldn't tell if she was angry because he was forcing her to think, upset because she hadn't realized Ngaire was in so much trouble, or annoyed because he was still turning her car seat into a damp sponge.

"She knew who they were?"

He held his hands out to either side, palms to the ceiling. "I don't know how much she knows, but her reactions are off for everything relating to her attack, and that's the only explanation I came up with. Either she knows who they were, or she knows enough for them to be found."

He experienced a sudden surge of guilt that he'd laid Ngaire's secrets bare for someone else, instead of keeping them close, like a true friend. But he couldn't get her to engage with him, and it was plain to him that she was eating herself alive with regret, recriminations, and worry. How long until she broke? Would a true friend let that happen?

"Fuck this. She's at the compound, clocked out at ten o'clock." Deb started the car and backed into the rain. Finlay leaned over, clunked his door shut, and buckled himself in. "If she'd still there, it's not because she found out some fascinating new angle to pursue."

"And you'd go there alone?" Finlay asked. "Thinking she's in trouble?"

"I shouldn't have let her go off by herself to begin with," Deb said. "I've got a radio if there's trouble, and I've checked out a Taser."

"Lucky I came along, then," Finlay said, not turning to see the expression that provoked. "Man to the rescue."

"Man to wait in the car unless I call for help," Deb said in contradiction. "Understood?"

Finlay nodded. The gesture a courtesy, not the truth.

He waited for three minutes in the car, then followed along behind Deb. She'd traveled off, with her hand on the canister of pepper spray. A cumbersome radio, which she'd tested before she left the car, was attached to her belt.

Finlay added concern for Deb to his anxiety about Ngaire. His dad had brought him up to believe that women needed to be protected. No matter how many times they'd kicked his ass and shown him otherwise, a nagging voice in the back of his head still insisted that he couldn't let this woman head into the foreboding darkness alone.

Deb was lost in the darkness. Finlay carried a penlight that he used for writing notes in his darkened car when he was on a stakeout. Not turned on yet because he wanted to use his own vision as long as he could. Otherwise, he wouldn't be able to see without it.

Finlay stopped and listened for Deb's footsteps. The rain had eased, but it was still heavy enough to cover any sounds she might be making.

He'd been out to the commune before, many times, when he was putting together the story that every paper had turned down. Isaiah had been around then. Finlay had seen the dog and man across the fields or yard several times, but they didn't come near, so he hadn't bothered them. The Maples, a couple who'd lost a child as stillborn on the commune, had given him permission to come out here. The farm harbored no fond memories for them.

Where would Ngaire go? Finlay hadn't talked to her since he'd gotten her drunk and slept on the couch. Well, mainly on the couch. There'd been the wake-up surprise of finding himself in Ngaire's bed with her clutching onto him for dear life. Clothed, so his first assumption didn't last.

When she'd talked through her visit to the commune, she'd focused on her abuse of Deb, her shame. Later she'd mentioned setting up an interview with Isaiah to find what happened during Magdalene's last days. She'd obsessed about the extraordinary wall art that captured Magdalene's mind and heart.

He headed to the housing block, feeling his way with the toes of his boots. Careful, but not so slow that he didn't make good progress.

To be out of the rain was a relief, but the wetness dripping from his body soon grew just as bad. He shook his head, imitating a dog to the best of his ability, but his fringe was still sopping wet when he finished.

The penlight went on. Outside plants blocked the windows, so any natural light was filtered even further. Dim outside turned to dark inside.

There were no wet footprints, apart from his own. No one had walked here in the past few hours, then. He moved at a slow pace through the different rooms. Thank the Lord the puritan nature of the commune meant there were no wardrobes or cupboards to check through. In Magdalene's room, he did a twirl and realized he was disappointed not to find Ngaire there. In his mind, he'd constructed a perfect picture, which burst apart when the light illuminated blank space.

A whine sounded. Finlay whirled to face the doorway. The hairs on the back of his neck stood upright, and his jaw clenched painfully tight. The sound repeated, sounding more plaintive on the rerun, and Finlay moved to the door, laying each foot flat before shifting weight onto it, to reduce the noise.

The whine sounded again and, this time, ran on for half a minute before the sound trailed downward and stopped. Finlay edged around the corner, sure it was the friendly dog he'd seen, sure it was a monster until he saw a dark shape. Red eyes reflected in his penlight, glowing. He reached behind him for the wall. Not scared, but just in case he needed to propel himself forward or twist back and around.

Finlay shone the light farther along, leaving the

eyes and the bright-white teeth, to see the long furry body, brown with gold highlights even in the torchlight.

"Trev?" he called out, unsure whether his memory was correct. "Good dog?" he asked with the same hesitation.

The beast whined again, then tilted his head back to howl. The noise sent Finlay's stomach rolling, but he held the light firm. "Never show a dog you're scared," his dad had often told him. "If they smell it on you, they'll attack."

At the time, it had had the ring of bullshit, but alone in the dark, it became plausible.

"Good dog, Trev," he called out, keeping his voice high and light. Memories from a colleague's recount of training a puppy. Low voice to tell them off, high voice to reward them. "Who's a good dog?"

Finlay inched forward, his hand stabilizing him against the corridor wall, fighting his nerves to keep the penlight nice and steady. When he was within a meter of the dog, he tucked in his chin so as not to expose his throat. "Good dog, Trev. Who's a good dog?"

There was a movement to his side, and Finlay turned the light to track it. The dog's tail was wagging. It thumped against the wall and floor in the confined space, but the gesture was still full of enthusiasm.

"Good dog," he said, holding out his hand and contacting the dog's ears. He scuffed the short hairs on the top of Trev's head, then stroked the length of his body.

The dog was damp. A smell more than something Finlay's wet body could feel. Even though the corridor wasn't warm, the dog generated enough heat for evaporation to release the unmistakable scent.

Finlay crouched by him, put the penlight on the floor, and patted the thick ruff of his neck. "Good boy. Good boy."

There was a note underneath the collar. Its edges poked out on either side, and his hand brushed it as he stroked the dog. "What's that you have there, boy?" he asked as he wiggled the paper free. "Somebody make you wear directions home, did they?"

Trev barked—once, twice—and growled low in his throat. He jumped to his feet, and Finlay saw the dragging hind leg, black blood drying around the wound where the dog's bone poked free. "Poor boy," Finlay said as he stroked the length of the dog again. He shone the torch straight at the leg, to see more of the wound, see what could've caused it.

He shone the light straight into the open eyes of a man lying on the ground behind him.

Finlay yelped, ran, twisted, caught his own leg with his other, and fell to the floor. The penlight rolled away, an arch of light spinning over and over on the corridor walls. As he kicked, he felt sure there'd be the clutch of a hand around his ankle. The stab of a knife in his back.

Commando-style, he dragged himself to the torch, picked it up, and shone it back along the corridor. The man lay in the same position. Eyes open. Mouth shut. Mouth taped shut?

"Christ, mate, are you all right?" Finlay said as he got to his feet and hurried to the man's side. "Are you hurt?"

When he ripped the tape off the man's mouth, he emitted a bellow of pain.

"Sorry," Finlay said and tried to flick the tape from his fingers. He scanned the length of the man, head to toe, then saw that his legs were bound with the same tape, from ankle to thigh. Arms pulled back and taped together.

Finlay searched his pockets for a knife but came up with his pen instead. "Here, hold still," he ordered, punching a series of holes through the tape binding the man's legs, then running the pen hard on the line until the holes merged into a tear.

He wriggled behind the man to get at his hands

and couldn't use the same method. With care, he worked the pen under the outermost layer of tape, then levered it upward with his full strength. It tore, and Finlay repeated this until he freed the last scraps of tape.

As soon as he was able, the man buried his face in the dog's fur. The dog ecstatically licked his face.

"This your dog, mate?" Finlay asked. Even to his own ears, it sounded redundant.

The man nodded but offered nothing further. Finlay shone his torch on the man's face, careful to avoid shining it straight in his eyes, and confirmed his original thought. The same man he used to see in the distance on the commune.

"What happened?" Finlay asked, sitting next to him. The flash of white paper on the floor caught his eye, and he picked it up, expecting to see a message from Isaiah written upon it.

Finlay read the message, and his mouth dropped open, "Oh, fuck." He sprang to his feet and ran out of the back door, the rain an encumbrance he'd stopped noticing.

"Deb," he shouted, the wind tossing the sound waves behind him as soon as they emerged. "Deb! Ngaire's in the slurry!" he screamed.

He ran along the muddy ground where the rainwater pooled. The ground had hardened over the preceding hot and dry weeks, so it couldn't absorb.

"Deb!" he yelled, his voice trampled by the rain. "Deb!"

He tried to turn, to veer right toward where he remembered the slurry being, but his feet slipped out from under him, and he staggered to one knee. His kneecap popped out of place, then, when he stood, popped indignantly back into position. Finlay ran, his useless penlight making him blind in the night, the weak beam too dim to navigate by.

He bounced off a tree, the weight of a full bough

of water dumping on his head. How long had it been raining? Six hours? Longer? Enough to fill a concrete pond in the middle of a farm?

Finlay caught movement from the corner of his eye, skidded to a halt, and, off-balance, slammed into another tree. "Deb!" he yelled as loud as he could.

The figure turned at the sound, and he waved the penlight. "What?" Deb asked as she joined him. The rain and the dark not seeming to have treated her any better than it had him.

"The slurry!" he said, pointing to where he thought it was. "Ngaire's in the slurry."

Deb didn't stop to ask questions but took off at a clip that outpaced him, holding her flashlight and spray the same way an American cop would carry a gun. Fuck, he wished the police carried guns.

He chased her, but he was winded, the drag of fast food and alcohol holding him back. Once, in high school, he'd been a sprinting star, but then he discovered the delights of smoking behind the bike sheds, a beer sneaked from his dad's pantry downed in the park on his way to school. Being übercool had taken a terrible toll.

Finlay forced himself to move forward quickly, ignoring his burning calf muscles and the knot of stitch in his side. His lungs heaved in air and raindrops and heaved them back out again along with his energy. He caught up to a few meters behind Deb, then kept pace. When she stopped, he careened into her back.

The walls of the slurry were a foot and a half high from the ground, seven feet from inside. Finlay walked to the edge, his heart triple-jumping in his chest. He didn't want to see.

"Ngaire?" Deb called out. Finlay strained for an answer as he scanned the slurry. His eyes still hadn't adjusted, and his penlight was useless at a distance. He waited for Deb to shine her torch across and back, moving farther along each time. "Ngaire?"

Finlay spotted her the same time as Deb and leaped over the wall to drop into the slurry before he could think. The water was over his knees. Where the fuck was the drainage? Why was this abomination even here?

"Ngaire!" he called as he splashed closer. The figure was bent forward, the ends of her hair trailing like sodden reeds in the water. He reached an arm out to touch her, found skin icy cold.

"No, no, no!" he shouted and seized her by the shoulder, turning her to face him, his penlight within range. "Ngaire."

When he shone the light in her eyes, it bounced off the open whites. One eye looked to the side, while the other stared straight ahead. A thousand horror movies couldn't engender this level of fear.

Finlay pulled her stiff body closer to him; she was icy. Colder than the rain falling out of a condensed cloud, colder than the dread in his heart. He pressed his fingers to her throat, hard against her jugular. Pressed against her clammy skin, her hard jaw.

Then he waited. Waited while the freezing Southerly poured its bounty over their bodies. He waited while Deb shouted again and again, "Is she all right?"

Waited, until at last there was the faint tremble, the soft whisper of a pulse.

"I'm her colleague, and this man is her husband," Deb lied to the nurse blocking them. "Course you can give us an update on her condition."

Finlay was so tired, he couldn't even muster a smile at the elevation of his status. From stranger to husband in one evening.

He'd exchanged his clothing for a gown and blankets when the nurses realized he was determined to stay, and he couldn't stay dressed in his soaking outfit. Deb had offered to drive him to get a change of clothes, but without enthusiasm, and he took it the same way. Neither of them wanted to leave until they understood Ngaire's condition better. Neither wanted their unspoken fear to come true.

He'd knotted a blanket at his waist, wanting most to cover his exposed rear. The other he slung over his shoulders.

The muscles in his arms and back were seizing. No one had examined him, but Finlay imagined that when he'd hefted Ngaire up to Deb's waiting hands, he'd pulled something. Or just exercised a muscle that hadn't known it was alive. When she'd leaned back to help him out, he'd shouted at her, "Go! Go!" As he waited in the night for help to arrive, the water's chill sank into his skin, his muscles, his bones. How long must Ngaire have lain there? By the time the ambulance pulled into the commune, the only warm part of him was the tears that streaked his face.

"I don't know. Do you have some ID?" the nurse asked Finlay.

He held his hands out to his side, and the blanket slipped from his shoulders. "I seem to have misplaced my wallet," he said.

"How about this for ID, and you take my word for him," Deb said pulling her badge. "My station number's 045699, if you want to call in. I'm based at the Christchurch Central Police Station." When the nurse continued to wait, she spat out, "Phone 363 7400 and ask."

Finlay appreciated her brusque manner when Deb pulled up her shoulders straight and loomed over the nurse. She only had an inch on her in height, but she knew how to use it.

"No, that'll be okay. Would you like to come into the Whanau Room?"

"No," Finlay and Deb said in unison.

"Okay, well, your wife has some extensive injuries to her head. There's swelling in her brain, and we must operate." She looked at Finlay. "The surgeon will bring a consent form out to you. As next of kin, you'll have to sign it before we can proceed, and he'll talk you through the specifics of the operation."

"Why isn't he here, telling us this?" Deb asked.

The nurse shifted her weight onto her back foot and stared at a point somewhere behind Deb's chest. "We've had to call him in, so he hasn't arrived yet. There isn't a neurosurgeon on permanent standby."

"What else?" Finlay asked when it appeared that Deb would speak again. He didn't need a tangential conversation going through the whys and wherefores of their not having the people that Ngaire needed on duty at the time she needed them.

The nurse shifted her gaze to behind his chest, instead. It freaked him out; as a journalist used to interviewing people, he liked his eye contact big, bold, and friendly. "Your wife is suffering from hypothermia. We're trying to raise her body temperature back up to normal with heated oxygen and saline. These treatments will continue throughout her surgery. But our focus at the moment is relieving the pressure on her brain."

"What are her chances?" Deb asked. Her face was still and hard, the muscles in her jaw stuck out in tightened bunches.

"Until the operation is performed, we won't know anything. The surgeon will give you a better idea of her prognosis. From just the hypothermia, I'd expect her to make a full recovery."

"Can we see her again?" Finlay asked. Deb had been with her in the emergency department, but to assess Ngaire's condition they'd taken her away for tests and treatment elsewhere. She was gone by the time Finlay arrived.

"You'll be able to see her after the neurosurgeon arrives, before she's prepped for surgery." The nurse held out a hand and placed it on Finlay's arm. With the continued lack of eye contact, it was an emotionless gesture that gave no comfort. "Don't worry too much. It won't help your wife."

"I thought nursing was supposed to be a caring profession," Deb said after the nurse had pushed out through the double doors and away. "They should screen out people like her."

"Bet she's great at her job," Finlay said and rubbed the side of his nose. "Sluicing out Bedpans Champion of New Zealand."

"Chief Drug Dispenser Gold Medal Winner 2010."

"Number One in the World at Cataloging Inventory."

They laughed together, earning a head turn from the row of people waiting beside them. "Once she's in the theater, I'll take you home, and you can get dressed," Deb offered again. This time, it sounded like she meant it.

"That'll be great. Thanks."

"Well, I can't have a naked man wrapped in just a blanket sitting next to me for too long," she responded. "I could get ideas."

"How bad did she look?" Finlay asked, stopping the flow of easy camaraderie in its tracks. "In the ER?"

Deb turned her head to gaze at the double doors. *So he wouldn't be able to read her expression?* "She looked like she was asleep. There was blood on her face, but that's all."

Finlay thought of her wall-eye and the lack of response to his touch. The way her skin had the same texture as a wet version of the cadavers he'd touched over the years in pathology when he was working a murder story.

"She looked okay, then, yeah?"

Deb nodded, her face still turned in the opposite direction. "She looked fine."

Chapter Sixteen

After William had scanned the hallway outside his office to make sure it was empty, he locked the door and sat behind his desk, staring at the newspaper in front of him.

The office hadn't started off with locks on the doors. A break-in where thieves had breached multiple rooms and rifled through multiple client files led to the change. Locked at night, unlocked in the morning. No one else used the locks during the day.

Breakfast had been the usual shambles. Amanda was still cool, so she spent most of the morning at the kitchen sink rather than across the table from him. It was one thing he'd tried to implement after Emma arrived, making sure they sat around a family table for morning and evening meals. He'd read somewhere that it helped child development. Amanda had agreed with him, yet now she was ignoring her own advice to shut him out.

Emma noticed nothing. If William didn't respond to her, she carried on conversations with her food or her plate or her cutlery—he wasn't sure which—while attempting not to eat a single thing. This had become her primary goal at mealtimes. A picky eater, according to his generation. When he mentioned it into idle conversation at work, two nineties babies told him to watch out that she didn't have anorexia. His protestations about her age falling on deaf ears.

"Oh, it can start at any age, you know," one of them replied with confidence. "We're bombarded with images from the media from birth, these days."

These days. As though she had other days to compare them to.

He hadn't even tried to read his paper. If Amanda didn't take part in family life, then he accepted that he'd have to. It wasn't until he reached the office and spread it out on his desk that he saw the article.

Police detective assaulted and left for dead.

William skimmed, then read the article with increasing horror. He knew Mikel could sometimes stretch boundaries when he was chasing a lead, but he didn't think the man was a monster.

Sure he wouldn't be interrupted, William dialed Mikel's number and paced back and forth as he waited for him to answer. As the phone continued to ring, he sat and swung his chair around to face the window. Viewing offices where people sat in cubicles in front of computers in a mirror image of his side of the street.

The handle to his room turned, followed by a flurry of knocks. William stood and peered through the side window into the corridor. Geoff's face stared back at him, a frown taking center stage. He pointed at the door in case William didn't realize he'd been knocking. A man and woman stood behind him. The woman was one of the detectives who'd been questioning Paul. Debra Weedon?

Shit.

He hung up the phone, unanswered, and hurried to unlock the door.

"What's your door doing locked?" Geoff asked as he strolled through. "That's against office policy." The policemen followed him through, and Debra nodded to him.

"I was making a private phone call, so I didn't want to be disturbed," William said, trying to force his voice to be light and breezy. "Last time I made a call to my wife someone wandered into my office and wouldn't stop talking until I hung up the phone."

He glared an accusation at Geoff, who stared back without a flicker of recognition.

"These officers are here to see you," he said. A redundant sentence from a redundant man. "They want to have a chat."

"Thank you, Mr. Waters," Debra said. "You've been very helpful, but we won't take up any more of your time."

She stared until he left the office and closed the door when Geoff left it ajar. "I don't know if you remember me, Mr. Glover."

William nodded. "Detective Weedon. I remember."

"And I'm Detective Sergeant Gascoigne, Mr. Glover. Can we take a seat?"

William gestured at the chairs, and they sat, Detective Weedon leaning forward and placing her elbows on the table. He frowned. William's mother would have scolded her and knocked them from the table; a childhood of etiquette remained when little else stuck.

"How can I help you?"

"We're questioning people about an incident that occurred with one of our officers," Gascoigne said. He was dressed in full uniform, epaulets gleaming from his shoulders, three white chevrons shining. "I believe you'd made her acquaintance. Detective Ngaire Blakes?"

William shifted in his chair, wishing he'd seen the bloody article earlier so he could have talked to Mikel. It would have been helpful to know for sure whether the incident involved him. Although at least this way he wasn't committing perjury, just obfuscation.

"I had met her once, with Detective Weedon. They attempted to interview my client, Paul Worthington, outside my presence."

Weedon glared at him—*if looks could kill*—but

she didn't contradict his statement. Another worm of worry wriggled through William's nervous system to join its buddies. If she was holding her tongue, it meant this interview was important. Bringing along her sergeant showed that, too.

"Quite, quite," said Gascoigne. "And have you met with Detective Blakes on any other occasions?"

William shook his head. "No, that was the only time."

"As you stated, you were Paul Worthington's lawyer. How did he contact you for representation?"

William looked from Gascoigne to Weedon. "I don't understand why that's relevant."

"Understand, Mr. Glover, that we're following up on the assault and attempted murder of a police officer. What you do and don't understand is not of our concern. Would you answer the question?"

"No comment" came crawling up his throat, but he swallowed it back. If he started that game, they'd just take him in, and then he'd be even worse off. His history wasn't a sealed record, so they'd already know his connection to Paul; they weren't idiots.

"I contacted him after I saw an article in the paper that said he was confessing to murder. We were good friends when we were young, and it concerned me that he'd got himself in a spot of bother." He forced a laugh. "The crime he was trying to confess to wasn't even a crime. I knew that girl, Magdalene Lynton, and I remember when she disappeared. The coroner ruled that she drowned in an accident on her parents' farm. Hardly a murder."

"And why would your client confess to a murder he didn't commit?" Weedon spat out.

William turned a calm gaze on her. His anger was back, slowing his movements to make him appear oh, so reasonable. "Why does anyone?" he asked with a shrug. "I don't understand the psychology of it, Detective Weedon, but I understand that false confessions are a common occurrence. Even in this day and age. If you Google it, I'm sure someone has a theory."

"Did Paul Worthington tell you that the confession was false?" Gascoigne asked, holding a restraining hand on Weedon's wrist.

William smiled and sat back in his chair. "I can't tell you that, Sergeant Gascoigne, and I'd think you'd know better than to ask. Whatever Paul and I discussed is privileged."

"Except your client's dead, Mr. Glover. Privilege doesn't extend after death."

William held his hands out to his sides, palms empty and exposed. "It does if another party's interest would be affected. Now, I can't say if that would or wouldn't apply in this case unless I'm compelled to by a court justice, but I'll stick on the side of safety, if you don't mind." He looked from one to the other again. "Not in the public interest either way, is it? He's dead, so if he falsely confessed, he's not hurting anyone, and if he told the truth, he's still not hurting anyone."

"Your name comes up a lot in association with Paul Worthington," Weedon said. "In fact, someone suggested that you may have been the one to commit the murder yourself, not Mr. Worthington."

"Oh, I'm the one who committed the murder that wasn't," William said, crossing his wrists. "Quick, arrest me now before I don't murder someone else."

"Is there anything about Paul Worthington's case you'd be willing to share with us?" Gascoigne asked, ignoring him. "It would help us a great deal if we could cross it off our list."

For a moment, William saw a smooth path to freedom in front of him. Admit that Paul had told him his confession was false, and the whole thing would go away.

He glanced over at Detective Weedon, who now sat with her arms folded. She looked curious rather than pissed off, and he saw the path twist and reform into a gaping trap. "No, there isn't," he said. "There's nothing he told me that I can reveal to you. Nothing at all."

"Where were you yesterday, between eleven a.m. and midnight?"

William snorted. "What? You want to know everywhere I went that whole time?"

No answer came back across the table, and he ran his hand through his hair, thinking through his recollections to see if there was anything objectionable in the lineup. "I was at work from eleven until seven thirty, except for a lunch appointment at Baretta." He stopped as a frown appeared on Weedon's brow. "Two *t*'s," he supplied, grinning at her discomfort. "Then I went home and stayed there until work today."

"And who can verify that for us?"

"All my work colleagues," William waved his hand at the hallway window, which revealed an unusually high amount of foot traffic heading down the corridor. "There's CCTV in the lobby, and my wife will confirm that I was home all night."

After writing down her name and phone number, the detectives stood.

"You're not planning on traveling anywhere in the next week, are you?" Gascoigne asked. When William shook his head, he continued, "Good. I wouldn't want to have to track you down."

When William stood to escort them to the door, his chair whirled back to strike the window. Not hard, but it was over a meter back from his desk. He saw Weedon taking note and felt the worms burrow in again.

"Your wife'll be home at the moment?" Detective Weedon asked as he opened his office door. Loud enough so three staff members at various points along the corridor could hear.

"Yes. Or you can contact her on her cell phone,"

William said. Then, louder, for the onlookers, "I've got nothing to hide."

Weedon nodded and tucked her notebook into her breast pocket. "See you again soon, *Billy*."

William restrained himself from slamming the door.

He got hold of Mikel later in the day. Mikel assured him he had nothing to do with the incident; he'd been somewhere else, and William had no choice but to believe him.

"It's not my scene, man. I don't do violence," Mikel had protested. "Threats, yes. Snooping, easy. Violence, no."

There was support for his protestation in his physical form. Mikel was inches shorter than William and looked fifty pounds lighter. Pitting him against a woman would have been a fair fight.

He left him to get back to the job, couldn't afford to piss the man off now, but he regretted the hire. If he'd just left it alone, he wouldn't have a suspicious contact to hide, if anyone went snooping. The police, for example.

William kept up with the story on his work computer. When he couldn't click on a link because of security, he routed the request through a proxy. Ridiculous system, anyhow. To get the information he wanted, he had to cheat his own bloody firm's system, put in place to stop one or two employees wasting the day on Facebook.

A few tense client appointments followed. He'd been so distracted, he hadn't done the groundwork. The hours flew away from him each day; even having worked most of the weekend, he was running to keep pace. He'd gotten too old for this.

The secreted money called out to him. A siren song that asked him to "Pick, pick me, and we'll live a carefree life." Not enough stored away for that, though.

Not enough just to pack up and walk out without a job to go to. And there'd be no bonus ahead.

He felt cheated by his life. Maybe not to the same extent it'd cheated his dad, but still. At this point, his workload should be winding down, not up. His income should be trending higher, not lower.

Christ. And he had to remember that Emma's tuition check would be presented soon. The house was mortgage-free, but the rates bill kept climbing in a way that made his throat clutch and his heart pound. As a lawyer, he should be rolling in it. Instead, he felt a noose was drawing closer, closer.

He had a shower after he arrived home. Something he often left for the morning, but there was a sheen of sweat on his body, and he needed to clean up before he could play with Emma. Before he had a glass of wine with Amanda.

"Not for me," she said when he pulled two glasses out of the overhead cabinet. For a moment he debated, then pulled one out anyway. He needed a drink, and being companionless didn't make it any less necessary.

"How was your day?" he asked. After the first gulp, he closed his eyes and waited for the tingle on the back of his tongue. He'd read somewhere that alcohol was absorbed into the bloodstream from the minute it hit your mouth. There were even greedy receptors in the lining of your throat that helped it work its magic. He needed it to kick in.

"I went to the doctor," Amanda said.

"Are you ill?" William asked, touching her shoulder. It was stiff, and after a moment, she pulled away. He put his glass on the counter and examined her—saw the circles under her eyes, the sagging skin from the weight she'd lost. "Is it something serious?"

Amanda laughed. The sound was brittle and weak. "You could say that."

He put his arms around her and pulled her close.

Home should be safe and comfortable, not full of fear. "What is it?" he whispered into her hair.

"I'm pregnant."

William's arms loosened for a moment, his brain trying to fit the words into a sensible order, then he tightened them again in a fierce hug. When Amanda resisted, her twisted her around and pulled her close, pressing his body full-length against hers.

"I can't believe it. I'll be a daddy again."

He heard the sound of clumping footsteps behind him and turned to see Emma running toward their noise. "What's goin' on?" she demanded, stamping her feet, then holding her arms out to William. "Daddy?"

He let go of Amanda to pick Emma up under her armpits and let her loop her legs around his waist. He leaned her tiny body back, took her arm, and pretended to dance her the length of the kitchen. Ten years dropped away. "I'm going to be a daddy again," he told Emma, giving her a kiss. "And you'll have a little brother or sister to pester."

"Not a pest," Emma insisted. Her face screwed up in concentration, then her eyes opened wide. "They're not sharing my room. I got it how I like it." A house-painting experience that Amanda said through gritted teeth was the last time they would do any remodeling, ever.

William grabbed hold of both her hands and let her crawl down his legs to the floor. "Don't worry, Ems. The baby will have its own room."

Satisfied with her accommodation and seemingly uninterested in the rest of the conversation, Emma walked off. Placing her feet one after the other in a strict line, arms out for balance.

William turned back to Amanda and saw none of the pleasure spread upon his own face reflected on hers. "What's the matter? Is there something wrong with the baby?"

She shook her head and pinched her lips together. Bewildered, William kept watching her face, waiting for her to explain. A tear rolled down her left cheek, joined soon by a brother, a sister, a bunch of cousins.

"What is it?" he asked again, his voice peaking with worry. "What's wrong?"

Amanda tried to talk, but her sobs got in the way. William's worry increased with each hitch of her chest, each shake of her head. He pulled her into a hug and stroked her hair back from her forehead. Kept stroking it the same way he did with Emma when she had a fever, and they were waiting for the Panadol to kick in.

"We. Don't. Have. The. Money," she managed, a sobbing intake of breath between each word. "Not. With. Emma's. School."

William laughed with relief. "Christ, Panda. I thought it was something serious."

"It *is* serious." Amanda pushed away from him and wiped her eyes. "I don't want Emma to miss out just because my birth control didn't work."

"She won't miss out," William said, taking her hand and holding it tight between both his own. "I promise you that."

"Well, how's that going to work, then?" Amanda asked. "Are you planning to spend even more hours at work? Emma barely sees you as it is."

He bore the brunt of that one on the chin. There was no denying it. "No." He paused for a moment, then added, "I've thought about cutting back on my hours."

Amanda shook her hand free of his and crossed her arms in front of her chest. "And doing what? Are you going back to criminal law?"

He shook his head. "No." Even though she resisted, he pulled her close and nuzzled into her neck. "I've been thinking about buying a farm."

"A *what*? What are you talking about?" She stared at him with bewilderment, then rubbed her frowning forehead. "With what?" she demanded. "You think selling this place will give you enough money? It won't. And who would run it?"

"I would run it. Not a big place, just big enough. I've got enough money invested, so we could run it and rent this place out. We'd be able to earn enough rent only to need the farm to break even." He put his palm flat on her belly. It was rounded, the only part of her that carried any extra flesh. "If this is a boy, I could teach him how to ride horses and milk cows and muster a few sheep. He could take over for me when I can't manage anymore."

Amanda put her hand on top of his, her palm soft and warm. She left it there for a moment until the heat grew between them, then flicked him off her belly with a grunt of annoyance.

"You don't know how to run a farm, and you're too old to learn. It's just a pipe dream."

She turned back to the sink, picked up a vegetable peeler, and pulled wide, angry strips from the new potatoes. William reached over and pulled it from her hands.

"You don't peel those, you scrub them," he said. "And I know how to run a farm. I grew up on one." He elbowed her aside and reached under the sink for the scrubbing brush, then filled the sink with an inch of water.

"You never told me," Amanda said.

She sounded stunned, and William turned to her, his forehead creased. "I'm sure I did. I lived on the bloody thing until I went to university. Where did you think I grew up?"

"I don't know where I thought you grew up because you never told me. Apparently there're a lot of things I don't know about you." Her voice was tight, her throat clenched so hard he could clearly see her swallow. "What money do you have invested?"

"Oh, I've been putting away funds for a few years

now. Always pays to have a safety net."

William scrubbed the potatoes, his hands turning red in the water, the thought of a farm growing in his mind. He hadn't even known he was thinking about it until he said it out loud, but it made perfect sense. Kids should be raised out in the fresh country air. They should have chores and get their hands dirty. They should learn about life from watching it grow and fatten and die around them.

Emma could have a pet lamb. She'd love that more than she'd love a private school. She could sense joy in its wriggling tail when she was bottle-feeding it formula, keeping it alive when its mother couldn't.

He smiled and turned to share his thought with Amanda, but she'd left the room. He should check on her later, make sure she was taking care of herself. With Emma, she'd been sick in the morning for five months straight. By the end of it, William was sure that her growing belly must weigh equal to the rest of her. After that, she'd blossomed with her pregnancy. It had carried on for half the year after she'd given birth to Emma, smoothing the transition to their new, noisy, housemate.

There was a loud thump from the stairwell, and William walked out to see what was happening, wiping his hands on the dishtowel as he did so.

Amanda had a wheeled suitcase propped beside her and was holding her hand out to Emma, who trundled her elephant sit-upon case downstairs, taking delight in each bump.

"What's going on?" William asked. He still held the towel in his hand, and Emma pulled it so hard, it fell to the floor. Amanda looked at it, and William did, too, staring until Emma jumped on it and pronounced it dead. When no one responded, she tucked her thumb into her mouth and reached behind her for her mother's hand. She hadn't sucked her thumb in months. He and Amanda had rejoiced that they'd be spared the dentist's bills they were facing if she'd continued until her adult teeth came through.

"I thought Emma and I might pay a visit to Mum's house for a few days," Amanda said. Her eyes were bright; the traces of her earlier tears gone. "You'll enjoy that, won't you, Emma?"

Emma nodded and stared at William with big, round eyes. Her forefinger snuck over the bridge of her nose, falling into the dimple just before her nostrils flared out. William had had the same shape in his nose when he was her age, like a ski-jump ramp. Emma had gotten it from him, just as half her genes had come from him. Confirmed in traits from the shape of her chin, the dimple of her nose, to the rough patches on her elbows that flared into eczema. He hadn't spent a night away from her since her birth.

"But why?" he asked. He didn't understand. Half an hour ago he'd been twirling Emma around the kitchen in delight at the thought of a sibling, and now she was leaving for an indefinite period. "What's wrong? Why are you leaving?"

Amanda shot him a look he knew well. It prefaced such phrases as, "If you don't know, it's no use me telling you," or, "Why don't you ever think before you speak?"

He swallowed. His throat was dry. The glass of wine sat in the kitchen, one sip gone. He'd been going to tip it out after he finished the potatoes to show solidarity with Amanda being unable to drink. She would laugh and clap, and he would bow. That was how it would happen. What had gone wrong?

"I think it's best you don't call us for a few days," Amanda said. She gestured at Emma to pick up the plastic pull of her case, then pulled the child across her body to place her between them. "I'll call you when I'm ready. I need to think about things."

The plaintive cry, "What things?" only sounded in William's head. The door closed, the car engine started, then he heard it turn into the road and drive away. When the sound mingled with the general buzz of traffic, so he could no longer distinguish it, he realized his mouth was still hanging open. He shut it with a snap but continued to stand and look at the closed door that stood between him and his family.

When he moved, it was back into the kitchen. He drained the glass of wine in one long drag, then refilled it over and over until he'd emptied the bottle. And the next one. An old, drunk man alone in an empty house.

Chapter Seventeen

"Could you turn that down?" Finlay asked as he walked through to the living room. The radio was blaring at full volume, making the subwoofer rattle and the voices distort.

Ngaire was banging the remote with the back of her hand, and he grabbed it from her, pressing the volume button until it stopped assaulting his ears.

"The batteries need changing," she said. As he opened his mouth to answer, she flapped her hand at him. "Shh, I'm listening to this."

Finlay walked out of the room, taking the remote with him in case she tried again. The batteries were fine; it was Ngaire who had crossed wires. Her major movements were fine, a slight stumble as she walked, a lag when she moved her arms. But her minor movements were agony to watch. Her digits misfired, pressing next to things instead of on them. She was unable to grip a piece of cutlery or hold a pen to write a note.

Still, early days yet. The surgery, which took eight hours to perform, had only required a five-day hospital stay. Finlay was terrified when they signed Ngaire into his care. Like a new parent holding his baby and being pushed out the hospital door, he wanted to turn back and say, "I'm not equipped for this."

Ngaire's right hand was bandaged. She'd stirred into a frenzy when she couldn't do up her buttons one morning. Finlay had suggested she wear a T-shirt instead, had gone to the dresser to pull one out for her, and turned to find Ngaire's fist drawn back. A punch went straight through the wall, plaster dust puffing out, while lumps of the stuff fell to the floor.

Finlay had reassured himself that she had aimed for the wall. That his head had been in a similar position a second earlier meant nothing.

The neurosurgeon who released Ngaire had mentioned that she might have anger issues, violent fits. Finlay had thought he meant she might swear and sulk.

When the phone rang, he jumped, then ran to answer it before the shrill ring could disturb the household. "Hello?"

"Hello, is that Mr. Blakes?"

Finlay acknowledged it was with a smile; another person bestowing a relationship that didn't exist.

"I'm calling from Meridian Energy. Your current account is now in arrears, and I wanted to make sure you'd received our bill."

Finlay frowned. Not in concern at a missed bill payment, but as he realized that no mail came to the letter box. Circulars, in spite of the "NO CIRCULARS" sign spelling out Ngaire's request, but no personal mail.

In the living room, Ngaire was now dozing with her head on the couch back. The radio advertising the mad, mad prices you could expect to pay for meat at The Mad Butcher.

He touched her shoulder to wake her, and she smiled and placed her hand on his.

"Ngaire, I had a call from your electricity company wondering if you'd received their latest bill."

She shook her head, "I don't know. Have we?"

"Do you have a post office box, maybe?" he nudged her. Memories came and went with regularity, and he was never sure what she did or didn't know. He'd noticed her tricks to hide when she wasn't sure.

She continued to rub her head and looked at the bedroom.

"Do you have a file where you keep your bills?" he asked. "That might show whether you have a box rental."

"My laptop." Ngaire stood up and reached beside the sofa, pulling it out. "I keep all my bills on my laptop. Here," she said after signing in, leaving Finlay to deal with the finer detail. "It should be somewhere in there."

He scrolled through the saved items and located what he was looking for. He jotted the reference numbers the post office provided, then clicked through to her e-mails to see what new bills had arrived. The energy bill was in there, along with the current rates bill. Having given up the lamentable tenancy agreement on his own flat, he could swing the payments easily.

"Did you find the box?"

"Yup. Now I need to check your key ring and see if you've got the key. I don't think the post office would be too impressed if I tried to get into your box using just a bill."

Ngaire giggled. "I don't think they'd want to know anything about you trying to get into my box."

He laughed with her, half at the joke and half in relief. The moments when his Ngaire, the old Ngaire, shone through the injuries and the disabilities were few. If they kept coming, though, he'd keep waiting.

Finlay brought the whole key ring with him, just in case Ngaire's assessment of the right one was off. It took a few minutes of trial and error before he opened it. When he did, a stack of mail fell out, along with a card announcing that there was more to collect behind the counter.

The wonder of small suburban shopping malls meant there was only one customer before him. Finlay tried to balance the envelopes, but they slid against one another where he clutched them. As he approached the counter, the entire pile gave, and the teller burst into laughter as most of the mail fell to the floor.

"I can give you a plastic bag if that'll help," she offered and extended a supermarket shopping bag. Finlay took it and scooped the lot into the bag. He checked behind him, but no one had joined the queue to be staring daggers at the extended wait.

"I have one of these," he said, plonking the card on the counter. "Is there very much?"

The teller nodded as she registered the number. "There's a whole load," she said. "Are you parked close?"

"Close enough," he responded and waited to see what "a whole load" might represent in real terms.

There were fourteen parcels in total. One of them had a date stamp on the day after Ngaire's assault, along with the word "Perishable." Judging from the light odor seeping out of the tight packaging, that could now be amended to "Perished."

Finlay scooped up as much as he could, filling the bag and his arms, and then nodded at the rest. "Is it okay if I leave these here? I'll just be a minute."

"Oh no, sir," she responded with a smile. She waved her hand across the empty expanse of the post office. "That would inconvenience our other customers."

"Kelly," came the warning reproach from the senior teller standing behind the Kiwibank desk. "She's joking," the woman informed Finlay. "It'll be fine, dear."

He took three trips, not wanting to chance it on the second leg, in case it meant breaking Ngaire's gifts into pieces. He assumed they were gifts; the ones wrapped in cellophane with colored bows gave that impression.

When he was back in the car, Finlay pushed aside a piece of cellophane to wrestle a wrapped chocolate from the stuffed paper nest. Finder's fee.

* * *

"I'm sorry, but we've made no progress so far," Deb said as she took a seat on the couch next to Ngaire. "We chased down a lot of leads, but none of them came to anything. Have you remembered anything new?"

Ngaire shook her head. Finlay had left a half hour ago, and she wished he was back. She didn't like going to the toilet in the house alone, just in case she needed help somewhere along the line. It wasn't something she would be comfortable asking Deb.

"I don't think there's anything to remember," Ngaire said. "I was hit from behind, never saw my attacker, and there was nothing amiss at the property to suggest anyone else was there."

Deb shifted her glance from Ngaire to look around the room. Ngaire colored; it was a mess.

"Finlay told me you may know something about your attackers," Deb said. "From the party," she clarified when Ngaire stared blankly at her. "He suggested that you may have been holding something back from the investigation because you were scared."

Ngaire colored as a twinge of rage flared in her chest. She tried to keep her breaths steady and even, to keep herself calm. Since returning from the hospital, her anger flared and burned at the slightest provocation until it scared her. She'd punched herself in the thigh more times than she wanted to count, blaming the deep purple bruises on walking into things around the house. That also happened; minor injuries covered her body from not being able to steer herself, from dizzy spells, from sudden muscle weakness.

"Did he?" she managed after a few moments.

"Is it true?" Deb asked, turning to face her. Ngaire saw the frown of concern on her face and felt the rage twist and boil inside her. "I know it can seem dangerous to tell us everything, but you know it's better to inform us than to keep things secret?"

Ngaire remembered the brothel operator who'd paid her a visit. Bea, Bella, one of those. She'd told her not to worry; she hadn't informed the police. Was Deb so cloistered that she didn't understand the myriad of grays that existed in every event?

"I'm not keeping anything secret," Ngaire choked out. "I've told you everything I know. For God's sake, I was struck on the back of the head. Even the evidence should tell you I'm not hiding anything."

Deb smiled and reached over for Ngaire's hand. "I knew that. I just needed to check. You know how things are."

Ngaire couldn't keep up with the changes. Her mind worked at a slower pace now, had trouble tracking everything that happened. She recalled Isaiah's long pauses before providing an answer. Was his head messed up from birth the way hers was from being cracked open?

"We had to interview all the people that hold a share in the compound," Deb continued. "I'll see if I can get you a copy."

Ngaire tried to make her emotions adjust. The confrontation was finished; the conversation had moved on. How was she meant to respond to what Deb was saying now?

"Did any of them give you anything?" she managed after a pause. "Did they remember much?"

Deb shook her head. "They gave us nothing of value."

"Did you interview Billy?"

"Yeah." Deb shrugged. "We got little from him, either way. Gascoigne was there with me, so I wasn't comfortable asking him much about the Lynton inquiry. He was much more concerned with any connection with your assault."

"Gascoigne's working the case?" Ngaire asked with surprise. The DS fronted to media, and he chased up paperwork, but his position was mentor and rally for the troops, not getting dug into the fieldwork himself.

"Course," Deb replied. "He's upset that this happened to you, given that you were only just coming back from the last attack. He doesn't want to lose you, and he doesn't want whoever did this to get away with it."

Ngaire heard a car door slam and closed her eyes in relief. She was tired, had a thumping headache, and still needed to use the toilet. With the relief came a nudge that she'd been meaning to ask Deb something. What was it?

"Have they located my car, yet?" she asked, even though that wasn't it. She could tell from the expression on Deb's face that it wasn't the right question for her, either.

"We found it the day after, torched, out by the Waimak." Deb sighed, then asked, "Didn't we tell you?"

The signposts flashed that she had. Ngaire tried to remember. Sometimes she started off with one idea and ended up lost in a different one. Scattered thoughts, the way if you were winded, it took a moment for you to remember how to move. It took her a while to remember how to think.

Her hands. It had something to do with her hands. Ngaire looked at them, but apart from the obvious bandage on one, she couldn't place the thought. It was drifting further and further away.

"Blood," she blurted, and Deb jumped.

"What?"

Ngaire shook her head and held out her open palm, clean in the daylight. "I went back to my car because I found blood. Not wet," she struggled for a moment, clicking her fingers as though that would provide an impetus to her brain. "Flakes," she said at last and relaxed. Sometimes when a thought came through that she'd searched for, she'd cry with relief, but Ngaire had company, so that wouldn't do.

"I had blood flakes on my hands, from lifting the cross. They were old and brown, and I wanted to know if it was blood or just the wood."

There was a muffled knocking at the door, and Deb got up to answer it without waiting for Ngaire to try. Ngaire experienced a quick pulse of anger again—*I'm not a Goddamn invalid*—but she pulled it back. Nice, even breaths. Keep your mind on the main point.

Finlay stood there with his arms full of packages. He must have been knocking with his head because he couldn't use his hands.

Deb took a few before the stack could topple. Two gift baskets crammed full of colorful treats. She counted another four packages still with Finlay, and after he'd laid those on the coffee table, he headed back out to the car. "There's a heap more."

Ngaire felt her thoughts wander again and fought to stop them. "There was blood on the cross," she said again to Deb, as though Finlay hadn't just interrupted. "It was in the locked room next to the pulpit where we thought they stored the chairs." She shrugged. "Well, they did store the chairs, but they also had an enormous cross. Too big to hang above the pulpit or on the wall or ceiling." She stopped and smiled, pleased with herself for getting the full thought out. "There was blood on the cross."

Deb frowned at her. Ngaire felt sick. Once, on the day after the surgery, she'd asked the attending nurse if she could have a glass of water. When she received nothing, Ngaire tried to get out of bed to fetch it herself. The nurse had called a doctor, and Ngaire had heard her say she'd been speaking gibberish. Speaking gibberish, and she hadn't even known.

"There wasn't any cross," Deb answered at last. "At least, not a big one. There were smaller ones on the wall." She tilted her head to the side with her hands held a foot apart. "Is that what you mean?"

"No, it was enormous. Large enough to be a real

one, a crucifix." Ngaire held her arms out to each side and stretched. "This broad, and taller than me."

Deb's frown deepened, then she turned as Finlay arrived with another load. He passed the full lot across to her this time, then went back to the car again.

Ngaire ignored the presents being stacked in front of her and chased the thought, chased it. She wasn't tired or achy or busting to go. She was absorbed, her eyes closed against the unwanted world. After a moment, she pressed on her ears to shut the sounds out, too.

There had been blood. Old blood. She'd put tiny brown smears into a plastic bag.

"A bag!" she shouted excitedly.

Finlay stopped in the doorway, and Deb stared at her. Ngaire looked from one to the other, these two people she loved, and for an instant hated them both. Why didn't they understand?

"An evidence bag," she said. Ngaire mimed the act of putting something into one, pulling the imaginary plastic tab off the imaginary sealing strip, and fastening it. "I put it in my pants pocket."

Deb flicked a glance to Finlay, then back to her. "There was nothing in your pants pocket," she said. "We looked at your clothing strand by strand. If it'd been there, we'd have found it."

"It must be there," Ngaire said. Another memory flared. "When I pulled the notebook out of my pocket, it was still there. I put the note under Trev's collar and put the notebook . . ." She trailed off. Had she put the notebook back in her pocket? She should have. Had she dropped it when she finished, too eager to help Trev up and away to fetch help?

Ngaire had pulled the notebook out, felt the slide of the plastic on the back of her hand. Hadn't cared. Wrapped up in the task she needed to do. The one thing she could still do to save her life. She felt the slide of the plastic on the back of her hand, and she shook it off because it didn't matter. "The slurry," she said, the pieces locking themselves into place. "The evidence bag will be in the slurry."

Chapter Eighteen

Mary Lynton read the article from the paper again. She'd read it through at least four times every day since it had arrived. The newsprint had smudged and would soon disappear into illegibility. No matter, by that time, she'd know it by heart.

Martha had gone. She'd packed one day while Mary was out at the shops and left a note on the table saying thanks, but no thanks. Mary had expected the house to be empty without her, but Martha had spent so much of her time elsewhere, she just experienced relief that everything would be in its place when she returned from errands.

Abe missed her. He'd been angry when Mary showed him the note, then insisted that Mary get into the car and look for her while he drove them around town. She kept asking, "What's the point? If she doesn't want to live with us, you can't make her." But once Abe got a mission going in his head, he saw it through to the end, reason or no reason.

Mary had breathed a sigh of relief when they couldn't find her. She had been steeling herself for a big public scene. Everyone would stare, and someone would call the police. There'd be *those looks*, and after everything that had happened with her darling Maggie, Mary was in no fit state to suffer through *those looks* again.

When the police paid a visit, Mary felt tingling dread that it was because of Martha. That Abe had done something to Martha. When they said an officer had been assaulted, it came as a relief. She'd offered an alibi as soon as asked, not stopping twice to think. Abe hadn't got them into any trouble over Martha, so everything was clean and sweet.

But then Mary remembered that nice detective who'd come around with her big, brown eyes and her thick brown hair tied back in a bun. Her detective friend had an edge to her, but when Ngaire had come back alone, Mary had seen how gentle she was. What a good friend she'd be. Mary remembered the compliment, that Maggie looked like her, and felt the exquisite flush of pleasure again.

She hadn't bothered to tell her how Maggie wasn't hers any more than Martha was. Maggie had come to them so young that Mary not being her true mother felt like the lie.

Nice young thing. Smart, but still gentle. She'd seen Mary's secret stash, Mary had known it was okay to show her, and she'd never blinked an eye. Just gave her a polite nod of thanks when she extended the offer of a biscuit.

She'd given her the keys without question. When she'd told Abe after he got home, she'd expected he'd be angry, but he'd just muttered a few curses and gone out to the garage to fiddle with his tools. She hadn't seen him much the next day. His walk must've worn him out because he came in hot and sweaty and dripping wet. Served him right for going out when he knew there was rain coming.

The detective's injuries sounded awful. The paper didn't go into much detail, but enough for her to intuit the truth. Head injuries. Assault. Mary knew what that meant. That meant someone had banged her over the noggin until she was out for the count. Not that those injuries worried her.

Police officer with head injuries left for dead in concrete slurry. That was the bit that worried her. A nice, gentle woman being tossed into Maggie's grave.

At the time they'd located her darling girl, Mary had pretended to believe the lie they force-fed her. That they'd fished her from the pond, nice and clean. She'd nodded and accepted it, and even now she repeated it whenever anyone questioned her.

She could smell the slurry on them a mile away. Did the whole world believe her an idiot? She could find and read a coroner's report when she traveled to town. While Abe went off to the TAB—the local betting shop—and thought she'd just stay in the car for hours while he satisfied his own pleasure.

That lovely detective, being tossed into the slurry to die. The same way her darling Maggie had crawled into the slurry to die.

So many similarities between them, Mary could even believe for a moment that Ngaire was her girl reincarnated. So similar. The same spark. Ngaire might be a brown baby, but not dark enough to matter. She was strong and courageous and smart, just as Magdalene had been. Just like her daughter.

Mary smoothed out the article and read it through again.

The alibi had sprung to her lips without hesitation, smooth and easy.

When the phone rang, William pounced on it. "Hello?"

There was no answer, but he could hear muffled voices, the swish of a phone moving.

"Hello?" he called again, louder, in case the caller was deaf.

The call was from his wife's phone; the number was displayed right there on the screen. He'd blocked every other number from calling through, diverting it to voice mail instead. William hadn't made it to work for a few days, and he didn't need to answer the phone to have a client yell at him.

"Amanda!" he shouted.

Still no response. William looked frantically at

the phone, trying to see if he'd muted it by accident. With buttons so small and crammed, he wouldn't be surprised. He missed the dial phones from his childhood that you picked up to answer and hung up to disconnect. Difficult to get that wrong.

He heard muffled voices sounding from far away again and got angry. "Listen, if you think this is funny, then—"

"Daddy?"

William's tirade cut off at the sound. Emma's voice was thin and quizzical. It didn't sound the same as the confident child who stomped around the house intent on destroying whatever raging horde she'd invented that morning.

"Hello, darling," he said. "How are you doing?"

His voice echoed back to his own ears. She must have him on speakerphone, the cell phone lying on the floor in front of her. She had a toy cell phone that she played with in the same way, not understanding or accepting that people holding their phones to their ears were doing it right.

"Mummy's crying," she said. "She won't stop. Grandma's being mean to her."

"Grandma's mean to everyone, darling. Just ignore her, and try to do what Mummy tells you."

"I do," Emma said, her voice full of indignation. "I cleaned up all my mess from breakfast this morning without Grandma even having to nag me."

William smiled as he imagined just how many times Emelda had to ask his rebellious daughter to do something before she considered that it had reached the level of nagging.

"That's good. You're a very good girl, and I'm proud of you. Are you able to put Mummy on the line?"

"No. Mummy doesn't want to speak with you. She has told me and told me and told me."

William closed his eyes and tried to think. Emma was hard to manipulate because of her natural obstinacy. "But I need to tell her something about the party," William said. "I don't know what kind of cake to order."

There was a short silence. With Emma, the silences were always short. "Cake?"

"Mm. Are you sure Mummy can't come to the phone?"

William waited, holding his breath, hoping this small deception wouldn't end up being replayed in a custody battle. He released his breath when he heard the phone being picked up and his daughter stamping her way around the house.

"Mummy, Mummy." Her voice sounded muffled and indistinct, as though she held the phone flat against her body.

"Hello?"

It was Amanda. William wondered whether she even knew there was someone on the line or whether she was just playing along with another one of Emma's games.

"Amanda, it's William. I'm so glad to hear your voice. Are you and Emma okay?" The note of concern in his voice was genuine; he realized he'd been worried by the silence.

"William," she said, followed by a distinct sigh. "I told you not to call me here. I said I'd phone you when I was ready."

"I didn't," he began, then stopped as the disconnect tone sounded in his ear. "Call," he ended, speaking to no one. A common occurrence these days.

At least he'd spoken to his daughter. He'd heard that she and Amanda were safe and well.

William imagined Emma trailing her mother the rest of the day, pulling on her skirt and demanding to know when the "cake" was happening. As his mind added details to the vision, he produced a smile.

Five days home from hospital, and Ngaire was feeling

the frustration. Finlay had decimated the offerings, but she found a solitary wrapped fudge left forlorn and alone in one basket. In another, she discovered a box of Turkish delight she guessed must not be to Finlay's liking. It wasn't to hers, either. It had been a treat of her mom's, and the sticky kisses she'd bestow on Ngaire after an indulgence but before the trip to the bathroom to throw it up cast a shadow that shouldn't exist over candy.

Beggars can't be choosers, though. Ngaire made short shrift of the packet while she sat trying to concentrate on shopping TV. All the while a rapid-fire announcer attempted without success to sell her a vacuum cleaner with headlights. So she could vacuum at night? What kinky engineering feat was that?

Sitting on the couch and eating chocolates. If someone had put it to her a year ago, Ngaire would've thought it heaven, but her daily reality was something more akin to slow and draining torture.

She wanted to be out doing things. Inside, everything screamed to take action—with Magdalene's case, with catching her attacker. Instead, she got to sit and rest and pin a false smile on her face when somebody she didn't want to see came around to visit the "invalid."

Ngaire stood up and made the perilous journey over to the stack of gift baskets and mail again. She hadn't even opened half the letters scattered over the coffee table. If she had been a polite woman, she would have replied to every single one, but without a stern parent to watch over her, Ngaire abandoned that plan. She sorted them out: a pile for bills, a pile for letters, a pile for I-don't-know-what-but-they're-getting-read-last.

Ngaire lay back and opened the first letter. It was from her Aunt Winnie, a lovely gesture from a woman she remembered from her childhood and had never visited since. But when she got to the paragraph regarding police compensation, Ngaire threw it aside and selected another.

A woman she'd helped leave an abusive relationship years before had written words of support. That she remembered her touched Ngaire and made her feel worthwhile. Her words of sympathy and strength for Ngaire's physical complaints were heartfelt and valid. The woman had been through similar beatings, though at the hands of a lover, not a stranger.

She opened the last one. Written in an old-fashioned script where the letters joined up in strange but familiar patterns. Beautiful. By the time Ngaire got to school, printing was all the rage, and no one ever progressed from there except self-taught.

"For years I told myself that Billy killed her; it was his fault. In a way it's true. He never should have left me alone with her."

Ngaire's heart beat faster, her eyes wobbled into double vision. She blinked hard and turned the letter over. Double-sided, but the only writing on the back was a valediction and a name.

Sincerely, Paul Worthington.

Chapter Nineteen

"Don't tell me I should rest. I've been doing nothing but for the past week. I want to see." Ngaire pulled herself out of the passenger seat using the door frame to hold her weight. Who knew simple things like getting out of a car required so much damn coordination?

"Ngaire, if you end up hurting yourself again, Deb'll kill me."

Ngaire shot him a foul expression. Why was he always so interested in Deb's opinion? "So? If you can't protect yourself against a girl, that's your problem. Are you going to give me a hand, or what?"

Finlay sighed and walked around the vehicle. He let Ngaire transfer her weight from the car door to him and held her steady as she gained her balance. Even with his help, she still tottered. Stupid body. Stupid head. Nothing sent or received messages the way it should.

"Thanks, I'm okay. You can stop groping me now."

She watched as his face fell, and she felt the flush of guilt again.

"Thank you for bringing me here," she said to make it up. "I appreciate it."

"Yeah, well, you know my opinion. Tell Deb, and let the police handle this."

Ngaire snorted. "Whatever happened to your reporter instincts? Don't you want to be involved in the story, Gonzo?"

He laughed, and relief rushed through her. Since reading the confession letter, Ngaire had been desperate to come out here and prove it to herself. Prove her instincts hadn't been wrong, and Paul Worthington's confession hadn't been a wild-goose chase.

"So? Where to now?"

"The barn," Ngaire said, leading the way.

When she'd used Google Earth to locate Paul Worthington's childhood home, she had a stroke of luck. A small farmlet still existed there, complete with barn and silo. She'd felt the first twinge of hope. Before, she'd been so interested in Magdalene's home turf, she'd never got around to investigating Paul's side. His father's land had been chopped up into much smaller blocks over the intervening years, but the nineties craze for lifestyle blocks had saved this small pocket from intensive redevelopment.

A reverse phone directory she shouldn't still have access to provided a number, and the owners gave permission.

Finlay followed along behind at first, until his natural curiosity kicked in, and he overtook Ngaire. She watched the back of him as he strode across the grounds in long paces, looking like an overgrown version of the intense schoolboy he'd been.

Her notebook was in her pocket, and she pulled it out to check the instructions she'd written to herself when her mind was alight with the need for discovery. Paul's letter had detailed once more the events of the night Magdalene died; if she could corroborate part of his confession, no matter how small, she might get justice for the poor girl.

And yes, Finlay was right. She had no sanction to be here, investigating. Once again she was on sick leave until she felt able to return, a déjà vu experience that did nothing for her mood. Ngaire remembered a time when she hadn't had a page full of physical progress points to tick off before she could perform her duties.

Although her low terror had intensified after the latest attack, she still wanted to follow up on this case. She needed a resolution more than she needed to feel safe.

"Hair," she said, then said it again with greater volume so Finlay would take notice. "There should be a small coil of hair placed in the main vertical beam."

As they walked closer to the barn, Ngaire could see her goal. The owners were away at the moment, city job during the week, playing at farmers every spare minute. Her dad once dismissed these properties as "no lifestyle" blocks, and it fit.

"Where?" Finlay asked, reasonably enough. He stood aside as Ngaire entered the barn and smacked the supporting post.

"Paul wasn't specific," she answered. "Search around. There must be a hidey-hole somewhere."

She held onto the beam as she looked up its length. It was a foot wide and as deep. There were rough patches, iron attachments with unutilized hooks, rusting until the day they'd drop to the earth to disappear. Where the upper loft joined, there was a mishmash of wedges and bracing beams, holding the planks in place. Would it be that high up?

Finlay must have seen her glance, because he jogged over to the ladder and climbed. The resulting creaks on the mezzanine level made Ngaire's chest tighten, but he kept going. He leaned out over her, holding onto the beam to keep his balance, and smiled.

"Better behave yourself down there, young lassy," he said with a thick Irish brogue that sounded comically like his normal speaking voice. "Otherwise, I'll be dropping something on your head."

She flipped him the finger and bent to examine the base of the beam. Where it tucked into the earth, the wood was rougher, but she still couldn't see a hiding place.

Instead of continuing to scan the beam, Ngaire

ran her hands over it, her fingers searching for any oddities. The wood was so well worn by age and weather that she didn't need to worry about splinters, but she couldn't sense any irregularities in the surface.

She checked the letter again. Once she was dead, I cut a lock of her hair and tied it with a ribbon. I hid it in the main beam in the shed, and it's probably still there.

Ngaire walked backward out of the shadow of the shed and looked up. She ignored Finlay mugging back at her and saw the enormous crossbeam that ran the length of the roof. It was far too high for her to reach, but from the mezzanine level where Finlay had to watch out not to bang his head, it was well within arm's length.

She yelled and pointed at it. Finlay looked behind him, mistaking the direction for a pile of old blankets and hay left there. Ngaire yelled louder, and he worked his way forward, touching things, until she clapped her hands.

As she'd done, he trailed his palms along the length of the beam, checking to make sure his footing would land safely. In front of the piled hay and blankets he stopped and Ngaire gave a whoop of victory.

Not waiting to see what he'd discovered, she trotted inside, angling like a drunk, and grabbed hold of the ladder to pull herself up. As she reached the top where the ladder became the floor, Ngaire lost her balance, pinwheeling her arms against the pull of gravity.

"Christ, girl. Are you determined to kill yourself?" Finlay said as he caught her wrist and pulled her so hard her cuff button popped free. "If you don't watch yourself, I'll leave you at home next time."

"Shut up and tell me what you found," she said back, a grin splitting her lips so wide her teeth retracted against the cool air. She threw an arm around his neck, half to keep her balance in the dizzying height, half to press his skin against hers.

"Come on, then."

He circled his arm around her waist and helped her walk to the edge of the flooring. "Now, for goodness sake watch yourself," he said. "If you fall over, there'll be no saving you."

Ngaire kept as far away as she could while still angling close enough to see what Finlay had discovered. There was a piece of wood, a line marking where it didn't sit flush on the beam. Finlay wedged his car keys into the small crack and levered the piece out.

It didn't come out at once. Millimeter by millimeter it worked free. Paul must've had time to spare if he'd chosen this as his hiding place. Or, once he'd hidden his treasure, he hadn't felt the need to pull it free to examine it. For some, it was enough to know it was there.

When it was out a centimeter, Ngaire dug her nails into the exposed edge on her side and pulled in tandem with Finlay. The wood popped free, and she overbalanced, falling a step backward to recover. The piece clattered to the ground, exposing a hole with an inch of room resting behind the plug.

There was a curl of blonde hair tied with a blue ribbon.

Ngaire pulled her digital camera from her back pocket. She took a photo of the hole with the hair inside, then the piece of wood now lying on the floor. Too late she thought of taking a picture before they'd pulled the piece out.

There were plastic gloves in her back pocket. When she'd been getting ready, she'd thought she'd pull the sample out and place it into an evidence bag. The gloves would protect the hair from damage. Her thoughts hadn't been too clear.

"We need to call the police," she said. "They must collect this as evidence. Properly."

It was hard to ignore the smirk on Finlay's face,

which announced, "I told you so," but she tried.

The problem was she couldn't stop thinking of herself as a detective. And she'd forgotten that unless the police bagged and tagged the sample, it wouldn't have any continuity chain. No matter what photos she took or to who she testified.

"I'll call Deb," Ngaire said after a moment. "My phone's in the car." No one had recovered the cell phone she'd lost in the attack, but she had a battered green Nokia from the back of her bedroom drawer that still worked.

But Finlay was pulling his own out. "Ngaire, love. Why don't you take a seat? There's no way we're getting down the ladder with only me to help you, so we're in for a long wait."

"There won't be DNA," Ngaire said, pursuing her own thoughts as Finlay made the call. The hair was snipped, the curling strands only two inches long. Without a follicle, there'd be no skin cells to test. They'd be lucky to find mitochondrial DNA, given the age of the specimen, its storage, and the fact that the lock had been cut from the bottom. Even Ngaire's poor visual inspection caught a few split ends. Conditioner had not been an ordinary commodity in the seventies. Magdalene's DNA would have washed straight out of those strands in water. Dried up as it was bleached by the sun. Leached out into the wood of its captive home for the forty years it had lain still.

"You don't need it," Finlay said as he joined her. "You know it's Magdalene's because Paul said so."

Paul's letter now sat at home waiting to be collected as soon as Ngaire bothered to phone and tell anyone. She'd taken a scan on her printer and carried that in her pocket instead. The ink mixing with her greasy fingerprints to form smudges on the too-white surface.

Ngaire felt light-headed and reached a hand out to steady herself against the beam. Until now, part of her still hadn't believed the old man who'd sat across from her. The skeleton with skin stretched tight, tight, across its frame. The dying man whose face smiled and eyes twinkled with life.

Finlay steadied her with arms around her waist, then she felt his hand go frisking across her bum.

"Stop it," she said. He laughed and pulled the letter from her back pocket.

"Perfectly innocent, ma'am. Just looking for this." He waved it above his head, then sat to read it. Read through the lines describing a desperate girl, a boyfriend's feeble actions to help, and a teenage boy who fulfilled his own needs because that's what he wanted.

"Why was she wet?" Finlay asked.

Ngaire looked at him, puzzled, and he showed her the flowing script.

"She was wet, and her arms were bleeding," he read aloud. "Why would she be wet and bleeding? Everyone I talked to said she'd sworn at her dad, and he'd sent her off to think about what she'd done."

Ngaire frowned and nodded. The same refrain she and Deb heard when they first interviewed the remaining church members. "Mary said she went to check on her later, and she wasn't in the thinking spot, or whatever the hell they called it."

"The contemplation spot?" Finlay suggested. "Meditation point?"

"Doesn't matter. She was sent there, and when her mom checked, she wasn't where she should have been." She frowned as another thought occurred. "I assumed Paul meant it was raining. He said she was soaked in his first interview. But if Mary was looking for her outside and was surprised she wasn't there, that doesn't add up."

"So, what else happened to her? If Magdalene was hurt by the time she arrived here . . ." Finlay trailed off into silence.

Ngaire looked at the land spread out before them. To their side was a thicket of pine trees, marking off the back field of the compound. In front of them was a paddock with sheep gathered in cliques, wandering aimlessly in the sun. Beyond that a house built with nineties styling. Uniform bricks that, in spite of their manufactured imperfections, always looked mass-produced.

"Whoever attacked me at the compound wasn't trying to hide what Paul Worthington did," Ngaire said. "When Paul was first speaking, we thought he was covering for someone, for Billy, but now?" She gestured at the letter. "It's obvious that Billy did nothing wrong, that night."

"Except leave his girlfriend alone with a psychopath," Finlay said. There was an edge to his voice that confused Ngaire.

"I don't think that's a crime, Finlay," she said, not bothering to hide the chiding note in her voice. "He went to get help for his girlfriend. End of story. Which doesn't help with the question of who hit me? And why?"

"Let your colleagues sort that out," Finlay returned. "When Deb gets here, we can pass on this information, leave everything in her hands, and go back home."

Go back home. To her couch, her TV. Put her brain on hold so she could get through the day. Back to unexplained fits of anger, ingratitude, sloth.

"I'm going to the compound," Ngaire announced. She stood up and smacked her hands against her thighs, brushing off the dust. The walk to the ladder was over before Finlay realized she was serious and jumped to his feet.

"You'll fall," he stated with certainty.

"Finlay Ewan, I am a trained detective constable, and I will not sit in a barn waiting for someone to rescue me." She tossed her leg a few rungs down the ladder, holding her arms out to her side so her elbows supported her while she gained her balance before gripping the top rung with her hands.

Near the bottom she stumbled, so she jumped the last steps. As she landed, she fell to one knee when her leg buckled, but she broke nothing, sprained nothing.

"Coming?" she called up to Finlay, who was staring at her, his expression twisted in stern reprimand.

Ngaire set off without waiting for an answer and soon heard his footsteps running to catch up with her.

"If you hurt yourself again, don't think I'll look after you again," he warned. Ngaire turned and flashed him an enormous smile.

"Right back at you," she said.

Despite his protestations, Finlay helped her over the gate that separated the two properties. Grabbing her waist while she stood on the bottom plank, then hauling her full weight over the top. He had to bend over to recover, propping his hands against his thighs while he caught his breath.

Ngaire elbowed him in the side. "You should lay off the booze in the future if you can't even help a girl over a gate," she said. "Superheroes shouldn't take this much time to recover."

Finlay moved to place his hands on his hips instead, although he still continued to pant like a dog running in full sun. He tipped his head back and let the sun wash over his face. "So, you think I'm a superhero?" he asked when his breath was even again.

Ngaire laughed and started to walk. "I suppose I said that," she said.

He slung an arm over her shoulder and squeezed her for a moment before letting go. "Where are we heading over here, anyway?"

Ngaire pointed ahead. "Across the field, through the next lot of pine trees, then round to the church.

There's something I want to check."

"Your crucifix?" he asked.

Ngaire turned to him in surprise. "I didn't know I'd told you that."

"You were telling Deb when I came home from the post office. She said they hadn't found it."

"Yeah, she did say that," Ngaire agreed, glancing up at Finlay. His eyebrows had a long hair at either extreme that pointed off to his hairline. She wondered if he'd grow more of them, thick, black, as he grew older. If he'd end up with big bushes up there to scare the little kiddies when he leaned too close.

There was police tape around the entrance to the church. Ngaire saw Isaiah staring at them from across the yard and raised a hand to wave. He returned the gesture but turned to walk farther away.

Ngaire ducked under the police tape. "Come on," she said when Finlay paused. "What?"

He ran his hand along the length of tape as though he were displaying a piece of jewelry on the shopping channel. "You seem to have missed this," he said. "I believe the DO NOT CROSS applies to you, too."

Ngaire snorted and held the tape high for Finlay to walk underneath. "What are we going to screw up?" she asked. "A complete lack of leads on my assault."

"I remember when you were lying in the hospital bed," Finlay said as he followed her under. "At the time you were so nice, quiet, and still."

"I was unconscious, Finlay."

"Yeah. Good times."

She pushed her elbow back into his stomach in a warning nudge, then turned to the locked doors next to the pulpit. They were no longer locked.

"Here?" Finlay asked, pulling the doors open before Ngaire could do it herself. "Wow."

Ngaire turned to him, trying to see what he was seeing, then caught the tilt of his mouth.

"Cool chair collection," he continued. "What other wonders do you have to show me?"

"Shut up. It must be around somewhere," Ngaire said and scanned the room. "The bloody thing was enormous. You wouldn't be able to carry it out and dispose of it. You'd need two hefty lads and a flatbed to get anywhere."

"So maybe that's who the police should look for," Finlay said as he poked his head farther into the cupboard. "Two hefty lads with a Ford Falcon."

"Look," Ngaire said, pointing at the floor. "Do you have a torch or something?"

"Something," Finlay said and pulled out his cell phone.

"Scuff marks and chalk," Finlay said in summary, then directed the light in a circle to search for more. "There," he pointed.

Ngaire looked at the floor where he'd gestured and saw the deep groove of a heavy object being dragged on wood. The gouges and scuffs lasted for two meters before ending in a small pile of sawdust. There was a chalk trace to highlight it for a long-gone evidence team.

"Okay, so I'm starting to be convinced," Finlay said. Ngaire shot him a look, and he shrugged. "You've just suffered a head injury you know. I'm allowed to have doubts."

"So if you'd just cut up a bloody great cross, where would you put it?" Ngaire asked. She ducked back under the police tape and looked about her in a circle. "Is there some," she faltered and clicked her fingers, trying to think of the word, "place where you can burn stuff?" she ended lamely.

"There's a refuse pit down behind the ablutions block," Finlay suggested. "They would've used it to burn biological waste to stop it becoming a hazard."

At Ngaire's raised eyebrows, he explained, "Dead lambs, animal remains, you get the picture."

She got the picture. The ablutions block had been unused for so many years, any odor had gone long ago. Ngaire remembered campsites where it didn't matter how many times the owners cleaned, the concrete bricks of the walls smelled of urine and feces. As though the open pores of the concrete inhaled and exhaled it.

The barbecue pit was a different story. As she drew close, Ngaire could smell and taste the charcoal in the air. Whatever had been burned there had burned recently. A pile of dark-gray charcoal still retained the shape of the logs they'd been. Ngaire estimated they'd been six inches on each side, the length varying from one to two feet long.

"It was raining the night I was attacked," Ngaire said. She walked to the concrete barbecue and touched a piece of charcoal with her toe. Its form collapsed on one side, falling into a pile of dust on the ground. She pulled back before she caused any more damage. "This happened later."

"Police would've been all over the site," Finlay pointed out. "They were here for at least two days getting samples and trying to pin Isaiah down to a single storyline. Not a perfect environment to cut up an enormous crucifix and set fire to it."

"Someone could've cut it up at the time. And it leaves a week afterward when they could've burned it," Ngaire pointed out. She'd been in the hospital for five days; at home another five. Although it felt like months since her assault, in actuality it wasn't yet a fortnight.

She bent to look more closely at the fire pit. There was a shape in the ash and charcoal, uniformity in the natural lumps and bumps. Ngaire pulled a glove on and stretched her hand out to touch it.

Metal. It was a loop of metal. Ngaire closed her eyes and tried to remember what she'd seen when she looked in the cupboard. There'd been the chairs, the cross, and on the cross a bolt and a circular hook. Given the weight of the contraption, it must've been used to navigate the cross into position while it was pulled upright. It was definitely the cross.

Finlay's mobile phone buzzed in his breast pocket, and he pulled it out. "Oh. Hi, Deb," he said in answer to a yelled query that sounded to Ngaire like, "Where the fuck are you?" Finlay smiled and winked at Ngaire. "I love you, too, Deb. You know you gave my nipple a little thrill. Buzz, buzz, buzz."

He smiled as another shrill tirade sounded, and then he laughed. "We're over at the commune, if you must know. Ngaire wanted to check a few leads."

The volume increased, and Finlay pressed the disconnect button and popped the phone back in his shirt pocket. "Deb'll be here soon. She's over at the back neighbor's right now. She sends her love."

"It didn't sound like that's what she was sending," Ngaire observed.

Finlay shrugged his shoulders. "She made a sexual reference several times, so I assume that was the message she was trying to send." He looked around the fire pit and back toward the housing block. "Should we see if Isaiah's willing to have a chat?"

Ngaire followed his lead and walked behind him to the house. The cool air inside was welcome after the direct sun. If she had been lying on a beach, her legs would have welcomed the rays, but reflecting off her hair they just made her brain frazzle.

"Isaiah?" she called out as she moved toward the corridor. "It's Ngaire Blakes here. I wondered if I could have a word?"

Finlay frowned, and Ngaire realized how she sounded. "Have a word," had for many years been synonymous with "Interrogate" and given Isaiah's age, he'd make that association.

"Isaiah, I wanted to check that Trev's okay. Did the vet fix up his leg?"

There was a rustling sound from a room farther

along, then Trev popped around the corner, traveling fast, even with a cast on his leg.

"Good boy, Trev," Ngaire said as she bent to give him a pat. "You look like you're doing fine."

"Hey," Finlay said and raised his hand. Ngaire looked up and saw Isaiah step out of the shadows of a doorway. He'd grown a beard since she'd last seen him. When they'd interviewed him at the station he'd shaved clean, but it was now filling in thick and fast. Ngaire saw ginger tufts in among the salt-and-pepper hair. She hadn't picked him for a redhead.

"Mm," Isaiah said in return, then patted his leg so Trev raced back to him. He sat on his hind legs and looked up until Isaiah pulled a piece of chopped meat from his pocket and fed it to him.

"Are you okay, Isaiah?" Ngaire asked. "Finlay told me you were roughed up a few weeks ago."

She didn't know how much anyone had told him about her own predicament, but it must have been enough. Isaiah stepped forward until he was within a meter and held out his hand. Ngaire shook it, felt a firm grip and dry palm, then released it as he tugged away.

"I'm sorry to hear about what happened to you," Isaiah said. The formality of his language should've made him insincere, but Ngaire could read the struggle he had to form the sentences in his wavering eye contact, his throat-clearing, his weight rocking from foot to foot.

"Thank you. I'm much better now, though. Are you feeling better?"

Isaiah nodded. He looked behind him, as though he'd heard a noise that escaped Ngaire's ear, then turned back to gaze at her stomach.

"Did you see anybody burning something?" she asked. "It would've been in the last week."

"Mm," he mumbled, then turned to look back along the corridor again. "I've burned wood, but I haven't seen anyone else burning anything."

"Where did the wood come from?" Ngaire asked. She didn't understand. Isaiah hadn't attacked her, he'd been trussed up inside. The bonds weren't something he'd faked. Finlay had said that he looked like a mummy, with the number of times the masking tape had been wrapped around his arms and legs.

Isaiah rubbed his hand through his thinning hair. He gripped curled hairs that extended out from his right ear and shifted his weight to his right foot. "From the woodshed. Somebody cut it up," he gestured with his hand—one chop, two, three. "I burned it because it belonged to the cross."

Ngaire felt an ache seize the back of her throat at Isaiah's tone. His voice was always a monotone, but at that word, it turned flat and dead. The minute expressions at play across his face disappeared, his skin frozen into a mask.

"You told me about the cross," Ngaire said. "Do you remember that, Isaiah?"

A curl flicked up the corner of his mouth, and he looked up into the corner, a repetition of his display for the camera. "I remember. I thought you'd get it. You see more than the other lady."

"What was the cross used for, Isaiah?"

He shook his head. At first a small gentle gesture, it became larger, became violent. His hair and his beard whipping from side to side. He looked crazy. Ngaire wondered if he was.

"What was the cross used for, Isaiah?" She stressed each word and stepped toward him. When Finlay gave her a warning tug on the wrist, she shook it free, irritated. "Why was there blood on the cross, Isaiah? Who did it belong to?"

His eyes opened wide, but he froze in place. Ngaire took another step forward, encroaching on his personal space. His breaths turned into pants.

"Why did you have to burn it?"

"Are you in here?" Deb's voice shouted from the

kitchen door. "You'd better be in here," she muttered in a lower voice.

Isaiah turned and ran. Trev followed barking, nipping at his heels. Ngaire tried to follow, tried to run, but her coordination abandoned her, and she stumbled into the wall, bruising her hip.

"Shit," she said, then yelled, "Shit!" She could see Isaiah and Trev running along the path, across the yard, into the pine trees.

"Hello to you, too," Deb said as she walked in. "Thought you needed help getting down a bloody ladder?"

Chapter Twenty

"While I appreciate that you've had a difficult time of late, when you're not on active duty, it means you are not to be on active duty. Have I made myself clear?"

Ngaire nodded and tipped her head forward, hoping she looked chastised. Unfortunately for her and Finlay, DS Gascoigne volunteered to go along for the ride when Deb left the station saying she was out on the Worthington case. His interest piqued after the attack on Ngaire. What a time to take an interest.

She felt excited underneath. Ngaire had been so close with Isaiah, almost getting him to admit something useful. Everyone was covering up something, and that Isaiah was part of it, she had no doubt.

That cross. It tied back to that cross.

"Sir, did we get any results back on the evidence from the farm?"

Gascoigne gave her a stern glance, then looked at his wife's photo. His smiling daughters; drug-free. "Have you not been listening, Ngaire? I said you are not on active duty. You are, at the moment, a private citizen. What we may or may not have found as evidence is not your concern."

Ngaire opened her mouth to protest but fell silent when he gave her such a glare that she went into self-defense mode.

"If we found anything," he continued, "and I emphasize *if*, then when you resume your duties as a police officer you'll be entitled to that information. If you're put back on the case, and if I deem it relevant."

With each "if," he stabbed his forefinger on the desk so hard, his short fingernails scuffed the surface. "Until you're signed off as fit, you can go home and relax, and if there are any developments in your case, we'll inform you."

Ngaire put her hands on the arms of her chair and levered herself up. She turned to face the door, then turned back as a thought struck. "When you say, 'my case,'" she said before Gascoigne's raised palm stopped her.

"When I refer to your case, Blakes, I mean the case that involves you being assaulted while out on duty. While out *alone* on duty, I should add. Along with the caveat that this behavior is something we frown upon and that you've had drilled into you should only ever occur as a last resort."

Ngaire nodded. "So, not the Worthington case?" she clarified one last time.

DS Gascoigne sighed and rubbed his forehead with his hands. Like he was getting a headache.

"Not the Worthington case," he confirmed.

William Glover pulled his wallet out and sorted through until he found Mikel's contact number. He'd woken up this morning to the realization that if Amanda knew he had an investigator following a police officer—possibly assaulted her, no less—it would increase the breach between them.

Besides, what did he have to hide? Mikel was just a pointless expense at this stage. If the police had been interested, they'd have invited him to the station for questioning.

While the phone rang, William took off his tie. There was a stain on the front of it that must have happened sometime between yesterday morning, when he'd put it on, and now, but he hadn't even noticed it. He checked the couch in case there was a sauce packet or something similar lying on the cushions. There wasn't. Lucky, as the stain on his tie was so deeply yellow, it didn't look as though a wash could get it out. He had other ties. Not that he'd gone to work for a while anyhow, but replacing a sofa cushion was a task so difficult to navigate that his mind shied away from the idea.

There was no answer. Mikel's phone must have rung thirty times, and he wasn't answering. There wasn't even a message. What did that mean? Who left his phone on but didn't answer?

Was there someone there with him?

William looked over his shoulder at the thought. If the police had Mikel, maybe they were waiting for a trace on his phone? Was that possible with a mobile phone? Probably. He'd been out of criminal law for too long to be sure what could happen with the new smartphones, but it appeared a safe bet. They could track anybody and anything these days.

He poured himself a finger of scotch and sat to think about it. There was still a chance that Mikel had just left the phone somewhere, tossed it into the glove box, or lost it down the back of the couch. Did a phone ring at the caller's end when set to silent? William had stuck to landlines for most of his phone business. It was the technology he'd grown up using, so it felt more comfortable. If only he'd embraced cell phones when they'd first arrived on the market, he'd now be able to work these things out. He'd know things where now he could only guess.

Should he look it up? He could Google it. But if they were tracking his phone after connecting him to Mikel, then they'd be monitoring his Internet searches.

William pulled his special laptop out of his briefcase. He could do a safe search and locate information that way. As he waited for the OS to boot up he dozed, then jerked himself awake. Since Amanda left, he hadn't been sleeping well, and now he was napping throughout the day.

What had he been doing?

He'd been calling Mikel, that was it. William grabbed hold of his mobile phone, then remembered that Mikel wasn't answering. What if he tried from the landline instead? That was it. He'd told Mikel only to contact him through the landline, so he hadn't recognized the number when William had called from his cell phone.

Again William dialed the number, and again he waited. At twenty rings, he threw the receiver as though it were contaminated. Mikel wasn't going to answer. At best, William paid him daily to do a job, and he didn't even have the courtesy to respond to his phone calls. At worst, he was sitting in a police interview, spilling his guts to the police and informing them every time William called his number.

He pulled the jack out of the wall but still didn't feel safe. There was a knife sitting on the kitchen counter, and William grabbed it and sliced through the line. Backtracking to the living room, he stopped to gulp the last of his scotch, then slid off the back of his mobile phone, popped the battery out, and removed the sim card.

William twisted the tiny piece of cardboard and metal between his fingers, but it stayed intact while his fingertips dented from the pressure. He put it between his teeth, the small, wired components striking a metallic spark off his molar filling, and bit and tore until it was twisted and useless.

He flushed it down the rubbish disposal in the kitchen sink to be sure. There. The police couldn't trace his calls now.

Deb dropped by her desk to fish out any messages. She'd been out in the field collecting samples from the barn where Ngaire had uncovered the lock of hair, much to Gascoigne's disgust. It had made for an awkward phone call. Deb didn't enjoy shutting her out.

Even less so because Ngaire was the only reason anyone had taken the Lynton case seriously to begin with, but the DS had made things clear. Information was only to be shared with other officers.

If Ngaire hadn't passed her knowledge to Finlay in the beginning, perhaps he would have overlooked a few more incidents, but things were what they were. She'd never seen the DS as angry as when Deb informed him that Finlay was the one looking after Ngaire at the moment.

There was an e-mail from the lab, and Deb typed her password into the link it contained to access the information.

Ngaire's hair sample was useless. Pretty, strange, and awful, but useless. Hair without a follicle attached was chancy, even with the equipment they had now to magnify even the tiniest trace, but after being stored for forty years in a barn? Nothing. Even with the Minifiler DNA analysis.

There was no surprise there, but still Deb's stomach sank. Finding that piece of evidence was the first time they'd corroborated Paul's story. The first piece in a real case. Now, unusable. The hair could come from anybody. Anything, even. The only evidential weight it carried was in hers and Ngaire's minds. Something had happened that differed from the official version. A strange old man could have told them the truth.

Deb scrolled and saw another report attached. The evidence bag she'd retrieved from the slurry after she'd hung a rope ladder over the side. Her heart had beaten fast while she was down there. If it had been anyone but Ngaire propelling her forward, Deb would've forced someone else to do it.

The storm water had drained out of the slurry, leaving only a mess of twigs, dirt, and branches. Deb spent the whole time on edge in case somebody decided that a fun trick would be to sluice water along the base

of the milking shed. It had been a long time since she'd
been a probationary constable and subject to ribbing
and pranks, but there were still occasions where
someone would flex his or her funny bone.

Deb had little sense of humor at the best of
times. At the bottom of a slurry where her friend had
almost died didn't qualify as the best of times by any
stretch.

She'd found the packet lodged against the drain.
Other pieces of debris had washed up there, the
reflective glint of plastic catching her eye more than
once before she spotted the real thing. The plastic had
caught on a twig, and the packet tore as Deb pulled it
free. She recorded it in her notebook.

At first sight, there'd been nothing showing in
the packet. A slight stain on the right side. Deb had
lodged it with the ESR offices but hadn't been holding
her breath. She'd submitted Ngaire's results, too: as the
sample had touched her skin, they didn't want to target
her by accident.

It was blood. Human blood. Despite the
degraded state of the sample, the ESR had produced a
result. It matched nobody on file, but if it belonged to
Magdalene, as Deb assumed, it wouldn't.

"Sir," she called as Gascoigne walked out of his
office. "Could I have a word?"

The look he gave her reminded her that there
was a dog house, and she was sitting in the middle of it,
but he came over to look.

"Do we have anything to match it to?"

"Not at the moment," Deb answered. "You're
happy for me to approach the parents?"

He nodded once, then left. At least with him
angry at her, she got out of the building quicker. Doug
was hanging about the front desk, chatting with Genna.
Or, chatting up Genna, to be more precise. Deb
wondered whether there was a bet in place. If that was
why he'd put the effort in lately. If there were a wager,

she wouldn't mind backing him for a win.

"Want to come out on an assignment?" Deb asked. "Gascoigne just okayed it."

Doug sighed theatrically, and Genna laughed. He dragged his feet back to his desk to log the job, then again as he grabbed his jacket. Deb gritted her teeth and waited, even though it must be in the high seventies outside by now. Detective Doug Redding was a year less experienced than she. In the pecking order of seniority, she outranked him, even though she didn't outrank him. Some officers paid attention to that stuff. The police taught you respect for hierarchy along with interview techniques and arrest protocol, but it slipped when it came to the gender gap. Deb just kept thinking that if she gritted her teeth long enough, she'd get to senior one year before Redding, and then the ranking wouldn't be imaginary. It would be on her epaulets for everyone to see. One year of glorious comeuppance. One day.

"Where're we going?" Redding asked in the car. He'd insisted on driving, but impractically hadn't researched any of the details.

"Retirement home out Northfield way," Deb replied. She pulled the GPS over and typed the address in, then banged the screen back toward him with ill grace. If Ngaire hadn't got her head bashed in, then she would've fielded this one alone. It was unreasonable to hold her responsible, but it was hard to exercise reason when everything was turning into a pain in her ass. "It's one of the back units, past the hospital."

Redding nodded and started whistling. Deb leaned back against the headrest and wished for a pair of earplugs.

Mary Lynton smiled at Deb and bared her teeth at Redding. *A good judge of character, then,* thought Deb. She brought out her extragood manners as a silent thank-you.

"I'm sorry to trouble you again, Mrs. Lynton. I wondered if you still retained any of your daughter's personal possessions? A toothbrush or comb, maybe?"

The likelihood was low, but it'd be the easiest. But Mary was shaking her head. "Goodness no, dear. We gave away all of Magdalene's possessions when we left the church. The only things we carry," she said tapping her head, "are up here."

"In that case," Deb continued, "I wonder if you and your husband would submit to a DNA test. We've discovered evidence we think may be important to your daughter's case, but we don't have a sample to match it to."

Mary Lynton smiled and nodded. "And what does that involve, dear?" she asked. "What do you need?"

"We can take a swab from the inside of your cheek, like a large cotton bud. It doesn't hurt. Otherwise, if you're not comfortable doing that, I could take a personal item—a used toothbrush or a comb with hair on it—and we can try to get a sample from that."

Mary left the room, talking back over her shoulder. "I don't think Abe would be happy about the swab, nor me. If you stick something in our mouths these days, we both gag." She brought back two toothbrushes and put them into the bags that Deb held open, labeling each and confirming with Mary that she'd assigned the colored handles correctly.

"What's happening with that nice, young detective?" Mary asked. "The other one. Ngaire."

"She's recovering at home at the moment. Whoever hurt her did a lot of damage."

"But she'll be okay?" Mary pressed.

Deb looked at her, surprised at the level of concern. As far as she knew, Ngaire had only visited Mary once more than she had, but the woman had tears in her eyes.

"Given time to recover, we hope she'll get back to normal. She's had a nasty head injury, though," she stressed, watching for the reaction. "There's every chance she'll have permanent damage."

Mary flinched. Deb was sure of it. Mary had flinched. She looked back at Redding to see whether he'd noted the reaction, but he was staring at the plethora of knick-knacks cluttering the shelves. Tiny figurines that looked as though they formed part of a Mills and Boon collectible set.

"Is your husband around, Mary?" Deb asked. "We'd like to talk to him again about what he was doing the day Ngaire was attacked." She stressed Ngaire's name, her first name, trying to make a stronger connection. "In your statement you said he was at home all day?"

Mary nodded, and her focus moved to her clasped hands resting in her lap. "That's right. He was here all day."

"That's unusual for him, isn't it?"

"What do you mean? No."

"Well, he's not here now. When Ngaire visited to collect the keys, he wasn't here. Are you sure he was at home that day?"

Mary stared up at Redding, then her gaze flicked over Deb before returning to her lap.

"I'm sure," she said. Deb waited, looking for another way in. Mary was holding her shoulders set and stiff, her back upright. It could be from the questioning, or it could be from guilt.

"Ngaire's noted that your husband has to go for a walk each day, because of his hip operation, is that right?"

Mary nodded.

"But not that day?"

Mary shook her head.

"Does he take other days off walking? You said his hips would seize up if he didn't."

Mary just stared at her hands. No response. Deb waited for a full two minutes, hoping Mary would crack the uncomfortable silence, but she held still and silent.

"Okay," Deb said and stood up. "Well, thank you very much for your time today, Mrs. Lynton. I hope we'll be able to give you some news soon about Magdalene's case."

Mary nodded, then frowned and looked up.

"What's the DNA for?"

Deb sat again. She usually dealt with a younger generation steeped in *CSI* and *Bones*. Sometimes she assumed that everybody understood.

"We'll use the toothbrushes to establish a DNA marker for both you and your husband," she explained. "It's like a fingerprint, only a lot more detailed and a lot less likely to match with someone else. Once we have those, we'll compare it to the sample we believe came from Magdalene. Because she's your daughter, we'll then be able to compare her markers with yours and your husband's to see if we have a match."

Mary looked up and made eye contact again. "Does it matter that we'd adopted Magdalene?"

Deb sat very still. Her blood rushed through her body, pumping from her chest and flowing out to her throbbing fingertips. She glanced at the bags that Redding now held. There'd be no way to collect a match for Magdalene. The only evidence Ngaire had collected that might tie her to Paul's confession, to prove her murder, had gone. Even after making his confession, he'd gotten away clean.

"Yes," Redding said when Deb didn't respond. "That means we won't be able to match your samples to the ones we've retrieved." He put the bags on the table. "Thanks anyway," he said and gave Deb a poke in the back.

"Thank you, Mary," she said and stood once again. "I'll be in touch if we make any progress. Would you like to take my card?" She extended the business card with her mobile and work numbers. She'd given it to her once, the first visit they'd made, but she made sure that Mary caught her eye this time while she still held it between her fingers. "Call me if there's anything you need to discuss," she said. "Anything."

Mary nodded, and they left, Deb clutching the bags to her chest as though they'd be stolen away. Outside, she looked up at the ornate metal and glass lights that dotted the internal streets of the home. Made to look like gas lighting, as though it were better, classier, than electric.

There were also cameras. CCTV mounted on every street corner, pointed at an angle to catch the doorways. A precaution against residents collapsing unnoticed more than a defense against crime.

Redding followed her gaze and nodded. "Head office is back at the entrance," he said. "I'm sure they'll be happy to oblige with the footage."

They were.

Chapter Twenty-One

Deb knocked on DS Gascoigne's door, and he motioned her inside. "Any progress?"

"We may have found a lead in Ngaire's assault case, sir," she said. He waved his hand at the chair, and she sat, balancing her papers on her knees.

"What have you got?"

"Redding and I paid a visit to Mary Lynton this morning to get samples to compare with the ones recovered from the cross." Gascoigne flapped his hand at her, *hurry up.* "Turns out her and her husband aren't Magdalene's biological parents, so that was pointless, but during our conversation I got the feeling her alibi for her husband may not be reliable. We retrieved the CCTV footage from the retirement village on the day. It shows Abe Lynton heading out of the village at eight-thirty in the morning and not returning until almost nine o'clock that night."

Gascoigne leaned back in his chair and looked up at the ceiling. "What is he, eighty?"

"Seventy-six, sir."

"And you think he's capable of the attack? On Ngaire and Isaiah." He waited for a moment, then, when Deb nodded, he continued. "What about the crucifix? Ngaire said she had trouble maneuvering it, and she's half his age. How did he drag it out to cut it up into pieces?"

"Look, sir, I'm as ageist as the next person, but I think he's capable of doing it all." She thought back to meeting him. The way he'd towered over the table full of women, washing his greasy hands clean on an old cloth that started life as a singlet. "He looks strong."

"Pass his registration over to the motor squad to see if they can place his vehicle, then. I want more than 'he was out at the time' before you bring him in."

He turned back to his computer, but when Deb didn't jump to her feet he looked back at her. "What?"

"Well, the Lyntons are Magdalene's adoptive parents, sir. We won't be able to use samples from them to compare to the evidence Ngaire collected."

Gascoigne sat back in his chair and again looked at the ceiling before wiping his face with his palm. "And I'll guess from your silence they have no personal items hanging around in good condition for us to use?"

Deb shook her head. "No, sir. Mrs. Lynton told us they destroyed or gave away all Magdalene's possessions when they left the church. We could've tried to get something from her room, she painted all over the walls, but Isaiah's over-painted everything in there a dozen times. There won't be any traces left."

The DS tapped on his keyboard for a few moments, then used his mouse to click, click, click. "Here," he said and turned the screen so Deb could see. "It says here that there was a secret compartment in the floorboards. Would there be something there we could use?"

"For fingerprints, maybe, but not DNA. It was just a few packets of condoms and a twist of weed."

He rubbed his forehead with his hand. Deb noticed for the first time how much the dark brown of his hair was being replaced with white. Saw how the lines on his face that used to appear with expressions now appeared there at rest.

"So, where does that leave us?"

"I don't know, sir. The only way I can think to get a sample to match would be to exhume her body."

"No."

"Sir, there's also the matter of her pregnancy.

The confession note indicated that although Billy Glover was her boyfriend—"

"No."

"—he wasn't the father of her child. At the very least—"

"No."

"—we may be able to pin statutory rape on someone."

"No, no, no, no, no." Gascoigne got to his feet and leaned over the desk at Deb. She shrank back but didn't concede.

"Sir, I know it's not a popular option—"

"Stop, Weedon. Just stop. It's not an option at all. This is a forty-year-old case with no evidence to back up anything so far." He held up his hand to stop Deb's protest. "No evidence we could present in court. We will not alienate the Lyntons, not to mention enrage the public, by exhuming a body just to collect samples."

"Is there another way?"

He frowned at her, the muscles in his jaw clenched. "That's my question to you. You're the one heading the case. Is there another way?"

She shook her head and felt her lower lip trying to stick out. Deb bit on it to stop it. She didn't need to look like a sulky child in front of her DS.

"If there isn't," Gascoigne continued when she didn't answer, "then it's about time we wrap this up. Concentrate on finding Ngaire's attacker, and get the Lynton girl case closed off. We've spent enough time chasing ghosts."

Finlay came inside, hauling three plastic bags of groceries, to find Ngaire seated on the floor. Pages of files radiated out from her in a meters-long starburst on the newly cleaned carpet.

For a second, images from *A Beautiful Mind* and *Homeland* flashed into his head, Ngaire skipping into the land of full-blown mental illness, but then he saw that she'd laid them out in sequence. Everything she still retained of the Lynton case, the majority of it provided by him.

He thought of asking her what she was doing, but it was pointless because, from the look of it, what she was doing was obsessing.

"Need any help?" he asked instead.

"Come here," she said, gesturing him over. "What do you see?"

"Lots of paper," he said and kneeled next to Ngaire in her plague circle.

"Over there, that's the stuff that confirms the original coroner's verdict," she explained, waving her arm to her right. "In front is the stuff that supports Paul's version of events. The hair, the . . ." she trailed off. "Well, just the hair and his letter. Over here," she waved to her left, "is the stuff that fits nowhere."

Finlay looked closer at the layout. There were reports she shouldn't have in her hot little hands, and he wondered whether Deb was back on board with the "Ngaire can do no wrong" brigade. There were notes that Ngaire had written up herself; bullet points as though someone had talked while she scribbled phrases to help her remember.

"Deb doesn't think she'll be able to match the sample from the cross."

Finlay frowned. "Weren't they able to get results for it?"

Ngaire nodded, "Yeah, but there's nothing to compare it to. Apparently Magdalene was adopted."

Finlay sat back on his heels and frowned. He didn't remember that coming up in his research, and he'd talked to many people. "Is she sure?"

Ngaire looked over to him and shrugged. "I assume she checked."

"Don't they have something else they could test?"

"Not forty years down the track. The whole case is dead in the water." A single tear ran down Ngaire's cheek before she sniffed and wiped it away.

"What about Magdalene herself?"

"I don't think a judge will let them exhume just to test blood found on the property where she lived. We don't know if it belonged to her, and even if they could prove that, we don't know it had a bearing on her death. It'd just cause a big public fight."

"Maybe not," Finlay said and got to his feet. He'd written something down in his notebook, he was sure.

"Why not?"

"Just give me a minute," he said. The book was a disorganized scrawl of people, places, and things. Trigger words to prompt him to remember later. Sometimes the triggers were so vague he couldn't even work out which story he'd been chasing when he wrote them. "Here it is," he said, showing her. *Two against one?* he'd noted in his deplorable handwriting.

"And what does that mean?"

"You told me earlier it seemed odd the council would side with the Lyntons to keep the cemetery intact, two against one. That the other couples should consult a lawyer."

Ngaire held her hands up, she didn't remember.

"Well, I did it for them, as a hypothetical. Do you have the title deed?"

Ngaire nodded and looked among her spread of paper to pick up the title deed and the nonprofit incorporation forms.

She held it out to him. "Here you go."

He ran down the list of names and checked it against his notebook. "Kelvin and Margarite," he said. He pulled out his phone and scrolled through the ever-extending list of contacts until he found the number he wanted.

"Hey Marge," he said by way of welcome. "It's Finlay Ewan here. I don't know if you remember . . ."

He held the phone farther from his ear at her effusive insistence that she remembered exactly who he was and how lovely to hear from him after all this time. He was always charming when out on the road trawling for information. You never knew when it'd come in handy.

"It's lovely to speak to you again, also," he said. "But I was calling about something that's delicate. I hope you don't mind."

No, she didn't mind.

"Are you still pursuing an exhumation order to rebury your daughter in the Little River Cemetery?"

Marge sighed. "We've tried, but we can't get it through."

"What about the Gibsons? Are they still trying?"

She sighed again, but he was piquing her interest. "Yes they are. The last time they told us that unless something changed, not to bother again. Why? What's happened."

"If you and the Gibsons want to, you can wind up the church altogether," Finlay said. "The farm would no longer be a protected asset. You'd be able to sell it."

"But how does that help me with Hannah?" The name of her baby sounded strange in Finlay's ear. A word spoken so seldom, she hesitated at the pronunciation.

"If the land isn't a church asset, the cemetery won't be a valid spot for burial. They'll relocate it instead. It's done with private cemeteries all the time."

He might've stretched that too far, but he had his fingers crossed in case anyone was watching.

"And that'll work?" she asked, her voice sounding more hopeful than doubtful.

Finlay shifted his phone to the other ear, sweat building up on his right side. "I can't guarantee anything, but it's a good chance. I've got a few friends I can call on to help you," Finlay said. His phone was full of numbers from people who owed him a favor. "If you want to go ahead, that is. I don't want to force you into anything."

There was a rustle, and then Kelvin's voice came on the line. "You're not forcing us into anything, Finlay. Thank the Lord if he's helped us out of this tangle."

He hung up the phone and turned to see Ngaire clap her hands. "That was spectacular," she said. "Is there nothing you can't fix?"

He pulled her toward him and planted his lips on hers, his mouth open. He cupped her chin in his hands, wanting the moment to last, but she pushed away and wiped her mouth.

"My rent," Finlay said, stifling his hurt behind a joke. "Do you want to call Deb, let her know?"

It was just after midday, a week later, when DS Gascoigne strode out of his office and approached Deb's desk.

"We've got permission," he said and put the printed form on her desk. "The court let us rush it through, so we can go any time from now. Is someone from the Ministry available?"

Deb nodded. A representative from the Ministry of Health had to be present at any exhumation. Forty years after burial it was unlikely there'd be any public health issues to speak of, but stupid laws were still laws. "He and the cemetery crew are ready to go." She paused for a moment. "Are we doing this right now?"

Gascoigne nodded. "The sooner we can get it done, the less time the press has to get hold of it. Even with the camouflage of the other participants, it will not be pretty."

"Sir, can Ngaire come along to the scene? I know she'll want to be there."

He shook his head. "Until she's back on duty, I don't want her within a mile of this case."

"Just as an observer, though?"

Gascoigne sighed and rubbed the back of his neck. He looked back toward his office—Deb imagined he wished he was safe within its confines—then shrugged. "I can't stop her if she's got permission from the landowners to be there, but make sure she understands if her boyfriend's tagline ends up on anything scandalous, she's in deep. Got it?"

Deb nodded. "He's not her boyfriend, but I'll tell her."

"Whatever. Let me know when you've got a confirmed time. I'll square up a few uniformed officers to guard the main gate."

"Yes, sir."

Deb had worked out the technicalities for the exhumation the day before, so it was short work to organize the internment officers and the clerk from the Health Ministry.

Last, she called Ngaire to give her the news.

Chapter Twenty-Two

"Park the car on the berm," Ngaire said as Finlay complained for the third time. "Over there," she pointed to a wide spot that looked like it had plenty of room in front of the deep ditch.

"How many are attending this bloody thing?" Finlay muttered. "I didn't think it was a spectator sport."

There were a dozen vehicles parked along the road. The police had blocked off the drive into the compound with a chain and police tape, although two officers were letting people through on either side.

"The couples who still own the property, the police, the guys to supervise the disinterment, the men to perform the disinterment, the cemetery owner where the new interment will happen, you and me."

"Grave digging never used to draw these crowds," Finlay said. "These modern types, I don't know."

"Stop complaining, and give me a hand," Ngaire said, holding her arms out on either side for balance. With the rain they'd had, the berm was soft mud under the long overgrown weeds and grass.

The officers stopped them at the gate, but let them through when both Deb and Marge came running up in welcome.

"I'd watch out," Deb warned as she gave Ngaire, then Finlay, a hug. "Gascoigne's not happy about the whole thing, and sweet little Mary Lynton is on the warpath."

Ngaire watched Mary from a distance as she

followed along behind DS Gascoigne, dogging his every step. She was waving her hands in the air, and even from her position across the yard Ngaire could hear her voice raised in anger.

She gripped Finlay's arm tighter. Although she'd known that Mary and Abe Lynton wouldn't be happy with the plan, at a deeper level she'd hoped that they'd accept it. Or wouldn't show up to watch.

More uniformed officers were pulling a cloth barrier around the grave site. It was similar to the tents they used to cover bodies found outside, to keep them private and away from prying eyes, but there was no top. The diggers weren't two burly blokes with shovels but an actual digger.

Off to one side were three waiting caskets. They were larger than normal, in both height and width, as they were designed for the exhumed coffins to be placed inside before reburial. The originals would no longer be fit to be used, so they'd be put in the new coffins. The forensic sampling would then occur before they loaded them in the long, black hearse parked off to the side of the housing block, ready to carry them to their new resting place.

Scene examiners were standing by. They'd dressed in plastic suiting, masks, booties, and gloves in preparation, and Ngaire saw a mobile DNA analyzer, the size of a briefcase, at their feet. It meant they should know the results within a few hours, rather than the days or weeks a standard processed sample could take.

"Do they know about the baby?" Ngaire whispered to Deb, pointing at her own abdomen in demonstration.

Deb nodded. "They know. If there's enough of her left, they might take her back to the pathology suite and try to do as many tests on her as they can." She sighed and shifted from one foot to another. "No one's expecting that to happen, though. Even with embalming, there's little chance of tissue being left."

Ngaire felt a flow of bile up the back of her throat and tilted her head to stare at the clouds overhead until she could swallow it back. So easy to think of this process as solely to gather evidence, help the case, find new clues, but the reality of what they would be doing was becoming stronger.

They'd dig up a grave, pull out a coffin, then reveal a body that was decades old. As with what the grave robbers of earlier times did, there was no dignity in this procedure.

Ngaire saw the Maples, Kelvin and Marge, standing off to one side. They weren't talking, just holding hands while they tried to keep out of the way. Unlike Mary Lynton, Marge looked at peace—as though her stillborn daughter, who had never been properly buried, were not being unearthed for the world to see but rather was finally being laid to rest.

Deb explained that there were two cemetery managers on site. One from Little River, where both the Maples and the Gibsons had opted to lay their loved ones to rest. The community they'd forged ties with after the church decamped and left them without enough money to move to central Christchurch. And one from Yaldhurst Cemetery, the closest operating cemetery to the land they stood on. Without a directive from the family, this was the option chosen for Magdalene's remains—one of the oldest cemeteries in Christchurch. Used to dealing with bereavement and grief, they stood near the heart of the activity but drew no attention to themselves.

"Ngaire!" someone called behind her. Ngaire turned and saw both DS Gascoigne and Mary Lynton bearing down on her. It was Mary who was calling. "Ngaire, thank goodness you're here. Could you please tell these officers they need to stop? I won't have Magdalene disturbed."

Ngaire put her arm around Mary's shoulder and walked her away from the group. "I can't do that. I'm sorry. I'm not even on active duty at the moment. I'm just here to make sure nothing terrible happens."

Mary stopped walking and twisted her shoulder free of Ngaire's hand. "Nothing terrible happens? Do you know what they're doing? They're digging up my daughter's grave."

"I'm sorry, Mary. I can't imagine how distressing this is to you. Would you like me to take you home? You don't have to watch this happen." When Mary didn't respond, Ngaire leaned forward and touched her on the hand. "They'll take good care of her, Mary."

"Who will? The people who are cutting her up to take samples?"

"It'll only take a tiny sample, Mary, like taking a pinprick from your finger before you give blood. They won't disfigure or deform her." Ngaire turned back to check that the lab analysts were still available. "If it'll make you feel easier, I can introduce you to the woman who'll be processing the samples from your daughter. They can take you through everything step-by-step so you understand what's happening."

Mary sobbed in response and clutched her arms across her ribs as though she were holding herself together. "I don't need to talk to them to understand what's happening. My daughter is being dug up from the ground and exposed to everyone." She wiped her hand hard across her eyes, slapping the tears away. "She's my daughter, she's not a piece of evidence."

"But don't you want to know for certain how your daughter died?" Ngaire asked. "We may tell that from her body. If she was murdered, then we may prove it."

Mary stepped back from her and shook her head. "She's been dead for forty years, what does it matter now? Her so-called murderer is dead. Are you going to lock up his corpse?"

"No, but . . ." Ngaire trailed off as she lost the words to explain. She thought it was better to know.

Better to pinpoint a crime if one had been committed, regardless of whether it resulted in a conviction or punishment. Better always to know the truth, even when it hurts.

But that was a personal philosophy, and it would be no comfort to the shattered woman in front of her bearing the unimaginable torment of a legal grave robbing.

Mary walked away, and Ngaire felt her judgment as a cold fact. She was useless. Her pursuit of the truth was useless. Its fruit would be rotten.

"Ngaire," DS Gascoigne called out, beckoning her with his hand. "I hear you're coming back to work next week."

She nodded. Her progress with the physio had been strong enough to warrant her sitting at a desk in the station again. Ngaire hoped that there weren't any wiretaps ongoing.

"Just make sure you don't overstep your bounds today," he warned. "I'm happy for you to observe, but I want nothing further."

Ngaire nodded. "Mary was upset. She seemed to think I'd be able to stop this."

"No doubt about it," Gascoigne said. "This will be a rough day. Not only for the Lyntons."

An operator got into the digger and moved it near the graveyard. It trundled over the white stones marking the edge, into the circle. Ngaire saw the markers, the painted rock, the Buzzy Bee, which had delineated the graves now lay to one side.

The clerk from the Health Ministry walked over to them and introduced himself as Lionel Peters. He was pale-skinned, and his suit was at odds with the dress of everyone else. He didn't look like a man used to working outdoors.

"Hiya," he said to the group at large, the casual greeting belying the formal nature of his clothing. Then he turned and stood in a line with them to watch.

"Have you attended one of these before?" Ngaire asked. He'd ended up beside her, and she found it easier to turn to him and make conversation than to watch the proceedings.

He looked grateful for the distraction, too. "A couple, not this old. Most of the reburials we do are because the cemeteries stuff up the original burial. They catch those pretty quickly, most of the time."

"What do you mean, stuff up?"

"Bury the wrong body in the wrong plot. Then they go to bury the real owner and find it's already occupied." His face became animated as he talked, getting into the groove as he shared his knowledge. "It's about sixty percent of the cases. Or they're really, really old, and the council needs them moved for development reasons. Like this," he conceded. "Think of *Poltergeist*, but they actually move the bodies."

Finlay laughed and turned away from the burial site. Ngaire noticed that he looked green around the gills. "What about the earthquake damage? Did anything come out of that?"

Lionel shook his head. "Not involving us. Most of that the council handled in their day-to-day repairs. Headstones, cracks in the earth. Nothing major."

Sounds from the digger drew their attention back to the scene. It was struggling to lift earth that had compacted over decades, even though the recent rainfall had softened the topsoil. The fat metal lip of the digger cracked through the hardened topsoil and scraped a shallow path through.

Mary Lynton screamed. For a moment, Ngaire thought she'd throw herself in the path of the machine, and her muscles tensed for action. Instead, she stopped beside the operator cage and yelled at the poor man trapped inside. "Careful! You be more careful." She thumped on the metal side of the excavator in emphasis.

DS Gascoigne caught her arm and pulled her

away. She let him but kept her eyes fixed on the driver until the tent tarpaulin shielded him from her line of sight. Gascoigne escorted her back beside her husband.

Abe Lynton stood with his back fixed in place, a posture that reminded Ngaire of the army. His crossed arms and set expression of anger denied the link, however, as did his age. He didn't even acknowledge his wife's outburst or pay her attention.

Ngaire remembered the hidden packet of biscuits back in their house. The strict gender lines that had been enforced at the commune. Deb suspected him of being involved in the attack on her, and Ngaire could imagine the man striking a woman, overpowering her.

The Lyntons had built a new life for themselves. One that didn't intersect with their earlier life on the compound. Then, Ngaire had brought a stinking heap of a murder confession and dumped it into the middle of their contained household. Would that have been enough to drive him to attack her?

As though he felt her gaze as a physical reality, Abe turned his head and looked into Ngaire's eyes. For a moment she was back, lying on the ground. After being hit over the head or having her leg muscle sliced, she couldn't tell. She lay still with fear enveloping her because the next step would be the last step. The next thing that happened would be her life ending.

Ngaire gasped and took a step backward, the movement jerking her out of the flashback. Finlay turned, but she shook her head and took another step away. "Just having trouble catching my breath," she said. A sentence she wouldn't have been able to say if it were true.

The fear was back. She thought it had gone, left her an officer not only capable of doing her job but hungry for it. To have the panic, the fear, the terror, dumped back over her like a bucket of ice water shocked her. Cold fear cored into her center and left her empty. Left her bereft.

* * *

It was the Maples' stillborn daughter they lifted up first. The coffin was tiny, its own sad story told in the lines of the hand-carved wood. Thick layers of varnish had been applied to the solid oak panels. The joins had been planed until they fit perfectly and the joists sealed with glue.

Workmanship was love. Kelvin Maples had given his baby daughter the only gift she would ever use, and he'd poured his heart into it.

When they raised the coffin, the workmen having abandoned the machinery to stand at the grave with ropes to handle the move with delicacy, Marge stared across the grounds at Abe Lynton. Ngaire frowned, puzzled, and turned to see why, but there was nothing she could see. Marge waited until he looked back at her and gave a small nod, then she pressed herself into her husband. She stayed there, hiding the sight from her eyes until she couldn't stand it any longer and turned to look. She gave a cry, of despair, of hope, of love. Ngaire saw her muscles tense against the urge to run to her child. Poised, even now, she waited until the casket was laid inside the other one, and the men moved away, before she walked over to it.

There was no need to lift the lid to reveal the contents. Marge pressed her fingers to her lips, then pressed the kiss onto the wooden box. She wound her hand around her husband, and they closed their eyes, mouthing words that no one else could hear. A prayer for their little girl.

Then it was the Gibsons' turn. Samuel's father's grave was the second one in, deeper than the Maples' daughter because he was an adult. The digger took small, careful scoops, not wanting to impinge on the grave next door. Not wishing to knock a digger-size hole in Magdalene's side.

There was less emotion here. A child losing his parent was, at least, the correct order of progression for death, even though the man had still died young by the standards of the day. Finlay whispered to her that he'd moved to the farm to "help" his son when he first grew sick and died within the year. Ngaire imagined they held that time as precious, though the image of her own mother or father moving to live with her, if one of them grew sick, filled her with negative thoughts.

This coffin hadn't been crafted to last. The sides were standard pine and had been deteriorated by the elements, despite the oil finish. As the men moved in to dig around the edges and hook together the ropes and pulley to lever the casket out, Ngaire saw one cast a concerned glance back over his shoulder. Lionel Peters noticed, too, and walked over to the graveside.

After a short consultation, he moved back to his vehicle and pulled what appeared to be a fitted sheet out of the back. The rustle as it moved led Ngaire to the conclusion that it was plastic. He waited while the final excavation continued, then passed it to the men, who smoothed it around the edges.

He joined their group again, his face contained, but a shade lighter. "Didn't hold up so well," he answered when Finlay gave him an inquiring glance. "Forty years is a long time."

They attached rope and pulleys back to the digger, then the men stood back to watch the lift. There was no way for them to raise a grown man by hand. The excavator lifted and extended its mouth, and the coffin came free with a sucking sound. As the box moved level, then a foot above the ground, the onlookers seemed to hold their collective breath.

There was a damp crack in the morning air.

Lionel had time to say, "Oh, shit" under his breath before the bottom of the coffin gave way. The ropes holding it aloft had been placed a short distance from the head and foot of the coffin, leaving the middle open to crack and spill its contents. As the rotted wood sagged and splintered, it exposed satin lining eaten black by mold.

The operator turned as fast as he could, swinging his cargo low across the ground to the waiting casket. As he positioned it, there was another crack, and the base gave way, spilling its contents into the waiting coffin. Ngaire released the breath she'd been holding and felt like cheering the driver, *good job*.

Mary Lynton screamed. This time, it wasn't a word or a phrase, it was a low-pitched howl that pulled from her belly into the still air. She crossed her arms tight, the muscles bulging with the effort, but she couldn't contain herself. On and on it sounded, raising the hackles on Ngaire's neck in sympathy.

Abe Lynton stood next to her, seeming not to notice. Until he abruptly turned and yelled into her face, "Get ahold of yourself, woman." His arm raised back as if to strike.

It was Mary that struck instead. Pummeling his chest and arms and head with her fists. Continuing her heartfelt screams.

"Your fault," she said, words entering the doleful sounds she was making. "It's all your fault. Just tell the damn police what you did, and we can go home. Tell them."

A fist strike on Abe's ear drew blood. His nose was swelling, his collarbone and cheeks red where her blows had struck. He grabbed at her wrists, but she pulled free.

"Don't you let them do this, not to Magdalene." She punched him hard in the upper lip, and it swelled in immediate response. "Make them stop. Tell them what you did to my daughter," she screamed.

Marge ran to Mary's side and caught hold of her arms. Mary twisted free and spat at her face. "Get off me, you cunt. God saw what you did. Have a nice time in hell with your baby."

Abe punched her in the diaphragm, and Mary crumpled to the ground, her face coloring purple. DS

Gascoigne ran to her side, while the operator from the digger jumped from his cab and walked over. He was over six feet and stood toe-to-toe with Abe Lynton, outweighing him by a good fifty pounds. When Abe took a step sideways, to go around him, the man said, "You don't want to do that, friend," and grabbed Abe's shoulder with one massive hand to hold him still.

The workers from the graveside moved in as backup, one to either side. Lionel and the cemetery operators walked across to form a back line while DS Gascoigne moved Mary out of the circle, out of harm's way.

They remained in a standoff, one old man facing his younger counterparts, until Abe spat on the ground and turned to walk to his car. When it appeared the line would stop him leaving, he tooted his horn until they broke formation and stepped aside.

"Should we . . ." Ngaire began, then stopped as she saw Deb take her radio out, calling to the officers standing guard at the property's gate.

"Hold him," she ordered, then strode toward the exit. "I'm arresting him for assault, male on female."

Chapter Twenty-Three

Ngaire walked through the front door and dropped straight on the sofa. The air whooshed out of the cushions, and Finlay laughed from the doorway.

"Do you feel like pizza?" Ngaire asked. *I don't want to cook,* the obvious subtext.

"Sure," he said and pulled out his phone. A few button clicks later, and dinner was on its way.

Ngaire lifted the arm of her jacket and sniffed. "Can you still smell it?"

Finlay nodded. "We should put these straight in the wash. Otherwise, the smell will never come out."

Ngaire nodded but stayed where she was. Her eyes closed, and she couldn't be bothered to open them.

The day hadn't improved after Mary's outburst. Deb hauled Abe back to the station for questioning, ecstatic that she had a legal right to detain him. Gascoigne, meanwhile, coaxed Mary, Marge, and Kelvin into a ride to the station to clear things up.

Left to their own devices, the exhumation party continued on with their job as though nothing had happened, and they lifted Magdalene's coffin out of the packed earth. There were no dramatic developments, and the casket held together on its swinging path to the new coffin. The largest bother was for the lab techs to prize the lid off. After so many years, the nails and bonding glue had formed an impenetrable seal, and they had to attack it with chisels to leverage it up.

Curiosity overriding her squeamishness, Ngaire had strolled closer for a look. Magdalene had occupied her mind for so long now, she couldn't leave without catching a glimpse.

There was nothing much left to her. Embalming had toughened her skin, which had then worn paper-thin against her skeleton in the years she'd occupied her grave. The team working to gather samples shook their heads when Ngaire asked if they'd be able to decide a cause of death; there was not enough left to provide evidence, considering that the methods available would be difficult to use even in a recent victim. They had, however, found fetal remains inside the coffin. The techs had removed teeth buds to provide a DNA sample. Given Magdalene's age when she became pregnant, there'd be evidence to convict somebody of a crime if they could find a match to an older male.

Ngaire thought of Billy: both the man she'd met as Paul Worthington's lawyer and the neighbor's boy he'd written of in his letter.

"For years I told myself that Billy killed her; it was his fault."

Paul's logic was skewed by self-interest and denial, but perhaps a crime existed there. Maybe Paul had reason to blame Billy because of the actions Billy had taken, instead of the ones he hadn't. Actions like getting a fourteen-year-old girl pregnant.

As Ngaire had promised Mary, the technicians took good care of her daughter. Careful but quick, they finished taking their samples and released the casket for closure within half an hour. They placed the samples collected from Magdalene's skin into the portable analyzer, while they kept the fetal teeth for the lab. A more intensive process would be required to extract a DNA sample from them.

The cemetery men loaded the new coffins into the waiting hearse: two in one, one in the other, and drove out in procession before parting ways at the first corner. The Gibsons followed along after theirs, and

Ngaire watched the second until it was out of sight in the distance. Magdalene's funeral procession, one lone hearse.

Ngaire had been tempted to follow, but the light was fading out of the sky, and her head throbbed with each beat of blood through her temples. After standing all day, she was desperate for to sit, to rest.

Lionel came over to say good-bye and shook her hand, an oddly formal gesture, under the circumstances. As he walked to his car, he called, "See you," over his shoulder as though he expected to bump into them again.

"Do you want to scout around before we leave?" Finlay asked in response to a suggestion she'd made that morning. Back when she felt fit and healthy. He appeared when she shook her head. Home was the one place Ngaire wanted to be.

With a start, Ngaire opened her eyes. Finlay had banged the sofa with his leg, disturbing her light slumber. "Pizza's up," he said, placing the hot cardboard containers in front of her, then walked to the fridge with their desserts.

Sniffing decomposition on her clothing again, Ngaire went into the bedroom to change before she could put herself off eating. After throwing them into the washing machine, she took a piece of pizza and sat, legs crossed. A week ago she hadn't been able to do that. Her physical progress was picking up speed.

"I'm doing a story," Finlay said as he walked back and sat next to her. "On the case."

"You've already done a story," Ngaire pointed out as she scooped up mozzarella cheese falling from her slice and popped it back on top. "What more are you going to say?"

"Thought I might angle it more toward the Lyntons." He took a large bite of pizza and topped it off with a chug of coke that wafted an aroma of vodka toward her. When she pushed her lower lip out, he laughed and passed it to her. As the sip burned its way along the back of her throat, she hummed with appreciation, then passed it back before she could gulp another.

"Don't you think you should wait until we know what'll happen?"

He cocked his eyebrow at her, "When have I ever thought I should wait?"

A fair point.

"If I put a few teasers in now, then I'll be primed to write a big one when they announce an arrest."

"*If* they announce an arrest," Ngaire said. "You don't know it'll come to anything."

"Well, at the least I can suggest that he's a wife beater."

Ngaire uncurled her legs and stretched them out in front of her. She patted her full belly and decided that, yes, she could fit in another slice. "At the time she was hitting him pretty hard," she said as she reached out. "There's a chance they won't charge him at all, considering."

"I wasn't asking your permission," Finlay said in a soft voice. "I'm just letting you know what I'm doing."

Ngaire poked her tongue out at him, a line of unease chasing up her back. "And I'm just playing devil's advocate. Mary yelling accusations doesn't make them true. Paul confessed to her murder already, remember? And she's recorded as drowning of natural causes. How many times and how many ways could she die?"

"Rasputin died from drowning after being poisoned, shot, and beaten, so she's got one more up her sleeve."

Ngaire let Finlay's black humor go unchallenged, though she was sure his recital of history was questionable.

"Whatever happened to Magdalene, it must've been bloody terrible," she said. "If Mary thinks her husband was involved, she must have been going crazy living with him all these years."

"Mary always struck me as a little crazy," Finlay agreed with good cheer, now on his second vodka coke. At least. How had she ended up living with someone who drank? Not that she was *living* with him. Just cohabitating.

Ngaire closed her eyes and let her thoughts flow back and forth. Even with the small shot of alcohol she'd drunk, a buzz worked through her, relaxing her limbs. Every muscle in her body tensed as she felt a blow to the back of her head, her ankle. As she tried and failed to raise her hands to ward off another blow.

"What's the matter?" Finlay asked as she forced her eyes open. Her body flooded with adrenaline, her mild buzz hyped up to electricity level.

"Just a nightmare," Ngaire said and smiled in reassurance, her heart beating so fast and so hard her retinas were flashing. "Just a bad dream."

Article: in April 1988 Janine Law was raped and murdered in her own home. The original coroner's verdict returned a finding of accidental death, saying she stuffed her mouth with a tea towel during an asthma attack and accidentally suffocated as a result.

It sounds absurd, but this remained the official cause of death for another seven years until her family pressured the police into reviewing her death as a cold-case investigation. After interviewing 125 men from around the Ponsonby suburb where Janine Law was killed, including taking interviews and DNA samples from twenty prisoners, a DNA match identified her killer. James Tamata confessed to her rape and murder in 1995, and her official record was at last updated to show the crime that ended her life.

Magdalene Lynton's family isn't pressuring anyone, but after a string of investigative discoveries following an unprompted confession, the original verdict of accidental death by drowning is starting to appear just as unstable as Janine Law's. So the question begins to arise: why aren't the Lyntons pursuing justice for their daughter?

With police close to an arrest . . .

William stopped reading the article and tossed the paper aside on the table. It landed heavily against a teacup and sent it falling until it smashed into large white chunks on the floor.

Would this case never go away?

He stood and moved from the table to the living room, misjudging distance in the dim light and stubbing his foot on the side table. The light was dim because he'd pulled the curtains closed. William didn't need his neighbors staring into his house, spying on him. He had enough problems.

His fingers pulled an edge of the curtain away from the window frame, one inch, two. After putting an eye up to the gap to stare out, he jerked the fabric back into place.

The farm he'd grown up on had wide-open spaces and fields where he could run himself into exhaustion and still not reach the edge of the property. Now he'd trapped himself in a square box, windows covered, but he felt more exposed than he ever had.

Was everyone out there intent on his ruin? Was this the way his life would end? All his life he'd done good things. Performed good acts. Helped people when they didn't think they'd ever receive help. This wasn't something he'd earned, something he deserved. One mistake from his teenage years shouldn't be held against him for so long.

The papers said they were coming for him. Coming for him, and they wouldn't stop until they'd locked him up and taken his family away. Amanda wouldn't understand his part in Maggie's death, and he couldn't blame her. William had never squared away his involvement, so there should be no expectation that she could.

Emma's footsteps sounded overhead. William cocked his head to the side and listened intently. It was another of the games they played on him. Somehow they could mimic his daughter's tread and sound it at will, driving him closer and closer to the edge.

What more did they want from him before they arrived to drag him away in cuffs? What more could he give? His family had been taken away, his life's work. Were they after his memories now, the only remnants of a happy life?

William walked upstairs, placing his feet on the edge of the runner where it offered the most cushioning, before the bare boards. If he stepped with great care, they wouldn't be able to hear him, and one day he'd catch them at it.

The light was bright in his eyes. He'd left the curtains open up here, since his neighbor's houses were single-story, and they wouldn't be able to see. Still, he was careful, dropping to the floor and crawling on hands and knees to the wall. Keeping his head tilted back as he rose to look outside so they wouldn't see his hair poking up over the window's base.

The gun was on the floor underneath the window. He didn't need it yet—everything was quiet now—but when it came, he'd be ready.

No one was going to take him down while a thousand people laughed at his downfall. No one was going to haul him off in handcuffs, while his daughter stared, and his wife applauded.

He didn't have many shells. The gun was a relic that he'd never turned in at amnesty. A small reminder of his father, who'd used it to take his life and had shown William the way. No man waits for them to take you. A man takes action.

Only a few shells left, but it was a shotgun. He'd only need one.

* * *

Deb stared at the screen as the results came in. One after the other, each giving the ping of mail arriving. The DS had given a few people a flea in their ear about results and priorities and beaten officers and murder inquiries, and suddenly they had progressed.

She looked up to see whether Gascoigne was in his office and beckoned him over. He frowned, then shook his head and pointed at his computer. Deb bundled the files together and forwarded the email to him, waiting for a thumbs-up to show they'd arrived before she joined him.

"Shut the door," he said, a sentence that would usually have her thinking of what she'd done wrong but now was just a simple instruction. When she went to sit on the chair opposite, he said, "Come around here. It's your case more than it's mine."

"It's Ngaire's most of all. She should be here."

"We can wait if you like. It'll be another week or two."

Deb mocked a hit to his shoulder, and he laughed before she stopped to remind herself that he was her superior. "Okay, go."

"Magdalene Lynton, samples from a cadaver, nuclear DNA extracted." Gascoigne brought up the sample as though either of them had a clue what they were reading. "Matched to evidence sample from crime scene 82332."

"What about Abe's samples?" They'd taken a swab after his arrest for assault. Even with him now out on bail, adding him to the database would give her joy.

He flicked through the files, opening the next in sequence. "Match to multiple samples from crime scene 82326. Match to Magdalene Lynton samples from a cadaver."

Deb frowned. "So, Abe was her father then. I wonder if Mary knew that?"

Gascoigne shook his head. "Not Magdalene's

father, there's another sample." He clicked on the link and brought up the photographs related to the sample location. "They extracted tissue from fetal remains in Magdalene's coffin."

Deb continued to frown for a moment, not understanding until he spelled it out for her.

"Abe Lynton was the father of Magdalene's baby."

Chapter Twenty-Four

"Ngaire, it's good to see you." Mary pulled her down to place a kiss on either cheek. "I'm so glad you could come."

"Any time, Mary. What did you want to see me about?" Ngaire hadn't stopped to think when Mary phoned her, just dropped her exercise routine and got in the car. Mary sounded breathless on the phone, and it crossed Ngaire's mind that the blow she'd suffered yesterday might have done more than wind her. Now that she'd seen that Mary was okay, it felt strange being here. She should have phoned the station to let them deal with it, but it was too late now.

"They've released Abe," she said. "He came here, but I told him he couldn't stay. The police said I had protection to keep him away from me."

Ngaire nodded. It was standard procedure to issue a protective order in domestic abuse cases. Even if Mary's was in a gray area of reciprocation. The orders allowed people time alone to decide whether to apply for a full court order and meant that any contact would be flagged to priority response.

"Was he okay with that?" Ngaire asked. She'd formed her opinions of Abe from the short glimpses she'd caught of him, not more than ten minutes total. "Are you scared he'll return?"

Mary shook her head, "No, he's gone. He won't be back."

"That's good," Ngaire said. "Did you need help with something else?"

"I wanted to see you again, dear. I missed our chats."

Ngaire shifted in her seat, moving her weight from one buttock to another. Her thigh muscle started to twitch into a cramp. What chats? She'd only ever seen Mary because of the case, and they hadn't been the most pleasant conversations in the world.

"I'm sorry about yesterday," Ngaire said. "I know it was hard to see your daughter's grave tampered with, but she's now where she belongs."

Mary tilted her head to one side as though listening. "No, she isn't. She shouldn't be below ground at all. Magdalene should still be alive."

There was no disputing that point. "Hopefully we'll have enough evidence now to determine whether Paul Worthington caused Magdalene's death," Ngaire said. "I know we can't convict him, but at least it will bring closure."

"Closure?" Mary asked, her head still tilted to the side. "I didn't need closure, dear. I already know what happened to my girl."

Ngaire couldn't think what to say. She felt awkward and trapped but didn't know how to leave without causing offense. Gascoigne was right, she should learn to leave well enough alone.

"Would you like a cup of tea?" Mary asked, moving into the kitchen without waiting for a response. "I'm sure a nice cup of tea and a bikkie will help."

A refusal would be rude. "Yes," she said. "That'll be nice." After a moment she crossed the room to lean on the Formica counter and watch Mary work.

There was a large glass jar with a cork-edged lid full of biscuits on the counter. Mary Lynton took a few for each of them and sat them on the sides of their saucers. The china she'd used was different from the other times, with rich patterns glazed into the surfaces. Her best china. No chips in these cups.

"I never told you about what happened before

Maggie died," Mary said with her back to Ngaire. Her hand pressed to the top of the kettle, checking the temperature. "I suppose nobody did, because it was a secret." She turned with her finger up to her mouth, keeping it buttoned, then dropped her hand away and turned to the teapot again.

"They had little to say," Ngaire agreed. "Just that there was an altercation between Maggie"—she used the abbreviation for the first time and saw Mary's shoulders stiffen—"and your husband. Each one said she was swearing at him, so he sent her off to think."

Mary laughed—a high note that lent an air of falsehood to the sound. "Sent her off to think, did he?" She took her hand away from the kettle as the sound of the boil grew louder and put a few teaspoons of loose tea into the pot.

"What happened, then?" Ngaire asked. She wondered whether this was the reason Mary called her around. If this secret was something she needed to tell and had nobody else to listen.

"Do you know why we followed the Prophet into farming?" Mary asked, changing tack. "The only one of us with outdoorsy skills was Kelvin. His skill was in carpentry. Just like our Lord."

"I don't know. I suppose I thought it was something to do with going back to the land. Weren't a lot of communes springing up around that time?"

"Oh, yes," Mary said. She poured hot water over the leaves, swirled the pot, then poured the water back out before filling it to the brim again. "Communes were all the rage. The Prophet told us that if we embraced a rural lifestyle, our children would flourish."

Ngaire frowned. "But there were only two of you with children. Wasn't it just Isaiah and Magdalene?"

"The Prophet promised there'd be more at any second," Mary said. "Magdalene wasn't ours, and Isaiah wasn't normal. Joseph told us if we got back to nature, then the Lord would bless us all with offspring, and our children would grow to be safe and clean."

Ngaire nodded, trying to follow. "Isaiah said something about that," she said as she worked it through in her memory. "He said The Prophet insisted the community close itself off because otherwise the Devil would get in."

Mary turned with a smile of recognition, and a touch of joy danced in her eyes for a moment before they fell into shadow again. "Yes, he said that if we could keep the Devil out, then we'd all be blessed with children."

Ngaire traced the pattern of large flowers that decorated the surface of the Formica. "Could none of you have kids?" Finlay had told her the Prophet was infertile due to mumps. The Lyntons had adopted Magdalene.

"None of us could," Mary agreed. "Until Marge got pregnant. That showed we'd made the right decision. The church farm was magical, and the Prophet had been right all along."

"But the baby died," Ngaire said, a tremble running down her arms before her fingers froze to stillness.

"The baby died," Mary confirmed. "Hers was the second body buried in the graveyard. Samuel Gibson's dad was the first and then the baby. Stillborn."

"That must have been hard for everyone."

There was a snort in response. "Hard? Four couples who thought they'd wrought a miracle and then, poof," she blew air over her fingertips. "It's gone. We were devastated."

"Is that why you all left so soon after Magdalene's accident?"

Mary stared at her with a look of disappointment on her face. "Magdalene's accident? But you're the one who told me, dear."

Ngaire shook her head, not following.

"Magdalene was murdered."

* * *

"I checked with the property managers, and he came home last night after we released him," DS Gascoigne said.

"Despite us warning him he couldn't go anywhere near his wife?" Deb asked.

"Yeah, well, did you really think that admonishment would stick?" He pulled his seatbelt across his chest and started the car again. "Abe Lynton knows that we took those samples, and he knows that he's about to be in trouble. His wife is the one who's been protecting him all these years, so she's the one he's running to."

The car rolled along the sloping driveway. As they turned the first corner, Deb pointed at the end of the street the Lynton's residence was on.

"How many houses down is it?" Gascoigne asked as he glided to a smooth stop. "Are we close enough to go in on foot?"

Deb shook her head. "No, they're right down the end. There's a clear view of us coming either way."

"Isn't there a back road to this place?"

Deb pulled the GPS unit toward her and scanned their surroundings. "If we go in on Bountiful Street, we can get closer. A house they back onto has its front entrance there."

Gascoigne swung the car around and drove back out of the village. There might be a grim set to his face, but Deb could see by the quick glances and the skillful handling of the vehicle that he was enjoying himself. Fieldwork was a rare occurrence at his level, no matter how good he was at it.

"Next right," she instructed as they drove closer. "Three houses down."

He pulled over in front of the house and turned to Deb. "Redding told me that Mary Lynton responded well to you the last time you attended, so I want you to go to the front. I'll stay out by the garage in case he's hiding out and tries to run for it. Radio if you need help."

She nodded, and they walked up the path to the house. A curtain was jerked aside, and someone peered out. Deb walked over to the side door and knocked.

"Police," she said showing her badge. "We're just doing a few checks in the neighborhood and need access across your property. Okay?"

The old woman who'd answered looked terrified and hunched over.

"Nothing to worry about," Deb said, attempting to reassure her. It didn't work too well. "We're just following up a few kids we think might have committed minor vandalism. Nothing violent."

The woman straightened, and her lip curled. "Taggers, eh? Well, you can tell them from me they need a bloody good hiding. Just look at my garage door."

Deb looked at the door in question but couldn't see any marks. "Right, I see," she said. It never hurt to agree with someone. "Just stay inside, and we'll be out of your road in a few minutes."

As she joined Gascoigne, he pointed at the side of the back fence, nearest the corner. They'd have to jump over, and that was the strongest point. "This thing looks like it's on its last legs. I'll give you a leg up."

He bent and hooked his hands together to form a step. Deb placed her right foot in it, then grabbed at the top of the fence and hopped up, letting the lift from Gascoigne propel her over the back. She turned to see him boosting himself over.

Around the side of the Lyntons' house, Deb ran crouched over. The windows started at one meter above the ground, and she kept out of the line of sight with ease. When she was at the corner, she turned to check on Gascoigne, who was standing with his hands on his hips. Legs planted steadily.

He nodded, and Deb strode up to the front door

and knocked.

"Mary Lynton?" she called out in a loud voice. "Mary Lynton, open the door. It's the police."

"Who murdered her?" Ngaire asked. She should've stayed at home and let the cops deal with this. At least, she should've told someone where she was going.

Mary laughed a joyless bark. "They all did. They killed her so they'd be able to continue their work."

"Their work?"

"The babies," Mary explained and rolled her eyes. "I told you. That's why we were there. Abe spotted it, you know. Magdalene was always running around, getting into trouble. He thought she needed to be taught a lesson, and the Prophet thought she'd brought evil into the church."

She carried the cups of tea through into the living room and sat at the table as though she were having a catch-up, discussing a holiday or the weather. Picked up a chocolate biscuit from the side of her plate and smiled with pure pleasure. Ngaire sat opposite her, placing her hands flat on the table for balance.

"Magdalene was a lovely girl, so willful. Always getting into trouble; always mouthing off. She got expelled from primary school, did you know?"

Ngaire shook her head, the conversation getting away from her. "Didn't she like school?"

"She hated anybody telling her what to do," Mary said. "From the moment I first picked her up. She cuddled right into my shoulder and made a bubbling noise. Mary pushed out her lips in imitation. "Abe told me to hand her over, and she howled." This time, when Mary laughed it sounded genuine, her eyes tearing with good memories. "She didn't like him one bit."

"That must've caused a few issues." Ngaire wondered whether she could get her cell phone without Mary spotting her. The bag was on the floor at her feet. She moved her right foot so it made contact.

"Oh boy, yes. Abe never spoke but to order her about. Maggie never spoke but to mouth off at him."

She looked over Ngaire's shoulder, and Ngaire turned to see the connecting door to the garage. When she turned back, Mary had tilted her head to the side again, so Ngaire focused on listening. Was a sound coming from there?

Ngaire kicked her bag with her foot again. "So what happened at the church?"

"She told me she thought she was pregnant. Much too late for me to help her get rid of it, too, the scallywag. That was after I'd given her some condoms. And she'd smoked weed out in the back fields when she thought no one was watching. Nothing but trouble."

The same warm smiled played across her face, and Ngaire felt a rush of anger toward her. How could she talk about her daughter with that loving tone while doing nothing to help her? Pregnant at fourteen, and the response is, 'Pity I can't help you get an abortion?'"

"Is that why you killed her?"

Mary's lips thinned. "No, my dear, it wasn't like that." She took a sip of her tea and wiped the chocolate stains from the corners of her mouth. "Maggie upset Abe by calling him some name in church. I was sick in bed, so I don't know what. He decided she needed to be taught a lesson.

"Marge was keen, too. Had her eye on Maggie's baby, what with having lost her own, and she wanted the community against her, so she could help herself. Joseph—" Her voice cracked and she put a hand to her mouth, repeatedly swallowing until she regained control. "I expected more from him. Magdalene deserved more. But he fell into step like the sheep he was. Bahhhh."

The animal noise was violent, full of hate. Ngaire held a hand out to Mary and waited for her to reciprocate. "What did you do?"

"Not me, dear," Mary grabbed her hand. Her

nails dug into Ngaire's skin, drawing blood. "I wasn't involved." She gasped for breath. "Magdalene was going to marry that lovely boy, Billy. Have a baby and make a real life for herself. Not like I did. She was too intelligent to marry a selfish monster and spend her life afraid."

Mary released Ngaire's arm as suddenly as she'd grabbed it and picked up her second biscuit. Ngaire watched her chew. Watched as the crumbs gathered on her lower lip, then fell off into her cup of tea. Her teeth were weak, and she sucked in a sip of tea to help her break the hard biscuit into a soggy mess.

"They tied her to the cross. Then they got buckets of water to wash her clean. Pouring it over her as though it was infused with the Holy Spirit rather than some crud from the trough tap."

Tears welled up in Mary's eyes and fell over the lower lids. She didn't move to wipe them or blink to shake them off. They enlarged until gravity pulled them over.

"I went to the church to see why they'd been away so long. She was sopping wet. They'd tied her with ropes, and the bindings cut into flesh in her attempt to get free." Mary's hand encircled her own wrist as though to sooth her dead daughter's wound. Her nails were flecked with Ngaire's blood. "I saw her, and for a moment, I mistook her for the Lord God on the cross. They'd laid it down on the floor. Then Abe tipped a bucket of water down on her. There was a towel in her mouth, so she couldn't scream. Her eyes were bulging with white. She looked like a horse in full panic . . . froth was pouring out of her nostrils." Mary wiped the final crumbs from her mouth with a shaking hand. "No wonder they kept going. She looked possessed."

Ngaire experienced the room sliding away from her. She felt the constriction of being bound, the sharp bite of open wounds as she struggled to break free.

Struggled and failed. The fear of her mouth being gagged and the threat of drowning as water was poured over her, again and again. Poured over her until her inhalations pulled water down into her lungs, her exhalations mixing it with air and forcing it out as froth. The pain of breathing liquid like fire in her chest. She gasped, fighting for air, and the room reasserted itself.

As Ngaire fought back the tears and panic of a girl long dead, Mary noticed her cup of tea again. She picked it up and took a sip, then tilted her head back to drain the cup. Tears rolled over her upturned cheeks and flowed into her ears.

Finished, she wiped at her face and tipped her head to the side again.

"Is there somebody there?" Ngaire asked. "Is someone in the garage?"

"Gosh no, dear. Nobody here but you and me."

Mary stared into space, an odd point somewhere in the middle of the table between Ngaire and her. When Ngaire shifted in her chair, Mary's gaze snapped back into focus, and she looked at her untouched tea and biscuits.

"Have something, dear. I don't want you to go hungry."

Ngaire picked up a biscuit by its edge and looked at it. The chocolate was melting from the heat of the cup. Her fingers pressed in and slid on the fatty surface. She took a small bite to appease her host, then another when Mary nodded at her eagerly.

The biscuits were store-bought, Ngaire reassured herself. There's nothing wrong with eating a packaged biscuit.

Still, her throat tightened against the small bites. Bile rose in protest.

"I screamed at them all to stop. They looked like someone had caught them at an orgy. All sucked up into the moment, then filled with shame at their animal behavior. I sent them back to the house, and then I told Abe that I was taking my daughter, and we were leaving, and I was never coming back.

"When I untied Maggie, I told her to get herself clean and dry and to pack a bag. We walked over, and I sent her down to her room. Everybody had gathered in the kitchen, eating the supper I'd laid out as though they'd just finished up with church and needed refreshment after the sermon."

Her face reflected the surprise she must've felt. Muscles lifted the skin of her forehead until it was free of wrinkles and pulled her ears back.

"I said I'd report them to the police. I told Abe Maggie was pregnant, and she needed to be cared for, not tortured. With Marge, I told her she was a greedy, child-hungry witch, and she deserved to burn in hell. Told the Prophet he was a sad, old man who wasn't capable of fulfilling our spiritual needs any more than his wife's physical needs."

Mary's face animated with a dozen quick emotional caricatures and settled on a mother cub protecting her young.

"When I finished, they left to go do the chores. The cows were calling out to be milked, and the evening deliveries needed to be made. I went to collect Maggie, to head off in the car, and she wasn't there."

Mary's wrung her hands together, hard enough that her paper thin skin turned red and then purple as she broke the capillaries under the skin. Her knuckles shone white at the pressure, and the bones in her wrists gave a sharp crack as the movement expelled air in a violent burst.

"For the next three days, I thought she'd run away. She was alive when I dragged her from the church. Alive when she went to her room." Mary stopped talking and stared at nothing, her hands working against each other. "Isaiah told me he scooped her out of the pond instead of the truth, but it was a gesture of apology. Making up for what he'd done."

She sighed, the effort shaking her body. One edge of her thumb gave under the pressure of her fidgets, and a thin line through to the flesh below showed, then filled with blood.

"The Prophet said it was a terrible business, but now we'd have a productive future. I told him I'd make sure he went to prison for torturing my daughter, and he tucked his tail between his legs and ran away."

Ngaire tried to imagine Mary as a strong woman dictating the lives of others with vengeance in her heart. She couldn't see it. Maybe there were mild flashes of animation beneath her docile features to lend weight to the argument. Mostly she was just simple placidity, being pushed and pulled by the will of others.

There was a flurry of banging on the front door, and Ngaire recognized Deb's voice as she yelled, "Mary Lynton, open the door. It's the police."

"Would you get that, dear?" Mary asked. "I'm exhausted."

Her face was pale, and her cheekbones arched over dark shadows. She looked ill, gravely ill, and Ngaire felt a tight knot in her stomach.

She opened the door just as Deb went to knock again, throwing her off balance, so she stumbled a step.

"Ngaire, what the . . ."

Ngaire shook her head. "I don't know. She rang me. She's talking about Magdalene."

Deb walked into the room and stood opposite Mary, the table between them. "Mary, we know Abe's here. We've enough evidence to arrest him. Can you tell me where he is?"

Ngaire's eye's widened as she walked closer to the table. Mary had spit bubbling in the corner of her mouth. When her tongue slipped out to lick it away, she saw more foam inside. Her tongue was a dark purple.

"Mrs. Lynton," Deb said, banging her knuckles on the table. "Where is your husband?"

Ngaire looked from the garage door back to the kitchen. Mary said Abe had gone. Her biscuits were out on public display. She'd used the good china.

Mary opened her mouth as if to speak but heaved breath into her lungs instead. She coughed it back out, blood and foam spraying across the tabletop. Against the side of Ngaire's untouched cup.

Ngaire turned and fumbled on the counter for the phone, calling back over her shoulder to Deb, "The garage. He must be in the garage."

There was another glass on the counter. A tumbler with a trace of amber fluid in the bottom. A man's drink. It was scotch.

She pulled the landline phone across the counter and dialed 111. "Ambulance," she shouted as if the operator were deaf. "We need an ambulance."

Deb pulled her radio free and signaled for Gascoigne. She flattened herself against the wall with the connecting door to the garage. When he ran through the entrance, she pointed to the door, and he took position on the opposite side while she reached for the handle.

Mary's head fell forward onto the table, striking it with a dull thud. Her arms fell to her side, limp.

Deb turned the handle slow, slow. When the latch shifted, she pushed it open. It slammed against the wall, and Deb turned into the doorway, holding her pepper spray in front of her as she scanned. Near corner, far corner, wall, floor.

"We need an ambulance to the Northfield Retirement Village. We have an unconscious woman in her late seventies. Possibly poisoned," Ngaire said.

She paused, while Deb called out to Gascoigne. "Here, on the floor." They disappeared from view.

"We may have a second victim, male."

Ngaire dropped the receiver to the counter and ran to the garage door, edging around the corner until the room was in view. There was a man on the floor, his mouth opened, a spume of froth from nose to chin. Gascoigne knelt by his head, two fingers against his neck. He shook his head, then pulled one of the man's eyelids up. Even from the doorway, Ngaire could see the pupil fixed in full dilation. It was Abe Lynton.

"He's dead," Gascoigne said.

Chapter Twenty-Five

"Don't leave without seeing me," DS Gascoigne said as he passed by Deb's desk. It was Ngaire he was talking to. Together, she and Deb were piecing the case into a semblance of finality. Already, she'd given a formal statement detailing what Mary Lynton had said to her when no one was sure Mary would survive.

She had scraped through. Abe Lynton, however, had been dead for hours by the time they found him. Ngaire hoped he'd done the things Mary accused him of, although having proved at least one crime, Magdalene's rape, she could allow herself to believe the others.

"Anyone would do it," Mary protested when they arrested her at the hospital. "Abe deserved it."

She seemed unaware that the provocation defense had been abolished by law. Something her lawyer would have the pleasure of telling her, so no policeman need bother.

That she'd attempted to kill herself would be a point in her favor. The balance of her mind and all that good stuff. Insanity was easier to demonstrate in court when you tried to off yourself after killing your husband of fifty-six years.

"Who's this?" Deb asked, sliding the file across to Ngaire.

"Bea," she said. "Or Bella, if you want her work name. Paul used to avail himself of her personal services."

"Yuck, thank you. I didn't need that image."

Ngaire laughed. "You should read it to the end. She came in to tell us about Paul saying Billy murdered a girl, but many of the things Paul made her do aren't fit for bedtime reading. In the end, I think she was glad when he beat her, and she had the chance to get rid of him."

"No, keep going, Ngaire. Make it better."

When Ngaire opened her mouth again, Deb shoved her palm in her face to stop her, laughing. "Mind me, girl."

The echo of an older generation's speech flashed Mary and Abe into her head. and Ngaire shuddered.

"Is it too cold for you?" Deb asked.

"No, I'm all right. What's happening with the other couples? Any charges?"

Deb shrugged. "We've recommended charges of manslaughter, but the prosecutors are reluctant to proceed based on your statement alone, and Mary's shut her trap now. Besides, from what she told you, Magdalene was alive when they finished."

"On her way to dying," Ngaire countered.

"With our luck, they'll just claim religious belief nuttery and get off anyway," Deb said. "Like those guys who killed Janet Moses. The only solid case was against Abe, and Mary sorted that out on her own."

Ngaire scanned the files on the screen. Ordered, they presented a picture of how Magdalene Lynton's life ended. From a start of statutory rape and impregnation, through to being pulled out of the slurry.

"We still don't know what happened there, do we?" Ngaire asked and pointed. "Magdalene ended up with Billy and Paul, but in his letter Paul wrote that he didn't throw her in the river like he'd told us. Just dumped her body over his back fence onto their land so he wouldn't get in trouble."

"One more genius tactic from a criminal mind."

"Worked in this case." Ngaire sat back and twirled around in her chair, her thinking position. "If I paid Billy a visit, I wonder if he'd tell me anything?"

"He knew how to keep his trap shut when

Duncan and I went to see him," Deb said.

Ngaire's mouth fell open at the statement, and Deb gave her a quizzical look. "What?"

"When did DS Gascoigne become 'Duncan'?"

Deb colored and shook her head. "Just a slip of the tongue. Anyhow, you're here on limited grounds to help me compile the case. I doubt the DS will let you go skipping off to interview people."

Ngaire shrugged her shoulders and spun the chair again. "Not a formal interview. As far as anyone is concerned, this is case closed. I'm more wondering for my peace of mind."

Deb shook her head. "Not your best idea. Course, if you wanted to go, nobody's gonna stop you. Just don't say you ran it by me."

"Course not," Ngaire said. "Look away, girl." She typed a few search terms into the computer and noted the resulting address. In a loud voice, she said, "I'm off now. I have mail to collect and grocery shopping to do."

Deb snorted and turned to her computer. "Don't try out for undercover work, eh? We don't want to endanger the entire force."

Ngaire walked to the DS's door and gave a quick knock. "You wanted to see me, sir?"

Gascoigne, or *Duncan*, as she couldn't help thinking, nodded at the door, and she closed it before taking a seat.

"I received confirmation from your physio that you're fit to come back on duty," he said.

Ngaire nodded. Adrianna had told her the same after her session the day before.

"However, I haven't received word back from your psychiatric assessment because you seem to have missed every appointment that he's set up for you."

"Yes, I've been very busy, sir."

"I know you've been busy, Ngaire. You've also been skating close to the edge of what is and is not legal, considering you don't have full sign-off to return to your duties." He tapped his finger on the folder in front of him, her name upside down on its cover. "You have an appointment tomorrow, and I want you to make a concerted effort to get to that appointment. Otherwise, we'll be reconsidering whether you're coming back to work at all. Is that understood?"

Ngaire felt one foot tall as she nodded.

Gascoigne sighed and pushed his chair back from the table to stand. "It's not that we don't want you to come back, Ngaire. I've had to tell your mates on the team not to pester you with questions because they had so many. But you have to comply with the conditions. Otherwise, you place the whole department at risk, and I don't just mean because of the paperwork. Do you understand?"

She nodded again and rose to leave. At another time, she would've defended the implication that she'd place other team members at risk, but of late she couldn't make that claim. "I'll get to that appointment, sir."

No matter how scared she was.

Ngaire pulled up outside Billy Glover's house and peered up into the windows. The house was a beauty, an old- style villa but made with materials that wouldn't give in to the elements as easily. There was a dormer window popping out of the ceiling line and a bay window on the ground floor with eight paneled windows offering a panoramic view.

A veranda ran the length of the right side of the house. In a notable difference from houses built in the same era, it faced the right way to capture the sun, rather than being built to the specifications of a different country, which ended up plunging it into the shade.

Ngaire exited the car and walked to the front door. As she knocked, a woman and a young girl walked up behind her.

"Can I help you?" the woman asked. Her voice sounded ragged, as though she were coming down with a cold. An impression heightened by red-rimmed eyes and ashen skin against her bright cornflower-blue scarf. "I live here," she continued, jutting her chin out in defiance.

"Hello, my name is Ngaire. I was looking for a Mr. William Glover? I tried phoning, but he didn't answer."

"You and me, both. I'm Amanda Glover," she extended her hand, and Ngaire shook it. "Will is my husband." She pulled a bunch of keys from her purse and tried the lock. Although the key turned, when she pushed against the door, it wouldn't open.

"Do you want me to try?" Ngaire offered. It looked as though Amanda were on the verge of tears. She pushed the keys at Ngaire and stepped back, her eyes scanning the neighboring properties.

Ngaire glanced around. There were lots of cars in driveways. For such a wealthy area, there were many people home during the day. She flicked through the keys until she reached the one Amanda had tried.

Again, the key inserted into the lock. There was no clicking sound because Amanda had unlocked the door, and when Ngaire turned the handle and pushed with her shoulder, the door held firm.

"Has he put in a deadbolt?" Amanda asked. "Will always threatened to beef up security, but he never got around to it. Said our nosey neighbors would be enough protection."

With the number of shadows standing at curtains that Ngaire could see, she agreed. She pushed her foot as hard as she could against the base of the door. There was no movement. "It's not a deadbolt," she said. "If it were, the bottom of the door would have some give." She pressed hard against the top instead, and there was an inward movement before the door stopped and bounced back as her pressure released. "I think there's something propped up against it. A chair or a dresser or something."

Amanda took another step backward, the hand that was not holding tight to her daughter fidgeting at her scarf and collar. "You think he's barricaded the door?"

Ngaire shrugged. After she'd walked along the front of the house, she held her hands up to the glass to see in through a window. "The curtains are pulled," she said, then continued around the corner, trying each one.

By the time she circled back, Amanda was being pulled along by her daughter. "Emma, please," Amanda said, shaking herself free. "If you don't want to wait here, then for goodness' sake go wait in the car."

"I want to see Daddy," the girl said. In lieu of either choice presented by her mother, she tilted her head back and yelled. "Daddy! Daddy! Daddy! Let us in!"

Amanda put her hands up to her temples and massaged in little circles. Ngaire sympathized. Emma had a set of lungs on her and the amazing ability to reach notes so high that only small children and Mariah Carey knew them.

A window opened above them, and Ngaire could see movement from the curtain. It wasn't drawn, but whoever was upstairs was hiding behind its folds.

"Darling, I think it's a good idea if you and Mummy go away today. Why don't you go on a picnic? You'd like that, wouldn't you?"

"William. Get down here at once, and let me in. I'm sorry I left, but this is getting ridiculous. Why have you cut your phone off? Work's driving me crazy, calling me night and day."

"Tell them to go fuck themselves," he yelled back.

Amanda put her hands over Emma's ears, but far too late.

"Is that a bad word, Mummy?" she asked. "Fuck, fuck, fuck." Her cheeks glowed red with delight.

"William Harold Glover, you come down and let me in. This is childish and stupid and I will not stand out in the street yelling at you."

There was movement again in the upstairs window. By the time Ngaire's conscious mind worked out the image, she'd pushed Amanda and Emma off the front path and into the shade of a large willow tree.

"What are you doing?" Amanda asked, shoving Ngaire back off her.

"Gun," Ngaire said. Her breath came in short pants, and her heart rate sped up. "He's got a gun."

Amanda held her gaze for one terrible second, then the words registered, and she picked Emma up and ran for her car.

"No!" Ngaire shouted, but too late. Amanda's car was in front of the house. In a direct line of sight with the upstairs window.

Ngaire ran, bent in half to present a smaller target. In her hand, she still clutched Amanda's keys. A fact Amanda had discovered for herself, judging by the repeated thumps on the passenger side door. Ngaire pressed the "Door Open" button, and the car beeped its cheerful response. Amanda pushed Emma into the back while she clambered over the passenger seat into the driver's seat, her body lowered away from the window.

"Here," Ngaire said, handing the keys inside. "Do you have a phone?"

Amanda nodded as she slotted the key into the ignition with shaking hands.

"Call 111 as soon as you get around the corner," Ngaire said. "Don't forget, and don't wait for someone else to do it, okay?"

"Yes. Yes," Amanda called, and the car pulled away from the curb, the open passenger door thumping shut as it built up speed. Ngaire was left exposed on the street. She sprinted to the side of the house, cursing that the windows were blocked. *Where the hell is he?*

She poked her head around the corner to survey the window. There was still a shadow of movement there. Ngaire bolted behind the house, scooping up a brick from the edge of the garden on the way. She shielded her face with her left arm and threw the brick as hard as she could through the largest window.

The curtain billowed out through the smashed gap. Ngaire pulled it farther out and used the ends to clear away the jagged pieces of glass. Not stopping to think, she crawled over, dropping to the floor and rolling away from the window inside. Out of the corner of her eye, she caught sight of a sofa, and as she scrambled to her knees, she moved over and crouched beside the end of the sofa.

A coffee table was covered with empty bottles and food wrappers. There was a jar used as a glass, and shards on the floor to show where another had met its end. Ngaire kneeled, trying to listen above the pounding of her own heart and her ragged breathing.

A creak sounded above her. William was moving about, but he was still upstairs. Shit. If only she knew the layout.

Her phone vibrated in her bra. Without pockets, she carried it in the only other place that was always handy. Caught tight between her breasts and her armpit, the sound was muffled, and Ngaire didn't think William would've heard.

She pulled it out and looked. The number was private. She flicked the bar to answer and spoke as quietly as she could.

"Ngaire, here." If this were a cold call, someone would get his ass reamed.

"It's Deb. Are you okay?"

"I'm in William Glover's house," she whispered. "He's armed. Did Amanda make the call?"

"She did. Get the fuck out of there, Ngaire.

Armed defenders are on their way."

"Just give me a minute. I might be able to talk him down."

The floorboards creaked again. This time near the stairwell.

"Get out of there! That's an order." The DS had replaced Deb on the phone and was yelling at her. Ngaire flicked the phone off, scared the sound had carried.

Another creak. There was definitely someone on the stairs. Ngaire got to her knees again and crawled to the neighboring room. A dining room with an open connection to the kitchen. As she swung beneath the table, behind the counter, Ngaire could just see the bottom step of a staircase. She held in position; held her breath. A shadow fell onto the step, then a foot followed it into view.

Now, you stupid bitch. To negotiate, you need to open your mouth now.

All Ngaire's will drained away. Her mind went blank, then flashed with red. Blood red. Her blood spilling out. The glint of a knife edge coming toward her. The knowledge of death.

Ngaire's heart pounded so fast and hard, she thought it would explode. Her mouth dried as if it had filled with sand. As she shook her head, she saw the dining room again. Her vision clouded in from the edges, and her panting was the loudest sound she'd ever made.

"My name is Ngaire Blakes." Her voice sounded weak. It shook and trembled. Ngaire pushed with her feet, driving her body back under the lip of the counter. "I'm with the police, and I just want to talk to you. There's no need for anybody to get hurt."

Her training kicked in now, and her rote memory drove her voice out, loud and strong. Ngaire cocked her head to the side, trying to get a better view without exposing herself. She wanted a sound to know where he stood.

"I didn't order it," he said. "I don't know why he did it."

Ngaire's mind spun as she tried to make sense of his words. Focus, focus. Keep your mind clean. Let him tell you what he needs to. Don't interrupt unless he's descending.

"I never ordered my investigator to hurt you. I just meant for him to keep tabs on you. On the investigation," he said. There was the sound of a sob and a stumble.

Ngaire shook her head, trying to place the sentence in order. Was he drunk?

"Who's your investigator?" she called back.

"Mikel shouldn't even have gone to the farm. That wasn't part of his brief."

Ngaire rubbed the skin between her eyes, hard. What, what, what? Was he talking about her assault?

"Abe Lynton attacked me at the farm. Was he your investigator?"

She leaned her head back against the counter. When she closed her eyes, pulsating lights flowed across her vision.

"Abe Lynton attacked you?" William sounded unsure.

Good. He's processing information. "Yes, he left his DNA all over the scene."

There was a series of muttered words. Ngaire couldn't make them out.

"Why do you have a gun?" she asked. Keep him talking. Keep him focused. Get out alive.

"It's my dad's," he said. "The only thing he left me."

"Is it loaded?"

"Oh, yes. It wouldn't work otherwise." He sounded calm. Calm and sure.

Ngaire thought of the Billy that Paul had described to her. From the start, when he pretended to hide the man's existence, to the letter where he placed his blame. Billy, the terror. Billy, the cruel and abusive friend. Billy, who forced him into burglary and speeding and rape and murder.

One man's opinion had colored her thoughts from the beginning. Unchecked. It was only Mary's voice that offered a different version. A dissenting opinion. She'd talked of Billy, whom she'd thought her daughter was lucky to find. A nice young man, she'd called him, over and over.

Which Billy held her at gunpoint now?

Ngaire used her feet to push herself higher against the back of the counter. She turned and duckwalked to the edge. The door from the living room was covered in square panes of glass, six inches by six inches. The panes reflected a gentle version of the kitchen. Soft and fuzzy. He was standing on the other side. Less than a meter away. Ngaire sank back on her haunches again.

"Would you put the gun down so we can talk?"

"We're talking now."

Ngaire gritted her teeth as her leg cramped. As the pain tightened, she clenched as hard as she could until her jaw joined in the protest. She gasped when the cramp let go. As blood flowed back through her muscle.

What had they been saying?

"I'm not much of a conversationalist when there's a firearm pointed at me."

There was a clunk as he laid something on the floor. In the muted reflection, she saw William sit with his back to the counter. He was no longer holding the gun, but it was within reach.

"Why did Abe Lynton attack you?"

"I was looking at the cross in the church. There were traces of blood on it. He tried to kill me to hide what he'd done."

"What had he done?"

"He and the other church members tied

Magdalene to the cross to perform some kind of exorcism. They killed her."

There was a gentle laugh and the shake of movement in the glass. "They didn't kill her. I killed her."

Another confession. Magdalene had waited, dead in her grave for forty years, and now people were fighting to claim responsibility.

Paul's version of Billy would have her believe him now. Lock him up and throw away the key. Paul's version ignored long years of service defending the underdogs of society. His service as a criminal lawyer so easily transformed into a mantra that he got criminals off. But when Ngaire had looked him up on the Internet she'd found a snippet from a victim's family. They'd come into court day after day and watched while Billy freed the man they believed responsible for their daughter's death. Hatred and resentment only to be expected.

Instead, they'd praised him for his thoughtfulness. The only person in the courtroom who took the time to introduce himself, explain his role. The only one who informed them of what would happen, where they should sit, when it was okay to leave. The one who took care to check on them when a piece of testimony hit hard.

In the end, he was Mary's Billy. Had always been Mary's Billy. That nice boy from the farm.

I killed her. Ngaire closed her eyes to watch the pulsing colors once more. She'd looked at the evidence again and again. Worked through the angles, one after the other. There was nothing she was more sure of in Magdalene Lynton's case than this. "You didn't kill Magdalene."

There was a rustle of movement and the sound of a muffled sob. "I left her alone with Paul," he said. "Even knowing what he was like. I should've known what he'd do. It was my fault. I killed her."

"You didn't kill her," Ngaire repeated.

"As good as. I left her alone with a killer."

"You ran off to fetch help," Ngaire said. She didn't know for sure, but it was the only thing that fit. His agreement fixed it in her mind. "You went to fetch help, and when you came back, she was dead, right?"

"Yes. I should've called an ambulance."

"Why didn't you?"

A strangled sob again. "Claire was scared if I called an ambulance they'd bring the police."

Ngaire nodded. A pregnant teen with an abusive father. They would've whipped her out of there and off to a foster family as far away as possible.

"I tried to get hold of Greg's grandmother. She was a nurse and I thought she'd be able to help. But she was out at the Bingo." He gave a cry of pain and anger. "I was so stupid."

"You think that Paul Worthington killed her while you were gone, and that's why you're responsible?"

This time, the answer was so faint she could barely understand the word, "Yes."

"Paul Worthington didn't kill her, either."

The evidence had been available to her for so long that Ngaire couldn't believe she hadn't put it together earlier. It was Deb, this morning, going through the case, who'd seen it. As she'd gone through the sex worker's statement, containing the details of the peculiar arrangements that her client demanded.

"She was already dead when he raped her," she said. "She was dead before he touched her."

Bella had told her what her client wanted. Sometimes he talked, but only at the start of the session. While she was getting ready. Bella specialized in unusual practices. Her bread and butter lay in babying grown men, but she fulfilled other fetishes, too.

"There was a prostitute he saw for years," Ngaire

said. "He made her take a cold bath and use ice to cool down her skin. Even inside. In her mouth, in . . . other places. She had to lie still while he had sex with her."

"I don't want to know what Paul was into," William said. This time, he didn't muffle the sobs. "I already know what sort of sick bastard he was."

"He asked her to do all that so he could pretend she was dead," Ngaire said. "Once, during a session, he insulted her. She insulted him back, and he beat her. Not because of what she said but because she spoiled the fantasy."

There was a sigh from the other side of the counter. The light of the sky through the curtains was shifting. Soon she wouldn't be able to see William's reflection anymore.

"I don't—"

"Fetishes aren't something you're born with, Billy. They're made up from sexual impressions you gain throughout your life. Especially when you're young. Especially your first." Ngaire waited a moment for him to work it through in his own mind. "Magdalene was dead when he had sex with her. Had been dead for a while. She would've died even if you'd had a full ambulance at the shed when she arrived."

William gave another strangled sob. "You're just saying that to make me feel better. To make me get rid of the gun."

"When they strapped Magdalene to the cross, it was level. They poured water over her. She had a towel stuck in her mouth so she couldn't scream. It was like waterboarding, but they didn't pause, they weren't careful. She would've inhaled a lot of the water they poured over her."

"People don't die from waterboarding."

Ngaire dug into her eyes with her knuckles. Colored lights replaced the flashing pulse of her retinas. "People would, if they did it like that. Your lungs aren't built to breathe water. If you inhale even a small bit, it hurts. The surface of your lungs gets damaged. It swells." She paused for him to catch up with what she was saying. "It didn't matter that they stopped. They'd already done the damage."

She'd looked it up back at the start. After she'd read through the autopsy the first time. Forms of drowning and their pathology. Dry drowning, where your lungs froth up a plug to stop you inhaling. Wet drowning, where your lungs inhale water and feed it through into your blood stream until your brain dies. And secondary drowning when inhaled water damages your lungs, so you die hours or days later.

"I thought you were coming to arrest me," William said. His voice was quiet and his breathing heavy. Weighed down with tears. "I thought it was time for me to pay."

Ngaire leaned her head against the wall. "There's nothing to pay for, Billy. You did nothing wrong."

He laughed again, low. Without humor.

"Did you know my wife left me? Amanda's pregnant and doesn't want to keep it. That's how much she hates me."

"Amanda? She was outside yelling to be let in an hour ago."

"Yeah, to get her things." He paused, and Ngaire could hear him wipe the tears and the snot away from his face. "I always knew if I told her the truth, she'd leave me. And as soon as I tell her a few things about my childhood—poof!—she's gone."

Ngaire shifted on the floor. Her bum was going to sleep. "I don't know your wife, but if I was living with someone for years, then found out they'd hidden large portions of their life from me for all that time, I'd be mad, too."

"It's all too late." There was a shuffle and click. Ngaire couldn't see, but it sounded like he'd picked up the gun again. Another flush of adrenaline coursed through her body, but she was growing too exhausted to respond. The thought of a bullet in her brain was a soothing one. Put an end to her struggles. Peace. Quiet. All her misdeeds and mistakes wiped out in one last action. Who would cry at her gravesite if she let him take her now?

Ngaire fell forward onto her hands and panted. A strangled cry issued from her throat. She fought back against the pull of nothingness: for herself, for Billy.

"Do you know what happens if you pull that trigger?" she asked. "Then it really will be too late. Until you die, there's always hope."

He laughed again, his only response.

"You could go back outside and introduce yourself. Let her get to know you." His problems seemed so easy to solve compared with her own. Her problems were the ones that were insurmountable. "Let your wife choose, knowing all the facts about you."

"Too late," he said. "I've lost my job. I would buy her a farm, but she acted like I was crazy."

"It's a big change. You should give her time."

So easy to fix William's problems. Could it be that easy to fix hers as well? Do the thing you should've done from the beginning. Go to the therapist you'd avoided. Give a statement without editing it first. Go back to being the person you always believed yourself to be.

There was another sigh, and Ngaire heard another click. "Wait," she called, coming around the corner to face him. "Your father killed himself, right?"

William tilted his head back against the counter and smiled. "Is this you trying to make me feel better?"

"Is that why you kept the gun?" Ngaire looked at the weapon, and her mind spun. She felt the slide of a knife, the slam of a bat, the choking fear of death. The barrel grew larger before her eyes, the center spinning like a top. Hypnotizing her. The end was coming, it was coming now, and she should just close her eyes and let it happen because she'd never be of use to anyone again. She used her friends, she endangered her colleagues. Death was too good for her.

William had spoken, but she hadn't heard. Nothing existed except the gun in front of her. The shells loaded. The trigger pulled back.

Air whooshed through her head, and Ngaire inhaled deeply, turning away. For a moment there was nothing but white light exploding in her vision, then the room span back into focus. Sharp and clear.

William had turned his head to her to make eye contact. Bloodshot capillaries were swelling throughout the whites of his eyes. He looked as though he hadn't slept in weeks. "Like father, like son," he agreed.

What? What were they talking about? *His father?*

"Children of suicides are always more in danger of killing themselves," Ngaire said. She cleared her throat when her mouth gummed up. The fear was coming up on her again. Ready to ride her shoulders like a demon. She spoke to drive it away. "What do you think will happen the first time Emma strikes trouble? Is that what you want for her? To sit here, in your position one day, because you didn't bother to show her there's an alternative?"

His body sagged back against the cupboards, his fingers releasing the shotgun. Ngaire pulled it away and slid it across the slick lino surface. Out of harm's way. She stroked the barrel, a moment's fetish, then pushed it away from herself, too. In reality and in her mind.

She chose life and gathered the crying man into her arms to rock him. Calming him. Calming herself.

Poor Billy Glover, who thought he'd marry his teenage sweetheart, not knowing or guessing at the madness that surrounded her. Poor Billy Glover, whom Paul found so easy to blame because he blamed himself.

"Maybe your wife married you because she suspected who you truly are," Ngaire whispered. Her pulse was slowing to normal. Her vision back to twenty-twenty. "Maybe she always wanted a nice farm boy, and she's pissed off she got a lawyer."

His tightly wound shoulders loosened. William pulled away from her grip so he could stand, then reached to help Ngaire to her feet. Together they walked to the front door, supporting each other like wounded soldiers.

"Also," Ngaire said. "I think you just taught your daughter to swear. You can't leave your wife alone to deal with that."

William laughed, and the sun broke free of clouds to bathe them in its light.

Chapter Twenty-Six

"This is a beautiful cemetery," Deb said as she and Ngaire walked back to the car. Established trees were dotted throughout the site, and in one corner space had been roped off for a farmer to graze his animals.

"Awesome. I know a perfect birthday present for you."

"Maudlin. And too expensive. I'll stick to chocolate, thanks."

Magdalene's gravesite had lost its air of newness. When Ngaire had first visited, there'd been fresh dirt from the recent internment. Now the grass was growing alongside the plaque, and the grave was settling to level.

"Where should I drop you off?" Deb asked. She was driving. Ngaire had surrendered her license on her shrink's suggestion. PTSD could strike without warning, and city traffic was a terrible place for that to happen.

"Finlay said he'd meet me at the McDonald's."

"Nice," Deb said, pulling out into a gap in the flow of traffic.

"Oh, not to eat. Just, he can find it, and few cars stop outside."

"Well, perhaps if you dated like a normal couple, he'd buy you a meal once in a while."

Ngaire and Finlay still hadn't determined the edges of their relationship. He'd moved out the month before, saying she didn't need him there, since she could look after herself now. She would've liked to keep him there and charge him the rent he was happily withholding from another landlord, but that would've been even weirder.

Although they were closer now than they'd been before her attack, Ngaire still wasn't sure they'd ever be an item. The tension that sometimes existed between them was due to pig-headedness, not sexuality.

"The DS is still pestering me," Deb said. "Always wants me to make sure you know you can come back."

Ngaire laughed. "Tell him that every time he asks you, it postpones my return by a month."

"How is it going, anyway?"

Ngaire saw no progress. Not when she woke at night, drenched in sweat and sure death was a second away. There were still days when an innocuous sound or a glimpse in her peripheral vision would flash a terror sequence into her head.

"It's getting better," she lied. She might not believe it herself, but it did no harm to have others believe it on her behalf.

"The DS would like you and Finlay to know he's owed a couple of favors, and he may cash in when he needs a good run in the press."

A side-effect of Finlay's feature on "The Three Deaths of Magdalene Lynton" had been work flowing through to him thick and fast. Instead of his having to call on newspaper editors and keep his hand in everything that happened around him, magazines were now interested in articles formed from long hours of research and offering informed critiques and opinions. It was more work than he'd put in before, but it was reaping him bigger rewards. His rent might still be late, but he was no longer rooting through people's rubbish bins looking for evidence of sexual transgressions.

"How are you and the DS getting on these days?" Ngaire asked.

Ever since Deb had slipped his first name into conversation, Ngaire had been on the lookout for a blossoming relationship. If it existed, then they were both better at keeping it covered up than anyone else in the station.

Perhaps she could enlist Finlay to go through their rubbish bins . . .

"*We* are getting on fine," Deb said, "and *we* are close to making an arrest, *we* are."

"Anyone I know?"

"Yes, as a matter of fact. A certain scumbag and his missus who may or may not have been near a party where somebody got herself stabbed."

Ngaire felt her shoulders curl forward, her chest caving in to avoid an attack. She swallowed hard and her throat felt dry and scratchy. "Would that arrest be likely to result in a successful prosecution?"

After working with her doctor for a fortnight, Ngaire had gone into the station to make a full and frank witness statement for her own assault. She'd done it to show her therapist she was doing fine, but the reservations that had stopped her from making the report still lingered. Even when she wasn't holding a therapist grudge.

"We think it's likely. We also think there are now a few more witness statements than there were, so someone's testimony may never have to enter a courtroom."

Because Ngaire had hidden the truth during her first interview, her second was on shaky ground. Corroboration was a blessing.

"Here you go," Deb said as they pulled up outside the restaurant. "With ten minutes to spare."

"Thanks," Ngaire said and swung her legs out of the passenger seat.

"Ngaire," Deb called. Ngaire crouched to look back at her friend. "We miss you, you know. No matter what troubles you're going through, you're a great officer. Remember that."

Ngaire's face flushed with color and warmth,

and she nodded. She couldn't swallow now for a different reason.

"I will," she said. "I miss you, too."

Deb pulled away from the curb, and Ngaire waved after her until she was out of sight. The sun was hot and high in the sky above her, so she moved along until she was in the shade of an awning.

She did miss Deb. Missed the job, too. Sometimes Ngaire wanted to scream with frustration at herself for not just picking up and getting better. At times, it felt like she was wallowing in talk, talk, talk with her therapist, while criminals were out committing crimes she should be preventing.

"You'd give yourself time to heal from a physical injury," her doctor had pointed out weeks ago. "When your leg was cut, you didn't go out running the next day. Give your mind the same time to heal. Just because it's not bleeding doesn't mean it's not hurting."

She'd picked up work at a lawyer's office in the meantime to make money. Her bank didn't care that she was going through a few issues at the moment. One of her conveyancing jobs had been for William Glover's purchase of a dairy farm out near Culverden. It was small and made artisanal products to supply the local restaurant markets.

Ngaire had been driven past the driveway one day and saw Emma running along, fetching something from the gate. She didn't ask Finlay to stop, didn't check to see whether the arrangement was permanent or Billy's daughter was there on a shared custody weekend. Just watched the young girl with red apples of exercise blooming in her cheeks and a smile of joy. Flaxen hair flew out behind her, despite being tied back with a blue ribbon.

There was a toot, and Finlay's arm was out the driver's window, gesturing her to hurry because he was double-parking. Ngaire ran to the door and jumped in, giving him a kiss on the cheek because it was a nice day, and she was glad to see him, and sometimes it seemed like everything could turn out okay.

"It's busy," he said, signaling to pull back out. "I thought you wouldn't see me."

"Not a chance. The traffic should ease on the way out to the compound."

She'd asked Finlay to let her go out there one last time. They'd found out how Isaiah Haldrem looked after himself, despite being incapable of buying his own food. Mary Lynton had been sending supplies out there, first taking them herself, and then setting up a permanent order with the supermarket. Another way she tried to atone for her lapses.

"Watch it," Ngaire said as they turned into the drive. "He's put the gate across again."

Between the potential buyers and the press and public wanting glimpses of a crime scene, the compound had gained a lot more foot traffic of late. Isaiah tried to be polite, but the constant contact was a strain. Sometimes he locked himself away.

"What's he going to do when they sell this place?" Finlay asked when Ngaire got back in the car. "I doubt he'll integrate well."

"There's a firm looking for a farm placement for him," Ngaire said. "They may have a slot out in Oxford, which suits. It's basic, but . . ."

"Yeah, I think basic suits Isaiah."

Ngaire pulled two bags from her side, then waited for Finlay to grab his. She dropped them on the kitchen counter, flexing her hand to work out the deep grooves that formed, then walked along the corridor.

"Isaiah, are you here?"

Trev barked and ran to greet them. Isaiah would follow along behind soon enough.

"You know the one thing I don't understand?" Finlay said.

Ngaire briefly thought of a rude retort but kept her lip buttoned. "What's that?"

"When they found her body out in the back field, why did they dump her into the slurry? How could they do that, on top of everything else.?"

"It made the hay grow," Isaiah said from the doorway.

Ngaire looked at him, a smile on her face. "What did?"

"The waste from the slurry," he said.

He walked through into the kitchen and took an apple out of a bag. He didn't offer to help with the groceries, didn't say thank you. Ngaire understood that it would never occur to him to do so, but it made her worry how he'd get on, even on a remote farm.

"It made the hay grow, and we put it on the flowerbeds around the house, so I thought if anything could work, it would be that."

Finlay frowned at him. "What?"

Ngaire felt a tingle light her hands and worm through her body. Her skull filled with helium; her ears buzzed. "You thought it would help Magdalene grow?"

Isaiah nodded and took another bite of the apple.

"I gave her three days, but she didn't come back, so I had to tell everyone she was dead."

And a pathologist came out and found a drowned body floating in a pool of sludge, the case self-evident. Ngaire felt a wave of sadness lump up her throat. What would've happened forty years ago if the pathologist examined a girl whose dead body had been found dumped in the back field instead?

She reached out a hand and patted his arm.

"The Bible's bullshit," Isaiah said with the heat of anger, backing away from her touch and walking along the corridor to the clean air outside.

Your free e-book is waiting . . .

There was more than one person involved in Magdalene's death, but there's only been one who paid with his life.
So far.

Marge Maples thinks everything will finally be easier: there's money from the farm sale, she's no longer on her feet ten hours a day, and Kelvin's about to retire. Life is coming good.

Pity karma's such a bitch.

"The Cup That Made You Stagger"
A Magdalene Lynton Companion Story

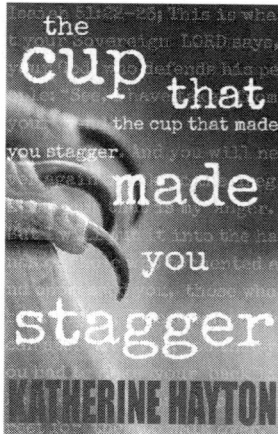

www.magdalenebonus.com

Also by the Author

Found, Near Water

Rena wakes from a coma into a mother's nightmare. Her daughter is missing, but no one's noticed, no one's complained, no one's searching.
Can Christine help her through the maelstrom of her daughter's disappearance?

Skeletal

Ten years ago Daina Harrow stole a secret that people had killed to hide. Now that her bones have been found on a building site, can a coroner's inquest uncover the truth behind her death?

Breathe and Release

Elisabet wakes with amnesia. Her husband's care quickly descends into aggression and violence. Lillian lies hog-tied in an underground cell. Forget about escape. Without water, she'll be dead within days.

About the Author

Katherine Hayton is a forty-two-year-old woman who works in insurance, doesn't have children or pets, can't drive, has lived in Christchurch her entire life, and resides a two-minute walk from where she was born.

For some reason, she's developed a rich fantasy life.

She can be found on **katherinehayton.com** or whiling her time away on twitter **@kathay1973**

Printed by Amazon Italia Logistica S.r.l.
Torrazza Piemonte (TO), Italy